# Jonathan Swift and Popular Culture ~

# Myth, Media, and the Man

*Ann Cline Kelly*

palgrave

*To Sophia and Alice*

JONATHAN SWIFT AND POPULAR CULTURE
Copyright © Ann Cline Kelly, 2002.

First published 2002 by PALGRAVE™
175 Fifth Avenue, New York, N.Y. 10010 and
Houndmills, Basingstoke, Hampshire, England RG21 6XS.
Companies and representatives throughout the world.

PALGRAVE is the new global publishing imprint of St. Martin's Press LLC Scholarly and Reference Division and Palgrave Publishers Ltd. (formerly Macmillan Press Ltd.).

ISBN 0–312–23959–9

**Library of Congress Cataloging-in-Publication Data**
Kelly, Ann Cline
Jonathan Swift and popular culture : myth, media, and the man / by Ann Cline Kelly.
    p.   cm.
  Includes bibliographical references and index.
  ISBN 0–312–23959–9
  1. Swift, Jonathan, 1667–1745.   2. Popular culture—Great Britain—History—18th century.   3. Mass media—Great Britain—History and criticism.   4. Verse satire, English—History and criticism.   5. Authors, Irish—18th century—Biography.   6. Church of Ireland—Clergy—Biography.   7. Satire, English—History and criticism.   I. Title.

PR3726.K452002
828'.509—dc21
                                                                    [B]
                                                            2001036569

A catalogue record for this book is available from the British Library.

Design by Letra Libre, Inc.

First edition: April 2002
10  9  8  7  6  5  4  3  2  1

Printed in the United States of America.

# Table of Contents

# Acknowledgments

This project has been so much fun, I almost hate to see it come to an end. The extravagance of mythmaking about Swift has been a constant source of delight, and uncovering Swift's role in enshrining himself in the lore of the culture has added to my admiration of his genius. Many people helped me along the way, contributing advice, information, opposing points of view, artifacts, printed materials, and moral support. My debts are many, and no doubt in the ten year period it took me to write the book, I may have forgotten some of my benefactors, for which I hope they will forgive me. My thanks to Stephen Ackerman, Vicki Arana, Joseph Bangiola, Kevin Berland, Frank Boyle, Marjorie Cline, Elizabeth Eisenstein, Carole Fabricant, Lynne Farrington, Judy Fontaine, Christopher Fox, The First Draft Club, The Folger Colloquium on Eighteenth-Century Women, A. C. Elias, William Horne, Cynthia James, Jennifer Jordan, Paul Korshin, Elizabeth Lambert, Sue Lanser, Mariam Lee, Hugh Ormsby-Lennon, Katherine Lesko, Robert Mahony, James May, Linda Merians, Ousmane Moreau, Ray Orkwiss, Deborah Payne, Leland Peterson, John Radner, Betty Rizzo, Johann Schmidt, Arthur H. Scouten, Sean Shesgreen, Mary Margaret Stewart, Charles Tita, Thorell Tsomondo, Charlotte Watkins, Tracey Walters, James Woolley, Calhoun Winton, Melissa Yorks. I owe particular debts to Claudia Tate, for helping me sharpen my focus; to Lorraine Henry and Pamela Volkman for making the book more readable; and to Hermann J. Real, for invaluable scholarly information. Some of the persons on the list do not accept some of the conclusions I have drawn, and it goes without saying that no one else but me is responsible for any errors in the book.

My home away from home has been the Folger Shakespeare Library, whose wonderful Reading Room and Reference staff have been essential to my work: Elizabeth Walsh (Head of Readers' Services), Georgianna Ziegler (Head of Reference), LuEllen DeHaven, Harold Batie, Rosalind Larry, and Camille Seerattan. The staffs at the institutions below have also been most helpful: Trinity College (Dublin) Library, Archbishop Marsh's Library, the Bodleian Library, the British Library, and the Library of Congress. Grants from the Folger Shakespeare Library as well as from the Faculty Research Fund in the

Social Sciences, Humanities, and Education and the Provost's Funds for Academic Excellence from Howard University were greatly appreciated. I would also like to thank the following for permission to publish excerpts from the following articles: Wilhelm Fink, "The Birth of Swift," *in Reading Swift: Papers from the Second Münster Symposium on Jonathan Swift,* Hermann Real and Richard Rodino, eds. (Munich, 1993); and "Swift's Battle of the Books: Fame in the Modern Age" *in Reading Swift: Papers from the Third Münster Symposium on Jonathan Swift,* Hermann Real and Helgard Stöver-Leidig, eds. (Munich, 1998); Rudolf Freiburg, "Swift's Enigma and the Mythopoeic Process in Print" in *Swift: The Enigmatic Dean*: Festschrift for Hermann Real, ed. Rudolf Freiburg, Arno Löffler, and Wolfgang Zach (Tübingen, Germany 1998); Associated University Presses, "Swift's Mythopoeic Authority," *Representations of Swift,* Brian Connery, ed. (Cranbury, NJ, forthcoming 2002). Not only for their expertise in marshalling a messy manuscript into printed form, but also for their patience and interest, I would like to express my gratitude to Kristi Long, Aimee Hartmann, Laura Lawrie, and Meg Weaver of St. Martin's/Palgrave Press.

My most profound gratitude is to members of my book-reading and book-writing family, both living and dead. Among the living, special thanks go to Henry Kelly, Sarah Cline, and most particularly, to my daughters, Alice and Sophie Kelly, to whom the book is lovingly dedicated.

# A Note on the Text

I have preserved the spelling in the texts I have used, but I have regularized the typography of ligatures, long s's, and superscripts. I have preserved the use of capitals, small capitals, and italics, but any other font has been rendered as italic.

The first citations to *The Poems of Jonathan Swift,* edited by Harold Williams, are included in text as (P), followed by the volume, page numbers of the poem, and line numbers of the citation. Subsequent references contain only the line numbers. Citations to *Prose Works of Jonathan Swift,* edited by Herbert Davis, are given as (PW), followed by the volume and page number. A similar procedure is followed for the *Journal to Stella* (JS) and the *Correspondence* (C), both edited by Harold Williams.

# List of Illustrations

# Introduction

An unheralded aspect of Jonathan Swift's genius is his use of print to make himself a legend in his own time and, it seems, forever after. The myths and legends (I use these two terms interchangeably) are legion and contradictory. Typically their truth cannot be verified with historical evidence, and their origins are forgotten, obscure, or suspect. Almost magically, they tend to reproduce, mutate, or stimulate entirely new narratives. Attributing to Swift thoughts, words, and actions, these stories, situated in an indefinite relationship to provable fact, primarily focus on his mysterious relationships with the women in his life, his madness, his religious apostasy, and his humorous eccentricities. Some of the stories evolve into chestnuts, retold time after time; other stories are more evanescent. Some have a cogent verisimilitude; others are overtly fictional.[1] The circulation of these stories in a wide variety of popular literature made Swift familiar to virtually every reader in the English-speaking world.[2] Swift's extraordinary celebrity results from several canny decisions he made about managing his career as an author: to write for the broadest possible audience rather than a discriminating elite, and to create an enigmatic and provocative print identity.[3] These two strategies reinforced one another. Strangely reluctant to write like a pious gentleman as befitted his class and vocation, Swift evoked constant criticism of his character that kept him in the public eye.[4] He translated that celebrity into power and glory.[5]

## Swift as a Writer of Popular Literature

Jonathan Swift, although he aspired to literary greatness, did not follow the prescribed script. Instead of writing in ways that would impress the self-styled Republic of Letters, Swift devoted most of his energies to publishing popular literature for a general audience that included minimally educated readers as well as highly literate ones. In the early eighteenth century, popular literature spanned the gamut from parlor fare, like The Spectator—whose implied reader is "polite," that is affluent, educated, and refined[6]—to cheaply printed street literature (ballads, almanacs, libels, prognostications, hues and cries) sold by hawkers, whose implied reader has less genteel tastes. Although Swift's publications often contain an odd mélange of witty erudition and coarse vulgarity, with irony always lurking as a possibility, Swift's contemporaries condemned his publications as "low" and questioned why an Anglican priest would taint his reputation by writing in that way.[7] The lowliness of Swift's works was signaled by their Grubstreet genres, their appeal to a broad audience, their offensiveness and sensationalism, and their reflection of the life and language of "the vulgar," or the underclass. Most scandalous, though, was Swift's complete lack of embarrassment about being known as an author of works "hawk'd in ev'ry Street, / [That] seldom rose above a Sheet" (P 1: 172, ll. 41–2). Swift's decision to publish for an inclusive rather than an exclusive readership and his popular successes made his peers uncomfortable. They worried that he was indifferent or hostile to the social, political, and literary hierarchies that ordered English culture and that he might use his powers as a writer to undermine them. Swift's inexplicable attraction to the lower classes of literature and people raised fundamental questions about his life and character.

Swift's success in writing popular literature can be measured by the demand for multiple editions of his works and by the numbers of responses they evoked—items with similar titles, imitations, parodies, and other spin-offs. Swift's celebrity is registered by the large amount of popular literature featuring him as a character or appropriating his name as a pseudonym. Because Swift was known both as a subject and an author of popular literature, he was mocked for his pretensions when he tried to present himself as an Augustan writer, that is, as a cultural leader committed to elevating taste and morality with works similar in form, tone, or style to those of classical Latin poets such as Virgil or Horace. Despite the avalanche of criticism it brought down on him, Swift continued to produce works that violated genteel standards of literary decorum and did little to correct his reputation as "King of the Mob."[8]

John Boyle, Earl of Orrery, one of Swift's first biographers, excoriates Swift for wasting his talent on outrageous trash rather than, by implication, publishing translations of Pliny like himself. Orrery is particularly troubled by the ease with which Swift could ventriloquize the underclass chat of servants, rustics, and homeless people as well as by the familiarity he seemed to have with hovels, dirty kitchens, and cheap inns. More in sorrow than in anger, Orrery concludes, "He delighted in scenes of low life. The vulgar dialect was not only a fund of humour for him, but I verily believe was acceptable to his nature; otherwise I know not how to account for the many filthy ideas, and indecent expressions. . . . that will be found in his works."[9] Unlike true men of letters with high personal standards, Swift, according to Orrery, was too "fond of seeing his works in print" and made public things that never should have left his desk (53). Orrery is horrified, for example, that Swift not only penned puns and riddles, but, without shame, published them. Orrery's judgment of Swift as an author prevailed until the late eighteenth century when Swift began to be re-packaged as an Augustan, a label that has stuck, although it obscures the nature of his writing career and the origins of his fame.

## Swift as Mythmaker

Swift's first popular successes—the anonymously published *A Tale of a Tub* and the Bickerstaff papers—revealed to him the way print instantly could transform the cultural landscape. Impressed with Swift's ability to grab the public's attention and change the way they thought, Robert Harley—first Earl of Oxford and Lord Treasurer in Queen Anne's Tory ministry—enlisted Swift's help in puncturing the hagiographic myths about the Duke of Marlborough, a victorious general and a Whig icon. Swift's *Conduct of the Allies* turned public opinion against the duke and dealt a stunning blow to his career. Fifteen years later in Ireland, Swift again used the power of the popular press to reconfigure political realities when he instigated a successful economic boycott against England with the publication of *The Drapier's Letters* (1724–5). Swift recognized that his ability to supplant old myths with new ones made him very dangerous to those invested in the status quo and kept him in the center of their attention.

Because of his lethal powers as a propagandist, Swift's enemies tried to destroy him just as he had destroyed the Duke of Marlborough. Rather than destroying Swift, the libels and caricatures merely served to give him a larger-than-life print identity that was much in demand. As a result, authors fathered sensational works on Swift or published fictional reports of scandals concerning him. The contrast between the thoroughly notorious behavior of the media-constructed Jonathan Swift and the clerical vocation of his flesh-and-blood double only enhanced the appeal of Swiftiana of all sorts. Observing that his notoriety inspired mythmaking, Swift seldom explained, apologized, or tried to amend his disreputable public image. As his late-eighteenth-century biographer Thomas Sheridan notes, "Perhaps there never was known a man whose true character has been so little known, or whose conduct at all times . . . has been so misrepresented to the world. . . . The chief source of all the erroneous opinions entertained of him, arose from Swift himself."[10]

## The Brass Trumpet

Of Fame's two trumpets, Swift most consistently sought the sounding of the brass rather than the gold. The gold trumpet delicately announces lofty achievements to the gods and the upper echelons of humanity, while the brass trumpet blasts out rumors to the general populace. The *locus classicus* of brass trumpet fame is Book Four of the *Aeneid*, where in a passage following an account of Aeneas's illicit rendezvous with Dido, fame/rumor (the

Latin *fama* carries both meanings) is described as a flying female monster with thousands of tongues spreading the news of the liaison. If the truth were not shocking enough, fame/rumor embellishes it: "Things done, [she] relates, not done she feigns, and mingles truth with lies."[11] The indeterminable mixture of truth and fiction allies rumor to myth for, in fact, myth can be defined as an enduring rumor.

The rumors or myths about Swift infuse the popular image of the man. For example, in Bartholomew Gill's mystery—*The Death of an Ardent Bibliophile* (1995)—the persistence of the legendary Swift plays a central role in solving the murder of Brian Herrick, Librarian of Marsh's Library in Dublin. Herrick, it seems, secretly enjoyed imagining himself to be Swift, an activity that involved dressing up in eighteenth-century clothes and watching pornographic movies. Finding out the truth about Swift, and consequently about Herrick, leads McGarr—the detective on the case—into a maze of contradictions and confusions.

> . . . Swift seemed to have purposely obscured the details of his life. To this day, it was not certain whether Swift had been celibate throughout his life or a womanizer, a confirmed bachelor or secretly married perhaps to his own half sister and the father of a child by her. All the while simultaneously conducting at least two long-term affairs with other women, one of whom might also have borne his child. In other words, he had been a "master of disinformation." . . . In Swift as in life, McGarr decided, there were no easy answers [. . . .][12]

The legendary Swift poses problems to scholarly biographers, who must clear away the thickets of error surrounding their subject, as well as to editors, who must decide whether works in question are Swift's or those of an author impersonating Swift. The general public, though, consumes Swiftiana of all sorts without much regard to its historical authenticity. Indeed, extravagant fictions seem to sell better than dry facts. Irvin Ehrenpreis, author of the standard biography of Swift, must warn his readers that they will not find their favorite stories: "Here, neither Swift nor Stella is made a bastard; Swift does not say, 'My uncle gave me the education of a dog'; Dryden does not say, 'Cousin Swift, you will never be a poet.'"[13] The fictions that Ehrenpreis dismisses have a persuasive verisimilitude and, because continuously repeated, an impressive authority.[14] The proliferation and persistence of these narratives testify to Swift's power to fire the imagination.

## Swift as Myth

Many people have temporary celebrity. Only a few become folkloric figures, whose words and deeds are familiar to the general public, generation after generation. What makes a man into a legend or a myth? Lord Raglan tackles this question in his eccentric yet useful book, *The Hero: A Study in Tradition, Myth, and Drama* (1936). Lord Raglan argues that the life narratives of mythologized figures share certain formulaic plot elements. From these plot elements, the qualities of character that foster mythmaking can be abstracted. Raglan itemizes the plot elements and numbers them:

1. The hero's mother is a royal virgin;
2. His father is a king, and
3. Often a near relative of his mother, but
4. The circumstances of his conception are unusual, and
5. He is also reputed to be the son of a god.
6. At birth an attempt is made, usually by his father or his maternal grandfather, to kill him, but
7. He is spirited away, and
8. Reared by foster parents in a far country.
9. We are told nothing of his childhood, but
10. On reaching manhood he returns or goes to his future kingdom.
11. After a victory over the king and/or giant, dragon, or wild beast,
12. He marries a princess, often the daughter of his predecessor, and
13. Becomes king.
14. For a time he reigns uneventfully, and
15. Prescribes laws, but
16. Later he loses favor with the gods and/or his subjects, and
17. Is driven from the throne and city, after which
18. He meets with a mysterious death,
19. Often at the top of a hill.
20. His children, if any, do not succeed him.
21. His body is not buried, but nevertheless
22. He has one or more holy sepulchres

In cheerleading style, Raglan ranks mythic figures by awarding them points based on how many (often very imprecise) approximations of the 22 elements listed above can be found in their biographies. Of Oedipus, Raglan notes, "We may award him full marks"; Theseus "scores twenty"; "We can give [Pelops] at least thirteen points"; "We can take [Apollo] no further, but he has scored eleven points."[15]

Implicit in Raglan's list are the attributes that mythologized characters have in common: power, mystery, contradiction, and heterodoxy. The power of Raglan's hero can be seen in items 1 (elevated status), 5 (divine heritage), 11 (victorious fighter), 22 (an immortal presence compelling worship); the mystery in items 4 (unusual conception), 7 (spirited away to foster parents),

9 (absent childhood), 18 (mysterious death); the contradictions or paradoxes in items 1 (virgin mother), 5 (human and god), 16 (ruler and exile); and the heterodoxy in items 3 (incestuous relationships), 4 (strange conception), 12 (unusual marriage), 13 (legacy in question), 16 (condemned by the gods), 21 (unburied body). These elements—power, mystery, contradiction, and heterodoxy—are the same ones that fuel gossip. People talk about people who are in control, seem to be hiding something, act inconsistently, or engage in unsanctioned or irregular behavior. Rumors spread and multiply because sharing them allows people to speak of the unspeakable (revolution, secrets, lies, sex) and to fantasize about the freedom of figures whose actions seem unconstrained by conscience, morality, law, or fear of exposure.

The lore surrounding Swift and Robin Hood is similar in many ways and supports Raglan's thesis that certain patterns and attributes are characteristic of popular legends. Raglan synthesizes the disparate Robin Hood narratives into a coherent history and keys it to his numbered list of plot elements:

> [Robin Hood's] father is a Saxon yeoman, but he is also (5) reputed to be the son of a great noble. We (9) hear nothing of his youth, but on reaching manhood he leads a life of debauchery until compelled to fly (10) to Sherwood, where he (11) gains victories over the Sheriff of Nottingham, (12) marries Maid Marian, the Queen of May, and (13) becomes King of May and ruler of the forest. For a long time he reigns, and (15) prescribes the laws of archery, but eventually illness overtakes him, and he (17) has to leave the forest, and meets (18) a mysterious death in (19) an upper room. He (20) has no children. The place of his death and burial are (21) variously given, but (22) miracles were performed at his tomb at Kirkley, in Yorkshire. We can give him thirteen points.[16]

Like those of Robin Hood, the mythologized versions of Swift's life fall into Raglan's formula. While Robin Hood (if he were a real person) had little to do with the creation of the folklore about him,[17] Swift self-consciously mythologized himself or spurred others to do so. Swift imbued his self-constructions with the four qualities abstracted from Raglan's list: power, mystery, contradiction, and heterodoxy.

Swift's enormous power derived from the massive influence of his works and his reputation for complete autonomy. He presented himself as one unbeholden to church, state, family, or patrons. Fostering a public image of himself as one indifferent to the judgments of both man and God, Swift's print alter ego was unashamed to play the fool or to violate taboos. He was a dangerous man, who brazenly insulted bishops, judges, and even King George with impunity, because he had demonstrated that his power over the populace was superior to theirs. His overt and covert threats to officialdom resulted in calls for his arrest, jail time for his printer, surveillance of his correspondence, and constant attempts to defame him. Swift bragged about being a wanted man because it showed how much he was feared and how little the authorities could do to control him. At one point, Swift implicitly contrasts himself to a Dr. Gee, who traveled in disguise because he was afraid that an obscure little essay he published would make him a target of violence. The truth, Swift says, is that "not a creature would hurt him, or had ever heard of him or his Pamphlet" (*Thoughts on Various Subjects,* PW 4:250). Through his writing, Swift acquired significant political power, but his ultimate power was defeating time by immortalizing himself in popular culture.

Crucial facts about Swift's life are cloaked in mystery, including who his father was, what his childhood was like, whether he was married, and how he died. Swift seems to have created much of this confusion, and certainly he did little to clear it up. Because Swift was a posthumous child (Raglan item 4, "unusual conception") and his father was not alive to confirm Swift's legitimacy, stories sprang up about his paternity. Orrery alleges that Swift himself started the rumor that he was the bastard son of Sir William Temple, a nobleman with ambiguous connections to the Swift family and for whom Swift served as secretary. Another rumor was that Sir William's father, John Temple, was Swift's father. Swift is silent about his early years. One exception is a story he tells about his being kidnapped (Raglan's item 7, "spirited away") by his nurse and taken to England, where he claims to have learned to read the Bible before the age of three. Victoria Glendinning, author of a recent popular biography of Swift, is openly skeptical about this often-recited "fact," and in essence, accuses Swift of self-mythologizing.[18] Swift encouraged rumors about his love life by simultaneously publishing affectionate poems to two women: Hester Johnson, whom he dubbed Stella; and Hester Vanhomrigh, whom he dubbed Vanessa.[19] Despite the eyebrows they raised, Swift never explained his mysterious relationships to these women. Mystery also surrounded Swift's death. Becoming mentally incompetent at the end of his life, Swift remained secluded for three years before he died, but not before rumors that he was mad had become part of his legend. To plumb their secrets, Swift's bones were exhumed several times and examined (particularly the skull), a variation on Raglan's item 21, "the body is not buried."

The mysteries about mythologized figures also derive from fundamental contradictions in their characters that make it impossible to know exactly who they are. These contradictions generate a dynamic dialectic of theses and antitheses that do not result in syntheses but open up new narrative possibilities. Swift obviously took delight in confusing his public image by accentuating his paradoxical or protean nature as an unchristian priest, a vulgar gentleman, an elite populist, a misanthropic philanthropist, a serious trifler, a Grubstreet Apollo, an pro-Irish Englishman. Such inconsistencies are simultaneously outrageous and awe-inspiring, because they suggest that Swift successfully resists conventional definition.

Raglan emphasizes that violation of social or moral norms is a central feature of narratives about mythologized characters, who are by nature not like ordinary men and women. Swift seems to have taken pains to publish objectionable works that set him apart from the rest of humanity. He publicly insulted his superiors, to whom he owed deference, as well as his friends and allies, to whom he owed consideration. He was openly disloyal to England in urging the Irish to resist English policies and took no pains to dispute the charges that he was a Jacobite, that is, a traitor who wished to depose the Protestant line of succession and put a Catholic on England's throne. Swift also projected himself as a traitor to his class by seeming to sympathize with the underclass and rejecting genteel literary proprieties. Relishing the role of outlaw and rebel, Swift twice provoked the authorities to seek his arrest for his "crimes of writing"[20] and inspired libelers to depict him as a lowlife, demagogue, felon, disciple of the devil, or the devil himself. In addition to his crimes of writing, the mysteries about Swift's love life and that of his parents gave rise to all sorts of stories embellishing his reputation for heterodoxy—including those charging him with incest, adultery, promiscuity, and illegitimacy.

Mythologized figures, like Swift, thwart categorization, refuse disclosure, and resist all measures to limit or control them in narrative form. Their extraordinary plenitude of possibilities inspires storytelling that "coils back on itself ceaselessly driven to articulat[e] a narrative other than the ones it has already generated since each inherently poses the possibility of saying otherwise."[21] Each story about Swift seems to evoke another, different one, and in so doing, evaporates the comforting, yet constraining, regimes of decorum, predictability, certainty, coherence, intelligibility—an experience Roland Barthes defines as "bliss." By implication, myths are bliss-producing texts, arising "out of scandal" and presenting a "subject [that] is never anything but a 'living contradiction,'" who is ultimately unknowable because he is always in the process of disintegration that leads to reintegration in new forms. Mythic characters take on lives of their own quite different from those of the flesh-and-blood namesakes. As Barthes notes, myth "leaves . . . contingency behind; . . . history evaporates, only the letter remains. . . . One must firmly stress [the] open character [of myth] . . . [I]t is a formless, unstable, nebulous condensation. . . ."[22] Myth's freedom from the rigid exigencies of the quotidian makes it so appealing.

To encourage stories about himself, Swift seems intentionally to have mystified his life and works with highly charged statements, crucial silences, and mixed assertions that have made basic questions about him impossible to answer. In this darkness, myths breed. Swift's authorial strategy was opposite to that of his self-promoting contemporary John Dunton, who confessed in print more than anybody wanted to know. Analyzing why he failed to ignite the interest of his audience, Dunton realizes in a rare flash of insight that he had defined himself too clearly and too fully: "[H]aving made [my life] so excessive plain. . . . the Publick has admir'd it less than they might have done, [I should have] just FLESH'D THE HINTS, and left 'em undetected, in Order for others to apply the Game home themselves, and to take the Pleasure of doing so a little more than was already offer'd to their view."[23] Dunton belatedly understood what Swift quickly learned: that readers and writers enjoy letting their imaginations have free play, which can only happen in the absence of established fact or authoritative explanation. As Andy Warhol says, "Always leave them wanting less."[24] Even if Dunton had been more reticent, though, his account would have remained stillborn because it lacks what journalists call "Hey, Martha" material—news so amazing, amusing, or shocking that it must be conveyed to someone else.[25]

## Mythmaking and Popular Literature

Swift published things that made news and made him news. Swift's self-representations and the attacks of his enemies combined to build the public image of a man with threatening power, cloaked vices, inconsistent principles, and subversive ideas. Endowed with these qualities, Swift became a legend in the emerging print culture of the early eighteenth century, during which time an avalanche of popular publications in broadside or pamphlet form became the equivalent of Virgil's many-tongued monster, *fama*. One author of the time, Tom Brown, provides a detailed description of the process by which print generates myth when he mocks a prostitute who has been denied this *"Immortality."* She was driven to suicide by unrequited love but saved at the last moment by her maid. If the death had occurred, it would have been the talk of the town, for what could be more of a "Hey, Martha" story than a prostitute who dies for love?

[T]hee wouldst have been immortalized in all the News-papers about town, and thy phyz [= face (slang)] most curiously engraved in wood . . . to adorn the Walls of every coffeehouse in Drury Lane. . . . Then there would have been the half a score of mournful Odes made upon thee, that's certain, sung most harmoniously at Holbourn-bar and Fleet-ditch: The Ballad-Women would have cried Here's a new and true Ballad of a miss of the town, that hang'd herself in Great Queen Street. . . . [N]ay, who knows but a City-Poet, in a few Years, would have brought thee into Smithfield [where chapbooks were published], where thou wouldst soon have overtopped Jeptha's Daughter and Bateman's Ghost [two perennially top-selling chapbook titles]. Or lastly, who can tell, but thou mightiest [*sic*] have been prefer'd to the almanac [the top seller of all works printed in England].[26]

Unlike Brown's prostitute, who missed being made a celebrity, Swift was represented during his lifetime in Grubstreet fare of all sorts; and after his death in biographies, novels, magazine articles, jestbooks, newspaper features, melodramas, self-help guides, textbook anthologies, and now, websites on the Internet. Unlike Brown's hapless prostitute, Swift did not leave his fame to chance, but carefully engineered his own immortality.

The first part of *Jonathan Swift and Popular Culture: Myth, Media, and the Man* addresses the decisions Swift made as a writer that gave him his unique power in popular culture. (Chapters 1–3). Swift's authorial strategies can be inferred from what he decided to publish and how he chose to characterize himself. Particular attention is focused on the way in which Swift fostered rumors or myths about himself. The second part of the book surveys the production of lore from Swift's death in 1745 to the present and emphasizes how successful Swift was in creating a self-replicating print identity destined to live on into the future. Although romantic, tragic, comic, and epic threads often are woven together in representations of Swift, I have analyzed them in four separate chapters to show the incremental accumulation of material in each category as well as to understand the effect of generic conventions on characterization, plot structure, and thematic focus.[27] Treating each genre in a chapter also dramatizes the multiplicity and inconsistency of Swift's print-constructed identity.

Through the early biographies written by Laetitia Pilkington, Lord Orrery, Patrick Delany, Deane Swift (Swift's confusingly named cousin), Samuel Johnson, Thomas Sheridan, and Sir Walter Scott, the now-standard elements of the Swiftian life narrative fell into place—the strange birth, the thwarted ambitions, the eccentric behavior, the Stella-Vanessa-Swift triangle, the patriotism, the madness, the grotesque death. Arguing with one another over the authenticity of their accounts, these biographers introduce contradictory details and alternative narratives that are subsequently re-circulated in numberless permutations. Swift created himself as a character whose story compels retelling and, because the truths of that story are both elusive and provocative, there will be no end of speculation. Despite the scores of biographies to date, including the exhaustively researched three-volume work by Irvin Ehrenpreis, new ones keep appearing, each one trying to bring order out of chaos but, in the process, adding new scenarios to consider. Swift is a miraculous well of narrative possibilities that can be dipped from endlessly but never runs dry.

In *The Frenzy of Renown: The History of Fame,* Leo Braudy urges scholars "to investigate the process by which fame becomes a matter of premeditation, a result of media management as much as of achievement, as well as how the great of the past behaved in such a way as to project larger-than-life images of themselves that would last longer than any specific action."[28] This book responds to Braudy's challenge. Although some may take umbrage at the idea that Swift self-consciously managed his authorial career to achieve power and glory, analyzing his brilliant success at so doing reveals new dimensions of his extraordinary genius and sheds light on the nature of fame in modern media-constructed culture.

# Chapter One ∼

# Republic of Letters versus Republica Grubstreetaria, 1690–1711

## Laureate Ambitions

In the 1690s, when Swift began writing, he mistakenly looked to his cousin, John Dryden, and to his employer, Sir William Temple, for guidance on how to make his mark as an author. Sir William Temple had achieved his fame as a courtier, diplomat, *belle lettrist* in another age, before the cultural center of England shifted from the country estate and court to the City of London, when printed literature targeted to a general audience became the most influential force in English-speaking cultures.[1] Swift was unaware that the model Temple offered him was anachronistic. Swift's other beacon was his cousin John Dryden. On Temple's Moor Park estate in Surrey, Swift, removed from the London scene, might not have realized that although Dryden had once been Poet Laureate and the epitome of Augustan high culture, he had, in essence, become a professional writer working in more popular modes by the 1690s.[2] With Dryden and Temple as exemplars, Swift attempted to do what the "self-crowned laureates" (Richard Helgerson's term) of the Renaissance (Spenser, Jonson, and Milton) had done before him: boldly define himself as the voice of his generation.[3] Because times had changed in the quarter century since Milton wrote *Paradise Lost,* Swift's early annunciations did not have the dramatic effect for which he might have hoped. In apprentice pieces, Swift started to understand the new world constructed by the popular press and, through trial and error, eventually learned how to make himself an important part of it. However, from 1691, when he first began to publish, until 1711, when some of his controversial anonymous works were publicly laid at his feet, Swift was virtually unknown to the general public.

## Hoaxed: The Athenian Society

Even though they were distant from the hustle-bustle of London, Sir William Temple and his secretary, Jonathan Swift, felt connected to other men of letters by periodicals circulating for that purpose.[4] Temple was particularly attracted to *The Athenian Gazette,* later called *The Athenian Mercury* (1691–97), published by John Dunton. Purporting to be the official organ of an Oxbridge collective called the Athenian Society, *The Athenian Mercury* supplied answers to questions sent into it, for the enlightenment of the reading public. The image of an elite Athenian Society dispensing information to the huddled masses is emblematized in the frontispiece engraving of *The Young Students Library . . . by the Athenian Society* (1692). The upper-class nature of the Society was underscored by the rhetoric of their publications. In the preface of *The Visions of the Soul, before it comes into the Body. In several Dialogues, Written by a Member of the Athenian Society* (1692), for instance, the author apologizes to his "bretheren, the Members of the Athenian Society," because he did not have time to consult with them before they left town to "go to their Estates in the Countrey."[5]

Through media management, John Dunton made the Athenian Society and its publication, *The Athenian Mercury,* known nationwide. Dunton understood that in a print-constructed world concepts achieve prominence when they appear in print, are read by other print-producers, who then incorporate them in subsequent publications. The more often concepts are repeated in print, the more pervasive they become, until they seem as though they have always been there. In other words, they are famous.[6] Sir William Temple, eager to join the conversation mediated by the Athenian Society, sent in his contributions from the hinterland,[7] and his secretary, Jonathan Swift, offered an ode praising the Athenian Society, asking that it be used as a preface to the next collected edition of *The Athenian Mercury.* Hooking his fortune to Dunton's star, Swift no doubt looked forward to a prestigious debut.

Swift did not understand until later that the Athenian Society was a print mirage or myth. While John Dunton created the impression that the Athenian Society was a large, exclusive, academic organization, it was, in fact, a Potemkin village propped up by Dunton and two brothers-in-law. Among the three of them, only one had any university training. While flying the flag of learning, the periodical addressed indecorous or bizarre topics that might otherwise be associated with Grubstreet productions. A sampling of a few questions gives the flavor of the whole: "What sex was Balaam's ass?," "How does a horse produce a square turd when its fundament is round?," "What are the best remedies for fleas in the hair?," "Why are prostitutes seldom or never with child?," "Is there such a thing as changing sexes?," "Do the deceased walk?," "Would Lazarus's estate belong to the next heir or himself

1.1.   Frontispiece, [John Dunton], *The Students' Library . . . By the Athenian Society* (1692). Swift may have learned much from Dunton, whose mythical Athenian Society inspired his second published work. By permission of the Folger Shakespeare Library.

after he rose from the dead?,", "If a man gives his wife the pox, can she quit his bed?," or "What became of the Ark, when the Flood was over?"

Dunton's *Athenian Mercury* began to be the butt of jokes and rumors, most of which centered on the plebeian nature of its authors and readers. In February 1692, just at the time Swift was completing his ode, Thomas Brown sneers at *The Athenian Mercury* for being full of "*impertinent Questions of Apprentices and Chamber-maids*" about "*Receipts for Fleas &c. and other such like wise Lectures.*"[8] The next year, Elkanah Settle's *New Athenian Comedy* (1693) depicts the Athenian Society as four men, none with classical knowledge. Among the four are a "Grubstreetonian" and a "Quack," who debate whether the flea or the louse is the nobler creature and give advice to Dorothy Tickleteat, a milkmaid, on her bed-wetting problems.[9] While he was writing his ode, Swift was obviously unaware that the Athenian Society was falling from respectability.

Swift put his name to the "Ode to the Athenian Society" as well as to the prefatory letter that accompanied it. Both of these items are exercises in self-mythologizing. Despite his modest circumstances and dependent position, Swift created a print persona who is Sir William Temple's peer: his letter refers to his "living in the Countrey" and to his passing his manuscript around in scribal copy for the private perusal of other men of letters. In the ode, Swift alludes to himself as a cosmopolitan, widely published author, and—laureate-style—professes to articulate the concerns of the nation and the age. The genre of the poem reinforces Swift's pretensions. It is a Pindaric ode—a lofty, emotional form that brought renown to John Dryden and Abraham Cowley.[10]

Swift's grandiose ambitions are evident in the first stanzas of his poem, where he compares the biblical deluge to the cultural devastation of England resulting from the military conflicts of the late-seventeenth century. When "victory and peace" restore learning, the "*Dove-muse*" brings a "*Laurel* branch" to make "an *Humble Chaplet\* for the King*" (P 1:16–25, ll. 27, 31). In a side note signaled by an asterisk, Swift identifies this laurel chaplet as "*The Ode I writ the King in* Ireland." Appropriating the laurel bays to himself, Swift imagines that his poem was the first "to Crown the happy Conqueror" (19), William, and that the flowering of his own wit is the only green spot in the battle-ravaged wasteland. Swift's "Ode to the King" was so obscure that no printed responses appeared in 1691 when it was published anonymously in Ireland, and no copy of this "lost poem" was discovered until the year 2000.[11] In referencing his reputation as a poet, Swift shared with Dunton an understanding of how new "realities" insinuate themselves into the common culture through repeated citations in print. Dunton's Athenian Society had qualities that evoked reaction and created a demand for publications that kept its name before the public. Although Dunton pro-

duced many of those publications himself, others joined in and created a craze for all things Athenian. In contrast, Swift and his inaugural works were hardly noticed.

Swift, however, was convinced he was on the road to glory because his Athenian ode not only appeared in print but also was cited in another publication. To his cousin Thomas, Swift writes that the poem "is so well thought of that the unknown Gentlemen [Dunton] printed it before one of their Books, and the Bookseller writes me word that another Gentleman [Charles Gildon] has in a Book called the History of the Athenian Society, quoted my Poem very Honourably (as the fellow calld it) so that perhaps I was in a good humor all the week" (C 1: 8). Little did Swift realize that Gildon's totally fabricated *History* had been commissioned by John Dunton as a way of giving the Athenian Society prestige. The myths propagated by Swift and Dunton complemented each other. Swift's ode supported Dunton's fiction that the Athenian Society was adulated by the Republic of Letters, and Dunton's publication of Swift's ode reinforced Swift's fiction that he was a prominent poet.

The nature of print-based fame was very much on Swift's mind as he wrote the Athenian Ode. His speaker asks, "[*W*]*hat is Fame?* where shall we search for it?" (176). Perplexed by the relationship of typographically created authors to their flesh-and-blood namesakes, Swift wonders what future generations will know about the men whose works they read.

> Although they praise the Learning and the Wit,
> And tho' the Title seems to show
> The Name and Man, by whom the Book was writ,
> Yet how shall they be brought to know
> Whether that very Name was *He, or You, or I?* (164–9)

The answer to Swift's question is "They usually cannot." To have more than a nominal existence, authors must create themselves as compelling characters by what they write and by what they stimulate others to write about them. In this way, their lives and characters become vivid realities familiar to readers. It is some time before Swift learned how to put this idea into practice.

In the "Ode to the Athenian Society," Swift tries to exalt himself as a laureate by writing in a solemn, elevated, prophetic, self-consciously poetic way. None of these qualities was much in demand in a print marketplace dominated by prose genres targeted to a broad audience (periodicals, biographies, autobiographies, essays, digests, narratives, sermons, instructional guides, political and religious tracts, memoirs), all of which challenged the privileged place of poetry and a classical tradition that enshrined conservative values. No wonder Swift's attempt to generate responses to a "laureate Swift" was a failure. His first signed publication stimulated no print reactions from anyone but Dunton and Dunton's hireling, Gildon. Without allusions, attacks, imitations, rejoinders, or public speculation, an author does not continue to be of interest, and, as far as most of the world is concerned, he ceases to exist. Swift's initial self-projection was dead on arrival.

## Superiority Complex

The prominence of his Kilkenny schoolmate, William Congreve, probably made it harder for Swift to bear his own obscurity. Worse still, Swift's cousin Dryden had publicly anointed Congreve as his successor in the laureateship. Swift, though, seemed to be under the delusion that despite having published only two unremarkable works, he was a contender for the position. Swift's third work designed for print publication, the "Ode to Congreve" (1693), makes the strange argument that Swift is more worthy of laureate status than Congreve. Early in the ode, Swift's mouthpiece makes clear his intentions to hitch a ride on the soaring fame of Congreve and to display his superior talents: He will "surmount what bears [him] up, and sing / Like the victorious wren perch'd on the eagle's wing" (P 1: 43–50, ll. 37–38). With this goal in mind, Swift writes his cousin Thomas in London, asking him to report how Congreve's latest play was received, "since I onely design that [these verses] should be printed before it" (C 1: 14), just as his Athenian Ode prefaced the collected edition of *The Athenian Mercury.*[12]

In the "Ode to Congreve" Swift differentiates himself from Congreve and calls specific attention to the "mighty gulph" (32) between the two worlds they inhabit as writers.[13] Swift's world is the unpolluted English countryside, where personal relationships and traditional moral values are the norm. Congreve, though, is situated in the vice-ridden, artificial world of London, where few know him directly, but crowds of "Goths" (83) are familiar with a media-constructed personality bearing his name. Swift's ode presents such fame as degrading, the product of a corrupt urban "Babel" (122) full of "whores" (125) and "stews [brothels]" (16). In contrast, Swift depicts his rural society as orderly and decorous, a place where he carries on a chaste love affair with the clear-speaking Muse by the crystal water's edge. Singing in a "primitive cell" (195) he is a modern-day "druid" (191). Because Congreve's plays are wares sold in the print marketplace, he must "stoop to fear" (86) displeasing boorish consumers. Swift, however, can avoid "*the dirty paths where vulgar feet have trod, / [And] give the vigorous fancy room*" (205–6). These lines, Swift notes, are excerpted "Out of an Ode I writ, inscribed The Poet. The rest is lost." As in the "Ode to the Athenian Society," Swift cross-references himself to foster the myth that he is widely renowned. By implication, "The Poet" is himself, a laureate capable of recovering the strengths of ancient Britain in an age increasingly beset by commercialism and the collapse of hierarchical distinctions. Throughout the poem, Swift's print alter ego implies that he has been divinely gifted with a "prophet's voice and prophet's pow'r" (1) that endows him with godlike ability to lead England out of its moral wilderness: *"My hate, whose lash just heaven has long decreed / Shall on a day make sin and folly bleed"* (133–4).

The ode's conclusion foreshadows an end to Swift's solitude, because it suggests that the success of his poem will make him famous in the way Congreve is, bringing the evils of the city to his doorstep and destroying his pastoral idyll.

> Whilst thus I write, vast shoals of critics come,
> And on my verse pronounce their saucy doom;
> The Muse, like some bright country virgin, shows,
> Fall'n by mishap amongst a knot of beaux;
> They, in their lewd and fashionable prate,
> Rally her dress, her language, and her gait;
> Spend their base coin before the bashful maid,
> Current like copper, and as often paid. . . .
>
> . . . . . . . . . . . . . . .
>
> *Sham'd and amaz'd,* [the Muse] *beholds the chatt'ring throng,*
> *To think what cattle she has got among;*
> *But with the odious smell and sight annoy'd,*
> *In haste she does th'offensive herd avoid.* (213–26)

Swift fears that popular fame will despoil all that is valuable about his world, but the influx of "*th'offensive herd*" and the departure of the muse are merely imagined scenarios. Perhaps the reader is supposed to hope that Swift will find a way to maintain his visionary power, his purity, and his isolation from oafish clods with filthy lucre, so that he can continue to produce odes like this one, which contains nothing "common or unclean" (233). Swift uses both the "Ode to the Athenian Society" and the "Ode to Congreve" to explore the relationship of the separate but intersecting universes of media projection and empirical reality. Swift notes, for example, that the real Congreve, whom he knows personally, is pure "bullion" (53), but the public image of Congreve is "counterfeit (56)." Despite his claims to authenticity, Swift himself was busy creating a counterfeit identity—one, however, that was in no danger of being sullied by popularity. Ironically, Swift did not get a chance to publish this fiction of himself as the true laureate because a poem by John Dryden, a laureate in fact, was chosen to preface Congreve's play.

After the "Ode to the Athenian Society," Swift's name next appeared on the title pages of Sir William Temple's *Letters* and *Miscellanea*,[14] which Swift, as Temple's literary executor, published after Temple's death in 1699. Swift used these occasions to establish his presence as a litterateur. In the preface to Volume I of Temple's *Letters,* for example, Swift repeatedly alludes to his intimacy with Temple and assumes a magisterial stance as he instructs his readers on the aesthetics of letter-writing and English style. Although Irvin Ehrenpreis finds Swift's dedication of this volume to King William oddly unpragmatic, the move makes sense if one considers Swift's laureate desires. Judging from the lack of any printed responses, the Augustan version of Swift did not impress the Republic of Letters and was of no interest at all to the average reader.[15]

## Changes

The turn of the century brought profound changes to Swift's life. The death of Sir William Temple forced Swift to leave Moor Park and take a position as chaplain to Charles, second Earl Berkeley, Lord Lieutenant of Ireland. (Swift had been ordained as an Anglican clergyman in 1694.) Accompanying Berkeley on a visit to London in April 1701, Swift discovered the exhilarating vortex of national politics and the publishing industry that kept it spinning. There Swift must have seen the irrelevance of his bardic maunderings, for he immediately jumped into one of the "paper wars" that dominated the popular press—in this case, a controversy concerning the impeachment of four Whig Lords, several of whom Swift hoped would advance his literary and churchly ambitions. With his anonymous publication of a pamphlet entitled *A Discourse of the Contests and Dissensions Between the Nobles and the Commons in Athens and Rome* (1701), Swift left capital "P" Poetry behind, but still retained his Augustan sensibilities.

Pretentious in both form and content, the *Contests and Dissensions* begins with a Latin epigram. The pamphlet, although slender, is divided into chapters and contains marginal notes that reference classical historians. Its learned argument addresses the dangers of "popular Clamours" (PW 1: 226) stirred up by the "Orators of the People" (199) and reflects the attitudes of the governing class. Swift did not understand the conventions of political pamphleteering, writing the *Contests and Dissensions* more to please the educated classes than the eclectic coffee-house crowd, whose opinions increasingly determined taste and public policy. One contemporary reader explicitly condemns Swift's tract for its "Ostentation," which leads the "unlearned *Reader* out of his way."[16] A few contemporary writers allude to it, but within a short time both the controversy and the *Contests and Dissensions* disappeared from view. Although the pamphlet went through two editions—"the Book was greedily bought, and read," Swift later recounted with some exaggeration (*Memoirs Relating to the Change . . . in the Queen's Ministry,* PW 8: 119)—it did not make readers curious to know more about its anonymous author, who seemed, based on the style and content of his pamphlet, to be a dull snob. Even Swift's modern editor, Herbert Davis, complains about the "colorlessness" of the *Discourse,* saying it is "exactly what might be expected from the editor of Sir William Temple's letters."[17] The direction Swift took after *Contests and Dissensions* indicates that he enjoyed the freedom offered by anonymous or pseudonymous publication and had begun to appreciate the relationship of controversy to market demand. Most important, Swift saw that in a print-constructed world, texts create authors, not the other way around, and that to become a commanding presence in English culture, he had to create an authorial persona whose works were in demand and whose character was memorable.

Swift's next experiment was to publish a book containing three texts— *The Battle of the Books, The Mechanical Operation of the Spirit,* and *A Tale of a Tub.* In this collection, he continued his analysis of print culture and tried out a variety of genres and authorial personae. Each of the three works in the 1704 volume is so different from its fellows that it appears that Swift was running various flags up the pole to see which would be saluted. The anonymity of the collection allowed Swift to assume fictive identities and escape from the roles of Anglican priest and Sir WilliamTemple's protégé that constrained him. Swift used all three of the works in the volume to search for answers to questions that obviously were on his mind. How can authors achieve power and glory in a print culture where novelty drives the market and works quickly sink from view? Regarding Fame's two trumpets, do popularity and prestige have to be in opposition?

## Ancients versus Moderns

Swift uses *The Battle of the Books* to dramatize the clash of cultural forces occurring at the beginning of the eighteenth century and to help him decide which side to join.[18] From his involvement in "paper wars," Swift had seen the immediate effects that topical pamphlets could produce. While scholars usually assume that *The Battle of the Books* is a defense of Sir William Temple's position that nothing Modern thinkers produce can equal the achievement of the Ancients, *The Battle of the Books* actually reflects Swift's ambivalence.[19] On one side of the clash were the old courtiers and the authors they patronized, for whom allegiance to the ancient or classical authors was necessary to maintain the literary, social, and political hierarchies that ensured their supremacy. They blew the gold trumpet of prestige for themselves and looked down on Modern celebrities created by the popular press. These Moderns not to the manner born and ignorant of the legacy of the past, however, could achieve as much or more influence than "their betters."

Swift staged his battle in St. James's Palace. The setting is highly significant, for St. James's housed the Royal Library, a symbol of English aristocratic prerogatives and High Art.[20] The hostilities in Swift's *Battle* are sparked by new library policies based on more democratic principles.[21] The specific cause of Swift's battle of the books is the application, by Richard Bentley, Keeper of St. James's Library, of policies outlined in Gabriel Naudé's *Instructions Concerning Erecting of a Library.*[22] Rather than shrines to ancient learning and the exclusive provinces of the noble or affluent, libraries, in Naudé's view, should be open to the general public and conserve the whole range of works produced by the culture. The battle in Swift's narrative is specifically incited by the implementation of Naudé's directive that topical pamphlets be accessioned. Naudé argues that although pamphlets are usually considered low ephemera unworthy of preservation, future scholars will need details of contemporary controversies. Besides, by dismissing them as "mean baubles, and pieces of no consideration, we happen to lose a world of rare collections, and such as are sometimes the most curious pieces of the whole Library."[23] Swift's battle is sparked because the Moderns, including the writers of this "new Species of controversial Books" (PW 1: 145) want to displace the Ancients from their position at the top of the literary hierarchy. The plot functions as an allegory to describe how the increasing influence of popular literature threatens the rearguard of the feudal order, which risks being swept away by the turbulent river of *"Disputes, Arguments, Rejoynders, Brief Considerations, Answers, Replies, Remarks, Reflexions, Objections, Confutations"* (144) pouring into the streets.[24] Despite Swift's unease about the Moderns, however, he does not decide the battle in favor of the Ancients but leaves the outcome in doubt.

The *Battle*-narrator notes that the Modern army has the advantage of numbers, its forces swelled by "infinite Swarms of *Calones*[25] . . . all without Coats to cover them," to which he adds a note: *"These are Pamphlets, which are not bound or cover'd"* (152n). Here the narrator underlines the class division between well-dressed leather-bound books, resident in the libraries of fine houses, and uncovered pamphlets, hawked in the streets, markets, and fairs. Self-styled members of the Republic of Letters, like Swift's narrator, have always degraded popular literature by associating it with poverty. A central part of the Grubstreet fiction is the idea of the starving writer willing to do anything for a few pence. As Northrop Frye points out, "[P]hrases emphasizing the cheapness of popular literature, such as 'dime novel,' or 'penny dreadful,' lingered long after inflation had made them archaic."[26] Grubstreet pamphlets and broadsides may have power but certainly no prestige. Perhaps to avoid the denigration associated with pamphlets, Swift published his three (he *Battle of the Books, Mechanical Operation of the Spirit,* and *Tale of a Tub*) together as a several shilling *book.*

In *The Battle of the Books,* Swift confronts the question of whether any author in a print-shaped culture can achieve enduring fame because of the rapid pace of change. In scribal culture, works supplanted one another, but at a very slow rate, so fame lasted a long time. Swift's narrator notes, for instance, how Duns Scotus and Aristotle "both concerted to seize *Plato* by main Force, and turn him out from his antient Station among the *Divines,* where he had peaceably dwelt near Eight Hundred years. The Attempt succeeded, and the two Usurpers have reigned ever since in his stead." In modern print culture, though, the revolution of authors takes place with lightning speed. The *Battle*-narrator describes how title pages, posted as advertisements for the latest publications, remain only "For a very few Days . . . in all Publick Places" (144). Neither do the few lucky authors ensconced in the library escape the inevitable annihilation that comes to all, some "in a few Days, but to others, later" (144).

Countering the idea of the library as a temple of immortality,[27] Swift's narrator makes it clear that even without the presence of warfare, the library is a place of death:

> I believe, it is with Libraries, as with other Cemeteries . . . that a certain Spirit . . . hovers the Monument, till the Body is corrupted, and turns to *Dust,* or to *Worms,* but then vanishes or dissolves: So, we may say, a restless Spirit haunts over every *Book,* till *Dust or Worms* have seized upon it. . . . (144)

By using books to embody their authors, Swift underscores the idea that authors "live" only as long as books by or about them continue to circulate and incite discussion. Unknown or forgotten authors are dead to the world. Subsequent editions of *The Battle of the Books* contain an engraving that shows Fame blowing one trumpet and holding the other. At the beginning of the eighteenth century, it was not clear which kind of trumpeting would persist longer, the gold or the brass.

In the midst of the death and destruction of the battle, Swift takes the opportunity to kill or castrate his literary fathers and clear a space for himself.[28] Dryden, spared death but dwarfed by his armor, is ridiculed as a "Mouse under a Canopy of State, or like a shriveled Beau from within the Pent-house of a modern Perewig" (157). Cowley is cleft in two, one half of his body trampled by horses and the other half dragged around a field. Although Swift plainly intends Temple to be a hero of the piece (163), he shows him unable to avoid a lance thrown by William Wotton, Bentley's ally. Cowley dead. Temple and Dryden impotent. Swift's infliction of wounds suggests his possible rejection of the exclusive literary modes these figures represent but leaves open the question of how to achieve lasting fame in a world constantly being remade by the media.

In the funereal gloom of St. James's library, Swift seems to look to the legendary figure of Aesop for some hope of authorial transcendence.[29] Aesop was very much present in the print culture of the early eighteenth century, when he had a "celebrity perhaps unrivaled by any other literary figure of the day, living or dead."[30] Aesop straddled the boundaries between the Ancients and the Moderns, for although Aesop had the respect of the literati and the enduring fame that qualified him as an Ancient, Modern writers, intrigued by his life and works, kept his name alive in popular literature by appropriating his character for new purposes and continuing to speculate about him.[31] To symbolize Aesop's ambivalent status, Swift notes that despite his alliance with the Ancients, Aesop is "chained . . . fast among a Shelf of *Moderns*" (150). Having "a thousand Forms," Aesop is a puzzling set of contradictions. Represented as powerful or enslaved, able-bodied or deformed, Greek or African, it was impossible to say with certainty who he was, leaving the reader "at Liberty to believe his Pleasure."[32] Aesop also had a reputation for unmannerly outspokenness. He was usually characterized as being extremely rude (in the service of truth) and indulging in scatological jokes. Because of their circulation in chapbooks as well as more elite forms, Aesop and his fables had become a part of English folklore. Far from being a static character, Aesop continued to assume new identities and to exist in the present. *Aesop in Europe, Aesop at Oxford, Aesop in Portugal, Aesop in Scotland, Aesop in Southwark, Aesop in Spain, Aesop the Wanderer, Aesop at Court, Aesop at Paris* all appeared between 1700 and 1710. Although Swift did not put them to use in *The Battle of the Books,* the lessons in mythmaking taught by Aesop's example were not lost upon him.[33]

As far as promoting Swift's career as a writer, *The Battle of the Books* was a failure. No one saluted this flag. Neither the substance of the work nor the life of its implied author were of interest to early-eighteenth-century readers. The Ancients versus the Moderns controversy, as the ubiquitous John Dunton expresses it in his *Works of the Learned,* was a "dry and insipid business,"[34] which did not inspire the coffee-house talk or pamphlet reactions that signified eighteenth-century celebrity.

The next work in Swift's anonymous three-pamphlet collection, *Discourse on the Mechanical Operation of the Spirit,* was another unsuccessful experiment but in a very different vein. The work addresses the threat of dissenters to the Anglican Church, a topic that had brought fame, for instance, to Henry Sacheverell, a firebrand preacher who published inflammatory pamphlets warning against religious toleration. While the narrator of *The Battle of the Books* has few identifiable qualities aside from his sympathy with the Ancients, the Discourser of Swift's *Mechanical Operation* is more sharply outlined. Swift makes the Discourser a novice writer, like himself. He is a member of the Royal Society, forthrightly in the Modern camp. Unlike that of the *Battle*-narrator, the Discourser for the most part has a rough, polemical style.

In the *Discourse,* Swift again returns to a contemplation of fame in modern print culture. His Discourser believes that he can make his name by following the fashion of the moment. To determine what that fashion is, he spends "three Days" doing research on current trends by looking at the title pages of new publications posted as advertisements. Based on this market survey, the Discourser observes that nothing "holds so general a Vogue, as that of *A Letter to a Friend*" (PW 1: 171). Although he determines to exploit the epistolary genre, the Discourser humorously undermines his choice by noting how inappropriate most published letters are:

> Nothing is more common than to meet with long Epistles address'd to Persons and Places, where, at first thinking, one would be apt to imagine it not altogether so necessary or Convenient; Such as, *a Neighbor at next Door, a mortal Enemy, a perfect Stranger,* or *a Person of Quality in the Clouds;* and upon Subjects, in appearance, the least proper for Conveyance by the Post; as, *long Schemes in Philosophy; dark and wonderful Mysteries of State; Laborious Dissertations in Criticism and Philosophy, Advice to Parliaments,* and the like. (171–2)

The first few pages of the *Discourse* are witty and urbane, although not particularly memorable, but the tone suddenly changes as the narrator opens his main business—a heavy-handed jeremiad against nonconformists. Through the *Discourse,* Swift seems to be mocking those who write to the minute, and at the same time, respecting the need for it. But nothing in the *Discourse* was amusing, amazing, or shocking enough to create a stir or even a flicker of response. As Phillip Harth puts it, Swift was "flogging a dead horse."[35] Irvin Ehrenpreis also condemns the satire, saying that it "takes a characterization which is heavy enough, and, without lightening its crudities, extends and labours all its applications."[36] Swift himself stepped away from the *Mechanical Operation* in a note to a later edition, in which he concedes that "This Discourse is not altogether equal to the two Former Treatises [*The Battle of the Books* and *A Tale of a Tub*]." No one saluted this flag either, not even its creator.

### Blockbuster

Whoever designed the 1704 title page—Swift, or the publisher, John Nutt—knew what he was doing. *A Tale of a Tub. Written for the Universal Improvement of Mankind* is printed in large letters and serves as the title for the volume as a whole. Smaller letters indicate the inclusion of *An Account of a Battle Between the Ancient and Modern Books in St. James's Library.* The

*Discourse on the Mechanical Operation of the Spirit* is not mentioned at all. Of the three items in the collection, *A Tale of a Tub* had all the earmarks of a potential bestseller. It was new, it was strange, it was going to be controversial. Clearly its publication would create a verbal furor that would generate multiple editions and continued reaction. Its author—whoever he was—would be the talk of the town. While Swift kept the narrators of his *Battle of the Books* and *Discourse on the Mechanical Operation of the Spirit* at arm's length, he embraces his *Tale*-teller as an authorial model. In writing the *Tale*, Swift seemed to have discovered the distinctive nature of his genius and first glimpsed the road toward immortality.

*A Tale of a Tub* has many of the features that Lawrence Lipking (in *The Life of the Poet*) identifies with authorial declarations of independence that announce a writer's rejection of his predecessors and his own past. Such a work is baffling and resists definition; it presents a radically new point of view; it moves the writer from "a backwater, province or enclave that time has forgotten" to the "focal point of all civilization. Making sense of history at last, he sees into the future."[37] That future, as viewed through the eyes of Swift's *Tale*-teller, is a plastic reality molded by the popular media. Augustans like John Dryden and his massive translation of Virgil are unknown except to a few scholars (PW 1: 22), while popular figures and popular texts define the culture. Perhaps for this reason, the *Tale*-teller chooses to situate his work under the "Classis" of "*GRUB-STREET*" (38).

Grubstreet literature not only includes topical pamphlets but also chapbook literature that never goes out of fashion, such as legendary stories of figures like Hercules, Dick Whittington, and Robin Hood. The "classis" also comprises jestbooks, like those mentioned by the *Tale*-teller—"*Six-peny-worth of Wit*, Westminister *Drolleries, Delightful Tales, Compleat Jesters*"—whose humorous anecdotes directly descend from the medieval fabliaux. In this context, the *Tale*-teller justifiably claims that the "Smithfield muses [Smithfield was a center of chapbook production as well as the site of a popular fair] have . . . nobly Triumphed over *Time;* have clipt his Wings, pared his Nails, filed his Teeth, turn'd back his Hour-Glass, blunted his scythe" (38). Characters and works that became Smithfield classics were those to which readers returned, time and again.[38] Although associated with the underclass, the readership of these chapbooks was universal.[39] By putting his opus under the classis of Grubstreet, the *Tale*-teller implies that he and his *Tale* might achieve the legendary status of a chapbook favorite like Aesop.

Whatever his expectations, Swift must have been overwhelmed by the amazing popularity of the *Tale* (four editions in a year and a half), and by the intense speculation about who its notorious author might be. The *Tale*-teller's identity was hard to discern because he defies categorization. While the allusions in the *Tale* reveal that its author is very well read, he lacks the basic discrimination that should accompany such learning. He, for example, sees no difference between High and Low literary Art, mixing folktale motifs, like the narrative of three brothers, with learned discourse. He is, by turns, coarse and refined, crass and subtle. He analyzes chapbooks as if they were arcane masterpieces—for instance, explaining that *Dick Whittington and his Cat* is "the Work of that Mysterious *Rabbi, Jehudi Hannasi*, containing a Defence of the *Gemara* of the *Jerusalem Misna*, and its just preference to that of *Babylon"*—and treating Dryden's *Hind and the Panther* like a simple tale (41). The *Tale*-teller's conflation of High and Low Art was objectionable, but his disrespect of religion was horrifying.

Pulling out all the stops, Swift's *Tale*-teller seems to hold Christianity itself up to ridicule, causing William Wotton in *Observations upon The Tale of a Tub* (1705), to condemn it as "one of the Prophanest Banters upon the Religion of *Jesus Christ*, as such, that ever yet appeared." In particular, Wotton recoils from the "Common Oaths, and Idle Allusions" that degrade the Word of God and the name of God as well as from the way in which the *Tale*-teller takes scriptural passages and concretizes them in ludicrous metaphors: "Can any thing be more blasphemous than his *Game at Leap-frog between the Flesh and the Spirit?*," Wotton asks.[40] In making analogies, the *Tale*-teller introduces into his text unseemly references to anuses, excrement, urine, fistulas, erections, flatulence, constipation, genitalia, orgasms, and other topics off-limits in polite discourse, especially one purporting to treat spiritual matters. In the fifth edition of the *Tale*, Swift published a disingenuous "Apology," in which he pretends to be surprised and disappointed that people misread his defense of the church. While he may have had the church's welfare at heart, his primary goal seems to have been the provocation of public reaction by being purposefully offensive. And react the public did.

One of the many responses to Swift's *Tale* is purportedly written by a night soil collector, who asserts that despite his underclass status and dirty job, he has more refinement than the *Tale*-teller. He castigates the *Tale*'s author for ignoring the "Bounds of Modesty" and presenting the "Lewdest Images" from ancient writings and the modern filth of "Dunghils . . . Ditches . . . and Common-shores [sewers]," which add a "Tincture of such Filthiness" to every part of the work. He is also appalled by the "Curses, Oaths, and Imprecations, that the most profligate Criminal in *New-Prison* would be asham'd to Repeat."[41] Indeed, the innovation of "Swearing and Cursing" in print caused comment by others as well because it was an unprecedented breach of the social code.[42] In the persona of the *Tale*-teller, Swift abandoned the restrictions that his sacred vocation and his genteel status imposed on him. He may have thought that the irony of the work would allow him to escape blame, but such was not going to be the case.

Immediately after the publication of *A Tale of a Tub,* the town was abuzz with questions about its anonymous author. Who would dare publish such a thing? And why? The night soil collector describes the speculation among his cohorts about the identity of the *Tale*-teller:

> One said, he believ'd it was a Journey-man-Taylor in *Billeteer*-Lane, that was an Idle sort of a Fellow, and lov'd Writing more than Stitching. . . . Why may it not be Mr. *Gumly,* the Rag-womans Husband in *Turnbull-street,* says another; he is kept by her, and [has] little to do. . . . But it was urg'd that his Stile was harsh, rough and unpolished, and that he did not understand one Word of *Latin.* Why then, cries another, *Oliver's* Porter had an *Amanuensis* at *Bedlam,* that us'd to transcribe what he dictat'd, and may not these be some scatter'd Notes of his Master's? To which all replied, that although *Oliver's* Porter was Craz'd, yet his Misfortune never let him forget he was a Christian. . . .

Suddenly, in the midst of this discussion, one man asks, "What if after all it should be a Parson; for who may make more free with their Trade? . . . Hold, cry all the Company, that Function must not be mention'd without Respect, we have enough of the dirty Subject, we had better Drink our Coffee, and Talk our Politicks."[43] That the *Tale*-teller might be a clergyman was the most sensational suggestion of all because it conjured up an unimaginable perversion—an anti-Christian priest with the mentality of a rag-woman's husband or Oliver Cromwell's crazy porter.

Other rumors circulated in print about the identity of the mystery man who dared to write the *Tale.* William Wotton, for example, relays what he has heard—"It is publickly reported that [Sir William Temple] wrote this Book: It is a Story, which . . . I neither made, nor spread. . . ." Wotton then introduces another rumor—that Thomas Swift (Jonathan's cousin), a clergyman, also had something to do with the *Tale.* If true, then Thomas Swift had bitten the hand that fed him by libeling the man—Lord Somers—who got him "a very good *Benefice* in one of the most Delicious Counties of *England.* "[44] Wotton calls on Thomas Swift to clear himself of suspicion, especially because he holds the public trust as a man of the cloth. Being linked to *A Tale of a Tub* would sink any churchman's career, because it had become synonymous with obscenity and blasphemy.

A hue and cry kept the secret *Tale*-teller in the forefront of public consciousness and created a rush on publications promising to reveal his identity. The anonymous author of *The Tale of a Tub, revers'd, for the universal Improvement of Mankind . . . With a Character of the Author* (1705) notes that information about the *Tale*-teller was in such demand that he could be sure his pamphlet would "Run like Lightning." This pamphleteer, like others, circulates the delicious gossip that a clergyman was responsible for *A Tale of a Tub.* One bit of evidence the pamphleteer cites is the lack of a frontispiece engraving before the *Tale.* On the one hand, this omission situates the *Tale* among cheaply printed chapbooks like "the *Seven Champions, Guy Earl of Warwick,* and *Hickathrift,*" but on the other hand, could mean that it was written by a "Reverend" author who is ashamed to be associated with the "compleat System of Divinity" in it.[45] The outlandishness of the *Tale* and rumors that a clergyman might be its author guaranteed that it would be read and talked about by everybody—"not only at Court, but in the City and Suburbs."[46] Anything *Tale*-related would sell, a situation that publishers and authors exploited.

William King, a priest known for his wit, beat down suggestions that he had written the *Tale,* but nonetheless rode its success by identifying his anonymously published *The Fairy Feast* (1704) and *Mully of Mountown* (1704) as "By the Author of a Tale of a Tub." Also piggybacking on the *Tale's* success were *The Second Part of The Tale of a Tub . . . by the author of The Tale of a Tub* (1708), *A Complete Key to the Tale of a Tub* (1710), *A New Tale of a Tub* (1710), and numerous other publications by "the author of a Tale of a Tub," "by a friend of the author of a Tale of a Tub," or "by one very near akin to the author of the Tale of a Tub" (1709). Before 1711, there were 28 *Tale*-related publications, a number that includes editions of *A Tale of a Tub,* imitations of the *Tale,* and works fathered on the *Tale*-author.[47]

Within a very short space of time, Swift's proxy, the *Tale*-teller, was a celebrity. And he remained famous for an eon in print culture, where titles and authors disappear quickly from public consciousness or fail to register at all. Thus, six years after the publication of his *Tale*—in the "Apology" to the fifth edition (1710)—the *Tale*-teller justifiably gloats that his "*Book seems calculated to live at least as long as our Language, and our Tast admit no great Alterations*" (1). Unlike the dead or dying authors in *The Battle of the Books,* the *Tale*-teller, thriving in new manifestations, remained very visibly alive, much like the everlasting Aesop. Like Aesop, the *Tale*-teller was powerful, mysterious, paradoxical, and heterodox—qualities that later became annexed to Swift's name and made him a legend.

While most critics believe that Swift condemns his *Tale*-teller, Swift's subsequent adoption of the *Tale*-teller's attitudes and identity reveal the opposite: that in the *Tale*-teller he found himself and saw his future as a writer of provocative popular literature. Swift knew that because he was an Anglican priest, such writing would be criticized, but he chose to do it, perhaps because he believed the influence it gave him would allow him to accomplish noble things. He presents this rationale to Stella, the young woman he befriended at Moor Park, whose name later became inextricably linked to his: "They may talk of the *you know what* [*A Tale of a Tub*]; but, gad, if it had not been for that, I should never been able to get the access I have had; and if that helps me to succeed, then that *same thing* will be serviceable to the church" (JS 1: 47). Like almost everything else written by Swift, the truth of this assertion is undeterminable.

## Hoaxing: The Bickerstaff Papers

Buoyed by his success in disturbing the universe with his *Tale of a Tub,* Swift—again with an authorial proxy—applied what he had learned to create another national sensation. In 1708, Swift set about to perpetrate a hoax that would destroy a cultural icon—John Partridge.[48] At all levels of society and in all parts of England, John Partridge was a familiar figure because of the popularity of his almanac and the subversive views he expressed in it.[49] Partridge was so alive in English culture that Swift may have been eager to see whether he could kill him—not through any violence—but by devising a fictional rival to Partridge, another astrologer/almanac writer named Isaac Bickerstaff, who would beat Partridge at his own game: hoaxing the public through print. In this match, Partridge is Br'er Fox, and Bickerstaff is Br'er Rabbit, the clever trickster who defeats him. As Swift creates the myth of Partridge's death, he creates the myth of Bickerstaff's power. Bickerstaff's first volley in his paper war against Partridge was the publication of an almanac that contained the prediction that Partridge would die on March 29, 1708, close enough to April first to make it appear as an April Fool's joke.

Ham-handed propaganda, doggerel verse, and homely advice were standard features of almanacs—the most popular of popular literature—but Swift's Bickerstaff nonetheless makes the bizarre claim that his will be a contribution to the Republic of Letters because he has proceeded "in a new Way" (PW 2: 143) that leaves the distinctive stamp of his genius on the form and elevates it—"I believe no Gentleman, who reads this Paper, will look upon it to be of the same Cast, or Mold, with the common Scribbles that are every Day hawked about. My Fortune hath placed me above the little Regard for writing for a few Pence. . . . Therefore, let not Wise men too hastily condemn this Essay" (PW 2: 149). As he did with the *Tale*-teller, Swift made Bickerstaff indifferent to literary distinctions, a technique, Swift discovered, that maddened the critics.

Projections of when prominent persons would die during the coming year were a staple feature of almanacs, but Swift carried his joke to extremes by following up on the prophecy of Partridge's death with "verification" that it had occurred. Two days after Partridge's "death," a Grubstreet pamphlet—*The Accomplishment of the First of Mr. Bickerstaff's Predictions*—appeared, offering "evidence" that Partridge gone to his reward. Swift's pamphlet masquerades as the account of a revenue clerk who was supposedly present at Partridge's deathbed and heard him confess that he did not have the visionary powers he claimed and was nothing but a fraud: "As to foretelling the Weather, [I] never meddle with that, but leave it to the Printer, who takes it out of any old Almanack as he thinks fit: The rest was my own Invention to make my Almanack sell" (PW 2: 155). Swift's revenue clerk reports that Partridge expired at 7:05 P.M., "by which is clear, that Mr. *Bickerstaff* was mistaken almost four hours in his calculation" (155). The next installment of Swift's serial fiction was a crudely printed broadside elegy replete with irreverent humor, jolting tetrameter, wrenched rhyme, and a concluding epitaph, which begins, "*Here Five Foot deep lyes on his Back / A* Cobler, Starmonger, and Quack" (P 1: 98–101, ll. 104–5). In the "Elegy" on Partridge, Swift abandoned (almost for good) any pretensions to writing Augustan poetry and began to use Grubstreet genres with frequency.

Swift's campaign against Partridge was an enormous success. Bickerstaff's *Predictions* were quickly pirated by half a dozen publishers and translated into Dutch, German, and French. Piracy, although ritualistically denounced by authors, was a signifier of their fame. The Bickerstaff hoax began as Swift's private property, but it soon became a community playground. Imaginative sequels poured forth, some purporting to be authored by Bickerstaff, others by Partridge, still others by purported friends of Partridge and Bickerstaff: *D. Pertridg's answer, to the wonderful Predictions set forth by Esquire Bickerstaff, for the year 1708. Wherein his several Prognostications are plainly confuted, by a special friend of Mr. Pertridg* ; *Doctor Pateridge's Answer to Esquire Bickerstaff's strange and impudent Predictions: or the Knave in Fashion; A Continuation of the prdictions* [*sic*] *for the remaining Part of the Year 1708. By Isaac Bickerstaff, Esquire;* and *Squire Bickerstaff detected: or the astrological Imposter convicted, by John Partridge, student in Physics and Astrology; Bickerstaff Redivivus; Bickerstaff's Prediction confirm'd in the Death of Partridge; A Letter from Mr. Isaac Bickerstaff to the Author of the Oxford Almanac.* Thanks to Swift, few persons living in England in 1708 could have been ignorant of Bickerstaff's name or Partridge's purported death.

Partridge cooperated in his own destruction by issuing assertions that he was alive and well, to which Swift responded with a *Vindication of Isaac Bickerstaff* (1709), giving further "proofs" of Partridge's death as well as answering Partridge's attacks on his style. Countering Partridge's view of him as a Grubstreet hack, Bickerstaff establishes his international reputation as a renowned litterateur by citing some of the numerous eulogies written to him in Latin, which he received from scholars in "several Parts of *Europe* (some as far as Muscovy)" (PW 2: 160). He professes his "Concern is not so much for [his] own Reputation, as that of the *Republick of Letters,* which Mr. *Partrige* hath endeavored to wound through my Sides" (159). Having a reputation as a popular writer (though he is one) is at odds with Bickerstaff's image of himself. In his words, "It grieved me to the Heart . . . [to see] Labours,

which had cost me so much Thought and Watching, bawled about by common Hawkers, which I only intended for the weightiest Consideration of
the gravest persons" (164). Like his proxy Bickerstaff, Swift, too, created a
provocative gap between what seems to be his own high estimation of himself and the way that others see him.

Swift's Bickerstaff, a gleam in his creator's eye a mere 12 months before,
secured a central place in the public's mind so definitively that he could declare total victory over Partridge by 1709. In a paragraph in *The Tatler,* Bickerstaff explains the nature of Partridge's death:

> [I]t is asserted by the said *John Partridge,* That he is still living, and not only
> so, but that he was also living some Time before, and even at the Instant when
> I writ of his Death. I have in another Place [the *Vindication*] . . . convinc'd
> this Man that he is dead. . . . For tho' the Legs and Arms, and whole Body, of
> that Man may still appear and perform their animal Functions. . . . [when] his
> Art is gone, the Man is gone.[50]

As a man, Partridge still lived, but his inability to counter Bickerstaff's myth
of his nonexistence signaled a failure of the "Art" that created his vital visi-
bility in the print media.

Bickerstaff's ability to kill Partridge through the press inspired imaginative fictions. In *Squire Bickerstaff Detected,* for instance, a sexton solemnly
denies the reality of Partridge's claim to life by telling him to his face, "It is
in print, and the whole town knows you are dead."[51] Daniel Defoe, in the
*Review,* tongue-in-cheek remarks that Partridge's "Elegy was cry'd about the
streets . . . and you know, Men's Elegies are never made till they are dead."[52]
Stories circulated about the problems that Bickerstaff's death warrant presented to Partridge. The *Dictionary of National Biography* reports, for instance, that Partridge wrote to the postmaster of Ireland and took out
advertisements in the newspapers to certify to his existence. (I have come
across no documents to support these assertions.) The story that Bickerstaff
forced Partridge to give up almanac publishing has also been repeated, often
by scholars, even though it is untrue. Partridge temporarily ceased publishing because of a lawsuit, not because of Bickerstaff's burying him. Myths of
Partridge's vanquishment by Bickerstaff's hoax keep circulating because they
are so much fun to read and repeat. Underneath the humor, though, may
lurk anxieties about the media's awesome power to create and to destroy.

Swift's Bickerstaff, like the *Tale*-teller, became a celebrity, his name on
everyone's lips. In *An Answer to Bickerstaff,* Swift creates a persona who sym-
pathizes with the embarrassment Bickerstaff must be experiencing as a gentleman who finds himself known as the author and subject of Grubstreet
literature. Through this vicarious exercise (which he did not publish), Swift

seems to be anticipating the day that his authorship will be discovered and sorting out his own responses to the criticism that would ensue.

> I BELIEVE it is no small mortification to this gentleman astrologer [Bickerstaff], as well as his bookseller, to find their piece. . . . immediately seized on by three or four interloping printers of Grub-street, the title stuffed with an abstract of the whole matter, together with the standard epithets of *strange and wonderful,* the price brought down a full half . . . and bawled about by hawkers of the inferior class. . . . [T]o comfort him a little, this production of mine will have the same fate: Tomorrow will my ears be grated by the *little boys* and *wenches in straw-hats,* and I must an hundred times undergo the mortification to have my own work offered to me . . . at an under-value. Then, which is a great deal worse, my acquaintance at the coffee-house will ask me, whether I have seen the Answer to 'Squire Bickerstaff's predictions, and whether I know the puppy that wrote it? . . . [As for Bickerstaff's next predictions], I suppose we shall have them much about the same time with *The General History of Ears* [an allusion to *A Tale of a Tub*]. . . . [I]t is very probable he will succeed as often as he is disposed to try the experiment, that is, as long as he can preserve a thorough contempt for his own time and other people's understandings, and is resolved not to laugh cheaper than at the expense of a million people. (PW 2: 197–9)

Although Swift criticizes Bickerstaff/himself for his "contempt for his own time and other people's understandings," he is plainly proud of his capacity "to succeed as often as he is disposed to try" and "not [have] to laugh cheaper than at the expense of a million people."

April Fool's Day became a cue for Swift's mischief making.[53] In 1709, the next April Fool's Day after the Bickerstaff hoax, Swift played a similar game by inserting a fake advertisement in *The Post Boy* of March 31 that announced an auction of books the next day. He sent readers on a fool's errand to "Mr. Doily's in The Strand" where offered for auction were "a small Collection of about a Hundred Books, of the choicest Kinds and Editions, all fair" as well as "7 Marco-Antonio Prints; proof Plates, a Porphiry Urn; two browse [*sic*] Lamps; and a small Parcel of Medals, some very Rare." In the next issue of *The Post Boy,* the editor prints a retraction, "That there was no such Auction design'd; and that the said Advertisement was taken in, and inserted by the Printer Boy's Inadvertency" (PW 4: 267). Years later, when one of Swift's enemies, Bishop Evans, saw his own obituary printed in the *St. James's Evening Post,* the first person he thought to blame was Jonathan Swift (PW 14: xiv) because of his reputation for media hoaxing.

Like that of the *Tale*-teller, Bickerstaff's name was used to sell publications. Among eighteenth-century publications, almost a hundred works have Bickerstaff included in the title or listed as author.[54] The most famous reincarnation of Bickerstaff is as the "author" of Richard Steele's *The Tatler.* In this mutation, Bickerstaff loses his association with Grubstreet and iron- ically becomes an arbiter of gentility. Although Bickerstaff and the *Tale*-teller were famous throughout England, the Continent, and the colonies, Swift was virtually unknown. That obscurity allowed Swift to try out different au- thorial strategies but prevented him from claiming his successes, although he covertly pointed to his authorship in several publications.[55]

From his Partridge hoax, Swift experienced firsthand the way Grubstreet genres could change cultural realities. Daniel Defoe—another genius of the popular press—attests to the profound effects wrought by lowly ballads, for example, by itemizing the revolutions ignited by them: "Did not the famous ballad of *Lilly-bulero* sing King *James* out of his three kingdoms? And . . . did it not form the Revolution [of 1688–89] of Blessed Memory? . . . The Riots in Scotland were ushered in with a Song, called *AWA, Whigs, AWA.* The mobs of Dr. *Sacheverell's* time had *Down with the Round Heads.* . . . [N]ay, even the Solicitations for the late *Callico Bill* were introduced with the Bal- lad of a *Call'ico Madam.*"[56] Swift could see from his own experiments with *A Tale of a Tub* and the Bickerstaff hoax that best-selling (and hence broadly influential) works combine novelty, irreverence, controversy, and mystery in ways that appeal to an inclusive audience of "the *Superficial,* the *Ignorant,* and the *Learned*" (PW 1: 117), to which the *Tale*-teller addresses his opus. Swift, however, needed to reconcile this epiphany with the expectation that as an Anglican priest with great literary talents, he was supposed to display his gifts in more elevated and elevating ways.

### Tables of Fame

Fame was very much on Swift's mind in 1708 and 1709. Although he no longer thought in terms of Ancients versus Moderns, Swift was still uncer- tain about what kind of a writer he wanted to be. He meditates on this issue in an elaborate fantasy called the "Tables of Fame," which appeared in two issues of *The Tatler* (September 13 and 15, 1709), written with his friend Richard Steele. In these essays, fame is a democratic popularity contest de- cided by votes sent in via the penny post. Readers were to list their candi- dates and submit them to "Mr. *Bickerstaff,* at Mr. *Morphew's,* near *Stationer's-Hall,*" where the results would be tabulated and "every Name. . . . rank'd according to the Voices it has" to determine at which table the person would sit. No "precedence [would be] given to the Ancients."[57]

Bickerstaff reports that his sister Jenny wants to nominate Aristotle, be- cause "he was a great Scholar, and that she had read him at the Boarding- School." Bickerstaff mordantly notes that "She certainly means a Trifle sold by the Hawkers, call'd *Aristotle's Problems.*"[58] A number of pamphlets bore

Aristotle's name as a come-on and had nothing to do with the ancient philosopher, for example, *Aristotle's Family Jewel, Aristotle's Legacy, Aristotle's Manual of Choice Secrets,* and *Aristotle's Masterpiece, or the Secrets of Generation Display'd,* the latter a racy sex manual. Bickerstaff is thrown into perplexity, thinking about the effect of "Excresences" on the "real Reputation" of an individual: to most readers at the time, Aristotle may have been more familiar as a pornographer than a philosopher. Swift had already seen that once the *Tale*-teller or Bickerstaff were widely known, they became public property—out of their creator's control—to be appropriated by others, who used the characters' celebrity for their own purposes. Swift's repeated returns to the issue of fame in print culture was part of his search for the ways in which he should conduct his life as an author.

During the period 1708–10, Swift was torn between seeking the quiet approval of the tasteful few or using the brass trumpet to rouse a general audience. He hedged his bets and, still under the guise of anonymity, published both Augustan and popular items in tandem. On the popular track, Swift possibly made some of his works available to Edmund Curll, perhaps through a third party.[59] Curll, the epitome of Grubstreet entrepreneurship, knew what would sell and how to sell it. He prospered for 40 years by giving the public what it wanted. *The Charitable Surgeon: or, the best Remedies for the Worst Maladies* (dealing with venereal disease) and *The Case of John Atherton, Bishop of Waterford in Ireland: who was convicted of the Sin of Uncleanness with a Cow* cinched Curll's reputation for never overestimating the taste of the English public. Curll was the first to publish Swift's *Meditation upon a Broomstick* and "The History Vanbrugh's House." He may have been the first to publish "Mrs. Harris' Petition" and "Baucis and Philomen," which appeared simultaneously with other editions in 1709. None of these pieces bore Swift's name, but all of them went through multiple editions, showing their wide appeal. Unable to contain his glee about his popular successes, Swift wrote to Robert Hunter in March 1709 to brag about his citizenship in the *"Republica Grubstreetaria,* which was never in greater Altitude, though I have been of late but a small Contributor" (C 1: 133).

At the same time he appeared under Curll's imprint, Swift was making sure that his verses were included in Tonson's upscale *Miscellanies,* a forum for Augustan laureates and would-be laureates.[60] "Baucis and Philomen" and "To Mrs. Biddy Floyd" appeared anonymously in Tonson's 1709 collection (and were simultaneously published by Curll). Without his name attached to his poems and huddled with numerous other poets in Tonson's collection, Swift must have been dismayed at his chances of being noticed. The contributors were all gentlemen or noblemen whose classical learning was evident, an exclusive club that would be shocked to know they were rubbing shoulders with the author of "Mrs. Harris' Petition," a low poem in the vulgar dialect of an

Irish servant woman. In *The Tatler*, Swift published several anonymous poems in the high style—"Description of the Morning" and "Description of a City Shower." Both are mock pastorals in iambic pentameter couplets, a more dignified meter than the Hudibrastic tetrameter Swift used in "The Elegy to Partridge." When the two "Description" poems first appeared, they elicited little or no printed response, and no one was interested in pirating them.

Others of Swift's experiments at this time involved creating personae—unlike Bickerstaff or the *Tale*-teller—that would not disgrace him as an Anglican clergyman. Seeming to enjoy the protean freedom of anonymous publication, Swift did not put his name to these works, even though they might have burnished his career in the church. His *Letter . . . Concerning the Sacramental Test* (1709) is purportedly written by a Member of the Irish House of Commons to protest the Sacramental Test, an official requirement that all officeholders take Anglican communion. Abolishing the Test, argues Swift's legislator, would severely undermine the authority of the Established Church, one of the pillars of English society. Embarrassed that he is writing a pamphlet, Swift's legislative gentleman takes pains to distinguish between his genteel tract and those "infamous weekly Papers that infest [the] Coffee-Houses" (PW 2: 111), although he has to acknowledge that "how insipid so-ever those Papers are, they seem to be levelled to the Understandings of a great Number. They are grown a necessary Part in Coffee-house Furniture, and some Time or other happen to be read by Customers of all Ranks, for Curiosity or Amusement. . . . One of these Authors (the Fellow who was *pilloryed*, I have forgot his name) is indeed so grave, sententious, dogmatical a Rogue, that there is no enduring him" (113). Sneering Defoe's being punished like a common criminal, Swift's speaker might pretend to forget his name (Swift supplies it in a footnote), but everyone else would have known it because, as opposed to Swift, Defoe was a celebrity.[61]

Also in 1709, Swift published another work with a similarly supercilious tone. The title page of the *Project for the Advancement of Religion* identifies the author as "A Person of Quality" and features an epigraph in Latin from Horace. (Latin epigrams became scarcer as the century proceeded, because the majority of readers could not translate them.) Swift's Projector expresses cosmic concern about the deterioration of the Established Church and proposes a plan of action, spearheaded by the Queen. In these two self-consciously high-minded pieces, Swift created laureate-style authors who address national issues and apparently bored everyone. There was virtually no response to either the *Letter . . . Concerning the Sacramental Test* or the *Project for the Advancement of Religion*. To rectify the situation, Swift seemed to have gotten Steele to puff the *Project's* anonymous author in *The Tatler*. Without naming Swift, Steele describes him as one "whose Virtue sits easy about him, and to whom Vice is thoroughly contemptible. . . . [T]he Man writes much like a Gentleman, and goes to Heav'n with a very good Mien."[62] Steele's promotion did not send readers stampeding to the bookseller and may have made Swift realize that defenses of the church would not make him famous.[63]

In 1708, Swift had drawn up a projected table of contents for a collection of his works, presumably to be published with his name attached, and solicited Richard Steele—renowned because of the success of his *Tatler*—to provide an introduction. This table of contents seems to reflect Swift's understanding that contradiction, indeterminacy, and transgression were most congenial to him and most likely to distinguish him as an author. The list of titles mixes coarseness with refinement, silliness with rational analysis, belles lettres with Grubstreet squibs. The items include "Essay on Conversation" and "On the Present Taste in Reading" as well as "Elegy on Partridge" and "Mrs. Harris' Petition." Swift's prevailing concern about fame can be inferred from the entry, "Conjectures on [the] thoughts of Posterity about me."[64]

Swift's authorship of several pieces was revealed in 1710, but the information produced little stir because his character was virtually unknown to the public. In *The Tatler*, Steele disclosed that Swift was the perpetrator of the Bickerstaff hoax as well as the author of "Description of a City Shower" and "Description of the Morning." Possibly to excuse the coarse elements (dead puppies, dirty mops, guts, dung, "filths of all hues and odours") in the two poems, Steele characterizes Swift as one who could take "obvious and common Subjects" and "treat them in a new and unbeaten Method."[65] Also in 1710, Edmund Curll published *A Complete Key to the Tale of a Tub*, which names Jonathan Swift and his cousin Thomas Swift as coauthors of the *Tale*. Based on Swift's possible associations with Curll, Swift might have had a hand in the authorship of *The Complete Key*, which rigorously defends the *Tale*'s religious orthodoxy and conveniently assigns the most scandalous parts of it as well as the failed *Mechanical Operation of the Spirit* to Thomas Swift.[66] None of these revelations had much consequence until Swift's behind-the-scenes political activities brought him into the limelight.

### Mythmaking for a Cause

Rebuffed by a Whig minister, Sidney Godolphin, Swift decided to get even by anonymously publishing a Grubstreet lampoon against him called "The Virtues of Sid Hamet's Rod" (1710). Associated with the Whigs before 1710, Swift's revenge signaled his disaffection. The publication of "Sid Hamet's Rod" reflects Swift's development of a distinctive style that blurs high and low elements in strange combinations, in this case, biblical and classical allusions with vulgar diction (*piss, breech, stink*). Swift reports to

Stella, then living in Ireland, "My lampoon is cried up to the skies; but nobody suspects me for it . . ." (JS 1: 59). No wonder. Clergymen were not expected to be authors of Grubstreet libels. When the Tories displaced the Whigs in 1710, Robert Harley, the new Tory Lord Treasurer, invited Swift to join the ministry as *chef de propagande*.[67] (Harley must have had private intelligence that Swift was "Sid Hamet's" author.) Swift's ability to rivet the public's attention and his absolute fearlessness recommended him for the job. Harley no doubt hoped that if Swift could create the myth that Partridge was dead, perhaps he could do the same with the Duke of Marlborough—the standard-bearer of the Whigs and commander-in-chief of troops fighting the War of Spanish Succession, a venture the Tories adamantly opposed. Harley assigned Swift the job of promoting the Tory point of view in the press and made him responsible for *The Examiner,* the ministry's periodical. Busy putting out brush fires for Harley, Swift had no time to think about the publication of his works or conjecture about what posterity might think about him.

Swift's apprenticeship in writing popular literature served him well in his new role as Tory spin-doctor, shaping day-to-day political reality through the popular prints. Of one Whig broadside, for instance, he writes Stella, "I must give some hints to have it answerd; 'tis full of Lyes and will give an Opportunity of exposing [the Whigs]" (JS 2: 656–7). When news of Tory emissary Matthew Prior's secret peace negotiations were leaked, Swift whipped up a hoax entitled *A New Journey to Paris* that served as a diversionary tactic and covered the embarrassment.[68] Advertised in *The Daily Courant* and *The Post Boy,* this "two penny pamphlet" went rapidly through three editions. Swift reports to Stella, "The printer tells me he sold yesterday a thousand of Prior's journey, and had printed five hundred more. It will do rarely, I believe, and is a pure bite [joke]" (JS 1: 358). So crucial was cheap print to Swift's authorial strategies, he opposed the ministry's plan to tax publications by the sheet. Writing Stella again, Swift tells her that "They are here intending to tax all little printed penny papers a half-penny every half-sheet, which will utterly ruin Grub-street, and I am endeavoring to prevent it" (JS 1: 177–8).

As Swift instilled the myths of Tory righteousness through the popular press, he also mythologized his *Examiner* persona as the first among equals in the Republic of Letters—a strategy that infuriated the Whigs. Although working under Harley's direction, Swift did not characterize Mr. Examiner explicitly as a Tory but, rather, as a laureate articulating the ideals of the nation; he did not refer to *The Examiner* as a common newspaper but as a transcendent work of art.[69] Mr. Examiner, for example, opens *Examiner* #40 with praise of his literary virtues: "I took up a Paper some Days ago in a Coffee-House; and if the Correctness of the Style, and a superior Spirit in it, had not immediately undeceived me, I should have been apt to imagine, I had been reading an *Examiner*" (PW 3: 147). Patronizing his opponents' attempts at irony, Mr. Examiner snidely notes, "*Irony* is not a work for such groveling Pens, but extream difficult, even to the best; 'tis one of the most beautiful strokes of *Rhetorick,* and which asks a Master-hand to carry on and finish with Success."[70] Responding to a query from Stella, who was unaware of his authorship of *The Examiner,* Swift pretends ignorance: "Yes, I do read the *Examiners,* and they are written very finely, as you judge" (JS 1: 208). The Whigs, of course, viewed *The Examiner* as a partisan tract written by a pretentious political hireling.

Mr. Examiner's masterstroke was his demythologizing of the Duke of Marlborough, who had been hailed as the agent of England's divine destiny by the Whigs. Joseph Addison's poem "The Campaign" (1705), sanctifying Marlborough, went through eight editions before 1711. In that context, Swift's Mr. Examiner exploits the market for nasty news about seemingly perfect people, revealing that Marlborough's conduct of the war was really a scheme to make him obscenely rich and dangerously powerful. Using economic arguments that would later prove so effective in *The Drapier's Letters,* Mr. Examiner/Swift published a balance sheet that compares the compensation given to Marlborough for his generalship with that given to a Roman counterpart for similar service. According to Mr. Examiner's calculation, Marlborough earned over 500 times more than the Roman—£540,000—an astronomical sum both then and now (PW 3: 23). To stoke anger against Marlborough's malfeasance, Swift devoted considerable energy to writing a longer tract—*The Conduct of the Allies*—that embellishes Marlborough's actions in the most inflammatory way possible. When *The Conduct of the Allies* (1711) appeared, it broke all sales records—11,000 copies in a few months.[71] Swift was elated, reporting, "[T]he pamphlet makes a world of noise" (JS 2: 424) and again, "The noise it makes is extraordinary" (JS 2: 428); and a few days later, "They are now printing the fourth edition, which is reckoned very extraordinary, considering 'tis a dear twelve penny book, and not bought up in numbers by the party to give away, as the Whigs do, but purely upon its own strength" (JS 2: 430). Just as he killed Partridge, Swift kills Marlborough. Public opinion turned against the general, who was deprived of his command and many of his perquisites. With *The Conduct of the Allies,* Swift may have changed the course of history. G. M. Trevelyan argues, for example, that Swift did more "to settle the immediate fate of parties and of nations than did ever any other literary man in the annals of England."[72]

Mr. Examiner's ability to topple the reigning gods was demonstrable. The Whigs had to find out who he was and destroy him. Speculation abounded until May 1711, when *The Present State of Wit* authoritatively declared that Swift was responsible for *The Examiner,* and by implication, *The Conduct of the Allies* as well as numerous other Tory tracts. Suddenly Swift was in the crosshairs of the Whig propaganda guns because he posed a deadly threat to their party's aspirations. The Whigs used the information that Swift was the author of *A Tale of a Tub,* the Bickerstaff papers, and *The Examiner* as a stick to beat him with, evidence that he was an apostate, a trickster, and a political hack. The Whig attacks did not make Swift disappear but, rather, ensured his prominence for the next four years.

# Chapter Two ∽

# Master of Surprises, 1712–28

A t the beginning of the period covered by this chapter, Swift had become a notorious figure through anti-Tory propaganda published by the Whigs. The Whig Swift fascinated readers with his insouciant disregard of the proprieties expected of an Anglican priest. In a typically ambivalent and provocative move, Swift responded to Whig caricatures by styling himself as an Augustan and at the same time giving proof that the Whig canards were not exaggerated. After the Tories fell from power and Swift moved back to Ireland to occupy the Deanery of St. Patrick's in 1714, he was virtually absent from print for almost six years. When Swift burst back on the scene around 1720, he started to plant the seeds of the stories that made him an enduring legend.

In mid-1711, the Whigs discovered the identity of the writer who was bedeviling them and launched an all-out assault on Swift. They vilified him as a political hack—motivated only by partisan zeal and capable of only Grub-street grandeur—and wondered openly about the lack of principle that permitted him to mock his religion in *A Tale of a Tub,* to switch his allegiances suddenly from Whig to Tory, or to associate with Tory Jacobites who sought to overturn the Protestant succession. The Whig media barrage had the effect of magnifying Swift's public presence and imbuing him with qualities that made him attractive. In this light, their accusations that he was an atheist, buffoon, renegade, opportunist, and traitor created a market for more works featuring these myths. Swift never directly answered the Whig charges. Instead, he outraged the Whigs by assuming the stance of an Augustan writer, who in concert with the heads of state, set standards for literature and morality. At other times, Swift presented himself just as the Whigs imagined him by combining the most notorious qualities of Bickerstaff, Mr. Examiner, and the *Tale*-teller.

Presuming that Swift would be ashamed of revelations that should embarrass a man of the cloth or a would-be litterateur, the Whigs painted his disgrace in lurid terms, perhaps hoping that he would beat a retreat into sermon writing. Commentary appearing in *The Protestant Post-Boy* (January 19, 1712) can serve as an example of the abuse with which the Whigs saturated the print media:

> [Swift is] one abandon'd Wretch, from a Despair of raising his Figure in his *Profession* amongst the Men of Distinction of one Side, fraught with Revenge and the Gleanings of *Politicks* which he pick'd up in exchange for his constant Buffoonery, and Rehearsing of merry *Tales of a Tub,* can best tell what glorious Fruits he has reap'd from his Apostacy, and brandishing his *Pen,* in defence of his new Allies, against the D—ke of M————h: It must be a melancholy Reflection to one who has nothing in View but the present Charm of *Profit,* to drudge on in *Renegado's* pay without Murmuring, and from being the *Buffoon* of One *Party,* become the *Setting Dog* of another. (Quoted PW 6: x)

Instead of shrinking from these criticisms, Swift acted as though they did not exist and made bids for high positions in church and state. Needless to say, Swift's actions infuriated the Whigs, which seemed to have been his intent.

## Swift's Augustan Myth

Proposing that all issues of his periodical be collected and published as a volume for the benefit of posterity, Swift's Mr. Examiner imagines that "if these Papers, *reduced into a more durable Form,* should happen to live until our Grand-children be Men; I hope they may have curiosity enough to consult Annals, and compare Dates, in order to find out what *Names* were then instrusted with the Conduct of the Affairs" (PW 3: 32). The Whig *Medley* does not let Mr. Examiner's visions of future fame go unchallenged. It greets with scorn the image of "our Grand-children" researching allusions in bound copies of *The Examiner:* "What a Present is here intended for the future Republick of Letters! The *Examiner* and our Grandchildren nam'd together in the same Paragraph! What fine work is here like to be! . . . [T]he more hast[e] he makes *to reduce it to a Durable Form,* the better"![1] That Mr. Examiner can mistake the Curllean trash he writes for literature that will endure the ages was, to the Whigs, more evidence of his inability to make essential distinctions.

Swift also asserted his literary superiority in the Preface to his anonymously published *Miscellanies in Prose and Verse* in 1711. Even though the volume does not name Swift as author, his authorship of the work it contained was obvious, for several items had been associated with him publicly. Swift praised himself by impersonating the publisher of the *Miscellanies,* who points to the unique excellencies of the works included in the collection and makes an explicit claim that their author stands—laureate style—

2.1.  "Curll in his Literatory." from *The Grub Street Journal*
(1732). A pile of Swift's *Examiners* are at the feet of Edmund
Curll, who is represented as a devil. Although Curll, the epitome of Grubstreet, did not publish *The Examiner,* he published
several of Swift's early works, some for the first time. Like Curll,
Swift understood the power of sensationalism to sell copy. By
permission of the Folger Shakespeare Library

above the rest: "[I]n every one of these Pieces [there are] some particular
Beauties that discover this Authors Vein, who excels too much not be Distinguished, since in all his Writings such a surprising mixture of Wit and
Learning, true Humour and good Sence does every where appear, as sets him
almost as far out of the Reach of Imitation, as it does beyond the Power of
Censure."[2] When Swift's role as Tory propagandist was revealed, the Whigs
mined the hawker's fare in the *Miscellanies* to illustrate the ridiculousness of

Swift's pretensions and cited items like *Argument Against Abolishing Christianity* as proof he had no respect for religion. Edmund Curll, always at the scene of a scandal, came out with his own *Miscellanies by Dr. Swift* in 1711 and another edition in 1714.[3]

No one publicly hailed Swift in the fulsome terms Swift bestowed on himself in the Preface to his *Miscellanies.* Negative depictions might be expected from Swift's enemies, but they also came from his friends. Swift's superior, Archbishop King, for example, refused to believe Swift was the author of the *Miscellanies:* "You see how malicious some are towards you, in printing a parcel of trifles, falsely, as your works. This makes it necessary that you should shame those varlets by something that may enlighten the world, which I am sure your genius will reach, if you set yourself to it" (C 1: 268). Although no one accepted Swift's view of himself as a great writer, Swift was not deterred. Despite these responses—or because of them—Swift continued to mythologize himself as an eminent author, even though his oeuvre consisted almost entirely of cheaply printed ephemera.

In 1712, after the Whigs had publicly branded Swift as a dangerous scallywag, Swift provoked more attacks by publishing under his own name the *Proposal for Correcting, Improving and Ascertaining the English Tongue.* Addressing the *Proposal* as a letter to "Robert, Earl of Oxford and Mortimer, Lord High Treasurer," he speaks "in the Name of all the learned and polite Persons of the Nation" (PW 4: 6) about the importance of distinguishing between great authors, whose "Words [are] more durable than Brass, and [will be read by] our Posterity . . . a thousand Years hence" (17) and writers for the popular press, whose "Scribbles of the Week" or "daily Trash" are the source of linguistic pollution (10, 12). The Swift in the *Proposal* turns his critical eye to the beauties of those texts that would be familiar to him as Anglican priest. Implicitly rebutting those who might doubt his reverence for sacred texts, this Swift magisterially commends the "great Strains of true sublime Eloquence . . . which every Man of good Taste, will observe in the *Communion-Service,* that of *Burial,* and other Parts" of the *Book of Common Prayer* as well as in the cogent simplicity of the King James Bible (15). In his *Proposal,* Swift characterized himself as an Augustan writer, who in concert with the heads of state, guides the nation toward greatness and goodness. Though he does not say so directly, Swift implies that his role as a cultural leader will result in his being chosen as the director of the academy he proposes.

Swift also reinforced the image of himself as an intimate of ministers with published accounts of his role in what came to be known as The Bandbox Plot. When a suspicious-looking parcel was delivered to Harley at his residence in the York Buildings on November 4, 1712, Swift, who happened to be visiting, volunteered to open it and discovered an explosive device. Swift, as eyewitness and major participant, spread the story. He apparently told everyone he knew and personally inserted the following account of the incident in *The Evening Post* and *The Post Boy.* Although his name is not mentioned, reactions indicate that everyone knew the identity of the "Gentleman in the Room."

> The Box was carry'd up to my Lord's Bed-Chamber, and delivered to his Lordship [Harley], who lifting up the Lid as far as the Pack-thread that ty'd it would give way, said, He saw a Pistol; whereupon, a Gentleman in the Room desired the Box might be given to him; he took it to the Window, at some Distance from my Lord, and open'd it, by cutting with a Pen-knife the Pack-threads that fasten'd the Lid. (PW 6: 196–7)

Inside were gunpowder, pistols, and nails primed to go off. Swift made himself the hero of his newspaper narratives, in which he courageously risks his own life to save Harley and protect the commonweal. Mirroring the closeness of Horace and Maecenas, Swift specifically mentions that the incident took place in Harley's bedroom.

Swift's characterization of himself as an Augustan laureate was implicit in his bid for the position of Historiographer Royal, a post created as a salaried position in 1661 and conflated with the Poet Laureateship by both Dryden and Shadwell.[4] While the Poet Laureateship fell into disrepute after Dryden's tenure, the post of Historiographer Royal retained its prestige. It was the highest possible official recognition of a prose writer—in essence, it was a Prose Laureateship. After the death in 1713 of the Historiographer Royal, Thomas Rymer, Swift began making his wishes known. Selection as Historiographer Royal would represent inclusion in the Temple of British Worthies as well as a chance to write the master narrative of the Tory ministry and, presumably, Swift's contribution to it. In this context, Swift penned a memorial to the Queen that is excruciatingly direct:

> [S]ome able hand should be immediately employed to write the history of her Majesty's reign; that the truth of things may be transmitted to future ages, and bear down the falsehood of malicious pens.
>
>     The Dean of St. Patrick's is ready to undertake this work humbly desiring her Majesty will please to appoint him her historiographer (PW 8: 200).

In making this request, Swift put himself on the same level as Thomas Rymer, who was renowned as a translator, critic, and historian. Rymer's multi-volume works, published in English as well as Latin, were designed for an exclusive readership. Although Swift did not publicly reveal his aspirations, rumors instantly carried the news to the coffee-houses. Through his experiences in place seeking, Swift saw that elevating himself generated an uproar that made him highly visible. It was a strategy he perfected as time went along.

## Whig Counter-myths

Swift's projections of himself as Director of the English Academy, Bandbox Plot hero, and Historiographer Royal, as well as rumors that he had demanded a bishopric as payoff for his services as Mr. Examiner, predictably galvanized the Whigs into an all-out effort to destroy his claims to authority. Instead of sinking Swift, the Whig libels spread his fame. Emphasizing the contradictions inherent in Swift's words and deeds, the Whigs delighted in cataloging his wildly divergent identities to reinforce the impression that he never was what he appeared to be and that he was without fixed principles. In one Whig-authored diary, a Swift character says, "[Although my] Three *Characters of* Clergyman, Critick, *and* Examiner, *may seem inconsistent . . . I can easily reconcile them.*"[5] Another Whig Swift writes in his *Real Diary,* "I must own that I have gone through as many Changes as my *Splendid Shilling,* and hope that I have many more to go through yet. . . . [The stars predicted at my birth that] I must be a *Whore,* if a *Woman;* a *P[arso]n,* if a *Man;* but was irreversibly determin'd to be . . . the Reverend Dr. *S—t;* a Boy, a Collegian, a *P[arso]n,* a Poet, a Politician, and a Lover."[6] Rather than rejecting or correcting Whig representations of his indeterminacy, Swift reinforced them.

The Whigs cast Swift in the mold of the folkloric trickster character, a shape-shifter who always tries to dominate by deception. In violation of the principles of distributive justice—the good prosper, the bad are punished—the trickster usually triumphs. If not, he bounces back to win the next time. Embodying the liberating idea that the universe is not governed by inexorable rules or authority, tricksters, such as Br'er Rabbit, The Sundance Kid, Wile E. Coyote, or Robin Hood, become subjects of popular narratives (jokes, ballads, cartoons). Audiences like to hear about someone who has "gotten away with it," so inadvertently the Whigs only added to Swift's charisma through their attempts to discredit him.

Reacting to Swift's *Proposal* to establish an English Academy, the Whigs expressed their amazement that a moral bankrupt, a political timeserver, and a Grubstreet hack should set himself up as the czar of English Letters or an epitome of religious orthodoxy. John Oldmixon, in *Reflections on Dr. Swift's Letter to Harley* (1712), for instance, criticizes "*the Bold Manner of publishing the* Letter . . . *from Persons that were never thought to trouble themselves much about* Fine Language"—indeed, "this most Ingenious Writer has so great a Value for his own Judgment in Matters of Stile, that he has put his Name to his Letter." By parading forth Swift's popular successes, Oldmixon suggests that no one could be a more inappropriate Director of an English Academy: "I make no question he is Prouder of his *Elegy upon Partridge,* and his Sonnet on Miss *Biddy Floyd,* than all of His Prose Compositions together, or even that elegant Poem, call'd *The Humble Petition of* Frances Harris, which is the Pink of Simplicity. . . . in the true Stile of a Mrs. *Abigail."* Oldmixon implies that any man who can slip into the skin of an illiterate Irish housemaid is no gentleman, and is equally unqualified to be a Dean or Bishop, or an Augustan arbiter of letters. Oldmixon quotes Swift's *Tale* extensively, especially passages containing swearing and bawdry, pointing out that "these Florid Strokes came from the Pen of a Reverend Doctor, who has sollicited lately for a Deanery, and sets up mightily for a Refiner of our Tongue."[7]

Swift's language proposal causes Arthur Mainwaring, in *The British Academy* (1712), to question Swift's loyalties, not in regard to class but in regard to nation. In his proposal, Swift admires the French Academy and implicitly compares himself to Cardinal Richelieu as an embodiment of cultural and political power, which inflamed Mainwaring's fears that Swift was a Jacobite, who, like some High Tories, secretly desired to re-enthrone the Catholic Pretender, then exiled in France. To Mainwaring, the institution of an Academy with Swift at the helm would be the end of English letters and English liberty. Citing the censorship powers of the French Academy, Mainwaring raises the specter of Swift forbidding all publications but his own Tory tracts. What would happen, Mainwaring asks, if "our Academy may not be in a Humour to write any Thing these Hundred years, except a Trifle now and then, as an *Examiner,* a *Conduct* [of the Allies]"?[8]

Whig responses to Swift's account of the Bandbox episode heightened Swift's notoriety through street ballads inspired by the Smithfield muses. Viewing the Bandbox Plot as another of Swift's hoaxes, cynically designed to promote his fortunes and those of the Tory party, the Whigs ridiculed Swift's heroic vision of himself by depicting him as a wild man, jester, or con artist in clerical garb who seems strangely unaware of his own shamefulness. "Plot upon Plot: A Ballad" (1712), for example, concludes with the stanza:

> Now God preserve our gracious Queen,
> And for this glorious deed,
> May she the Doctor make a Dean,
> With all convenient speed!
> What tho' the Tub has hinder'd him,
> As common story tells,
> Yet surely now the Band-box whim
> Will help him down to Wells.[9]

Reeking with sarcasm, the ballad suggests that his "glorious deed" surely will absolve Swift of the sins of *A Tale of a Tub* and gain him the bishopric of Wells, a rumor that had become a "common story."

"The Plotter Found Out: or, Mine Arse in a Band-box, to the Tune of *Which No Body Can Deny*" (1712)[10] characterizes Swift in a similarly comic way and emphasizes that he is Harley's "tool," not his Augustan peer.

> . . . [B]y *Bob's* usual Luck the Mischief was mist all,
> For he knew where to look for't, and soon spy'd the Pistol;
> And then gave the Box to a Wit [Swift], that was his tool.
>
> · · · · · · · · · · · · · · · ·
>
> *Swift* Gogled and Star'd, and turned up his Whites,
> And ran with the Box to the Window to Rights;
> Where he fund out, what put us all into sad Frights.

Another broadside infuses Swift for the first time with unrestrained sexual energy—a feature that later becomes an intrinsic element of his public image.[11] In the satire below, *bandbox* clearly functions as a Freudian symbol.

> A *Plot* is lately broken forth, a dismal, deep, horrid, fanatical unheard of *Plot!* found out by Parson S . . . t in a Ban-Box,—Parson S . . . t found it there, and he swears it is a *Plot*, a curs'd, damn'd, fanatical *Plot* . . . Parson S . . . t['s]. . . . peeping into Ban Boxes has sav'd the Nation:—and may Parson S . . . t for the future—[be] the Grand Inspector of *Ban-boxes* in the Kingdom.—O ye Milliners Look to your selves when Parson S . . . t *Examins* your *Ban-boxes*. . . . Take Notice—Parson S . . . t has a Piercing Eye,—Parson S . . . t has a penetrating Judgement,—Parson S. t has a Great—— . . . Take this Advice with you,—Be sure you lay not *Plots* in *Ban-Boxes*,—for Parson S . . . t will *Examin* them, and *Pistols* and *Ink-horns*—will signify no more than a TALE OF A TUB.[12]

The strange image of Swift invading the milliners' shops emphasizes his barbarous impropriety. "Parson Swift" does not behave as a priest—or indeed as any civilized person—should.[13]

When the news erupted that Swift had put his name forth as a candidate for Historiographer Royal, more attacks ensued. Not surprisingly, the Whigs expressed incredulity that someone so overtly unqualified for the Republic of Letters would claim not only citizenship in it but leadership over it. In *Essays Divine, Moral, and Political*, a Whig Swift ironically argues that he deserves to be the exemplar of High Culture, or Historiographer Royal, because he has apprentice experience in writing "characters," or libels hawked in the street. He declares, "[S]ince I intend to set up for an *Historian*, I have began at the lowest Class." The satire imagines Swift addressing

Prince Posterity (whom the *Tale*-teller invokes) to tell him that he is no longer worried about the fleeting fame of modern publications because his "*Own Writings, and Actions, are Grav'd on Monumental* BRASS," a distortion of Swift's phrasing in the *Proposal For Correcting . . . the English Tongue.* Playing with the ideas of brass both as metal and effrontery, the Whig Swift tells Prince Posterity that given a choice between Fame's Golden trumpet (Noble Fame) and her brass trumpet (Scandalous Fame), he would prefer the brass. For the "Golden One *has a Loud, Shrill, and Agreeable Sound, but by Degrees it dies away, and can only he heard by a* Few" while the brass one "*is much* Louder, *which is sufficient to gain Attention from* Most."[14]

The travesty of Swift's being considered for the post of Historiographer Royal is also the subject of "An Epistle to Dr. Sw—t," included in *A Farther Hue and Cry after Dr. Sw—t* (1714). It is a fictionalized letter in verse from Matthew Prior in Paris to Jonathan Swift in Windsor, in which Prior congratulates Swift on his lasting fame as an historian, a reputation that rests on *The Conduct of the Allies.* The tone is heavily sarcastic:

> Thee unborn Tories shall with Pleasure read,
> And bind Thy Sacred Pages with their Creed;
> To future Times Thou shalt recorded stand
> The Great Historian, who has sav'd the Land;
> In Bodley's Library shall be enroll'd,
> Thy Covers and thy Back be wrought with Gold.[15]

The idea that Swift's literary output would be read with reverence in the future, much less that it would be considered even worthy of binding, is scoffed at. The Whig Prior concludes by praising Swift's decision not to write for the Republic of Letters but to go after the Grubstreet market for almanacs, prophecies of Mother Haggy, and tales of apparitions. Another presentation of Swift as lowly hack with an underclass following appears in a verse narrative that dramatizes a "poetical contest" between Swift and a "minor poet." The two characters hurl invectives at each other in front of an audience of porters, apprentices, cobblers, and cookmaids until finally the bookseller Lintot orders them to cease their squalid brangling "Lest Civil Wars disturb your Country's Peace."[16] This Whig caricature underscores the idea that Swift is a street fighter rather than the laureate voice of national consensus.

While the prospect of Swift as Director of the English Academy, Harley's aide-de-camp, or as Historiographer Royal stirred strong negative emotions in the Whigs, the rumor that Swift might be made Dean of St. Patrick's as a reward for his work as Mr. Examiner caused the most consternation. In *History of Jacobite Clubs* (1712), a Whig Swift says, "*A Word's sufficient to the*

*Wise, / Know that we all expect to rise, / I to a Deanery.*"[17] Asked whether his name is Jonathan in the *Tryal and Condemnation of Don Prefatio* (1712), Swift responds, "Perhaps it is, and perhaps not, will you give me a Deanery if I tell you?"[18] One story, published by Abel Boyer, is that John Sharp, Archbishop of York, "strenuously opposed the promotion of Dr. Swift, one of the [Tories'] prostituted tools to a deanery in England: Having with becoming firmness, represented [to the Queen], what a scandal it would be, both to church and state, to bestow such a distinguished preferment upon a clergyman who was hardly suspected of being a Christian."[19]

The oxymoron of Swift as an unchristian priest stimulated wild scenarios. Supposedly "fasten'd to the Gate" of St. Patrick's on the day Swift was installed as Dean, a poem—written by another Irish Dean, Jonathan Smedley—shows the world turned upside down when an ungodly cleric, who spends more time publishing than praying, can become the spiritual leader of a great cathedral. The poem was included in *An Hue and Cry after Doctor S—t*, which went through more than nine editions in 1714, the year it was published.

> *This Place he got by Wit and Rhime,*
> *And many Ways most odd;*
> *And might a Bishop be in a Time*
> *Did he believe in God.*
>
> .    .    .    .    .    .    .    .
>
> *Look down St.* Patrick, *look we pray,*
> *On thine own Church and Steeple;*
> *Convert thy Dean on this great Day,*
> *Or else God help the People.*
>
> *And now, whene'er his D—n-sh-p dies,*
> *Upon his Stone be graven,*
> *A Man of God here buried lies,*
> *Who never thought of Heaven.*[20]

To libel Swift as well as to capture the market for confessions from this miscreant, Whig authors published diaries, purporting to be Swift's true thoughts. In one of several Whig-authored diaries, Swift confides his reaction to being passed over for bishop and getting, as a consolation prize, the deanship of St. Patrick's: "Fell into a Consideration of the Reasons why I must not prefer'd to the Bpk. of *Ra*[pah]*o*. Too Merry. Too Ludicrous. Too Fickle. Too loose. [My] Books Profane. What a Devil, is this a Reason? said I." In the conclusion of the diary, Swift addresses the "Gentle Reader": "I have ordered this my Journal to be published on *March* 17, being a Day consecrated to the Memory of St. *Patrick* (to whom I am indebted for my Conversion to Christianity, as my Predecessors and Countrymen formerly were)."[21] Swift never took any serious measures to rebut the charges against him or to construct himself as a Christian believer. Both his silence and his subsequent actions reinforced Whig myths of his atheism.

One of the first decisions Swift made after his installation as Dean of St. Patrick's in 1713 was to return to London and resume his work as a Tory propagandist. Swift clearly showed no desire to give up the journalistic skirmishing that his enemies found most reprehensible in a man of the cloth. In the period 1713–14, the particular objects of Swift's ire were two Whigs with whom he associated before he turned Tory: Richard Steele (his former friend, with whom he collaborated at times on *The Tatler*) and the Earl of Wharton (from whom at one time Swift had hoped for a chaplaincy). In a number of pamphlets, Swift attacked Steele for his failures as a writer, and Wharton for his failures as a man.[22] To demonize Swift for his assaults on their spokesmen, Steele and other Whigs depicted Swift as a man who would turn on his friends to gain his own ends. In *The Guardian,* for example, Steele refers to his adversary as "an estranged Friend" (May 13, 1713), and in *Essays Divine, Moral, and Political,* a Whig Swift confesses that he pursued Steele "*with a Violence inconsistent with the Character of a Friend, and unworthy of a Clergyman and* Christian." Swift's low scourging style, the author of the *Essays* notes, is no different from that of "*Porters, Carmen, Foot-Soldiers, Players, Bullies, Bawds, Pimps [and] Whores*"[23] and offers a sharp contrast the polite style of Steele. In one Whig elaboration of the lurid plot of brotherly love turned to hate, Swift seeks reconciliation with Steele by suggesting they both admit they cannot write, retire from politics, get drunk every night, and "Immortalize our *Dolls* and *Jennys*" like Tom D'Urfey and other Grubstreet poets (P 1:180–84, ll. 115–6).[24] Although the imbroglio with Steele created a public image of Swift that was hardly complimentary, Swift seemed to relish the controversy and did all he could to perpetuate it.

While Swift characterized Steele as an incompetent writer, he characterized Wharton as an immoral man, charging him with atheism, fornication, bribery, and altar defilement (PW 3: 28). His earlier libels on Wharton provoked few responses, but in 1713 Swift published a couplet about the Earl that became a flashpoint: describing himself, Swift says he was "In State-Opinions *a-la Mode/* He hated *Wh——n* like a Toad" ("Horace, Epistle 1.7, Imitated," P 1: 170–75, ll. 35–6). The Whigs seized on the couplet to epitomize the cold calculus that would allow Swift to vilify his former colleagues in order to forward his political ambitions.

In *Essays Divine, Moral and Political,* the Whig Swift makes clear to Prince Posterity that he is attacking Steele and Wharton to reap benefits from the Tories:

> *The . . . Accusation against me is, That I hate* W———n *like a Toad; and that I*
> *have Libell'd not only him, but the whole* Junta *round: And to make a Crime of*
> *this, they alledge, that these People were once my Friends and Benefactors. . . .*
> *[But they were out of power] and I assure your Highness, I am no* Fool, *and will*
> *not bestow my Attendance without a Prospect of a Reward.*[25]

In another purported confession, Whig-authored *Dr. Swift's Real Diary*,
Swift also reveals himself to be a godless machiavellian, who remains in relationships only so long as they benefit him and achieves advancement by
bullying or deception. In recounting his life, this Whig Swift itemizes its key
events:

> Born on a *Sunday,* and so broke the Sabbath. . . . Disobey'd my Father and
> Mother. Bambouzled my School-Master. Run in Debt with the Pye-
> woman. . . . Went to the University. . . . I studied little, broke all the Statues,
> and Made Lampoons. Commenc'd Batchelor of Arts. . . . Am made a Priest.
> Set up for some Religion. Make Love. Turn Wit. . . . Past five Years away in
> Poeming, Punning, Insulting, Idling, Tatling. . . . Resolve to be a *Whig.* . . .
> Ridicule the Church in *Baucis* and *Philemon.* . . . Drop St—e and Ad—n. . . .
> Take leave of [Wharton]. Turn Tory. Lampoon the Whigs.[26]

The Whig caricatures inevitably link Swift's moral degradation to his use of
vulgar forms and styles. In the *History of the Jacobite Clubs* (1712), the author (who confuses Wharton with Berkeley), notes that Swift "descended so
low as to . . . petition in *Doggerel* for my Lady's Women ["Mrs. Harris' Petition"] . . . turn'd Renegado [and] . . . from that Day forward commenc'd
*Malecontent* to his Lordship [the Earl of Wharton]."[27]

The couplet about "hating *W[harto]n* like a Toad" appears in "Part of
the Seventh Epistle of the First Book of Horace Imitated: and Addressed to
a Noble Peer" (1713), Swift's first major self-construction since his "Ode to
the Athenian Society" (1692). Although its classical form might answer
charges that Swift was no Augustan, the poem does more to elaborate Whig
myths about Swift than to present exculpatory counter myths. Indeed,
Swift reinforced everything the Whigs were saying about him: that he belonged on Grubstreet; that he was Harley's creature; that he was motivated
only by political ambition; and that he was disrespectful to his priestly vocation. In the epistle, Swift describes himself as a writer whose "Works were
hawked in ev'ry Street: / But seldom rose above a Sheet" (41–2); as Harley's
intimate, who "Came early, and departeth late" every day from Harley's
home (79); as a virulently anti-Whig propagandist ("He libell'd all the *Junta*
round" (37); and as a "Clergyman of special Note, / For shunning those of
his own Coat" (27–8). It is impossible to say whether Swift botched his defense or, more likely, that he wanted to give the Whig press something more
to chew on.

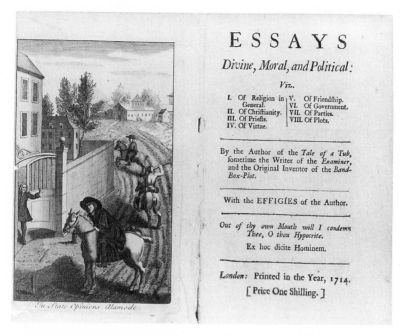

2.2. Title page and frontispiece,[Thomas Burnet], *Essays Divine, Moral and Political* (1714). The satire is one of the many Whig attacks on Swift, which made his name and supposed character known in popular culture. The frontispiece engraving of Swift arriving at Harley's gate is the first published image of him. By permission of the Folger Shakespeare Library.

The most inflammatory element of the epistle is a scene in which Swift humorously asks Harley to unprefer him as Dean of St. Patrick's because the costs of the installation ceremony and ongoing expenses threaten to impoverish him. The scene portrays Swift as one who is brazenly indifferent to proprieties and arrogantly asserts his power. A Whig propagandist, Abel Boyer, saw the poem as a bald attempt at extortion in keeping with Swift's general character: "Who else should be so *hardy* as to offer such balderdash to a *prime minister?*"[28] In a similar reaction to the epistle, William Diaper dramatizes Swift as a crass bully in his conversation with Harley:

> 'I want a thousand Pounds, my Lord,'
> 'Nay, instantly—but—say the Word;'
> If he denies, you tell him plain,
> 'E'en take your Deanery again.'[29]

The eyebrow raising nature of Swift's epistle to Harley made it a bestseller; it quickly ran through eight editions not only in London but also in Dublin and Edinburgh. The poem prompted the first published visual representation of Swift, one in which he looks like a highwayman on horseback arriving at Harley's gate.

The character of Swift—constructed in print both by Swift and his enemies—was that of a man who seemed scandalously unworthy to be an Anglican dean because of his unseemly interest in political power, personal gain, and popular journalism. The Whigs, however, added a more serious, accusation to disqualify Swift from assuming the Deanship of St. Patrick's by alleging that he might be a Jacobite, an enemy of the Church of England and the English Constitution who supports the claims of the Catholic Pretender to the English throne. Several almost-successful invasions made Jacobitism a near and present threat to English values. The Whigs routinely accused the Tories (with their High Church affinities) of being cryptojacobites, a brush with which the Whigs also tarred Swift. In the diary published in *An Hue and Cry,* a Whig Swift records for one day: "Went to dine at the *George,* with two *Papists,* three *Jacobites,* and a *Tory.* Damn'd the Cook, lik'd the Wine. No Wit. All Politicks. Settled the Succession [of the crown after Anne's death; she had no children]. Fix'd the Place and Time of [The Pretender's] Landing."[30] And in his *Real Diary,* under "Wednesday," another Whig Swift notes, "Prepar'd Matter for a Poem on the *Pre*[tende]*r's* Landing" and on "Thursday," "Finish my Poem. Make further Progress in my Tract in Favour of the Pretender."[31] Jacobitism challenged a key feature of England's self-identity as a nation—its Protestantism. With Catholic Ireland on one side and Catholic France on another, England felt very vulnerable.[32]

Swift's decision to continue to pursue brass trumpet fame might have been affirmed by the lack of response to two defenses of the Established Church he published during this period: *Mr. C———n's Discourse of Free-Thinking Put into Plain English for the Use of the Poor* (1713) and *A Preface to the Bishop of Sarum's Introduction* (1714). No one identified Swift as the author of these anonymous pamphlets, perhaps because he was known for eschewing ecclesiastical topics. Even though humorous and ironic, the implied authors of these defenses did not capture the public's imagination enough to inspire any published reactions. In contrast, the irreligion, disloyalty, opportunism, underclass inclinations, and nastiness of the Whig Swift were popular topics that Swift reinforced in his implicit and explicit self-depictions.

### Death and Resurrection

Whig pamphleteering kept Swift alive in public consciousness until Queen Anne died in 1713 and the Tories fell from power in 1714. At that point, Swift returned to Ireland to assume his duties as Dean of St. Patrick's Cathedral. No longer an immediate threat to their agenda, Swift ceased being the subject of Whig libels. In contrast to the flood of materials relating to Swift during his stint in London, there were only two works about him published between 1716 and 1718. Once a prominent feature in everyday discourse, Swift suddenly disappeared from the public scene reflected in the popular press. The first of the two depictions during this period is *St. Patrick's Purgatory* (1716), in which an anonymous author imagines how depressed Swift must be now that he has been exiled from the center of English politics and publication. Stuck in the purgatory of Dublin, this Swift declares himself "Dead and Buried"; his Jacobite dream of setting "the whole Kingdom on Fire by one *French Spark*" has evaporated. He laments his fall, saying "Why S—t is so hard a Fate to be thine? Pity! Was it to this end I excell'd in Prose, and flow'd in Rhime? . . . Ascend ye kinder Stars, and direct me to the Goddess, the true Goddess, SUCCESS." Declaring himself above the herd and bound for glory, the *Purgatory's* Swift declares he will begin to "Rhime and Write" again. In this Whig fantasy, Swift is shown as a tortured spirit in the netherworld, cut off from fulfilling his ambitions as a seditious writer.[33]

The second work about Swift that appeared during this period presents a very different image. In *A Decree for Concluding the Treaty between Dr. Swift and Mrs. Long,* published by Edmund Curll in *Letters, Poems, and Tales: Amorous, Satyrical, and Gallant. Which passed between Several Persons of Distinction. Now first Publish'd from their respective Originals, found in the Cabinet of that Celebrated Toast, Mrs. Anne Long, since her Decease* (1718), Swift appears in a flirty, playful role. Written by Swift between 1710 and 1713, the work is clearly a private joke that somehow fell into Curll's hands. In the piece, Swift dramatizes a facetious conflict between himself and Anne Long. He claims that because of his "Merit [and] extraordinary Qualities" he can make any demand he wishes of Anne Long. She reminds him that in her position as "Toast" it would be inappropriate to favor him in particular. A compromise is reached: Swift can have the exclusive attention of Anne Long for two hours, if she decides he deserves it (PW 5: 196–7). While the *Decree* does not make it clear, the treaty between Swift and Long somehow had great consequences for Mrs. Vanhomrigh and her daughter, Esther, who would later attain international celebrity as Swift's Vanessa. In 1718, though, Curll's revelation of a relationship between Swift and Vanessa had no market value and therefore generated no responses. Aside from *St. Patrick's Purgatory, A Decree for Concluding a Treaty,* two reprints, and two attributions, Swift was dead to the world for a while.[34]

In 1718, Swift was reborn—as a Whig! Despite its fulsome praise of George I, Whig statesmen, and the Duke of Marlborough, many assumed that the anonymous bestseller, *A Dedication to a Great Man,* was Swift's. *A Dedication* evokes memories of the *Conduct of the Allies, A Tale of a Tub,* and the *Argument Against Abolishing Christianity* because of its witty but often blasphemous rendering of spiritual abstractions into concrete terms; its emphasis on the relationship between economics and ideology (manifest in a satiric balance sheet); its startling novelty; its parody of publishing conventions; and its strange mixture of vulgarity and gentility, in particular, high-flown discourse studded with gross bodily imagery—all characteristics of the Swiftian style.[35] *A Dedication to a Great Man* was very popular (eight London editions, one Irish edition) and stimulated a number of comments that should have been gratifying to Swift, despite the misattribution. One author welcomes Swift's return to publishing after "not having set the three Kingdoms a-laughing in five years together," whereas before that time, he had been "tickling the Sides of Mankind once a Week, at least."[36] Another epistle from a bookseller pleads with Swift to return to London, "*For, I protest, since you left Town, / My Trade's so dead, I'm half undone.*"[37]

The reactions to *A Dedication to a Great Man* must have made certain things obvious to Swift about his reputation as an author: (1) that unless he shaped his own public image, others would represent him in ways he found anathema (such as being presented as a Whig); (2) that previous images of himself, constructed by both him and the Whigs, had been forgotten in the space of the few years since he left London in 1714; and (3) that the public appreciated him as a humorist rather than as a serious Man of Letters. At first, to clear his name, Swift intended to print an objection to having something as "insipid" as *A Dedication to a Great Man* fathered on him (PW 9: 34). Ultimately he decided not to, perhaps realizing that the attribution reestablished his public presence.

Having *A Dedication to a Great Man* fathered on him seemed to launch Swift into action. He began to define himself in new and surprising ways, which not only planted the seeds of myths about his life and character but also gave him power for which he was beholden to no one. Swift's publications during the 1720s situated him in a new setting—Ireland—and added to the outrageous inconsistencies associated with his name. Included among the paradoxes that dominate Swift's self-depictions and the responses he elicits from others are his political position (he is both an embodiment of revolution and the status quo); his aesthetics (he is represented as Apollo, yet he writes offensive and trifling works); his manners (although he is gentleman, he does not act like one); and his sex life (he is a priest who seems to be intimate with two women simultaneously).

## Subversive Authority: The Dean as Agent Provocateur

While the Whig ministry might have been initially relieved to see Swift sail across the sea, in the 1720s he began to vex them more at a distance than he had at close hand by exacerbating their paranoia about Ireland. Swift's identity as Jacobite had been a standard feature of Whig propaganda, and his ability to rouse public opinion was demonstrated by *Conduct of the Allies* and other pamphlets. What if he used his talents to foment a popular revolution that would inflame the Irish Catholic majority to join the French-based Jacobites in an invasion of England? Swift did everything he could to keep this worry alive. Even before he started publishing his anti-English/pro-Irish tracts, the Whigs feared he might be plotting sedition, as indicated by a poem called "The Ode-Maker," which appeared in both Dublin and London in 1719.[38] The poem's anonymous author takes Jonathan Smedley to task for failing to dish up the latest dirt on Swift, whose installation as Dean Smedley had entertainingly lampooned in "Verses Fasten'd to the Gate of St. Patrick's." The Ode-Maker imagines Swift's joy when "Packets bring a Rebel-Guest/Full fraught with News." Whether "Rebel-Guest" means the Pretender himself or Jacobite agitators is unclear, but after the packet boats' arrival, the Ode-Maker's Swift, abjuring his usually solitary and miserly existence, throws a clandestine party:

> . . . then ev'ry Door
> Being shut, they chat their Treason o'er
> And o'er again, full Bowls go round,
> And sprightly Mirth and Faction crown'd;
> And *John* is bid to cut, and cut on,
> . . . a whole Yard of Neck of Mutton.

The Ode-maker represents Swift's disloyalty not only by infusing him with a treasonous political agenda but also by emphasizing his rejection of values and aspirations he ought to hold as an upper-class Anglo-Irishman in a position of authority. Even though the "Ode's" Swift can afford to live in a genteel manner, he is parsimonious. For breakfast, he has "Water-Gruel"; for lunch, he asks his servant to steal a chop; and for dinner, he sups on "a Crust of Bread / A Pint of Wine, and so to Bed." He has no inclination toward marriage, but he has a strange interest in his servants' sexuality, "Thinking what often *John* and *Nell* do." Attracted to the underside of life, he loves to show "how well he can rehearse / The nastiest Thing in cleanest Verse." The Swift character in "The Ode-Maker" embodies heterodoxy and revolution—"He's always Odd and always New," which is exactly why he is "perfect Ballad-swelling Matter." English anxieties about Swift's capacity for dangerous mischief can also be seen on the title page of another work from the same period, *Miscellaneous Works, Comical and Diverting: By T.R.D.J.S.D.O.P.I.I.* [The Reverend Doctor Jonathan Swift Dean of Patrick's in Ireland] (London, 1720), "Printed by the Order of the Society *de propagando.*" It includes *A Tale of a Tub,* "By a Member of the Illustrious Fraternity of Grubstreet"; the *Argument Against Abolishing Christianity,* the Bickerstaff pamphlets, and other flippant or irreverent works "By a certain paultry Scribler."

Swift's first new publication in six years—*The Proposal for the Universal Use of Irish Manufacture* (1720)—was a bombshell. In it, Swift created an authorial persona who is the embodiment of English nightmares. Arguing that England is the enemy rather than the protector of Ireland and appealing directly to the Irish populace to resist English economic oppression, Swift slyly plants the suggestion that they should "*Burn every Thing that came from* England . . . *except their* Coals" (PW 9: 17). Even though the pamphlet was published anonymously, there was no doubt in anyone's mind about the identity of the author. The threatening nature of the pamphlet resulted in the immediate arrest of its printer. Much to the dismay of English officials, Swift's *Proposal* became a symbol of Irish opposition to English power. When the printer was brought before the King's Bench for prosecution, the authorities could not get a grand jury to indict him, although they tried nine times.[39] The *Proposal* presents a surprising new vision of Swift as a man passionately concerned with the welfare of Ireland's citizens and intensely critical of England, whose economic policies, in his view, caused their misery.

As Dean of St. Patrick's, Swift should have been acting in concert with the English Lord Lieutenant. Instead of supporting English policy, Swift condemned it. Instead of maintaining the peace, he fomented rebellion. Instead of publishing sermons, he published inflammatory pamphlets. "Dean Swift" was thus an oxymoron, "Dean" connoting authority and "Swift" connoting subversion. Swift never stepped away from either identity or tried to resolve them. Epitomizing the irreconcilable identities contained within Swift, *A Defence of English Commodities being an Answer to the Proposal for the Universal Use of Irish Manufactures . . . Written by Dean Swift* (London and Dublin, 1720) presents the bizarre spectacle of an upright "Dean Swift" denouncing a seditious scoundrel whom he does not name but who clearly is also Swift—a man who is "not a Christian; and by this Mark I have no body to suspect . . . but a *Tory* Doctor of Divinity . . . [who in the past sowed] the Seeds of Discord and Contention, under the Cover of a Bandbox" (PW 9: 269, Appendix B). The *Defence's* "Dean Swift" reminds his audience that this unnamed malcontent is "the same evil Genius that set the People of *England* against *their best and most faithful Allies* [alluding to Swift's *Conduct of the Allies*]. . . . He has a Variety of Shapes; sometimes he is a Priest, sometimes a Philosopher, and at other times a Tradesman; but for the most part, a Ballad-Maker, a Punster, and a Merry-Andrew; unchangeable in this alone, that his constant End is to do Mischief" (276). Several of Swift's editors have thought the *Defence of English Commodities* is his. If true, it would not be the first or last time Swift attacked his own work to heighten the controversy surrounding it.

In the 1720s, Swift established himself as an expert on economics. Reducing the traditional relationship between England and Ireland to a balance sheet, Swift breached a profound taboo by making visible the ways that commerce and empire depend on the exploitation of the have-nots by the haves. It is no wonder that Swift was later honored by some Soviets. Through his satires, the destructive power of money, especially as it affects the underclass, is treated in diverse ways. In a Grubstreet elegy "On the much lamented death of Mr. *Demar,* the famous rich Man" (1720)—which went through multiple editions, both in Dublin and London—Swift lightheartedly celebrates the death of a usurer. (Although anonymously published, it was quickly attributed to Swift.)[40] Demar refused to lend to the poor, who needed money more than the rich. Instead, his customers were members of the governing class: "*Lords, Knights,* and *Squires* were all his humble Debtors. / And under *Hand* and *Seal* the *Irish* Nation / Were forc'd to own to him their *Obligation*" (P 1: 232–5, ll. 16–18). The poem describes how, after death strikes him, "[Demar] that cou'd once have half a Kingdom bought, / In half a Minute is not worth a Groat" (19–20). This humorously leveling verse became a perennial favorite and one of the first of Swift's works to be incorporated in the universally read jestbooks.[41] Following the "Elegy on Demar," Swift published another one of his most popular poems (although little read now), also on the subject of financial immorality. "The Bubble" (1721) treats the disastrous collapse of the South Sea Company stock and warns about the dangers of paper credit, which allows the rich to get richer at the expense of everyone else.[42] In one of the last quatrains of this lengthy ballad-like poem, Swift offers a prayer:

> May He whom Nature's Laws obey
> Who *lifts* the Poor, and *sinks* the Proud,
> *Quiet the Raging of the Sea* [referring to the South Sea Stock Crisis]
> And *Still the Madness of the Crowd.*
> (P 1: 248–59, ll. 209–12)

When England's plans to establish a bank in Ireland met with resistance in the Irish press, everyone assumed Swift's hand was at work because of his newfound interest in money matters. One broadside refers to "a paper of Scandal handed about by the Hawkers, as Swift as Lightning, that will blast your favourite Bank, tho' you love it as *David* did Jonathan" (qtd. PW 9: xx). Modern editors are less certain of Swift's authorship of the many squibs designed to stir up opposition to the bank, but contemporary attributions tell us much about the public identity Swift had developed for himself during the early 1720s: he was anti-English, concerned with economic equity, and excited by the imaginative possibilities of excrement. One of the most popular antibank works attributed to Swift, for example, is *The Wonderful Wonder of Wonders Being an Accurate Description of the Birth, Education, Manner of Living . . . of Mine A—se,* containing a sustained metaphor that graphically describes the bank's operations in terms of the lower intestine and anus. ("He has the Reputation to be a *close, griping, squeezing* Fellow; and that when his Bags are *full,* he is often *needy;* yet, when the Fit takes him, as fast as he gets, he *lets it fly"* and so on (PW 9: 282–83). First published in 1721, the pamphlet was much in demand, going through at least six editions in Dublin and London. In some editions, the title mutates to *The Wonderful Wonder of Wonders: Or the Hole-History Of the Life and Actions of Mr. Breech . . . by Dr. S—t.* Clearly inspired by the *Wonderful Wonder* was *The Swearer's Bank: or Parliamentary Security for Establishing a New Bank in Ireland, wherein the medicinal Use of Oaths is consider'd* (at least four editions, one by Curll); *An Account of the Short Life, sudden Death, and pompous Funeral of Michy Windybank* (at least three editions); and *The Benefit of Farting* (a whopping 14 editions), all of which were fathered onto Swift. Whether or not he wrote *The Wonderful Wonder of Wonders,* Swift could observe how its flamboyantly low humor sold copy. The *Wonderful Wonder of Wonders* (and its spin-offs) firmly annexed the sustained appeal of bathroom humor to Swift's name. One popular example was *The Grand Mystery, or the Art of Meditating over an House of Office* [privy] . . . *Published by the Ingenious Dr. S—ft,* which was first printed in 1726, but went through multiple editions (in French and English) by 1760. The generative effect of excrement on Swiftian mythopoesis is evident in the numbers of works in the scatological vein attributed to him. At the same time Swift appeared to be reveling in vulgarities, his name graced the title page of *A Letter to a Young Gentleman, Lately enter'd into Holy Orders* (1720), in which Swift, speaking as an Augustan, laments the decline in verbal decorum evident in the writings of "Scholars in this Kingdom" and advocates a return to "Proper Words in proper Places" (PW 9: 63). This stuffy, pedantic Swift was not as popular as his racy counterpart, so the *Letter* was seldom reprinted.[43]

The self-involved playfulness of the antibank propaganda posed no real threat to the Whig ministry. Swift's *Drapier's Letters* (1724–5), which returned to the seditious theme of the *Universal Use of Irish Manufacture,* were another matter entirely. Swift in the guise of M. B. Drapier, a manufacturer and seller of linens, sounded the alarm to his fellow citizens about England's imposition of a half-pence copper coin produced for the mint by William Wood. In an overtly demagogic style, the Drapier vividly describes the economic devastation that will ensue if Wood's debased coinage circulates in Ireland. He tells the "Shop-keepers, Tradesmen, Farmers, and Common-People of Ireland" as

# THE

# WONDERFULL
## Wonder of Wonders;

Being an Accurate Defcription
of the Birth, Education, Manner of Living, Religion, Politicks, Learning, &c. of
mine A--fe.

## By Dr. Sw - ft.

With a PREFACE, and fome few Notes,
Explaining the moft difficult Paffages.

*Then as a Jeft for this time let it pafs,*
*And he that likes it not, may kifs my A---*
Jo. Haynes

The FOURTH EDITION.

## LONDON:

Printed from the Original Copy from DUBLIN,
and Sold by *T. Bickerton*, at the *Crown* in
*Pater-Nofter-Row.* 1721. Pr. 4*d.*

2.3. Title page, *The Wonderful Wonder of Wonders; Being an Accurate Description . . . of Mine A[s]se* (1721). This work may not have been written by Swift, but it permanently annexed scatological themes to his name and encouraged similar *jeux d'esprit* to be fathered on him. By permission of the Folger Shakespeare Library.

well as the "Nobility and Gentry" that it is their duty to God, Ireland, and their own families to boycott the coin and to sign petitions against it. The Drapier assures the citizens that they will not be at fault for resisting English authority; rather England is to blame for violating the LAWS OF GOD, OF NATURE, OF NATIONS by treating the Irish so unjustly (PW 10: 63).

Through a steady stream of nearly twenty newspaper reports, broadsides, and pamphlets (the publication of some subsidized by Swift to keep the price at a minimum), Swift riveted the attention of both the English and the Irish on a relatively inconsequential issue by dramatizing it as the battleground of freedom against tyranny, Irish rights against English profit. As publications by others swelled support for the Drapier's cause and revolution presented itself as a possibility, the English quickly jailed Swift's printer, John Harding, and put out a proclamation offering a reward of £300 for information about the identity of the Drapier. Of course, everyone (including the agents of the Crown) knew Swift was responsible. That no official dared arrest him, that no one betrayed him by turning state's evidence, and that no jury would indict his printer showed that Swift was more powerful than the King of England. Completely autonomous, he derived his power directly from the citizens of Ireland, who supported a cause he made clear to them through the popular press. When the patent for Wood's half-pence was withdrawn, the Drapier's decisive victory over the English juggernaut infused Swift with almost-supernatural power and inspired multiple elaborations of his heroic character. One title, *Fraud Detect'd: or, the Hibernian Patriot* (1725) provides an anthology of Drapier-related items, including "Songs Sung at the Drapier's Club in Truck Street."

The names of Swift and the Drapier are used interchangeably during the mid 1720s. One poem, for example, equates Swift with God, who protects the ship of state:

> Till you, whose Voice, the proudest Waves obey,
> Brings it, at last unto the quiet Key.
> . . . . . . . . . . . .
> Our Gratitude, with Ease, may be express'd,
> We'll strive to be, what you would make us—bless'd.[44]

During and shortly after the Wood's half-pence controversy, Swift's birthday was used as an occasion to celebrate him and his liberation of Ireland from slavery to England, a metaphor Swift persistently used to characterize the relationship of the two nations. "A Poem on the Drapier's Birth-Day: Being November the 30th" (Dublin, 1725) characterizes Swift in godlike terms as an "Immortal Man, from whose unbounded Flame / Nature's inferior Sons are warm'd to Fame"; a drinking song salutes him for the "convincing Paper

/ [that]Set us, gloriously, / From Brazen Fetters free"; and a birthday poem, published in 1726, argues that Swift is much more than an Irish hero: "He was born for all Mankind."[45] Most of these pro-Irish/anti-English broadsides were not republished in England but certainly must have alarmed the representatives of the Crown situated in Dublin, who no doubt reported their concerns to the ministry.

Letting the English know that he had no intention of retiring his colors after *The Drapier's Letters,* Swift kept up his drumbeat, emphasizing that the misery of Ireland's underclass was not a natural state, but rather the result of cold-blooded economic policies designed to make sure the English governing class got a good return on their Irish investments. In *A Short View of the State of Ireland* (1728) Swift chastises the affluent English for their blindness to the misery of the Irish poor:

> [There is] general Desolation in most Parts of the Kingdom. . . . The Families of Farmers, who pay great Rents, are living in Filth and Nastiness upon Buttermilk and Potatoes, without a Shoe or Stocking to their Feet; or a House so convenient as an *English* Hog-sty, to receive them. These, indeed, may be comfortable Sights to an *English* Spectator; who comes for a short Time, only *to learn the Language,* and returns back to his own Country, whither he finds all our Wealth Transmitted. (PW 12: 10–11)

In his masterpiece of irony, *A Modest Proposal* (1729), Swift also indicts England as the purposeful perpetrator of underclass suffering.

> It is a melancholly Object to those, who walk through this great Town [Dublin], or travel in the Country; when they see the *Streets,* the *Roads,* and *Cabbin-doors* crowded with *Beggars* of the Female Sex, followed by three, four, or six Children, *all in Rags,* and importuning every Passenger for an Alms. These *Mothers,* instead of being able to work for their honest Livelyhood, are forced to employ all their Time in stroling to beg Sustenance for their *helpless Infants;* who, as they grow up, either turn *Thieves* for want of Work; or leave their *dear Native Country, to fight for the Pretender in* Spain, or sell themselves to the *Barbadoes.* (PW 12: 109)

The reference to fighting "*for the Pretender in* Spain" is designed to inflame English fears that the Irish poor would love to wreak revenge on Protestant England by aiding the Jacobite forces.[46]

Because of his Irish tracts, Swift was asked by various groups in Ireland to arbitrate issues brought to him by the poor and exploited. Some publications expressing gratitude or asking economic guidance include *An Account of the Journey-Men Weavers Grateful Congratulation of the Rev. Dr. Swift Dean of St. Patrick's Safe Arrival [in London], with his kind Answer and Bounty to their Corporation* (Dublin, 1726); *A Letter to M. B. Drapier, Occasion'd by the Late Oppressive Villainy of the Br[ewe]rs, in Raising the Price of their Malt Liquors* (Dublin, 1729); and *The Memorial of the Poor Inhabitants, Tradesmen, and Labourers of the Kingdom of Ireland* [To the Reverend Dr. Jonathan Swift] (Dublin 1728), which asks Swift's help in convincing the Lord Lieutenant to raise money to import grain as a relief measure.

Swift's success in uniting an Irish audience was very ominous to the English, for they had always counted on the Irish to dissipate their energies fighting each other. Lord Orrery remarks that "The Papist, the Fanatic [Presbyterian], the Tory, the Whig, all listed themselves volunteers under the banner of M. B. Drapier" (73), a vision of unusual unity also captured in "A Poem to the Whole People of Ireland" (Dublin, 1726) that describes the Drapier's consensus-building among the mob:

> But let those consider, how firmly united,
> Were *Whigs, Tories, Trimmers,* and the *H[anoveria]ns;*
> And with what Delight he all others invited,
> Even *Quakers, Conformists,* and the *Presbyterians.*[47]

In another broadside, the recently deceased Judge Whitshed (who had tried to indict the printer of *The Drapier's Letters)* comes back to tell Swift why he hates him so much: "[T]is not enough for you to see and be exempt from the Miseries with which your Country is involv'd, but you must be daily opening the Eyes of the *Ignorant Vulgar,* and letting them know, from what Springs their Calamities proceed. . . . [and] the reasons why they have been so long deny'd the Blessings of Ease and Plenty."[48]

### Yahoo Laureate: Apollo and Gulliver

Swift sardonically observed that Ireland was a place where a writer who "hath been the *common Standard of Stupidity in England . . .* could put on a *Face of Importance and* Authority . . . [and] be admired and followed as the Pattern of *Eloquence* and *Wisdom"* (PW 9: 20). Like a whale in a fishpond, Swift easily assumed the status of laureate in Ireland during the 1720s. He was asked to write prologues to plays, advise aspiring writers, and be a public spokesman. In what might seem conventional praise, Irish poets mythologized Swift as the viceroy of Apollo, the god of literary creativity. But as Pat Rogers points out, the image of Swift as Apollo's viceroy or vice-regent "had a special potency" in Ireland, a country governed by a Lord Lieutenant representing the Crown.[49] As Apollo's viceroy, Swift's divine power trumped the temporal power of the King's viceroy. Against the backdrop of Anglo-Irish relations, the poems featuring Swift characters linked to Apollo (written by

Swift and others) had revolution as a subtext. "Apollo's Edict" (1721),[50] for example, portrays the vision of a new political order brought to earth by the heaven-assisted Swift. In the opening lines of the poem, Apollo explains that

> *IRELAND* is now our royal Care,
> We lately fix'd our *Viceroy* there:
> How near was she to be undone,
> Till pious Love inspir'd her Son?
> What cannot our *Vicegerent* do,
> As *Poet* and as *Patriot* too?
> Let his Success our Subjects sway
> Our Inspirations to obey,
> And follow where *he* leads the Way. (P 1: 269–272, ll. 1–9)

In response to these and numerous other poems joining Swift with Apollo, Jonathan Smedley, Swift's Iago, ironically acknowledges Swift's skill in writing but naively questions why he would use it to shape public opinion:

> But pray, *Great Sir,* (our Isle's *Apollo*)
> From what dull Logic, does it follow,
> That, 'cause in Writing you have Skill,
> Can joke off Hand, have Wit at Will,
> That *a whole People* you must cully.[51]

Smedley's attack against Swift-as-Apollo immediately provoked a number of counter broadsides from Irish citizens eager to defend their advocate. One anonymous author, for example, produced "A Scourge for the Author of the Satyr, Gibing on . . . the Reverend Dean Swift, Hibernia's Apollo" (Dublin, 1725).

Seeing how incendiary it was, Swift reinforced and amplified the linkage of his print persona with Apollo in "Apollo to the Dean" (1724) and "Stella's Birthday" (1728). In these poems, Apollo is characterized as one of Swift's familiar acquaintances.[52] In "Apollo to the Dean," Apollo complains that Delany has stolen his poetical fire and that Stella has spurned him as a lover "some ten Years ago" (P 1: 262–66, l. 44). In this poem, Stella (the mythologized Esther Johnson) appears in print for the first time. Swift depicts himself in a sexual rivalry with Apollo, thus implicitly underscoring his creative power. In "Stella's Birthday," Swift facetiously tells Stella that Apollo worked with him "Hand in Glove" (26). Notwithstanding his joking claims of being inspired by Apollo, Swift did not have fame as an Apollonian writer. His name appeared on publications that were topical, earthy, objectionable, or trifling. Some of these Swift wrote; others were attributed to him.

After a career of broadsides and pamphlets that made him famous, in 1726 Swift finally published a book—*Gulliver's Travels*. Although it was presented as the narration of Lemuel Gulliver, no one was fooled. Swift's trademark style was immediately spotted. Swift knew *Gulliver's Travels* would be the media event of 1726. He hand-carried his manuscript to London to make sure it reached the printer and perhaps to relish firsthand the effect it had on the English public. Overnight, Lilliput, Brobdingnag, Laputa, and Houyhnhnmland became familiar to readers of all ages and ranks. An enormous groundswell of *Gulliver*-related items appeared. The *Annotated List of Gulliveriana 1721–1800* lists 26 publications for 1726, quite remarkable considering *Gulliver* appeared in October. For 1727, 68 publications are listed. In 1726, *The Penny London Post* and *Parker's Penny Post* began serializing *Gulliver* for those unable to afford the book. Still in England after the *Travels'* publication, Swift bought a print of Gulliver in a teacup from a hawker (C 3:257). *Mist's Weekly Journal* carried an advertisement for fans displaying "Quinbus Flestrin or the Man Mountain, at full Length."[53] A celebrity, Swift himself was characterized as one of the popular shows of London in one pamphlet that lists "*the Copper-Farthing Dean from* Ireland" among the current attractions that include "*a White bear, at the House of Mr.* Ratcliff *in* Bishopsgate-Street . . . *and the wonderful Wild Man that was nursed in the Woods of Germany by a wild Beast, hunted and taken in Toyls* [nets]."[54]

Contemporary commentaries on *Gulliver's Travels* reveal how much its broad appeal was viewed as a threat to hierarchies embedded in the status quo. In the hands of unsophisticated readers, who could not tell the difference between *Tom Thumb* and the *Aeneid,* some feared the book might be very dangerous.[55] These reactions underline the anxiety generated by Swift's decision to reject the modes of writing expected of him and, by implication, blur class distinctions. The author of *Gulliver Decypher'd* notes that Swift "never produced any thing in his own Profession," but rather spent his time "alluring the common people . . . by Omens, Predictions, and Odes, which he caused to be sung in publick Places." This pamphleteer sarcastically notes that *Gulliver's Travels* could not possibly be written by an Anglican dean since there is "not one Word of true Christianity in it, but several ludicrous and obscene Passages, which are shocking even to common Decency" and that surely Swift must be too busy to engage in such nonsense: "Doubtless he, *good Man,* employs his Time to more sacred Purposes than in writing Satyrs and Libels upon his Superiors, or in composing *Grub-street* Pamphlets to divert the vulgar of all Denominations"[56] The author of *A Letter from a Clergyman* also worries about the populist rhetoric in *Gulliver's Travels* and the Irish tracts, which contain "Terms the Rabble use in their Contests with one another in the Streets," which lead "the People into Disaffection and Disloyalty." In particular, the anonymous author of this *Letter* is appalled at Swift's leveling tendencies—calling the "best Gentlemen in the Kingdom . . . Pedlars, Pickpockets, Highwaymen, and Bullies. . . . He spares neither Age or Sex, neither the Living or the Dead; neither the Rich, the Great, or the Good."[57] Jonathan Smedley adds his condemnation, saying, "Poor *Curll's* Head was stuck in a Pillory for a Book [the pornographic *Nun in her Smock*] which could not do a hundredth Part of the Mischief, as not having had a hundredth Part of the Readers [as *Gulliver's Travels*]"[58]

Swift chose to write his chef d'oeuvre as a humorous satire filled with many offensive elements, particularly sexual and excremental motifs, a strategy that accentuated his lack of respect for polite proprieties. Swift had seen the powerful attractions of excrement in the astonishing popularity of the *Wonderful Wonder of Wonders*. A letter to the *Flying Post* criticizes Swift's lack of "Delicacy" for revealing Gulliver's problems with waste disposal in Lilliput as well as having Gulliver make "use of a new Fire Engine," referring to his urination on the fire at the royal palace.[59] One of the most popular spin-offs from *Gulliver* was William Hogarth's invented scene, "The Punishment [an Involuntary enema] Inflicted on Gulliver [for urinating on the Lilliputian palace]," which appeared in 1726 and periodically after that through the end of the century. In a fake biography, Smedley alleges that excrement had been an early and constant passion with Swift—that "the first Instance he gave of his Genius and Spirit, was sh[ittin]g in his School-Master's Slippers, which afterwards gave him the Hints of there being such Creatures as *Yahoos*."[60] Associated with elements of low comedy, Swift became a natural subject of jests as well as the putative author of coarse squibs.

Despite his reputation as the epitome of literary lowliness, Swift published (with Pope) three volumes of *Miscellanies* (1727–8). The "Preface" to Volume I (signed by both Pope and Swift) states that the authors want to forestall Edmund Curll from more piracies (he had published a two-volume *Miscellanies* in 1726) and that they will print all that they have, no matter the quality, since even the worst things by great authors show their "distinguishing marks of style, or peculiarity of thinking." Although Swift and Pope present themselves as arbiters of the English Republic of Letters, some of the works they publish, especially in Volume III, are trash by any standard of judgment. One poem, for example, has the elegant refrain

> So Ditton and Whiston
> May both be bep-st on;
> And Whiston and Ditton
> May both be besh-t on.[61]

Pope wrote many of grossest and most idiotic pieces in the collection, but since none was labeled as to author, Swift was equally blamed.

If Swift and Pope wanted to disgrace themselves in the *Miscellanies,* that was one thing. But they had the breathtaking effrontery—by including *Peri Bathos, or The Art of Sinking in Poetry*—to label as pathetic some of the most acclaimed English poets. An uproar ensued. The most extended response was Jonathan Smedley's *Gulliveriana: or a Fourth Volume of Miscellanies. Being a Sequel of the Three Volumes published by Pope and Swift* (1728), in which Smedley compiles 344 pages of printed attacks on the two authors, as well as supplying some of his own. Smedley dismisses Swift's verse as "*Doggerel* and *Burlesque*" and also finds him falling far short of the great prose writers of the age—"a Thousand more . . . Qualifications cannot enable him to write like *Barrow*, in *Divinity*; like *Hoadly*, on *Government*; like the *Spectators*, in *Wit* and *Humor*. . . ." The only people who think Swift's "*Ribaldry* and *Low Life*" are commendable, Smedley implies, are the benighted Irish, who "huzza'd [him] in *Dublin*." Outraged that Swift and Pope might think their *Miscellanies* constituted a "*Temple of Fame*," Smedley declares that they cannot hold a candle to the true inhabitants of "*Palaces* for *Apollo* and the *Muses*." Smedley's frontispiece shows Swift and Pope on a "stage itinerant," which the *Tale*-teller associates with Grubstreet. By implication, notes Hugh Ormsby-Lennon, Swift and Pope are mountebanks, gulling the public with their impostures. In the foreground of the engraving, a satyr shakes hands with Jack Pudding, the merry-andrew or buffoon who is the mountebank's accomplice.[62] Once again, Swift's assertions of his superiority open the floodgates to responses designed to puncture his inflated self-mythologizing.

Many authors predicted that the embarrassment of *Miscellanies* had effectively ended the careers of Pope and Swift. One poem muses on the ironies of human fate, using the two authors as examples—"Who would be Witty, Wise or Great? / When *Sw—t* and *P-p-e*, so fam'd for writing. . . . / Are *Names* now, hardly worth reciting."[63] Another poem prophesies that Swift's "hum'rous, oft obscene, undelicate" writing will inevitably situate him where he ought to be:

> Unheeded, and unknown amid the Filth
> Of *Billingsgate*, the Waterman's lewd Jest,
> And tattling Gossip's Tale; fit Company
> For such a vulgar Taste![64]

That Swift had sunk himself was wishful thinking. As the compendia in *Gulliveriana* demonstrates, the publication of the *Miscellanies* elicited narratives and attributions that reflected and magnified Swift's prominence in popular culture.

## Ungenteel Gentleman

As an author, Swift had a reputation for disregarding polite decorum. What was he like in private? Swift satisfied the natural curiosity about the hidden

GULLIVERIANA:

OR, A

FOURTH VOLUME

OF

# MISCELLANIES.

BEING A

SEQUEL of the THREE VOLUMES,
publiſhed by POPE and SWIFT.

To which is added,
ALEXANDERIANA; or, A Compariſon
between the *Eccleſiaſtical* and *Poetical* POPE.
And many Things, in VERSE and PROSE,
relating to the latter.

With an ample PREFACE; and a CRITIQUE
on the Third Volume of *Miſcellanies* lately
publiſh'd by thoſe two facetious Writers.

*Sequitur pede, pœna, claudo.*     HOR.

LONDON:
Printed ·for J. ROBERTS, at the *Oxford Arms* in
*Warwick-lane,* M.DCC.XXVIII.

2.4. Title page and frontispiece, [Jonathan Smedley], *Gulliveriana* (1728). This work is a compilation of attacks on Swift and Pope for *Miscellanies* (1727–8), which arrogantly imply they are two of England's greatest writers, notwithstanding the low trifles contained in the volumes. The two are depicted on a montebank's stage. Swift's hooves are visible beneath his clergyman's gown. His titillating relationship with Stella is referenced in the star above his head. By permission of the Folger Shakespeare Library.

lives of celebrities by depicting himself at home or in the homes of his friends. Self-consciously he characterized himself or elicited characterizations of himself as a man indifferent or hostile to the manners and tastes that a person in his position should possess. On the one hand, such depictions added to the scandals already connoted by his name—his lack of respect for received opinion, his selfish ambition, his attraction to nastiness and lowliness. On the other hand, Swift's indifference to what others thought and his ability to thrive in the face of their hostility, testified to his extraordinary existential strength.

Initiating a line of mythmaking that centers on Swift's rude behavior as a guest, "Journal of a Part of a Summer" was published as an anonymous broadside. The poem, in which Swift portrays himself as a comic character, recounts a visit to his friends, the Rochforts, who lived in Gaulstown. In the poem, Swift shows himself relaxing out of the public eye—roaming the house in his nightgown, eating breakfast, fishing, or playing backgammon. The poem caused a commotion when it appeared in Dublin (the exact date is uncertain) and then was soon republished in several London periodicals in 1722–3.[65] While the poem obviously seems like an affectionate joke, Swift's enemies inferred the worst about his manners and motives. Swift was accused of extreme ingratitude toward his host and hostess, for repaying their hospitality with public humiliation. In the poem, for instance, Swift depicts Mrs. Rochfort as a shrewish mother: "At Ten, my Lady comes and Hectors, / . . . and scolds us down to Breakfast" (P 1: 278–83, ll. 13, 16). At one point the arrival of more houseguests necessitates an embarrassing reallocation of domestic resources, which Swift describes as follows:

> The *Dean* must with his Quilt supply,
> The Bed in which these [new guests] lie:
> *Nim* lost his Wig-block, *Dan* his Jordan [chamber pot];
> My Lady says she can't afford one. . . . (121–24)

By implying that the Rochforts did not have enough linens and chamber pots to accommodate all their guests, Swift, it was alleged, shamed them. It is not clear how the poem first got into print, but Swift's attackers assumed (I think correctly) that Swift had arranged to publish it. Swift's possible responsibility aside, "The Gaulstown incident" became a shortcut way of referring to Swift's lack of respect for his friends, because he was willing to make matters public that should have remained private.

Swift's enemies spiraled the "Gaulstown incident" into a lurid scenario of betrayal. One commentator, who calls himself Philoxenus, reports that the "malevolents among us cast invidious reflections on the Dean for writing this poem . . . that it was ungrateful, after having sucked all the *Sweets* of *Gallstown*, to leave the following *Sting* behind him." Philoxenus elaborates the plot by adding that Swift—whom he calls "Dr. *Celer*" [celer = Latin for swift], "rudely disappeared in the middle of the night, *sans Ceremonie*." Another writer rekindles the associations of Swift with the blasphemous *Tale*-teller, by condemning the perfectly innocent "Journal" as a burlesque of the Day of Judgment.[66] Even though the charges of irreligion against Swift are entirely unwarranted in this case, writers and publishers realized that any fictions about Swift would sell—the more sensational the better.

William Percival, who was caricatured in Swift's "Journal" as a pedantic boor, retaliated with a broadside published in Dublin. His painfully inept poem presents a Swift who is willing to eat out lavishly at others' expense, but is too miserly to be a host himself, for in "the *Dean's Kitchin*. . . . / . . . there is no Fire, / Or wine . . . ." When allotted £5 to give his church chapter an annual feast, Percival's Swift uses it as an opportunity to make a profit. Percival's Swift is so cheap that he will avoid paying for food at any cost, and so

> As for himself, with draggled Gown,
> Poor Curate like, he'll trudge the Town,
> .   .   .   .   .   .   .   .   .   .   .
> Sometimes to *Gawls-Town* he will go,
> To spend a Month or two or so,
> Admires the *Baron, George* and's Spouse,
> Lives well, and then Lampoon's the House.[67]

Percival's characterizations of Swift's cheapness, the lack of amenities at his house, the "draggled" condition of his clothes, his failures as a host and guest are not rebutted by Swift. Rather, he elaborates these ideas in his own writing, for example, in a later poem in which he describes his stay with Sir Arthur and Lady Acheson at Market Hill. As with "The Journal," what appears to be a private joke mysteriously found its way into print. One anonymous author hyperventilates on Swift's betrayal of the Achesons as evidence that he does not deserve to be revered as an Irish Patriot:

> O! had ["The Journal"] ne'er appeared to mortal eyes,
> Unsully'd then had stood the D[rapie]r's Name,
> And unborn Tongues, proclaim'd the Patriot's Fame:
> Now fresh alas! The black Remembrance lives,
> *Gallstown* again in *Market-Hill* revives.
> A secret Poison lurks within his Breast[. . . .][68]

The condemnation of Swift's behavior for writing the "Journal" obviously did not deter him from producing many more poems in which he insults hosts, and particularly, hostesses. He knew the pieces would evoke strong reactions, and he was right.

William Percival was Swift's enemy, but Swift's own friends also emphasized his failures as a host. Patrick Delany published two poems that comment on Swift's parsimony with his guests. One notes the similarity between Dean Swift and his predecessor, who was also cheap—"Are the Guests of this House still doom'd to be cheated?"—and the other playfully imagines Apollo occupying the guests so they don't realize what they have been "fob'd off, with Sheer-Wit and Sheer-Wine."[69] Thomas Sheridan, another friend, authored an anonymous poem that pretends to be an inventory of the house at Laracor that Swift loaned to the Bishop of Meath. Frequently reprinted, this poem describes furnishings that would mortify any proper householder:

> An Oaken, broken, Elbow-Chair;
> A Cawdle-Cup, without an Ear;
> A batter'd, shatter'd Ash Bedstead;
> A box of Deal, without a Lid;
> A Pair of Tongs, but out of Joint;
> A Back-Sword Poker, without Point;
> A Pot that's crack'd a-cross, around,
> With an old knotted Garter bound;
> An Iron Lock, without a Key;
> A Wig, with hanging, quite grown Grey. . . . (P 3:1044–5)[70]

Depictions (by Swift and others) of a Swift character indifferent to material comforts and shows of wealth—such as good clothes, suitable amenities, and generous hospitality—developed a demand for further evidence of his eccentricities. Jests, epigrams, and light verse were generated to supply this desire.

### Priestly Satyr: Bedroom Fantasies

The most electric revelation to emerge about Swift during the 1720s was that he had a love life—and not an orthodox one, either. Whig caricatures had shown him cursing, drinking, and plotting—but not copulating. With the appearance of "Cadenus and Vanessa," Swift became sexualized, for the poem portrays an intimate relationship between Cadenus (=anagram of Decanus), soon identified as Swift, and a passionate young woman, soon identified as Esther Vanhomrigh. As a clergyman, Swift should have presented himself as a model of married life, but instead he had chosen to remain a bachelor, and possibly—as the poem implies—not a chaste one. The poem metaphorically opens the door to the most private space inhabited by Dean Swift—the bedroom.

In the year it was published, "Cadenus and Vanessa" went through an astonishing 15 editions in London, Edinburgh, and Dublin. A high-profile sex scandal was just what Swift's enemies might have hoped for as a dramatic way to undermine his authority. Instead, it endowed Swift with Dionysian potency. The questions raised by the poem about Swift's relationship with Vanessa have never been answered. Swift certainly made no attempt to do so. Vanessa died in 1723. When the poem appeared in 1726, rumors circulated that she had been killed by unrequited love or that she had published the poem in revenge for Swift's not marrying her. "Come Cadenus, come with haste /. . . . or I like Vanessa die," sighs the author of a broadside entitled "A Young Lady's Complaint for the Stay of Dean Swift in England" (1726). The central question was, How far did they go? Almost immediately after the poem was published, titillating lines that hinted at the answer mysteriously appeared in some versions. To this day, it is uncertain whether Swift or one of his enemies inserted them. In the insertion, Vanessa tells Cadenus that she will teach him how to love—"But what success *Vanessa* met, / Is to the World a Secret yet: / . . . . [It] must never to Mankind be told, / Nor shall the conscious Muse unfold" (P 2: 686–714, ll. 818–19, 826–27).

How this compromising poem got into print is an enigma. Most modern scholars believe that several manuscript versions of the poem existed, and that one of them fell into the hands of a printer. I am convinced, however, that Swift is personally responsible for the public appearance of this work. From London, where he had taken *Gulliver's Travels* to be printed in 1726, Swift writes to Knightly Chetwode, a friend concerned about the hubbub stirred up by the poem's recent publication. Swift replies that given the number of circulating copies, it was only a matter of time before it became public: "I know several copies of it have been given about, and [the] Lord Lieutenant told me he had one. . . . I am very indifferent what is done with it." (C 3: 129–30) If the poem had been floating around Dublin for several years, why did it suddenly appear shortly after Swift had left for England? Lobbing bombshells and then leaving town was a typically Swiftian move. Could Swift himself have made manuscripts available to the printer? Although Chetwode's letter has been lost or destroyed, Swift's denial implies Chetwode's accusation: "[P]rinting it myself is impossible, for I never saw it since I writ it. Neither if I had, would I use shifts or arts, let people think of me as they please" (C 3: 129–30). The Swift-Vanessa liaison became the talk of the town. Curll immediately scraped together a two-volume *Miscellanea* that contains a rebus supposedly written by Vanessa. In this rebus, Swift reproves her for being so carried away by an "Amorous Fit" that she stoops to write in a low genre (rebus) on a low subject (himself).[71]

The furor surrounding "Cadenus and Vanessa" was clearly not embarrassing to Swift. When Pope asked whether he wanted to include the poem in their 1727–8 *Miscellanies,* Swift readily agreed. Even more puzzling, though, was the fact that Swift also gave Pope poems he had written to Stella. One of them, "To Stella, Visiting Me in My Sickness," is set in Swift's bedroom, suggesting the closeness of their relationship. Swift's connection with one woman was shocking enough, but his decision to create the spectacle of himself as a bachelor Dean linked in print simultaneously with two different women made heads spin. What was he thinking? One more surprise from the master of surprises! The nature of the relationships was not clear, and never became clearer, although one author after another claims to know the truth. In *Gulliveriana,* for example, Smedley declares the following, after quoting the passage about "the conscious Muse" never unfolding her hidden knowledge:

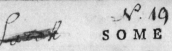

SOME

# MEMOIRS

### OF THE

*Amours* and *Intrigues*

#### OF A CERTAIN

# IRISH DEAN:

Who LIV'D and FLOURISH'D in the
Kingdom of IRELAND, not many Hundred
Years since.

#### INTERSPERS'D

With the GALLANTRIES of Two *Berk-shire*
*LADIES.*

### IN

Which will be inserted several Original Letters of the said DEAN, that will be well known
by Those that may be now living, who have
ever seen the DEAN's Hand-Writing. By a
LADY, who in those Days was well acquainted
with him.

The THIRD EDITION.

### *LONDON:*

Printed, and *Dublin* Reprinted by *R. Dickson*, in *Silver-
Court, Castle-street*, opposite the *Rose-Tavern*, and
Sold by the Booksellers. M DCC XXX.
(Price, a *British* Half Crown.)

2.5.   Title page, *Some Memoirs of the Amours and Intrigues of a Certain Irish Dean* (1728). By simultaneously publishing affectionate poems to Stella and Vanessa (while seeming to be married to neither), Swift set in motion rampant mythmaking about his love life and sexuality. By permission of the Folger Shakespeare Library.

This passage wants no Comment; but I must add to it, that whatever happen'd between them two [Vanessa and Swift], the *Captain* [Swift] and *Stella* * * * * all this while—and I think this Circumstance lets the Reader into the *whole Secret,* without any other Help of his *conscious Muse.*"[72]

Once Swift opened the door to bedroom fantasies about him, it could never be closed. Following the publication of the poems to Stella and Vanessa in the late 1720s, Swift's sex life became a popular topic, with all sorts of lurid suggestions offered in print.

The contrast of Swift's seeming libertinism with his priestly vows produced wonderful copy. The frontispiece to Smedley's *Gulliveriana* depicts Swift with satyr's hooves peeking out beneath his clerical gown and a star labeled "Stella" shining above him. One poem caricatures Swift as a man "who left his Prayers, / His Church, his God, to holy Drudges, and / Let loose his passions for the world. . . ."[73] Another imagines Swift's love nest:

> So when *Vanessa* yielded up her charms,
> The blest *Cadenus* languished in her Arms;
> High, on a Peg, his unbrushed Beaver hung,
> His Vest unbutton'd, his God unsung,
> Raptur'd he lies. . . .[74]

It wasn't long before Swift's reputation as a lover landed him as a protagonist in a romance, which rapidly went through three editions. Its title is provocative—*Some Memoirs of the Amours and Intrigues of a Certain Irish Dean. . . . By a Lady, who . . . was well acquainted with him* (1728). The Swift in the *Memoirs* has goat-like appetites. Although he might seem like a proper clergyman, he is *"very gross in his* Amours, *only sought after new Faces to gratify himself in the easiest and cheapest Manner he could."* The narrator quotes Swift as saying that he would not be satisfied by "half the Women in Ireland," whom he seeks to ensnare with games of "Hot Cockles, Push Pin, [and] Smutty Stories *of his own Invention. . . .*"[75]

By the end of the 1720s, Swift had created identities that would grow into mythic figures after his death—the epic freedom fighter, the comic eccentric, the polygamous lover. His power, his mysteries, his contradictions, and his heterodoxy would keep people talking and writing about him. In 1729, though, Swift did something that might have seemed impossible—he became even more outrageous in print than he ever had been before. At the same time, conscious of his own mortality, he began erecting noble monuments to his memory. These opposing efforts added to the paradoxes at the core of his public identity and heightened the rumors that made him into a lasting legend.

# Chapter Three ∾

# Intimations of Mortality and Immortality, 1729–45

With the publication of "A Libel on Dr. Delany" (1729), Swift entered a new phase in his self-mythologizing. Nearing the last decade of the biblical three score and ten allotment of years, Swift appeared to become very conscious about making sure his mark on the world would endure. His focus on himself as a subject is evident during the 1730s in the number of references in his poems to *Dean, Drapier,* and *Swift*[1] as well as the appearance of Swift's name on his title pages. In his last years, Swift devised dramatic self-representations that would imprint his life, character, and works on history in indelible ink. His strategy was paradoxical. On the one hand, Swift elicited the sounding of the gold trumpet, by emphasizing his identities as the brave Drapier, the conscientious dean, the great author, and the noble benefactor of his city. On the other hand, he escalated the scandals about himself to a new level, with shocks that would bring forth the blasts of the brass trumpet. In this regard, Swift's print-constructed character in the 1730s was radically different from that of the 1720s. His indirect criticism of the Crown and the ruling class bloomed into open contempt; his offensive imagery became nauseatingly graphic; his rudeness, especially to women, verged toward degradation; once merely ungodly, now he seemed positively satanic; his jaundiced view of human nature sank to misanthropy; his interest in the underclass took a perverse turn; and his eccentricities began to look like madness. The diverse representations of Swift in the 1730s—by himself and others—were often ironic or rhetorical, but combined together to produce an image of extremes. In light of the problematic qualities associated with him, Swift's enemies viewed his claims to greatness and nobility as ludicrous.

As Swift's letters from the 1730s show, mortality and immortality were on his mind, yet he did little or nothing to remove doubts about his character.

Rather, he seemed intent to heighten the clash of theses and antitheses in his portrayals, presenting himself as an unresolvable conundrum rather than a definable individual. At the end of the decade, Swift published his own elegy, "Verses on the Death of Dr. Swift" (1739), which does little to clarify who he was or how he wanted to be remembered. A typically Swiftian production, it raises far more questions than it answers with its oxymoronic depiction. After Swift died in 1745, biographer after biographer attempted to answer the questions that Swift refused to, each assembling the contradictory evidence in different ways.

### Impudent Traitor

In *Gulliver's Travels* (1726) and *The Drapier's Letters* (1724–5), Swift took care not directly to defame the king, his ministers, the aristocracy, or the rule of English law. That deference disappears in "A Libel on the Reverend Dr. Delany and a Certain Great Lord," a poem in which Swift expresses a hatred of the King and English institutions, particularly the English class system. Swift does not mask his voice in the "Libel," but speaks as himself to his friend Patrick Delany about the lack of distributive justice in a society where worthless aristocrats have wealth and privilege, while the meritorious—for example—literary geniuses, suffer neglect. As cases in point, Swift itemizes the atrocities: William Congreve, abandoned by Charles Montagu, Earl of Halifax; Richard Steele, "left to starve, and dye in *Wales;* John Gay, exiled from "*St. James's* in Disgrace"; Joseph Addison "by Lords Carest, / Was left in Foreign lands Distrest" (P 2: 480–86, ll. 33–82). Of the poets Swift mentions, only Pope has been unaffected because he "Refus'd the Visits of a Queen" and would not stoop to "lick a *Rascal Statesman's* Spittle." In this light, Swift ironically urges Delany not to believe that the new Lord Lieutenant of Ireland, John Carteret, has his best interests or those of Ireland in mind.

> He comes to *drain a Beggar's Purse*:
> He comes to tye our Chains on faster,
> And show us E[ngland] is our Master:
> Caressing Knaves and Dunces wooing,
> To make them work their own undoing.
> (124–28).

To speak about the King's representative in this way was flabbergasting. Although Swift makes Lord Carteret an exception to the rule that those in power are the lowest of the low, Swift does not step away from his contention that rank and merit are in inverse relation.[2] Those with the highest rank are really the lowest on the scale of being, an injustice that causes him to "sincerely hate / Both [Kings] and *Ministers* of *State*" (173–4). Such sentiments rekindled speculation about Swift's strange desire to take the part of the underclass and also about his view of humankind in general.

In the conclusion of the poem, full of insights "Fresh from the *Tripod* of Apollo," Swift creates an analogy that implies that the King's relation with his Irish viceroy is parallel to that of Beelzebub with one of his under devils. Swift highlights his traitorous insult in the final lines of the poem:

> . . . [N]o imaginable things
> Can differ more than GOD and [Kings]
> And, *Statesmen,* by ten thousand odds
> Are ANGELS, just as [devils] are GODS.
> (196–200)

The shocking yet exhilarating rebuff to authority made this poem a best-seller, with at least four editions within the year. Joshua, Viscount Allen, publicly denounced Swift at a meeting of the Privy Council as "a man who neither feared God nor honored the King."[3] But despite Allen's threats to punish Swift and his printer, the Crown made no moves against them even though the "Libel" generated large amounts of commentary in both the London and Dublin press. No doubt the ministry was alarmed at Swift's antimonarchical harangues, which evoked the horrors of the Regicide and the English Civil War. Swift wrote more like a Presbyterian roundhead than an Anglican dean, who by definition, should be staunchly royalist.

Besides Swift's brazen disrespect, another shocking aspect of the poem was his seeming hatred of all mankind, an idea that also lurks beneath his ambiguous representation of the Yahoos in *Gulliver's Travels.* While the upper classes viewed themselves as vastly more civilized than the underclasses, Swift inflames their emotions by implying that both classes are equally Yahoo-ish. This view imbues Swift with the political agenda of a leveler and the unchristian religion of one who does not believe that man is made in the image of God. In light of Swift's "Libel," the anonymous author of the "Panegyric on the Reverend Dean Swift" (1730) suggests that Swift has lost his bearings. He once appreciated the men he now equates to Yahoos, and he once "despis'd the *Beast* with *many Heads* / And damn'd the *Mob,* whom now he leads," but all is now changed (P 2: 491–98, ll. 161–2).[4] Another poem, professing to be from a friend, admonishes Swift to step away from his libel because it destroys all the glory he had attained as the Drapier—"No more let such Subjects your Virtue destroy / . . . . give over your LIBEL, / Apply to RELIGION, and think on the BIBLE."[5] Swift's seeming inability to acknowledge obvious hierarchies and essential distinctions laid the foundations for myths of his madness.

Unlike those given power by birth whom Swift excoriates in his "Libel," Swift created his own power through publications that influenced a mass readership. With that power, he could openly flout official disapproval, and, indeed, demand to be honored by those to whom he was anathema. In the midst of the brouhaha sparked by his "Libel on Dr. Delany," Swift began to lobby for official recognition from the City of Dublin for his efforts on behalf of the Irish people. In particular, he wanted to be publicly recognized with the presentation of the Freedom of the City in a gold box, equivalent to the modern ceremony bestowing the keys to the city. Seeking reward from agents of the Crown for his attacks on the Crown, Swift's lobbying was an inflammatory move that put the city fathers in a difficult position. While they did not want to honor a traitor, as Anglo-Irish they might have admired Swift's resistance to imperial authority or they may have feared mob violence if Swift's petition were rejected. One of Dublin's upper crust, Marmaduke Coghill notes in a letter that it took "three years earnest solicitation" by Swift to get the box and that "the Dean and his Friends" wrote the proposed inscription for it, which celebrated Swift as "the most eminent patriot and greatest ornament of this his native city and country." Coghill snorts, "Such an arrogant inscription desired by a man himself is surprising, but the man is so well known that nothing of this nature is new. . . ."[6]

In the end, the city fathers awarded Swift the gold box, but without an inscription on it, for they were reluctant to spell out honors for an author of treasonous works. To counteract the damage of awarding Swift a gold box, the city fathers at the same time (May 30, 1730) also awarded one to Bishop Hoadly, an extreme Whig and one of Swift's worst enemies. "A Panegyric on the Reverend Dean Swift" sarcastically links Swift's gold box to the infamous Bandbox, which the poet claims was "More precious far than ev'n the Gift / Of our *Metropolis* to *S—t*" (46–8). A number of other popular prints focus on the inappropriateness Swift's award.[7] No doubt Swift knew that seeking and getting the gold box would cause a stir.

The hostile responses to the "Libel on Dr. Delany" were signs to Swift that he had succeeded magnificently in vexing the world. Writing to Benjamin Motte, he called the poem "the best thing I writt as I think" (C 4: 83) and urged Motte and Pope to include it in the 1732 *Miscellanies,* something Pope was loathe to do for fear of government reprisals. Invigorated by the commotion caused by his "Libel," Swift published two more seditious poems in 1733 that resulted in the dramatic arrests of those responsible for printing them.[8] Both "Epistle to a Lady" and "On Poetry: A Rapsody" attack the English prime minister, Sir Robert Walpole and repeat the implications in the "Libel" that kings are among the lowest life forms. In "Epistle to a Lady," Swift characterizes himself in the third person as "the Dean," who asks why he should show respect to the King—"Shou'd a Monkey wear a Crown, / Must I tremble at his Frown? / Could I not, thro' all his Ermine, / Spy the strutting, chatt'ring Vermin?" (P 2: 628–38, ll. 149–52). In "On Poetry: A Rapsody," the speaker implies that only Grubstreet hirelings would be willing to praise the King:

> O, what Indignity and Shame
> To prostitute the Muse's Name,
> By Flatt'ring [Kings] whom Heaven design'd
> The Plagues and Scourges of Mankind.
> Bred up in Ignorance and Sloth,
> And ev'ry Vice that nurses both.
> (P 2: 639–659, ll. 405–10)

Swift's lambasting the court and the ministry caused some people to admire him for speaking his mind without regard to class distinction; the same attribute made others fear and despise him, seeing his actions as a threat to the social order.

## St. Drapier

In the late 1720s, Swift joined with his friend Thomas Sheridan to publish an anonymous periodical in Dublin they called *The Intelligencer*. One of its overt aims was to mythologize Swift-as-Drapier as a popular hero, a move that had the effect of reinscribing the Drapier's epic victories in public memory and discomfiting the English, who dreaded the thought that Swift might spark a Jacobite uprising in Ireland. Because *The Intelligencer* was a joint project of Swift and Sheridan, one assumes its hagiography had Swift's full endorsement. The nervousness of the English about Swift's intentions boosted *The Intelligencer*'s sales in London, where collected editions of a thousand copies each appeared in 1729 and 1730—an unusual demand for a periodical printed in Dublin. Lending credence to rumors of Swift's subversion, two London periodicals with Jacobite leanings—*Mist's Weekly Journal* and *Fog's Weekly Journal*—reprinted issues of *The Intelligencer*. *Mist's Weekly Journal* had an estimated circulation of 8,000 to 10,000.[9] One contemporary commentator explicitly decries Swift's efforts "to inflame the *Irish* Nation against the *English,* and to make them throw off the Subjection to the *English* Government . . . and, in fine, to pave the way for a new or Popish Revolution. . . ."[10]

Through *The Intelligencer,* readers were reminded that Swift and the Drapier were one and the same. Several broadsides declared that Swift had sullied the "Divine" image of himself-as-Drapier with publications showing his crasser, coarser side, and by the late 1720s, the Drapier started to take on a life of his own in publications, separate from that of Swift. The Drapier was a noble symbol of self-determination every Irish citizen could salute, while Swift was a name that connoted scandals of various kinds. Ironically, as one author put it, "none but S[wif]t, [could] Eclipse the D[rapie]r's Name."[11]

The bond of the Drapier with Swift is cemented in *The Intelligencer* by the interchangeable use of their names and the addition of narratives that show Swift exemplifying the fearless courage of the Drapier, who fights for justice against those of superior force and rank. One story, for example, concerns Swift facing down an unrepentant bully, a country squire named Abel Ram, whose coach almost runs Swift down in the town of Gorey. Instead of apologizing in person to Swift, Ram sends a servant with a brief note of regret. *The Intelligencer* denounces the gesture as a travesty, considering that Swift is a gentleman "to whom the Nation hath in a particular manner been obliged" for his *Drapier's Letters*. In retaliation against Ram, according to the story, Swift has his servant deliver a note to the squire, in which Swift threatens to accuse Ram of attempted murder unless he fires his coachman.[12] A folktale about the incident became part of the oral tradition in Ireland. The story describes Abel Ram forcing Swift into a ditch. Extricating himself, Swift is supposed to have uttered this couplet: "England's pride [in some versions, dread] and Ireland's glory / Was thrown in the ditch by the Ram of Gorey."[13]

*Intelligencer* #18 (November 26–30, 1728) proposes a reinauguration of the popular celebrations of Swift's birthday on November 30, to honor him for his role as the Drapier. While such celebrations seemed to have taken place immediately after the publication of *The Drapier's Letters* in 1725 and 1726, no record exists of one in 1727, a lapse that *The Intelligencer* finds lamentable:

> It has been the Custom of all wise Nations, not only to confer immediate honours upon their Benefactors, but likewise to distinguish their Birth-Days, by Anniversary rejoycings. . . . It is for this reason, that I recommend Saint Andrews Day [November 30] unto you, to be Celebrated in a most Particular Manner, being (as I am well-informed) the DRAPIER's Birth-day.[14]

The ensuing festivities were reported both in the Dublin and London papers, perhaps the result of plants by either Swift or Sheridan.[15] In another effort to encourage adulation, *Intelligencer* #15 hyperbolically admonishes the Irish to read the Drapier's *Short View of the State of Ireland* every day, have their children memorize it, and hang every page in frames on the walls of their houses. By analogy, Swift is God, and *The Drapier's Letters,* his gospel. Shrines with statues should be built to him "in those Memorable parts of this Kingdom, where our Heroes have shone with the greatest Lustre," so the populace can pay homage.[16]

*The Intelligencer* eventually became too much work for its authors. After it ceased publication in 1728, Swift joined forces with George Faulkner to keep Irish autonomy and its champion, the Drapier/Dean Swift, in the fore-front of public consciousness, both in Dublin and London. Faulkner's ini-tial interest in mythologizing Swift as the Drapier was manifest in his publication of *Fraud Detect'd, or The Hiberian Patriot,* which he published in 1725 and then republished in 1730.[17] It contains *The Drapier's Letters* as well as "Songs sung at the *Drapier's Club* in *Truck Street.*" Stories about Swift in Faulkner's *Dublin Journal,* which far outnumber those in other Dublin papers,[18] increased Swift's fame and Faulkner's fortunes.

In the *Dublin Journal,* the Dean/Drapier is glorified as a popular hero, one who risks danger to fight against England on behalf of Ireland. Swift took an active role, it seems, in feeding Faulkner information about his ac-tivities or even writing stories about himself that would appear in the *Dublin Journal.* Several unpublished manuscripts in Swift's hand are jour-nalistic pieces he seems to have prepared for Faulkner, for example, the *Ad-vertisement Against Lord Allen* (PW 12: 140) and *The Substance of What was Said by the Dean* (PW 12: 144–48), both of which attack those who doubt his worthiness to receive the honorary gold box in recognition of his patri-otic service. In these accounts, Swift, pretending to be an observer, writes about his actions in the third person. In "The Substance of What was Said by the Dean," Swift's reporter describes Swift's speech on receiving the gold box. In it, Swift rehearses his good deeds—obtaining benefits for the Church of Ireland, lending money to the poor, and battling English eco-nomic oppression by daring to print *The Drapier's Letters*—"Although a certain person was pleased to mention those books [*The Drapier's Letters*] in a slight manner at a public assembly, yet he (the Dean) had learned to be-lieve, that there were ten thousand to one in the kingdom who differed from that person; and the people of England, who had ever heard of the matter, as well as in France, were all of the same opinion" (PW 12: 148). Perhaps because they had a defensive tone, Swift decided not to have these items printed.

A steady stream of materials about Swift appeared in the *Dublin Journal.* Some items, like the report of dog lost by one of Swift's friends or the theft of fruit from his orchard, appear as tidbits about the private life of the local celebrity. Other stories dramatize the Dean/Drapier's continued battles for the welfare of Ireland and record the populace's gratitude for his sacrifices. One example is the serial narration of Swift's confrontation with a hard-nosed Whig, Richard Bettesworth, whom Swift had offhandedly slurred in a broadside by referring to him as "Booby Bettesworth" and rhyming his name with "sweat's worth." Apparently Bettesworth went to the Deanery and threatened Swift with bodily harm, after which, as Ehrenpreis notes,

"The *Dublin Journal* (prompted, one assumes by Swift) carried the tale further." On Saturday, January 5, 1734, it was reported that a group of citizens massed at the Deanery to pledge protection to the Dean. The next Friday, they massed again, incited by information "that a certain person had openly threatened in all companies to stab or maim" Swift.[19] They left a "suspiciously well-worded document" (Ehrenpreis's phrasing) signed by 31 persons, which promised to shield the Dean against Bettesworth and "all his Ruffians and Murderers" (PW 5: 341). This document was published as a broadside, and the next week, a thank you from Swift appeared in the *Dublin Journal.* No doubt there was animosity between Swift and Bettesworth, but as Ehrenpreis's skepticism suggests, it is hard to know the degree to which Swift or Faulkner enhanced the reports to cast the contretemps as an epic battle. The Bettesworth saga, like that of the "Ram of Gorey," became part of the legendary lore associated with Swift.[20]

To underscore the idea of Swift as the favorite son of Ireland, indeed as a mythic hero about whom poets sing, Faulkner's *Dublin Journal* published a number of seemingly spontaneous poetic infusions. These items were usually authorless, implying that Swift already had folkloric status. On November 26, 1737, this one appeared:

A Pun on Dr. Swift, D.S.P.D. Proving Him Immortal

If DEATH denotes to be at rest,
Of SWIFT he'll never be Posess'd
As Sure As Water's in the Ocean,
While SWIFT is SWIFT, he is in motion;
Then while in motion 'tis confess'd;
That SWIFT will never be at rest:
What's SWIFT is QUICK, then on this head,
SWIFT can't at once, be QUICK and DEAD.[21]

The doggerel nature of most of the verses about Swift in the *Dublin Journal* suggests that they represent the heartfelt sentiments of plebeians.

In the 1730s, Faulkner started publishing stories about the birthday celebrations honoring the Drapier. As the proposal in *The Intelligencer* reports, these events had ceased after the Wood's half-pence issue was resolved. It might be that Faulkner himself organized these new expressions of gratitude as a publicity stunt to augment the reputation of Swift, whose collected works Faulkner was planning to publish. Accounts of the birthday bonfires appear in the *Dublin Journal* in 1732, 1734, 1737, 1739, and 1740.[22] Faulkner's narrative of the evening of November 30, 1737, at St. Patrick's Cathedral, runs as follows:

The bells rang as usual on the most solemn occasions, nineteen patataroes fired several rounds, four large bonfires were upon the steeple . . . and the windows illuminated: Such extraordinary rejoicings have not been practised on that occasion these several years past, by which it appears, that the people are now more sensible than ever of the many obligations they lie under to so great a lover of his country.[23]

This description of the citizens' outpouring of joy is formulaically repeated in many articles concerning Swift in the *Dublin Journal.* Another typical example is a report of events that occurred after the defeat of an excise bill detrimental to Irish interests, against which Swift had lobbied: "[A]bout a dozen young men of the liberty and St. Patricks, joined together to have a bonfire on the steeple, and another before the Dean's house; where they gave a barrel of ale in tubs to express their joy, and the following healths were drank with great solemnity, and at the close of each, [']A health to that *worthy patriot the DRAPIER, who saved our nation from ruin*[']."[24]

While Faulkner showcased Swift-as-Drapier in his newspaper, Swift himself was publishing poems with similar aims in Dublin and London. In "Traulus, A Dialogue Between Tom and Robin" (1730), Swift has Tom ask why Traulus (Swift's name for Lord Allen, who wanted Swift punished for the "Libel on Dr. Delany") calls the Dean a "paultry Scribler, / *Papist,* and *Jacobite* and *Lib'ller.*"

> Why must he sputter, spaul and slaver it
> In vain, against the People's Fav'rite?
> Revile that Nation-saving Paper
> Which gave the D[ean] the name of *Draper?*
> (P 3: 794–99, ll. 4–5, 9–12)

"Drapier's Hill" (1729) is another poem published by Swift that forges the link between himself and the Drapier. Widely reprinted, the poem narrates Swift's purchase of a piece of land from his neighbor, Sir Arthur Acheson, which he names Drapier's Hill. The persona muses that when the Drapier is forgotten, the hill will remain as a memorial, vying in fame with Cooper's Hill, the subject of one of the most admired poems of the age. The speaker's long list of Drapier memorabilia, though, undercuts the *ubi sunt* theme by making it impossible to think of a time:

> . . . when a Nation long enslav'd,
> Forgets by whom it once was sav'd;
> When none the Drapier's Praise shall sing;
> His Signs aloft no longer swing;
> His Medals and his Prints forgotten,
> And all his Handkerchiefs are rotten;
> His famous Letters made waste paper. . . .
> (P 3: 875, 11–18)

As Drapier, Swift possessed the qualities of an epic hero, who bravely defends his tribe or nation against its mortal enemies. In this case, though, the "mortal enemy" is England, the mother country. Facetiously explaining Swift's unnatural hatred, one anonymous English wit put him down as the author of "Ub—Bub—A—Boo: Or, The Irish Howl. In Heroic Verse," giving the impression that Swift had "gone native" in Ireland.[25]

### Liberationist Theologian

One of the most surprising developments of the 1730s was Swift's explicit portrayal of himself as a defender of the Established Church. Primarily the butt of jokes about being a godless Dean, Swift had published a few anonymous pamphlets in support of the church, but they had provoked little or no response that identified him as author. In a new emanation, Swift merges the Dean of St. Patrick's with the Drapier. As Dean of St. Patrick's Cathedral, Swift theoretically was an agent of the Crown, but he used his ecclesiastical position to lash out at the English and, more specifically, the Whigs in power, for their hostile attitudes toward Ireland.

One of the issues Swift-as-Dean addressed in print was the Whig policy on toleration, in particular, their efforts to repeal the Sacramental Test in Ireland (the requirement that all officeholders take Anglican communion), a move that Swift characterizes as an affront to the Irish Church.[26] Swift's aggressive attacks on Whig attempts to repeal the Test resulted in Faulkner's arrest and imprisonment.[27] Another flashpoint for the Dean was the ministry's policy of appointing English Whigs as bishops in Ireland, thus denying preferment to native-born priests and generally exploiting the lower orders of the clergy, who tended to be Irish. Swift's sympathy with the Irish underdog is made clear in a note to his *Considerations upon Two Bills . . . Relating to the Clergy of Ireland* (reprinted by Faulkner in 1738) that says its author (previously identified as Swift) "hath always been the best Friend to the inferior Clergy." Swift's close relations with church underlings seems to have inspired two often-reprinted poems (probably not written by him) entitled "Verses Spoken Extempore by Dean Swift on his Curate's Complaint of Hard Duty" and "The Parson's Case," both of which made their first appearance in 1734.[28]

Striking pro-Irish chords similar to those of the Drapier, Swift-as-Dean characterized the actions of the English-dominated church as a form of cultural imperialism. In the anonymous "On the Irish Bishops," Swift describes how "Our B[ishop]s puft up with Wealth and with Pride, / To Hell on the Backs of the Clergy wou'd ride" (P 3: 803–805, ll. 17–18). While Jesus had only one traitor among his apostles, Swift says that among the Irish bishops, it is "Six Traytors in Seven" (32). Swift extends this analogy in a poem entitled "Judas," published in 1735. The violence of the imagery conveys his anger and disgust.

As antient *Judas by Transgression fell,*
And *burst asunder* e'er he went to Hell;
So, could we see a Set of new *Iscariots,*
Come headlong tumbling from their mitred Chariots,
Each modern *Judas* perish like the first;
Drop from the Tree with all his Bowels burst;
Who could forbear, that view'd each guilty Face,
To cry; Lo, *Judas, gone to his own Place:*
*His Habitation let all Men forsake,*
*And let his Bishoprick another take.*
(P 3: 806, ll.17–26)

Questionable church appointees are also the focus of Swift's widely reprinted "An Excellent New Ballad," which chronicles the adventures of the Dean of Ferns, who was accused of rape in Ireland: "A Blessing upon [the Whigs, they] have sent us this Year, / For the Good of our Church a true En[glis]h D[ea]n. / A holier Priest ne'er was wrapt up in Crape, / The worst you can say, he committed a R-pe" (P 2: 516–20, ll. 3–6). Josiah Hort, Bishop of Kilmore, was another one of Swift's targets, attacked by name for his sycophancy and corruption.[29] Many of these anonymous poems were linked to Swift in Faulkner's publication of the collected *Works* in 1735, but there is no doubt when first published they were identified as Swift's work by their extravagantly expressed outrage against his ecclesiastical superiors.

As Dean of St. Patrick's, Swift not only accused the English bishops of undermining the Irish church but also placed heavy blame on the absentee English Whig landowners, who resented the taxes required to support the church and pressured the Irish parliament to repeal them. Moves to reduce church income motivated Swift's *Some Reasons Against the Bill for Settling the Tythe of Hemp, Flax, &c by a Modus* (1734)—a bill supported by Richard Bettesworth. Several years later, Bettesworth led another charge in the Irish Parliament to reduce the tax income of the church, a move that incited Swift to write "The Legion Club," one of his most sensationally seditious broadsides. Swift, always exceeding himself, reached new levels of virulence with the poem. In it, he equates the members of Parliament to inmates in an insane asylum:

While they sit a-picking Straws
Let them rave of making Laws;
While they never held their Tongue,
Let them dabble in their Dung;

. . . . . . . . . .

Let them stare and storm and frown,
When they see a Clergy-Gown.
(P 3: 829–39, ll. 49–52, 55–56)

The poem was too radioactive for any Dublin printer to touch, so it was published scribally—Swift says in a letter that there were "fifty different Copies" (C 4: 501). Almost immediately, the work was printed in London in *S—t Contra Omnes* (1736), a title that underlines the oppositional qualities that Swift associated with himself. To Sheridan, Swift joked about the possibilities that the author might be summoned before the Privy Council to explain himself (C 4: 492). Swift clearly reveled in being perceived as a menace by officialdom.

Swift dramatically united his Dean and Drapier personae in March 1733 when he used St. Patrick's Cathedral as a site of resistance to a recent devaluation of gold by the English ministry. Ehrenpreis says, "Swift's *grand geste* this time got into the London prints only; I suppose those of Dublin were intimidated. . . ."[30]Even though the following description, quoted by Ehrenpreis, was not published in the *Dublin Journal,* its style is identical to Faulkner's adulatory blurbs about Swift, suggesting that it may have been written by him and/or Swift and sent to the London newspapers:

> We have received several anonymous letters [inspired by Swift? (Ehrenpreis's query)] concerning the display of a black flag on St. Patrick's steeple, the muffling of the bells, which rang mournfully all day, the sexton of St. Patrick's being sent for by a tipstaff, and the retiring of the merchants to a tavern, and their drinking long life to Dean Swift and confusion to the enemies of Ireland. All we can say is that the citizens were greatly alarmed when they saw the black flag, imagining that our patriot, who had been ill, was dead. Many of them ran in great consternation to the church, where they learned that their Dean lived, and to their great consolation was happily recovered from his late illness. The signs of mourning were on account of the lowering of the gold.[31]

Despite their apoplexy, the ministry could do little to stop Swift's rabble-rousing. How could anyone arrest the Dean for expressing his concern about the economic well-being of his parishioners? Besides, he was capable of raising the mob against them.

Swift's ostensible concern for the church provided a way to humiliate Lord Fitzwater and Lady Holderness, prominent English aristocrats and absentee Irish landlords, who had refused to supply the Dean with funds to construct a proper monument in St. Patrick's Cathedral to memorialize the lady's grandfather, the Duke of Schomberg, a hero of the Battle of the Boyne. When the Lord and Lady were not forthcoming with money, Swift threatened to expose them (C 3: 390). They continued to ignore him. True to his word, on a large marble slab placed near the altar, Swift had inscribed in Latin a memorial designed not so much to honor the Duke as to shame the Duke's family. An English translation reads as follows:

The Dean and Chapter earnestly and repeatedly requested the Duke's heirs to undertake the erection of a monument in memory of their father. Long and often they pressed the request by letter and through friends. It was of no avail. . . . The renown of his valour had greater power among strangers than had the ties of blood among his kith and kin.[32]

Swift made sure that this public embarrassment got wide coverage. Faulkner's *Dublin Journal* carried the initial story as well as several other follow-ups. In addition, Swift bragged that he "took care" to have his Schomberg epitaph published in seven (!) London newspapers (C 4: 410). If Swift wanted to rile the sensibilities of the English governing class, he succeeded. In a letter to the Countess of Suffolk, Swift chortles, "I hear the Queen hath blamed me . . . and that the King said publickly, I had done it in malice. . . . But the publick prints, as well as the thing it self will vindicate me" (C 3: 483).

Swift was well aware that the humiliations and damnations he called down on his enemies in the name of the church would subject him to counterattacks, not the "vindication" of which he writes to the Countess of Suffolk. Yet he seemed to believe (rightly) that such attacks only added to his preternatural power. With the hellish imagery in his satires of the 1730s as well as the intensification of his identity as an apostate priest, Swift inspired his enemies to consign him to the devil's party. Swift highlights himself in this role by publishing "The Place of the Damn'd by J.S.D.D.D.S.P [Jonthan Swift, Doctor of Divinity, Dean of St. Patrick's]" (1731), which appeared in both London and Dublin. In it, he presents himself as one with an intimate knowledge of hell, where he places lawyers, ignorant prelates, timeserving priests, and privy councilors. In response to "The Place of the Damn'd," the author of "The Devil's Gratitude" says that the humorous tone of the poem "make[s] men's fears less, and religion a jest," hence the devil's gratitude to Swift for doing his work.[33]

In another poem, "A Curry-Comb of Truth for a Certain Dean," Swift is arraigned for his crimes—mainly satirizing the governing class and encouraging a mass readership to share his views, for "Tis Treason to be *popular.*" The poem concludes with an ambiguous compliment—that no one can hurt or destroy the invincible Swift because "the very Devil himself / Is come to Patronize the Elf," implying that Swift is protected by the dark powers.[34] Also linking Swift and the devil, a sarcastic speaker in "Panegyric on the Reverend Dean Swift" contrasts Swift to other malefactors who excuse themselves by saying, "The devil did the deed, not they!" Swift, though, is not ashamed of his satanic capabilities and indeed can outdo "old Nick" when it comes to evil. Rather than the devil controlling Swift, Swift controls the devil. Addressing Swift, the poem's persona says:

> The Simile would better *jump,*
> Were you but placed on *Satan's* Rump;
> For if bestrode by you, *Old N—k,*
> Himself could scarce forbear to kick,
> And curse his wicked Burthen more
> Than all the Sins he ever bore. (136–41)

The image of Swift as the devil's clergyman is also conveyed in *Dean Jonathan's Parody of the 4th Chapter of Genesis* (1729) (which describes Alexander Pope's purported rape of his nurse) and demonstrates the kind of irreverent biblical exegesis "Dean Swift" might do. The seemingly out-of-control anger and viciousness of Swift's poems during the 1730s, especially "The Legion Club," caused some of Swift's biographers to date his madness (another form of possession) to this period.

### Underclass Sympathizer

In the 1730s, Swift accentuated his relationship with the underclass and aroused more questions about his attitudes toward them. He had seen what strong reactions "Mrs. Harris's Petition" had caused as well as his decision to bury his servant Alexander McGee in St. Patrick's and put up a marble memorial to him—a gesture Smedley characterized as a "Kind of burlesque *Apotheosis . . .* to Banter all Things of that sort,"[35] that is, class distinctions. Because of his rejection of Augustan modes, his familiarity with the lives and language of the vulgar, his contempt for the powers-that-be in church and state, and his penchant for rabble-rousing, Swift's loyalties already were under suspicion. Whether Swift actually held revolutionary or egalitarian ideas is indeterminable, but clearly Swift realized that fostering the development of such a public image was provocative in the extreme. His reputation as a opponent of economic exploitation of the underclass associated his name with publications such as *The Humble Petition of the Weavers and Venders of Gold and Silver Lace, Embroiderers, &c* (London, 1731), *A Petition of the Footmen in and about Dublin,* (London, 1733) and *The Humble Petition of the Colliers, Cook Maids, Blacksmiths, Jack-Makers, Brasiers, and others* (London, 1744).[36]

In "A Panegyric on the Dean in the Person of a Lady of the North" (1735), Swift takes pains to present himself as one comfortable among the common folk, particularly the servant class. In the poem, Swift situates Lady Acheson as the narrator. She describes Swift's activities at her estate at Market Hill, where he was a long-term guest. In this humorous and lighthearted poem, Swift amazes Lady Acheson by outdoing her Irish help at their own jobs. He is replete with the skills expected of butlers, chambermaids, farmhands, and cook maids, for he is able to fetch the right wine bottles, darn socks, hunt rats, build pig stys, sweep chicken coops, and make butter:

> How are the Servants overjoy'd
> To see thy D—nship thus employ'd!
> Instead of poring on a Book,
> Providing Butter for the Cook.
> Three Morning-Hours you toss and shake
> The Bottle, till your Fingers ake:
> Hard is the Toil, nor small the Art,
> The Butter from the Whey to part. . . .
> (P 3: 886–97, ll. 175–83)

In the poem, Swift's Lady Acheson notes that the Dean talks to everyone the same way, no matter who they are—"*Dermot,* or *His Grace,* / With *Teague O'Murphy,* or an Earl; / A Dutchess or a Kitchen Girl" (122–4).

Swift's concern for those on the bottom rungs of society was evident in the mid-1730s when he began publicizing in the *Dublin Journal* his intentions to bequeath money to build a mental asylum for homeless and indigent persons. Of course the news sparked reaction. Was this one of his hoaxes? Another "burlesque *Apotheosis*"? Swift did nothing to dispel the idea that the hospital was some kind of a joke, which encouraged others to joke about it as well. Faulkner published a humorous verse entitled "On the Revd Dr. Swift, D.S.P.D. leaving his Fortune to Build an Hospital for Idiots and Lunaticks": "The DEAN must dye?—Our Idiots to maintain? / Perish Ye Idiots!—and long live the Dean!"[37] In "David Mullan's Letter to Dean Swift" (1735), the impoverished Mullan facetiously questions Swift's allocation of "Pelf . . . to raise a . . . Madman's Mansion," for when Swift dies persecuted by "Dunces," the hospital will remind posterity "*That Wit in Madness shall for ever end.*"[38] Mullan's poem foreshadows the myth, emerging much later, that Swift was the first patient in his own asylum.

Swift's attitudes toward the poor or underclass are difficult to gauge because he assumes so many different perspectives, often within the same work, and because when Swift depicts the underclass in a very harsh way, it is difficult to say whether he is registering his disgust at them or at the people who caused their misery. In *A Proposal for Giving Badges to the Beggars in all the Parishes of Dublin [written] by the Dean of St. Patrick's* (1732), Swift indicts English colonial policies for causing the conditions that produce beggary, boldly asserting, for example, that the English actually export "large Cargoes of [beggars] from *Chester* to *Dublin*" (PW 13: 136). But although he purports to have sympathy for the homeless, he characterizes them as a "profligate Clan of Thieves, Drunkards, Heathens, and

Whoremongers, fitter to be rooted out of the Face of the Earth, than suffered to levy a vast annual Tax on the City" (139). The same ambiguity and ambivalence pervade *A Modest Proposal,* making Swift's real sentiments impossible to determine and encouraging a large number of stories about Swift and the underclass.

Swift's *Directions to Servants* (1745), published by Faulkner the year Swift died, generated some of the strongest reactions from its readers and consequently has been perennially popular.[39] Realistically portraying the resentments that those below stairs might feel and instructing them how to exact their revenge in subtle but devastating ways, *Directions to Servants* gains disturbing power by showing that the relationship of servants to masters should be characterized not in terms of feudal loyalty, but of guerrilla warfare. On the battlefield depicted in the *Directions to Servants,* the servants have the upper hand, both in terms of numbers and strategic advantage. Living on such intimate terms with servants and being so dependent on them, householders would be deeply unsettled by Swift's account of what might be said and done behind their backs.

The nurse is advised that "If you happen'd to let the Child fall, and lame it, be sure never confess it; and, if it dies, all is safe" (PW 12: 64). The laundress is advised to wash the linen until it is "torn to Rags" and told, "Always wash your own Linnen first" (64). The maid is advised to empty her lady's chamberpot when she goes to greet visitors at the front door and to break the coals on the marble hearth (60–1). The footman is advised to clean his master's shoes with the hems of curtains and to sample the food with his fingers before he serves it (36). The cook is advised not to wash her hands after she visits the "Necessary-house" because they will just get dirty again when handling the food (31). Because of its problematic contents, Faulkner was impelled to preface *Directions to Servants* with a statement that "*the Author's Design was to expose the Villanies and Frauds of Servants*" and to show the "*Vices and Faults, which People in that kind of low Life are subject to*" (PW 13: 5). Despite Faulkner's assuring readers that Swift had the attitudes toward the underclass that a gentlemen ought to hold and pointing the moral, the work creates serious doubts about where Swift's loyalties lay.

## Dung Dabbler

In the 1720s, Swift's name became associated with excrement, because of the *Wonderful Wonder of Wonders;* and with sex, because of his poems to Stella and Vanessa. As part of the shock tactics in the 1730s, Swift published works that perversely combine sex and excrement, or focus on excrement in a very tactile way that went far beyond anything he had done in the past, causing twentieth-century critics to characterize Swift's new perspective as an "excremental vision."[40] Some scholars have speculated that the death of Stella in 1728 plunged Swift into nihilism and negativism that he expressed with gross, graphic imagery, but there is nothing but circumstantial evidence to support this theory. In the context of my argument, I would put forth another possibility: that Swift's scatological escalation in the 1730s was in keeping with his seeming desire at that time to connect his name with distinctive, highly charged themes of transcendent interest that would make sure the brass trumpet continued to blast his name long after his death. Misanthropy, class warfare, and excrement were topics that would endure the test of time and had been claimed (for good reasons) by very few authors.

The most notorious work reflecting Swift's excremental vision is "The Lady's Dressing Room" (1734). It was one of the most popular poems Swift ever published, running through multiple editions not only in London and Dublin but also in Edinburgh and Cork. In the poem, Strephon, Swift's speaker, describes with exquisite precision the filth he finds when he invades the bedroom of his beloved, Celia:

> But oh! it turned poor *Strephon's* Bowels,
> When he beheld and smelt the Towels,
> Begumm'd, bematter'd, and beslim'd
> With Dirt, and Sweat, and Ear-Wax grim'd.
> No Object *Strephon's* Eye escapes,
> Here Pettycoats in frowzy Heaps;
> Nor be the Handkerchiefs forgot,
> All varnish'd o'er with Snuff and Snot.
> (P 2: 525–30, ll. 43–50)

The poem's climax comes when Strephon opens the lid of the closestool and sees what has been "plumpt into the reeking Chest." Choking with disgust, he cries, "Oh! *Celia, Celia, Celia* shits!" (110, 118). Swift's degradation of Celia and his union of love with excrement in the poem are in sharp contrast to the romantic idealizations featured in the novels of sensibility and sentimental drama beginning to flood the literary market and reinforce Swift's image as a misanthropist.[41] The queasiness the poem induces is heightened by the uncertainty about the author's attitudes toward the nastiness he has produced. Is he appalled or delighted?

Like most of the things Swift wrote, the poem sparked discussion of its author. The characterizations of Swift-as-author of "The Lady's Dressing Room" are completely divergent from the noble characterizations of Swift-as-Drapier. One critic chastises Swift for looking in "close-stools instead of the Bible / And writ[ing] on Caelia so dirty a libel; / How well must he preach the Word of the Lord, / Whose texts are a Shift, stinking Toes, and a

T—d."[42] In "The Dean's Provocation For Writing the Lady's Dressing Room" Swift is portrayed in the act of having sex with a prostitute. Unable to perform, he blames the smell of the woman's nearby closestool and demands his money back. She refuses, telling him "Perhaps you have no better Luck in / The knack of Rhyming than of————," but encourages him to keep writing to "furnish Paper when I Sh—te."[43] The "Lady's Dressing Room," then, not only reinforced Swift's association with unspeakable filthiness but also rekindled images of him in ladies' bedrooms, having illicit sex. As a response to the denunciations elicited by "The Lady's Dressing Room," Swift anonymously published a *Modest Defence* of the poem by comparing it favorably to those of Horace and castigating persons unable to "discover that useful Satyr running through every Line, and the Matter as decently wrapp'd up as the Subject could bear" (PW 5: 338, Appendix C). In this context, Swift's representation of himself as an Augustan seems purposefully inflammatory.

Another major foray into excrement is *City Cries, Instrumental and Vocal: Or, An Examination of Certain Abuses, Corruptions, and Enormities in London and Dublin. By the Rev. Dr. Swift* (1732). Purporting to be a satire on the way some people can read political implications into ordinary occurrences, Swift's speaker studiously examines piles of human excrement in the streets of Dublin in order to refute those who say the English have left the dung to deceive people into thinking (contrary to fact) that the Irish poor are not starving:

> [The disaffected say that the excrement comes from] *British Fundaments,* to make the World believe, that our *Irish* Vulgar do eat and drink; and consequently, that the Clamour of Poverty among us, must be false; proceeding only from *Jacobites* and *Papists.* They would confirm this, by pretending to observe, that a *British Anus* being more narrowly perforated than one of our own Country; and many of these Excrements, upon a strict View appearing Copplecrowned, with a Point like a Cone or Pyramid, are easily distinguished from the *Hibernian,* which lie much flatter, and with less continuity. (PW 12: 220)

To disprove the idea that British anuses and excrements are inherently different from those of the Irish, the persona hires a physician to stick his fingers up the anuses of persons of both nations. Not only does he find that their anuses are indistinguishable in structure, but the feces of each smell the same (PW12: 220–221). In this scene, Swift outdoes himself.

Swift waxes poetic on the "Copple-crowned" glories of excrement in a "Panegyric on the Dean in the Person of a Lady of the North," in which he has Lady Acheson describe Dean Swift's construction project at Market Hill—two outhouses, one for each sex, which he dedicates as temples to the

"Goddess *Cloacine.*" In 1704, Wotton criticized Swift's *Tale*-teller for comparing altar incense to fumes from a jakes, but in the "Panegyric" Swift carries the metaphor even further.

> Here, gentle Goddess *Cloacine*
> Receives all Off'rings at her Shrine.
> In sep'rate Cells the He's and She's
> Here pay their Vows with *bended Knees:*
> (For 'tis prophane when Sexes mingle;
> And every Nymph must enter single;
> And when she feels an *inward Motion,*
> Come fill'd with *Rev'rence* and Devotion.)
> (205–12)

Meanwhile, out in the fields, the farm hands "grace the flow'ry downs, / With spiral Tops, and Copple-Crowns . . ." (303–4).

By the 1730s, excrement had become a distinct marker of a Swiftian text and generated much imaginative mythologizing about Swift's character as an author. *Human Ordure, botanically considered. By Dr. S—t* (London and Dublin, 1733), for example, was frequently reprinted throughout the eighteenth century. Another attribution is *Dean Swift's Maw-Wallup, a Dainty-Dish, or Quality Mess* (London, n.d.), which uses the cover of Swift's name to talk about phlegm, scabs, diarrhea, and bedpans in a thoroughly unappetizing way. Far from being furtive or embarrassed about figuratively dabbling in dung, Swift, in addition to the items discussed already, also published "A Beautiful Young Nymph Going to Bed" (1731), "Strephon and Chloe" (1731) and "Cassinus and Peter" (1731), all of which are full of repulsive details about bodily functions that polite people should not discuss. These poems were all included in Faulkner's 1735 collection of Swift's work. Swift's embrace of excrement was another one of the scandals or mysteries that kept people talking about him after his death. His refusal to act as one defiled after touching pitch was inexplicable and, in a way, awe-inspiring.

### Great Writer

No longer hailed as "Ireland's Apollo," few were praising Swift as a great writer in the early 1730s. The exception proves the rule. Matthew Pilkington, a sycophant who parlayed his acquaintance with Swift into an endorsement of his own pathetic writing, published *Poems on Several Occasions . . . Revised by the Reverend Dr. Swift* (2nd edition, 1731) with a frontispiece engraving of the Temple of Literary Worthies, containing volumes of Homer, Virgil, Chaucer, Milton, Dryden, and Addison. Pride of place on the central altar, however, is given to Swift. Pilkington's estimation of Swift's place in the literary panoply is laughably at odds with his reputation at the time. When Faulkner decided to gather Swift's scattered publications into a collected edition targeted to an upscale audience, he does not justify the endeavor on literary grounds. Rather, Faulkner makes clear that market demand motivated his production of the four-volume set, to be published by subscription. Advertising in *Dublin Journal* (February 6, 1733), Faulkner justifies his enterprise by saying "It hath long [been] wished, by Persons of Quality and Distinction" (PW 14: 42). Whether Swift cooperated with Faulkner to bring out this edition (Swift denied it) is a matter of scholarly controversy.

The brisk sales of Faulkner's volumes to aristocrats and gentility validated Swift on his own terms: not as an Augustan but as a popular writer who loved to offend the very "Persons of Quality and Distinction" who subscribed to Faulkner's edition.[44] Ehrenpreis observes that "Faulkner must have beamed. . . . Of dukes and duchesses alone, [he] counted as many as fifteen. . . . the demand was so great that subscribers had to be asked to send small money with their messengers, 'it being impossible to get change for so much gold.'"[45] The enormous success of Faulkner's edition added to the sense that Swift lived a charmed life. For his offenses against Man and God, surely no one more deserved to be punished with failure and oblivion. Faulkner's edition demonstrated that Swift's brass trumpet fame gave him as much or more power and glory than he might have attained by seeking gold trumpet fame. It also suggested that, with the endorsement of the English governing class, the gold trumpet had begun to sound for Swift, despite his crimes against High Art.

The publication in Dublin of Swift's collected works predictably fueled protests by English publishers, who believed they had legal rights to some of the pieces. Writing to Benjamin Motte, who had threatened to sue George Faulkner, Swift refused to interfere in the fracas, saying "I am so incensed against the Oppressions from *England*, and have so little Regard to the Laws they make, that I do as a Clergyman encourage the Merchants . . . [to conceal their illegal imports and exports] from the Custom-House Officers, as I would hide my Purse from a Highway-man, if he came to rob me on the Road, although *England* hath made a Law to the contrary . . ." (C 4: 494). Reacting to these words, the normally sedate Irvin Ehrenpreis exclaims, "The open appeal to lawlessness astonishes me."[46] Swift mythologized himself as a modern Robin Hood, an outlaw boldly indifferent to the law and successful in tweaking the noses of English authorities.

Swift achieved a dignity in Faulkner's 1735 publication of the *Works* that made his enemies guffaw. For example, in "Momus Mistaken: A Fable, Occasioned by the Publication of the Works of the Revd. Dr. Swift," James Arbuckle takes pains to emphasize that despite the appearance of his works in

3.1. Frontispiece, Matthew Pilkington, *Poems on Several Occasions* (2nd edition, 1731). Although Swift had a reputation as a writer of popular Grubstreet fare, Matthew Pilkington, seeking Swift's support, gives pride of place to him in a Temple of Worthies containing Augustan writers like Dryden, Horace, and Virgil, whose writings targeted a more elite audience. Father Time is in the foreground, selecting the writers who will endure into posterity. By permission of the Folger Shakespeare Library.

an elegant form, Swift is no gentleman but a lowlife. The fable opens with the Dean, "as is his Wont," in "a dirty Lane," accompanied by Mercury, who instead of the messenger to the gods, is figured as a "Crier of the News." Seeing Mercury and Swift making "waggish Jokes, and sly Remarks, / On City Damsels," Momus decides as a joke to mistake Swift for Apollo in his lothario mode. Momus pretends not to understand why Apollo, accompanied by his "Scoundrel Pimp," Mercury, would be in "such a scurvy Place. . . . / Disguised too in that Garb of Grace [a priest's gown]" unless he were in pursuit of a woman. In former times, Momus notes, such amorous pursuits stimulated beautiful poetry that earned Apollo laurels from the other gods. By contrast, Swift's seedy encounters reflect the sordidness of his life, character, and works as well as the ludicrousness of considering him Ireland's Apollo. In this light, Momus asks Swift, "How will the Gods endure / To see you spawl their Azure Floor. . . . / To smoak your Honour sadly chewing / The filthy Rags of Caterwawing"? At the conclusion of "Momus Mistaken," Swift huffs off, leaving Mercury (representing the popular press) to tell the world that he and his works are elevated, not degraded. Mercury sarcastically performs this duty:

> The Volumes in my Hand behold:
> (In *Faulkner's Shop* they're to be sold)
> These shall to future Ages tell,
> The Drapier never sunk, or fell.

This conclusion is ironic, for the rest of the poem demonstrates that Swift (despite his association with the noble Drapier) is irretrievably sunken and fallen. Dressing his "spawl" [spit; coarse utterance] up in calves' leather, Arbuckle implies, will not convince anyone of Swift's worthiness as a writer.[47]

Swift's standing in English letters is the focus of a poem entitled "The Life and Genuine Character of Dr. Swift, written by himself," which first appeared on April 1, 1733, in London and was quickly reproduced in several editions. Although Swift published disclaimers denying his responsibility for "The Life and Genuine Character" in the *Dublin Journal,* most scholars assume he wrote it and meant to publish it, perhaps as another April Fool's joke. Whoever wrote the poem organized it as a debate on Swift's literary merits between one of his supporters and a Whig detractor. Swift's Whig attacker in "The Life and Genuine Character" itemizes the usual charges against his writings: they are trashy, seditious, misanthropic, vulgar, and self-promoting. For the first time in print, though, these charges are directly and substantially answered. To the charge that Swift damaged public institutions by exposing their leadership to ridicule, Swift's defender says that vice must be exterminated wherever it is found—"No *Vermin* can demand *fair Play,* /

But, ev'ry Hand may justly slay" (P 2: 541–50, ll. 126–7). To the charge that
Swift is a demagogue, the defender reminds his opponent that "our *Nation*
[is] in his Debt" (96) for what he accomplished with *The Drapier's Letters,*
and that "His *Principles,* of antient date" compelled him to rescue the church
and ministry by libeling their morally bankrupt leaders (146). To the idea
that Swift wrote to advance himself, the defender retorts that instead of
being rewarded, Swift was persecuted and punished for altruistically trying
to reform the world. To the charge that Swift's disappointments in life made
him so misanthropic that his views should be discounted, the pro-Swift
speaker says that Swift does not hate humankind in general, but is exercised
in particular by the corruption in key members of the governing class.

"The Life and Genuine Character" ends with antithetical assessments of
Swift's literary legacy. The Whig attacker asserts that Swift's writing consists
of only worthless ephemera like "*high-flown Pamphlets*"; libels "Against the
*Court* to show his *Spight*"; extravagant fictions like *Gulliver's Travels* ("A *Lye,*
at every *second* word")—"But—*not one Sermon,* you may *swear*" (180–93).
Swift's defender ignores traditional measures of literary greatness—profi-
ciency in dignified genres and the approval of the self-styled Republic of Letters—to claim that though Swift's methods might be unorthodox, "Tis
plain, his Writings were design'd / To *please,* and to *reform* Mankind"
(196–7). That critics generally misread his intentions and denigrate his reputation as a writer shows that they are degraded, not he—"The *Praise* is *His,*
and *Theirs* the *Blame*" (200), a sentiment that recalls one of Swift's most
popular aphorisms from his *Thoughts on Various Subjects* (1711)—"When a
true Genius appears in the World, you may know him by this infallible Sign;
that the Dunces are all in a Confederacy against him" (PW 1:242). Measur-
ing literary worth in terms of social and political effect, Swift's defender challenges the received opinion that popular writers cannot be great writers.

Whether his contemporaries would grant that Swift was an exemplary
writer, they could not argue with his popularity. Whatever was published
with Swift's name on it sold well, creating an incentive for publishers to market new works by and about him. Faulkner, for example, republished the
original four volumes of the *Works* in 1738, plus two more. In the 1746 edition, Faulkner added another two volumes, to make a total of eight. The
1763 edition contained 11 volumes, and the 1768 edition contained 19.
Many of the pieces in these volumes are of dubious authenticity. "The
Draper's Apparition to G—ge F————r," published the year of Swift's death
(1745), dramatizes the return of Swift's ghost to chastise Faulkner for "Be-
thinking of a hundred Shifts / What next to print and pass for *Swift's.*" The
specter charges Faulkner with jeopardizing Swift's fame in posterity: "Thou,
O avaritious Slave! / Not pleas'd my better Works to have, / Must tinker-like
recoin my Dross, / And half-form'd Embryo Works engross; / Works that can

never stand the Test / But rust and canker all the Rest."[48] The outlandish trash attributed to Swift and written about him had the opposite effect from that feared by the Draper's ghost. Instead of clouding Swift's greatness, the outpouring of questionable Swiftiana gave Swift a prominence that paradoxically elevated him into a figure of authority and an epitome of certain virtues, including those of the Augustans.

## A Living Legend

By the time Swift published "Verses on the Death of Dr. Swift" in 1739, he knew that he was a living legend, not merely a transient celebrity. His future fame, as he prophetically envisions it in this summary poem, rests not so much on the greatness of his literary oeuvre, but on a continued fascination with his character as an embodiment of liberty, an idea highlighted by the words in the "Verses," "Fair LIBERTY was all his Cry: / For her he stood prepar'd to die" (P 2: 551–72, ll. 347–8). The poem extensively portrays Swift as a freedom fighter for Ireland in the role of Drapier and also illustrates Swift's lack of deference to persons of rank, his indifference to wealth, and his autonomy—he is not dependent on anyone or any institution for his power. The Swift character in the "Verses" is unconstrained by social proprieties, saying and doing whatever he desires. He is also unconstrained by the need for consistency, feeling free to occupy contradictory identities without embarrassment. He feels no obligation to settle the arguments about his true nature.

While he lived, Swift knew that any major development in his life would be newsworthy, so he begins the "Verses" by imagining the gossip among his acquaintances as he deteriorates mentally and physically: "He cannot call his Friends to Mind; / Forgets the Place where last he din'd" (87–8); and later, "He hardly drinks a Pint of Wine; / And that, I doubt, is no good Sign" (109–10); and finally, "He hardly breathes. The Dean is dead." (150). His death sets the presses rolling until there is "Some Paragraph in ev'ry Paper, / To *curse* the *Dean,* or *bless* the *Drapier"* (168–9). Even after he is dead, Swift imagines (correctly) that there can be no consensus on him. In Swift's prophecy, the news of his death quickly leaps from Ireland to England, where it is greeted with loud joy by the members of the English governing class, including Queen Caroline, Sir Robert Walpole, and Lady Suffolk. The Queen says, "He's dead you say; why let him rot" (183). His card-playing "female friends" chatter about him in between bidding their hands. While he is alive or newly dead, Swift is the talk of the town, but what about after that? Is it true that "this Fav'rite of *Apollo?* / [has] Departed; *and his Works must follow"*? (249–50)

Once Swift is no longer a political player, the poem suggests that the London crowd, even his friends, will quickly forget him: A year after his death there is "No further mention of the Dean; / Who now, alas, no more is mist, / Than if he never did exist" (246–8). The bookseller Lintot declares that Swift's "way of Writing now is past; / The town hath got a better Taste" (265–6) and pushes the latest authors—Colley Cibber, Stephen Duck, John Henley, and Thomas Woolston—all of them bound for the slag heap of history. While urban trendsetters embrace the latest novelty, the "Verses" implies that Swift will remain in the memory of the less sophisticated. In this light, Swift envisions a "Country Squire" asking for "SWIFT in Verse and Prose" a year after his death (253). He also envisions himself the subject of a lively debate at the Rose Tavern, where some are for him and others against.

An "impartial" speaker rises to mediate the disagreement. Far from being "impartial," this character praises Swift in hyperbolic terms, blowing the gold trumpet with all his might. Swift would, of course, know that the "impartial" speaker's characterization—so contrary to his existing public image—would prompt heated commentary. Did Swift really see himself as the "impartial" speaker presents him? Was he being ironic? These are questions that cannot be answered, although many scholars have tried. Indeed, Swift wanted not to provide answers but to produce debates, and he succeeded amply at that. While Swift had been demonized as a writer of demagogic billingsgate, the "impartial" speaker puts a different spin on this characterization and portrays Swift as an epic hero drawing his power directly from the people, whose interest and support he brilliantly enlisted through his writing. That popularity allowed Swift to challenge oppressive or corrupt institutions. Swift, through footnotes he added to the poem and the speech of his "impartial" observer, stresses that despite the sneers of the critics, "all People" bought his works (312), and that some of those works, like *The Drapier's Letters,* brought about radical political change because they were *"read universally, and convinc[ed] every Reader"* (168n). Testifying to Swift's potential to overturn the status quo, the "impartial" speaker reminds readers that twice Swift had a price put on his head—"But, not a Traytor cou'd be found, / To sell him for Six Hundred Pound" (353–4)—and that the Crown could not find a jury that would indict Swift's printer. While the Whig ministry and the Crown might want to repress his memory by downplaying his impact, the poem attests that for his services as Drapier, he has become a folk hero in Ireland, *"celebrated in many Poems and Pamphlets . . .* [and] *His Sign was set up in most Streets of* Dublin *(where many of them still continue) and in several Country Towns"* (408n).

In his "Verses," Swift emphasizes his enormous power, both as a writer and as a generalized symbol of resistance. But he purposefully does little to clear up the mysteries surrounding him. Where exactly are his loyalties? He damns both the English and the Irish. What is this "liberty" for which he is prepared to die? The word was often found in the mouths of Whigs advocating latitudinarianism. What motivates him? Surely not the exaggerated altruism attributed to him by the "impartial" speaker. What kind of man is he? In the poem he displays both vitriol and equanaminity. Is he joking or serious in what he says? The indeterminate irony of the poem makes it impossible to say.

Swift's ability to look into the face of death and laugh reveals his assurance that his life and character would endure in posterity. The sales of "Verses on the Death of Dr. Swift" might have confirmed his expectations. 19 editions appeared within a year of its first appearance in 1739. By the time "Verses on the Death of Dr. Swift" was published, Swift knew he had created a larger-than-life print persona, whose sensational features would continue to inspire myths and counter myths. His existential freedom, his bizarre contradictions, his profound enigmas, and his flamboyant opposition to orthodoxy made Swift confident of Curll's success in publishing his "Will, [his] Life, and [his] Letters . . . / [And] reviv[ing] the Libels born to die" (203–4).

In 1737, Swift turned 70, but continued to send things to the press. In addition to the "Verses," he finished several other large projects. Still seemingly harboring laureate ambitions, he tried unsuccessfully to publish his *History of the Last Four Years of the Queen,* a work to which he had devoted much energy. But there was no market for an out-of-date chronicle of Tory triumphs. He wrapped up another longterm endeavor, *Polite Conversation* (1738), a whimsical set of dialogues in which characters speak to each other in proverbs, clichés, and aphorisms, many of Swift's coinage. Swift arranged to have the work printed in both Dublin and London. In May 1740, Swift made his will, declaring himself sound in mind, but weak in body.

Three years after the publication of "Verses on the Death of Dr. Swift," in 1742, news circulated that a number of Swift's friends had applied to the courts to have him declared of unsound mind. A jury of 12 men examined the evidence and concluded that Swift was not capable of taking care of his "person or fortune," so guardians were appointed to manage his financial affairs. Mrs. Ridgeway, Swift's housekeeper, looked after him at the Deanery, where he remained sequestered.[49] Rumors of Swift's madness started to flutter. In the absence of fact or Swift's authority, far-fetched stories could be told without fear of challenge.

The reading public may have been prepared for the news of Swift's incapacity because the year before, in 1741, Alexander Pope had published a volume of correspondence containing letters by Swift full of pathos, self-pity, and nihilism. Swift had opposed Pope's publication of these letters, perhaps because they undermined the legendary power with which he sought to charge his memory.[50] Vastly popular, Pope's edition appeared in at least ten different issues or editions, one by the notorious Edmund Curll, whose imprint was the sure sign of lurid revelations. Swift's letters—seemingly the first glimpses into his private thoughts—showed Swift not as a dynamic force field, but as a pitiable, tormented old man. He writes Bolingbroke, "I was forty-seven years old when I began to think of death, and the reflections upon it now begin when I wake in the morning, and end when I am going to sleep" (Letter 40). To Pope, Swift characterizes his life in Ireland as that of "a stranger in a strange land" (Letter 37) and vows that when he dies, "my flesh and bones are to be carried to Holy-head, for I will not lie in a Country of Slaves" (Letter 45). To Gay, he mournfully notes, "The best and greatest part of my life . . . I spent in England. . . . I am condemned for ever to another country" (Letter 5). To Bolingbroke, he laments his hopeless fate, "to die here in a rage, like a poisoned rat in a hole" (Letter 35). These letters suggest that Swift is profoundly depressed, on the brink of a nervous breakdown or suicide. At the same time that Swift is writing these dismal missives to his English friends—perhaps to flatter them on how much he misses them and their country—he is sending letters brimming with humorous bonhomie to his Irish friends. These playful, upbeat letters were not published until later, and when they did appear, could not erase the impression that Swift was in extreme mental distress toward the end of his life.

Swift's death on October 19, 1745, was an anticlimax, greeted in virtual silence by the press. Apart from Faulkner's eulogy in the *Dublin Journal,* there was one broadside elegy. By comparison, an outpouring of publications honored Pope, who had died the year before. The appearance of Swift's will in 1745, however, caused a considerable stir, prompting multiple editions of it in Dublin and London, as well as generating several parodies. The will had several startling disclosures. One was that Swift had not been joking about leaving his money to found a mental hospital for "idiots and lunaticks." Almost immediately there was speculation that his sympathies for the mentally ill sprang from his recognition that he was one of them. The next surprise in the will was the text of the Latin epitaph Swift had written for himself. Instead of soothing Christian pieties, the epitaph seemed to express anger and bitterness. In English, the text of the inscription he wanted over his grave reads as follows: "The body of Jonathan Swift, Doctor of Divinity, Dean of this Cathedral Church, is buried here, where savage indignation can lacerate his breast no more. Go, traveler, and imitate if you can one who strove his utmost to champion liberty." In death as in life, Swift intended to needle and vex the world.

Banquo asks "Who knows what seeds may grow" and bloom in posterity. After Swift died in 1745, biographers started writing their accounts of his life with great abandon. Rather than follow the plot of Swift's life laid out by the "impartial" speaker in the "Verses," the early biographers were more interested in supplying answers to the questions that Swift had raised in the public's mind about his breeding, his love life, his sanity, his loyalties, and his lack of embarrassment regarding the scandals associated with him.

Eighteenth-century and early-nineteenth century biographies put in place what came to be seen as the essential episodes in the telling of Swift's life story. As for the authenticity of these episodes or their details, the biographers contradict themselves as well as each other, undermining any hope of agreement about the facts of some matters. Despite their claims to truth, the biographies are full of myths—unverifiable stories, whose origins are forgotten, obscure, or suspect. As time proceeded, the Swiftian narrative was inflected by the publication of new evidence concerning Swift's life, such as the *Journal to Stella,* the letters of Esther Vanhomrigh, and records of his schooldays at Trinity College.[51] The information in these documents added new flourishes to existing myths about Swift and stimulated new ones. Because of his decision to write for the broadest possible audience and to create a powerful, enigmatic, paradoxical, and heterodox print alter ego that evokes imaginative responses, Swift remains alive in popular culture today, where he has a thriving existence, in print, broadcast media, and cyberspace.

The next four chapters focus on mythmaking after Swift's death. Although romance, tragedy, comedy, and epic often intermingle in narratives about Swift, I discuss them in separate chapters in order to trace the origins and incremental evolution of the different plotlines as well as to identify the influence of generic conventions on the stories Swift inspires. Directly or indirectly, all of these stories grew out of the seeds that Swift carefully planted in his own writing.

# Chapter Four ～

# Unconventional Love, Sex, and Marriage: The Swiftian Romance

Aeneas and Dido, Lancelot and Guinevere, the Duke of Windsor and Mrs. Simpson—stories about the unconventional or unsanctioned love lives of famous figures spread quickly through the general population. Not only Swift's sexuality, but also that of his parents became a subject of speculation. Was he illegitimate? If so, who was his father? Did Swift by accident end up marrying his sister, who might have been an out-of-wedlock child of the same father? By publishing unsavory pieces that linked sex with excrement and affectionately addressing two young women in print while seemingly being married to neither, Swift—a clergyman, no less!—stamped his character with taboos that generated gossip. Sexual irregularity or unlicensed love is an essential aspect of narratives concerning mythologized figures. Raglan's list contains implications of incestuous relations (3), unusual conception (4), unconventional marriage (12) and barrenness (20). Like other legends, Swift is depicted in multiple, often contradictory ways—in this case, as oversexed, undersexed, married, unmarried, chaste, libertine, gay, incestuous.

Swift's decision to situate himself in print with Stella and Vanessa permanently altered the way he was perceived and started rumors that evolved into the myths of the Swiftian romance. "Cadenus and Vanessa" as well as a number of poems celebrating Stella's birthday were published in the Swift-Pope *Miscellanies* of 1727–28. The poems construct Swift as the object of intense desire by two women much younger than he, but do not detail the relationships with any clarity. In "Cadenus and Vanessa," Swift professes to be surprised at Vanessa's passion for him and ostensibly tries to tamp it down, yet he does not foreclose the possibility that her passion found some release. The poems to Stella reveal the intimacy of people who have known each other a very long time. In one poem, "To Stella, who collected and

transcribed his poems," Swift tells Stella, though "With Friendship and Es-
teem possesst, / I ne'er admitted Love a Guest"(P 2: 727–32, ll. 13–14), a
statement that some people cannot believe. Those who accept it at face value
see the pathos of unreciprocated love swirling underneath.

Samson and Delilah, Eloise and Abelard, or Anthony and Cleopatra are
automatically coupled in discourse. Swift, however, is coupled not with one
woman but with several. While James Hay specifically titles his biography
*Swift: The Mystery of his Life and Love,*[1] in fact, most accounts of Swift de-
vote enormous space to the uncertainty of the arrangements among him,
Stella, and Vanessa. Because Swift left nothing but titillating clues behind,
his biographers fill in the narrative gaps with the evidence they have at hand
and with their imaginations. The first biographers—Laetitia Pilkington,
Lord Orrery, Patrick Delany, Deane Swift, Thomas Sheridan, and Sir Walter Scott—lay the foundation of the romance narrative, each adding
episodes that stimulated further elaboration or embellishment in novels,
melodramas, poems, magazine articles, newspaper features, medical treatises, and other popular biographies. From medieval times, romance has
been distinguished by its serious attention to the social and psychological dimensions of unsanctioned desire. I use the term *romance* broadly to reference explicit or implicit narratives about sex or love that are complete in
themselves or embedded in a larger narrative or discourse.

There are two main reasons why there has been so much mythologizing
of Swift's amours. The first is that Swift constructed himself as a means to talk
about sex, both by stimulating questions about his own sexuality and by publishing works that deal in graphic ways with sex and its infantile substitute,
excrement. As Michel Foucault points out in *The History of Sexuality,* the pu-
ritanical codes existing in European cultures since the eighteenth century
have not eliminated sex as a topic. Indeed, the opposite has occurred: "Rather
than the uniform concern to hide sex, rather than a general prudishness of
language, what distinguishes these last three centuries is the variety, the wide
dispersion of devices that were invented for speaking about it. . . ."[2] During
the eighteenth century, for example, what went on in the marital bed (or
what failed to go on) was off-limits in genteel conversation, but could be discussed under the cloak of legal affairs, such as in accounts of rape trials or
works like Edmund Curll's *Cases of Impotency,* which summarize divorce proceedings. Another cloak was reproductive health, which authorized such
tracts as Daniel Defoe's *Conjugal Lewdness: A Treatise Concerning the Use and
Abuse of the Marriage Bed* (1727), Nicholas Venette's *Conjugal Love reveal'd;
in the Nightly Pleasures of the Marriage Bed* (1720), *Onania; or the Heinous Sin
of Self-pollution* (1718) and *Aristotle's Compleat Masterpiece . . . Displaying the
Secrets . . . of Generation* (1684), all of which went through through multiple
editions during the eighteenth century and afterward, no doubt consulted

more by curious adolescents than by the married couples to whom they were theoretically addressed. As Foucault notes, "At issue is not a movement bent on pushing rude sex back into some obscure and inaccessible region, but on the contrary, a process that . . . arouses it, draws it out and bids it speak, implants it in reality and enjoins it to tell the truth . . . in a myriad of discourses . . . [reflecting] the interplay of knowledge and pleasure."[3] Swift created a public image that facilitated the modern desire to make sex speak and maintain propriety at the same time. A biography of Swift promises as much suppressed passion as any bodice-ripping novel, but under a more respectable cover.

The second spur to the mythmaking about Swift's love life is the hope that by learning the secrets of his bedroom or of his parents' bedroom, the baffling elements of Swift's character can be understood. As Foucault observes, "What is peculiar to modern societies, in fact, is not that they consigned sex to a shadow existence, but that they dedicated themselves to speaking of it *ad infinitum,* while exploiting it as *the* secret."[4] In the early novel, suspense about irregular sexual relationships—illegitimacy, incest, miscegenation, unknown parentage, polygamy, unnatural coldness, promiscuity—is at the center of the plot. In the novel's denouement, the secrets are revealed.[5] The belief that knowledge about an individual's sexuality might be a key to understanding his behavior inspired scientific study in the nineteenth century that laid the groundwork for psychoanalysis.[6]

Because Swift created his print persona as a provocative enigma, speculation about his sexuality, or that of his parents, promised to explain the strangeness of his words and deeds. In the first major account of Swift's character to be published after his death in 1745, Laetitia Pilkington introduces into print the plotline of Swift's problematic parentage. While she does not go so far as to say he was illegitimate, Pilkington casts a cloud on the moral character of Swift's father, whom she claims died of a mercury treatment for an "Itch" he "had brought home . . . with him, which he had got by lying in some foul Bed on the Road. . . . The Dean was a Posthumous Son to the Gentleman, but, as he said, came Time enough to save his Mother's Credit" (31). The report of Swift's father possibly having venereal disease (which required the mercury treatment) may indeed have issued from Swift himself as Pilkington claims, but this "fact," like most of the supposedly firsthand information relayed by Swift's early biographers, lacks any corroboration but the author's say-so.

Focusing primarily on her own amorous adventures, Pilkington, in the first two volumes of her *Memoirs* (1748), has little to say about Swift's sexual relationships, although about one quarter of her material consists of anecdotes that illustrate Pilkington's flirty but nonsexual relationship with an old and eccentric Dean Swift. In one story, she tells of being at the Deanery all afternoon reading Swift's unpublished manuscripts. When her husband appears around dinnertime, Pilkington's Swift taunts him: "'Well, Mr. *Pilkington*, . . . I hope you are jealous; I have had your Wife a good many Hours, and as she is a likely Girl, and I a very young Man [Pilkington's note: "he was upwards of Three-score"], you don't know what may have happen'd'" (36). Pilkington acknowledges that there would be great demand for any illumination she could shed on the "Dean's Amours, as he has not quite escap'd Censure, on Account of his Gallantries," but because, in her view, love seems to have been a "Passion he was wholly unacquainted with, and which he would have thought it beneath the Dignity of his Wisdom to entertain" (45), she can say little.

For the introduction of the major elements of the Swiftian romance, credit must go to Lord Orrery, whose *Remarks on the Life and Writings of Dr. Jonathan Swift* was published in 1751. The most sensational stories in Orrery's account are rumors that Orrery purportedly wanted to debunk, namely, that Swift was the illegitimate son of Sir William Temple; that Swift and Stella were secretly married; and that Swift and Stella might have been brother and sister. While ostensibly denying the truth of these rumors, Orrery adds information that either bolsters their credibility or makes Swift seem guilty of worse scandals. Orrery's revelations guaranteed that his book would be a bestseller and stimulated numerous printed responses, most of which blame Orrery for blackening Swift's memory.[7] The attacks on Orrery of course swelled the demand for his *Remarks* to even higher levels. Within one year of its appearance, there were five London editions, two Dublin editions (including one by Faulkner), one French edition, and a German edition.

Although stories of Swift's illegitimacy may have been the subject of gossip in some quarters, there is no evidence, except Orrery's unsupported testimony, that this was actually the case. Adding to the scandal of Swift's bastardy, Orrery claims Swift himself originated the rumor because he was ashamed of his common birth: "Like *Alexander*, he thought the natural son of *Jupiter* would appear greater than the legitimate son of *Philip*" (10). Outraged by these assertions, Deane Swift (Swift's cousin) later answers Orrery, saying that he doubts Swift "himself was ever apprized of that calumny, much less that he ever acquiesced in it"(76). Throughout his narrative, Orrery focuses obsessively on issues of class, a prominent theme in British popular fiction, like *Pamela,* for example. Unlike Pamela, Orrery's Swift lacks the nobility of refined sentiments, correct manners, and moral probity to compensate for his common birth, for, according to Orrery, "the vulgar dialect," "filthy ideas," indecent expressions, and low company seemed to have been "acceptable to his nature" (21). Presumably if Swift had any of Sir William Temple's blood running in his veins, he would not behave so boorishly nor tolerate conversation with the clientele of "cheap inns." Orrery's aristocratic superiority colors his rendering of Swift's life and character.

The drama of the bastard unacknowledged by his high-born father that Orrery introduces into the Swiftian legend had long been a popular feature of English literature. In the moralized depictions of the patriarchal family that dominated British literature of the eighteenth and nineteenth centuries, a character's uncertain origin—especially if it suggests the possibility of illegitimacy or base parentage—became a major plotting device. Examples include Steele's *Conscious Lovers,* Fielding's *Tom Jones,* Cumberland's *The West Indian,* Dickens's *Oliver Twist,* or Wilde's *The Importance of Being Earnest.* The frequent reprinting of Richard Savage's poem, "The Bastard" (1728), and of the biographical accounts of Savage by Samuel Johnson and others, reflect an intense interest in the subject of illegitimate birth. In his narration of Swift's life, Orrery slyly adds incest to bastardy by denying allegations of both. Orrery's account, for the first time, makes it clear that Swift and Stella met at Moor Park, where he was Temple's secretary and she was the young daughter of two of Temple's retainers.

Through Orrery, too, the reading public discovered that in 1716 the Bishop of Clogher secretly wed Swift and Stella (23), a "fact" that has been debated ever since by layman and scholar alike.[8] (No authoritative evidence has been produced that a marriage occurred.) Orrery's revelation of the marriage generated the obvious question—why did Swift keep his marital status secret? Always the snob, Orrery suggests that Swift was ashamed of Stella's low birth—"the flaw, which in Dr. Swift's eye reduced the value of such a jewel, was the servile state of her father, who . . . was a menial servant to Sir William Temple" (24). Orrery then adds that not only was Swift's marriage secret, it was celibate. How bizarre. Orrery reports that the couple lived entirely apart from one another and "that it would be difficult, if not impossible, to prove they had ever been together without some third person" (16). Swift's never having been alone with Stella is another often-repeated "fact," backed only by Orrery's assertion that it is true. Fanning the flames as he does so, Orrery beats down the suggestion that the reason for Swift's celibacy is that he and Stella discovered they were half-siblings after the knot was tied. To argue his point, Orrery snidely discounts Temple's paternity of Stella, saying that if she had been Temple's daughter, Swift would have bragged about her blue blood (16).

Like Iago, Orrery defames while pretending to defend. His dirty-minded insinuations prompted a reviewer in *The Gentleman's Magazine* (August 1752) to wonder why Orrery "could not suppress one passage in which *bawdry* is but half concealed."[9] Orrery's sexualizing pervades his account; for example, he refers to a group of Dublin women with whom Swift had literary discussions as his "seraglio." Despite arguments by Deane Swift and other subsequent biographers that the speculation about incest was without warrant, the story had an allure that kept it alive. Five years after Orrery put the idea of Swift's celibate incest into circulation, the lead article in the November 1757 *Gentleman's Magazine* added complex (and totally undocumented) detail to the myths about amorous doings at Temple's Moor Park estate and focused on the awful reality of the Swifts' marriage:

> He admired her; he loved her; he pitied her; and when fate had placed the everlasting barrier between them, their affection became a true *Platonic* love. . . . Can we wonder . . . that the Dean and *Stella* always took care to converse before witnesses? . . . Can we wonder that they should spend one day in the year in fasting, praying and tears, from this period to her death? Might it not be the anniversary of their marriage?[10]

This free indirect discourse imputed to Swift and the lurid account of the couple's sackcloth and ashes anniversary is overtly fictional. Historical authenticity is not the aim here but, rather, the satisfaction of desires to explore taboo breaking.

Why incest became such a prominent theme during the eighteenth century is unclear.[11] In the Republic of Letters, Enlightenment thinkers debated whether the aversion to incest was a product of nature or nurture and whether valid reasons existed for prohibiting it.[12] In popular culture, brother-sister incest is a recurrent theme in the late-eighteenth- and nineteenth-century-fiction, which often features couples unaware of their parentage who realize they unwittingly have (or are about to) commit sibling incest. Novels with this plot pattern are legion and include Defoe's *Moll Flanders,* Fielding's *Joseph Andrews,* and Lewis's *The Monk.* The focus on hearth and home in the sentimental literature of the period may have derived from transgressive fantasies or horrifying anxieties about endogamous relationships, reactions that also would feed the popularity of works focusing on the dark world of the gothic castle.[13] Incest, of course, has traditionally been one of the extraordinary features associated with mythological figures—Oedipus marries his mother and King Arthur fathers Modred by his sister Morgaine. At any rate, Orrery's implications of Swift's incest had a revolutionary effect on how the world viewed Swift from 1751 onward.

To develop the sexual scenario, Orrery draws in detail the torrid emotions involved in the Swift-Stella-Vanessa triangle (of which he had no firsthand knowledge). In introducing this plot for the first time, Orrery falls back on the conventions of the novel—dramatic confrontations, overheated rhetoric, strange coincidences, distributive justice, and the whore (Vanessa) and madonna (Stella) opposition. After Orrery reports that Swift and Stella were secretly married, he introduces Vanessa as the homewrecker. She was, in Orrery's narration, "happy in the thoughts of being reputed Swift's concubine: but still aiming and intending to be his wife" (68). Referring to the titillating lines of "Cadenus and Vanessa," which teasingly refuse to reveal the results of Vanessa's attempt to seduce Swift—"But what Success *Vanessa* met, / Is to the World a Secret yet"—Orrery blames Swift for being so ungentlemanly as to publish the fact that he might have had sexual intercourse with Vanessa (72)—another example of his lack of breeding.

In Orrery's rendition of events, Vanessa—unaware that Stella was already Swift's wife—steps up efforts to snare him for herself. According to Orrery, Vanessa makes a fatal mistake by writing Swift a letter, in which she demands that he marry her. On receipt of Vanessa's ultimatum, Orrery's Swift rides to Celbridge to tell Vanessa good-bye forever. Ignoring his own acknowledgment that "their particular conversation, as it passed without witnesses, must for ever remain unknown," Orrery imaginatively places himself in the room with the lovers and provides a scene of operatic intensity: "[Swift's] reply was delivered by his own hand. He brought it with him when he made his final visit at [C]*elbridge:* and throwing down the letter upon her table, with great passion hastened back to his horse, carrying in his countenance the frowns of anger and indignation"(73). In Orrery's account, the breakup literally kills Vanessa—and it is all her own fault. Orrery draws the moral: "Thus perished, at [C]*elbridge,* under all the agonies of despair, Mrs. *Esther Vanhomrigh;* a miserable example of an ill-spent life, fantastic wit, visionary schemes, and female weakness" (75). Orrery's account of the Swift-Stella-Vanessa triangle became the ur-text of the Swiftian romance—repeated, embellished, rejected—but always present in any account of Swift's life. The truth, as far as it can be discerned, is less dramatic. Swift wrote Vanessa affectionate letters up until the fall of 1722 when she seems to have become ill. She probably died of the same disease that killed her sister in 1721, not of unrequited love. That she does not mention Swift in her will caused some people to suspect a quarrel, but as Ehrenpreis points out, Swift would not have wanted his name to appear in that context.

Four years after the death of his mother and three years after the appearance of Orrery's *Remarks,* Jack Pilkington published the third volume of his mother's *Memoirs* in 1754. This volume, so different in tenor from the previous two, is, I believe, primarily the work of Jack Pilkington, capitalizing on the strong market demand for sensational scenarios involving Swift, as evidenced in the brisk sales of Orrery's *Remarks.*[14] Seeing the response that Orrery's suggestions of incest provoked in the reading public, Pilkington (whichever one) reiterates Orrery's statements about the celibacy of the Swift-Stella marriage by saying they "did not indulge the Desires of the Body" and supplying the reason in a footnote: "Mrs. *Johnson* [Stella] . . . [was] said to be his own sister." Pilkington then offers an outlandish reason for Stella's decision to live apart from Swift despite their marriage: she knew "that while she continued only a Visitor, he would treat her with Respect; which would cease, as his Temper was unpassive, if she lived intirely with him; and every Fault of the Servants would be attributed to her" (280, 280n).

In Volume III, Pilkington characterizes Swift as a man with an uncontrollable temper and brutal impulses. Fostering legends of Swift as a cruel lover, stories nominally narrated by Laetitia provide several outrageous displays of Swift's verbal and physical violence toward her. He repeatedly beats her, and at one point, throws her to the floor and forces a bottle of rum down her throat. A. C. Elias, editor of the Pilkington *Memoirs,* voices his suspicions about the authenticity of this last scene by pointing out the contradiction to Laetitia's testimony in the first volume of the *Memoirs* that Swift was a very light drinker, who only indulged in watered-down wine.[15] Pilkington's supposed abuse at Swift's hands foreshadows later allegations, primarily by Victorian writers, that because both Vanessa and Stella predeceased Swift, they died from his torture.

The market appeal of Swift's inexplicable relationships with the women in his life is evident from the title page of Patrick Delany's *Observations on Lord Orrery's Remarks* (1754), which announces that the volume contains "Several singular *Anecdotes* relating to the Character and Conduct of that great Genius, and the most deservedly celebrated *Stella.*" Delany, one of Swift's friends, adds fuel to the fires of Swift's amours by ostensibly providing insight into Stella's reaction to Vanessa's rivalry. In a story not found in any other source, Delany reports Stella's witty reply to someone who commented how well Swift wrote on Vanessa—"Mrs. Johnston smiled, and answered, that she thought that point not quite so clear; for it was well known, the Dean could write finely upon a broomstick" (58), alluding to Swift's *Meditation upon a Broomstick* (1710). Yet Delany implies that Stella was not really so philosophical, a point he illustrates by printing a poem called "Jealousy" that he ascribes to Stella, containing lines like, "Ah, Love, you've poorly play'd the hero's part, / You conquer'd, but you can't defend my heart" (69). The poem had originally appeared in Concanen's *Miscellaneous Poems* (1724), along with another one, both identified as the work of the same anonymous "Lady."[16] There is no bibliographic or textual evidence that Stella wrote "Jealousy."

Although he professes to be horrified that Orrery could impugn a man who once was his friend, Delany cannot resist telling stories about Swift's love life that do nothing to redeem his honor. Delany, for example, accepts Orrery's story of Swift's unacknowledged and celibate marriage, but asserts that the reason that Swift and Stella lived apart was to save money—that they would need a more lavish household if publicly recognized as man and wife (60–1). While rejecting Orrery's assumption that the Swift-Vanessa relationship was a sexual one, Delany adds suggestive details that undercut his argument. In particular, Delany reports that Bishop Berkeley (conveniently dying the year before the publication of the Delany's *Observations*), as the executor of Vanhomrigh's estate had to go through her effects and "found, upon examination, (as he frequently assured me) that they contained nothing, which would . . . bring the least reflection upon Cadenus. . . . [or suggest] the least hint of a criminal commerce between them" (123). Denying the accusation that they had a "criminal commerce" underscores the idea that most people think the contrary. Delany creates another ending to Orrery's story of Vanessa's demise. In his version, scorned by Swift, Vanessa became an alcoholic and sought revenge on Swift by requiring Berkeley, as her executor, to publish her letters as well as "Cadenus and Vanessa," a story that scholars have declared to be totally without foundation.[17] The relationship between Berkeley and Vanessa caused speculation, especially since it became known that she left £3000 to Berkeley, despite the fact they seemed never to have met. In Delany's version of events, Vanessa is not a self-centered vixen, but a woman overtaken "with all the warmth and violence, of the strongest Love-passion," which made her helpless to withstand her own emotions (123–4). Delany's reversal of the Petrarchan romance—here the woman rather than the man suffers from the cruel indifference of the love object—recalls the mysterious sexual magnetism with which Swift charged himself in "Cadenus and Vanessa."

In *Essay Upon the Life, Writings, and Character of Dr. Jonathan Swift* (1755), Deane Swift repeats some of the stories told by Orrery and Delany, rebuts others, and adds some new facets to the evolving lore. Quoting from a cache of unpublished documents (including the letters from Swift to Stella that will later be known as the *Journal to Stella* as well as Swift's terse autobiography), Deane Swift clearly has inside information, which he mixes with his own speculations. To the narrative of the Stella-Swift relationship, Deane Swift offers some bits of news: that a proposal of marriage was made to Stella by another man (the Reverend William Tisdall), which Swift, in essence, prevented Stella from accepting; that Stella acted as his hostess in the Deanery; that Stella, with her companion, Mrs. Dingley, would stay at the Deanery when Swift was out of town or when he was suffering with giddy fits; that Swift was a frequent visitor in the Vanhomrigh's house while he was in London and Stella was in Ireland; that while a student at Trinity College, he had proposed marriage to his roommate's sister, Jane Waring, whom he dubbed Varina. Deane Swift's reports of these events—later corroborated by publication of Swift's letters—added new permutations to the Swiftian romance with which future authors could play.

In opposition to Orrery, Deane Swift is unsympathetic to Stella, whom he portrays as a stalker. According to Deane Swift, Swift finally consented to marriage in 1716 when Stella went into a severe depression because she had been unable "to compleat her conquest" and because people were gossiping about her odd situation. In this light, Swift felt it necessary to "raise her spirits, and to secure the fame of her innocence from all possibility of reproach." Like Orrery, Deane Swift believes that Stella and Swift were secretly married and lived apart. Adamantly rejecting Orrery's insinuations of incest and providing a detailed chronology to show how it could not have occurred, Deane Swift presents a number of contradictory explanations of why Swift did not marry Stella earlier, and, once married, why Swift did not acknowledge the marriage: (1) that he would become a pariah if it were known he married a servant who once waited on his sister, a prospect that would have killed him within a year; (2) that he did not want to be married in the first place and so refused to live as a married man; and (3) that he already had all the advantages of marriage—Stella acted as his hostess and companion—without any of the obligations (85–95). Like Delany, Deane Swift expresses sympathy for Vanessa. Defending her against Orrery's assertions that she was a loose woman punished for her sins by an early death, Deane Swift eulogizes her—"Thus died at *Cellbridge,* worthy as a happier fate, the celebrated *Mrs. Esther Vanhomrigh,* a martyr to love and constancy"—and supplies a Lycidas-like elegy in which nymphs and shepherd swains decry the demise of one with "virtues uncorrupt and pure" (264–5). Like Orrery, Deane Swift knew Swift only in his later years, long after these events had taken place.

Letters between Swift and the two women in his life began to be published in the late eighteenth century and fueled new visions of the relationships among the three. Deane Swift used the so-called *Journal to Stella* as a source for his account. Not published until 1784, these letters, written by Swift to Stella when he was in London 1710–13, opened a window into the intimate lives of the two correspondents. Because of their self-dramatizations, ironic humor, and coded language, however, their meaning is difficult to interpret, opening the way to rampant mythmaking. The "little language" of the letters can be seen as the baby talk of a fatherly Swift to a daughterly Stella, or as flirty (and sometimes dirty) jokes between a man and a woman. In the letters, Swift occasionally alludes to their time together at Moor Park, which fed rumors of their incest.

The correspondence between Esther Vanhomrigh and Swift also trickled into print and provided new material for fictional accounts of her secret relationship with Swift.[18] In Vanessa's letters, the painful intensity of her love is revealed, although her physical relationship to Swift remains obscure:

> O——how have you forgott me you indeavor by severities to force me from you nor can I blame you for with the utmost distress and confusion behold my self the cause of uneasie reflections to you yet I cannot comfort you but here declair that tis not in the power of arte time or accident to lessen the un-

expressible passion which I have for- - - . . . don't flatter yourself that separa-
tion will ever change my sentiments . . . for heavens sake tell me what has
caused this prodigious change in you which I have found of late If you have
the least remains of pitty for me left tell me tenderly No don't tell it so it may
cause my present Death and don't suffer me to live a life like a languished
Death which is the only life I can leade if you have lost any of your tenderness for me[.] (C 2: 363)

The spectacle of an almost crazed Vanessa importuning an affectionate yet
frightened Swift brought the over-heated drama first revealed by Swift in
"Cadenus and Vanessa" to a much higher pitch.[19] For years, readers had only
Swift's side of the story. The letter above and others like it gave credence to
the myth of Swift as a ghoul torturing and killing his hapless victims.

Thomas Sheridan's *Life of Swift* (1784) was the next major source of stories about Swift's amours. Sheridan (the son of Swift's friend by the same
name and Swift's godson) celebrates Swift in epic fashion in the first five
chapters, but then, in the sixth chapter, turns to the hidden "facts" of Swift's
love life, "A subject, which, in one of his singular character, is more likely to
excite curiosity than any other" (284). Quoting from Swift's letters, Sheridan elaborates in his own way the Swift-Tisdall rivalry for Stella introduced
by Deane Swift, as well as the nature of Swift's relationships with Stella and
Vanessa. A popular addition to the scenario that ends the Swift-Vanessa relationship is Sheridan's assertion that it was precipitated because Vanessa
wrote a note to Stella (not Swift, as in Orrery's version), demanding to know
whether she and Swift were married. Swift finds the letter addressed to Stella
and is so enraged he rides down to Celbridge. Sheridan supplies the dialogue
of the encounter: "She trembling asked him, would he not sit down? No—
He then flung a paper on the table, and immediately returned to his horse."
When Vanessa opens the paper, she sees it is her letter to Stella. The trauma
of this encounter kills her. To give a sense of Vanessa's mental state, Sheridan
prints two poems supposedly written by her, one an "Ode to Wisdom" in
which she pleads for help "to soothe my griefs to rest, / And heal my tortur'd
mind" (356).[20] In addition to introducing Vanessa's letter to Stella into the
romance plot, Sheridan also provides more evidence of Swift's cruelty, in this
case, to Stella. Claiming to have reports from his father who supposedly attended Stella on her deathbed, Sheridan asserts that as a dying wish, Stella
plead with Swift to acknowledge publicly their marriage. "Swift made no
reply, but turning on his heel, walked silently out of the room, nor ever saw
her afterwards during the few days she lived." In Sheridan's version of events,
Stella rails bitterly against him, then sends for a lawyer to change her will,
which she insists on signing in her own name (284). Swift, Stella, the elder
Sheridan, and the rest of Swift's friends were all long dead when this account

appeared, so Sheridan could safely assume that anything he said would remain unchallenged.

Around the time of Sheridan's biography, a new allegation about Swift appeared in Nichols's supplement to Swift's *Works* published in 1779, and then in 1786, reprinted by both *The Tatler* and *The Gentleman's Magazine*. In *The Gentleman's Magazine* (August 1786), the story very authoritatively states that while a prebend at Kilroot, Swift attempted to "ravish one of his parishioners, a farmer's daughter." He had to quit his post and leave Ireland. Supposedly, a magistrate named Dobbs still had the transcript of the hearing and the facts were attested to by the current prebend at Kilroot. *The Gentleman's Magazine* later printed a retraction, but the story still continued to circulate.

Walter Scott's *Memoirs of Jonathan Swift* (1814), published as the first volume of his nineteen-volume edition of Swift's works, is the last major fount of anecdotes contributing to the lore surrounding the Vanessa-Swift-Stella relationship. For this biography, Scott consulted numerous persons, who contributed manuscripts or oral accounts that ostensibly shed light on Swift. Most of the sources of the oral reports fall into the following categories: someone folklorists call a FOAF (a friend of a friend), someone long dead, or someone with a suspiciously vague identity. There is no way to tell whether or not, following the practice of modern tabloids, Scott put words in the mouths of people who could not protest or has attributed fictional words to fictional characters.

Although Scott tries to create a unified narrative of the Swift-Stella relationship, competing versions shout from the footnotes and crowd his text to the top of the page. For example, Scott's declaration that Swift and Stella were married by the Bishop of Clogher in 1716 is contradicted by a long note that undermines the authority of the statement: "The Bishop of Clogher, it is said, informed Bishop Berkeley of this secret, and by Berkeley's relict [widow] it was communicated to Mr. Monck Berkeley. . . . But I must add, that if, as affirmed by Mr. Monck Mason, Berkeley was in Italy from the period of the marriage to the death of the Bishop of Clogher, this communication could not have place" (218n) and so on, for four pages. Adding further ambiguity to the Swift-Stella relationship is Scott's report that Dr. Tuke of St. Stephen's Green "has a lock of her hair, on the envelope which is written, in Dean Swift's hand—'Only a woman's hair'" (223n)—a detail that becomes a feature of almost every treatment of the love affair.

One of the most sensational rumors Scott retails is that Swift and Stella had a child. This story supposedly comes from Richard Brennan, "the servant in whose arms Swift breathed his last," who told it to George Monck Berkeley who told it to Scott. Brennan claims to have gone to school with Swift junior, who, according to the tale, visited the Deanery every Sunday for dinner. Sharing Orrery's snobbism, Scott dismisses the story, saying it is improbable "that so proud a man as Swift should provide no otherwise for his only child, than to board him in a school, where so mean a person as Richard Brennan was a scholar"(228–9n). Another innuendo Scott casually drops is that Swift had relationships with women other than Stella, Vanessa, and Varina. Without comment, Scott prints in a footnote a passionate letter to Swift from a "Sacharissa" found in the papers of a "Mr. Smith," which concludes, "You may easily imagine with what impatience I shall expect Friday; I can't add how much I am yours till the arrival of my doom!" (242n)

As for Swift's possibly incestuous marriage to Stella, Scott, on the authority of a friend of the widow of Patrick Delany (a typically tangential source), reports that just after the supposed wedding, Delany passed Swift as he was bolting out of Archbishop King's study. Entering the study, Delany "found the Archbishop in tears, and upon asking the reason, he said, 'You have just met the most unhappy man on earth; but on the subject of his wretchedness, you must never ask a question,'" to which Scott supplies a footnote: "It is proper to state, that Delany's inference from this circumstance, was a suspicion that Swift, after his union with Stella, had discovered that there was too near a consanguinity between them, to admit of their living together" (221, 221n). The anecdote became an obligatory element biographical accounts and the phrase in its final line, "the most unhappy man on earth," repeatedly used as a way of identifying Swift.

Regarding Swift's relationship with Vanessa, Scott paints a picture of what went on at Celbridge Abbey, thanks to the reminiscences of the 90-year old son of Vanessa's gardener, who heard the information from his father. Considering his advanced age and how long ago his father told him the story, the son's account seems unnaturally detailed.

> [His father] remembered the unfortunate Vanessa well. . . . He said she went seldom abroad, and saw little company: her constant amusement was reading, or walking in the garden. . . . [H]er society was courted by several families in the neighborhood. . . . But she avoided company, and was always melancholy, save when dean Swift was there, and then she seemed happy. . . . The old man said, that when Miss Vanhomrigh expected the Dean, she always planted, with her own hand, a laurel or two. He shewed her favorite seat, still called Vanessa's Bower. Three or four trees, and some laurels, indicate the spot. . . . There were two seats and a rude table within the bower. . . . In this sequestered spot, according to the old gardener's account, the Dean and Vanessa used often to sit, with books and writing-materials on the table before them. (231)

Following this description are two poems Vanessa supposedly penned while sitting at the rude table with Swift. Needless to say, Scott's ancient gardener is the only source of this tale first published 160 years after Vanhomrigh's death.

Victorian writers, particularly affected by what they perceived as Swift's cruel treatment of the two major women in his life, began to characterize them as "victims" of his fatal emotional abuse.[21] Both Francis Jeffreys (in his critique of Scott's biography in the *Edinburgh Review* [1816]) and William Makespeace Thackeray (in his essay in *The English Humourists* [1853]) describe Swift's relationships in such grotesque terms that future writers can only explain his actions as those of a madman or one possessed by the devil.[22] Francis Jeffreys, rendering Swift as a coldhearted monster, details how Swift killed Vanessa and then, "with this dreadful example before his eyes," moved on to torture "his remaining victim." Jeffreys has "no hesitation pronouncing him the murderer" of these "innocent and accomplished women."[23] Thackeray, for his part, apostrophizes Stella as a martyr: "Gentle lady! so lovely, so loving, so unhappy. . . . We know your legend by heart. You are one of the saints of English story." Responsible for her death, Thackeray's Swift is a "guilty, lonely wretch, shuddering over the grave of his victim."[24] The characterizations of Thackeray and Jeffreys set the tone for nineteenth-century depictions, many of which emphasize that Swift's rejection of God led to his depravity.

To probe the psyche of this "murderer," some Victorians looked to science. As Foucault emphasizes, scientific discourse provides a way to talk about otherwise taboo topics in a completely respectable way—as part of a seemingly objective search for truth. In this case, the topic was the nature of Swift's sexuality and sexual performance. While phrenologists who examined Swift's skull in 1835 determined that he possessed an excess of "amativeness,"[25] the most popular thesis produced by *scientia sexualis,* however, was that Swift was heterosexual yet frigid or impotent. This line of inquiry was fueled by Swift's supposed refusal to marry and/or cohabit with Stella, his seeming misogyny, and his obsession with excrement. Thomas Beddoes's contribution, *Hygeia: Or Essays Moral and Medical* (1835), puts into play the idea that Swift's abnormal relations with women resulted from, in Robert Mahony's words, his "pitiable secret vice—which Beddoes was too delicate to label as masturbation."[26] Beddoes's theory influenced a number of future commentators, who allude elliptically to Swift's "unnatural misconduct" or "the excesses of a secret habit."[27]

From the nineteenth century into the twentieth, Swift's triangular relationship with Stella and Vanessa was the frequent subject of articles appearing in periodicals. A few examples will suffice: "Jonathan Swift Marriage Questioned" (*New York Times,* March 4, 1883); "Was Swift Married to Stella?" by Alexander Leslie (*Anglia,* September 1895); "Further Light on the Stella Marriage Question" (*Irish Times,* February 17, 1906); "Some Irish Love Affairs: Dean Swift and Stella," *(The Lady of the House,* December, 1908); *Dublin Weekly Freeman* "Swift's Fatal Love Story: The Tragedy of

Stella and Vanessa" (*The Weekly Freeman,* December, 1908); "Swift's Relations with Women" by John Macy (*The New Republic,* November 16, 1921);
"The Mystery of Stella" by E. Barrington (*Atlantic Monthly,* March, 1922);
"The Web of Mystery; Faithful Stella and Tragic Vanessa" by J. A. Rice,
(*Evening Herald,* June 2, 1936); "The Most Unhappy Man on Earth" by Edmund Wilson (*New Yorker,* January 22, 1949). Mackie Jarrell's analysis of
materials collected by the Irish Folklore Commission in the 1940s shows
that tales about Swift's love life circulated not only in printed material but
also in oral lore. One legend is that Swift visited Celbridge nightly and wrote
*The Drapier's Letters* there, and that after Vanessa's death, her ghost attacked
people on the Temple Mill Road (fire came out of her mouth and she threw
people in the river).[28]

Because the Swiftian romance became one of English culture's most compelling stories, it endowed objects and places with new and special value.
Watches, rings, and pictures associated with the principal characters were
"discovered" and myths devised to explain their meaning. The author of "A
Relic of Swift and Stella" (1832), for example, weaves an elaborate story
around an ax found at a site once visited by Esther Johnson. Based on no evidence at all, the article asserts that the ax was presented to Stella by Swift
with an inscription "doubtless of Swift's own composition."[29] Another find
is a locket containing a portrait of Swift supposedly belonging to Stella, said
"to be lost after her death, but . . . recovered about fifty years ago by Mr.
Maguire, in whose family it now is. This is one of the few miniatures of the
Dean ever painted."[30] Stella also seems to have lost more jewelry, this time
in Quilca, where her gold ring and some earrings were retrieved from a rusty
iron box at the bottom of a pond.[31] Another person claims to have the ring
Swift gave Vanessa (*The Irish Times,* Feb 7, 1936). At regular intervals, news
reports tell of portraits with murky provenances, which have been unearthed
from attics and basements. The images of "the young Swift," Stella, and
Vanessa used to illustrate books and articles are all of dubious authenticity.

The storytelling of eighteenth-century and nineteenth-century writers
formed the bases of the myths concerning Swift's amours that emerged in
the twentieth century. Until then, few innovations had challenged Orrery's
innuendos that Swift and Stella might have been fathered by Sir William
Temple. Denis Johnston, however, advanced the argument that Swift's father
was really Sir William Temple's father and that Sir William was Stella's father, thus making Swift a half-brother to Temple and an uncle to Stella. Supporting this theory with ambiguous historical records, Johnston advanced
his arguments in journal articles ("The Mysterious Origins of Dean Swift"
[1941]); books (*In Search of Swift* [1959]*)*; and several dramatic works for
radio and stage.[32] A late-twentieth-century addition to the paternity myths
comes from Victoria Glendinning in *Jonathan Swift: A Portrait* (1998). After

rehearsing the contradictory opinions on the lineage of Swift and Stella, Glendinning says, "Stop."

> There is another hypothesis concerning Stella's parentage that no one, so far as I know, has come up with. It is this: that Stella was not Bridget Johnson's daughter [Johnson was Sir William Temple's housekeeper], but Martha Giffard's [Giffard was Sir William's sister, who lived with him]. Widowed almost as soon as she was married, Martha had many admirers. You can take this extravagantly further, incorporating the prevailing belief that Stella was Sir William Temple's daughter. What if Stella were Sir William's daughter by his own sister, brought up under their roof as the daughter of Bridget Johnson?[33]

For four or five pages, Glendinning mounts a very convincing argument for her thesis, but then tells the reader, "Stop again. You do not have to believe the incest story. I had much rather you did not.... I am absolutely not putting it forward as the truth, nor even as a possible truth."[34] With postmodern playfulness, Glendinning emphasizes that her depiction is merely a depiction—that the truth about the man, Jonathan Swift, is impossible to discern amid the jumble of competing narratives ungoverned by fact or probability.[35] In spinning her tale, Glendinning displays the pleasures of the imagination that inspire Swiftian mythopoesis.

The relationship of Swift, Stella, and Vanessa attracted the attention of twentieth-century dramatists, who manipulated the plenitude of plot elements (celibacy, libertinism, adultery, incest, betrayal, emotional abuse, illegitimacy) into various permutations. Scenes in which Swift and Stella find out they are brother and sister or scenes depicting Vanessa's receipt of the letter telling her Swift is married to Stella became staples of the genre. In Florence Bell's variation, *The Dean of Saint Patrick's: A Play in Four Acts* (1903), Vanessa sends Stella the letter, and Stella, taking pity on Vanessa, rides to Celbridge to solace her. In the meantime, Swift finds the letter, follows Stella to Celbridge, throws the letter on the table, at which point Vanessa dies.[36] Charles Edward Lawrence's *Swift and Stella* (1927) opens with the couple holding hands when the letter from Vanessa arrives. Stella tells Swift that even though it was not true, she had informed Vanessa they were married. Of course, the drama reveals the awful truth—that they can't marry because they are brother and sister.[37] In the Earl of Longford's *Yahoo* (1934), the letter from Vanessa forces Swift grudgingly to marry Stella, an act that by implication kills both women.

No letters from Stella seem to have survived, but those extant from Vanessa were intently analyzed and used as foundations for narratives detailing her relationship with Swift, as were Swift's letters to both women. In the early twentieth century, for example, the theory that references to

"drinking coffee" in the Swift-Vanessa correspondence represents a coded allusion to having sexual intercourse was popularized by a number of writers,
among them Stanley Lane-Poole in *The Fortnightly Review* (February, 1910),
Stephen Gwynn in *The Life and Friendships of Dean Swift* (1933), and, most
recently, Bruce Arnold in *Jonathan Swift: An Illustrated Life* (2000).[38] Arnold
recounts Swift's fanciful rehearsal to Vanessa of a history of their relationship, "from the time of spilling the Coffee to drinking of Coffee, from Dun-
stable to Dublin," and wonders how Swift could deny that he was
passionately in love with Vanessa: "What remote consistency is there between such a view and the loving words of a man to a young girl, as he tells
her his remembrance of the most agreeable chamber in the whole world, the
one in which the two of them, close together and alone, take coffee, or with
their lips and mouths savour the tart tang of a home-grown orange, dipped
for sweetness in a bowl of sugar, then crushed and sucked and swallowed
down?"[39] All that passion, according to Sybil LeBrocquy, resulted in the
birth of a child, whom Stella raised after Vanessa's death.[40] Reports of another out-of-wedlock child—in addition to the one purportedly borne by
Stella and Swift—appears in mid-twentieth-century oral Irish folklore containing "the tradition that the Rev. William Pilkington was Swift's son by
Mrs. Pilkington, and that he looked remarkably like the Dean and had his
satirical gifts."[41]

A set of modern myths with an opposing premise characterize Swift as a
man who is revolted by the physical implications of sex. In *Yahoo* (1932),
Swift tells Stella, "Why should I any more than Gulliver seek by union with
one of the Yahoo species. . . . No, no! I vow I'd swoon at a female's embrace
as readily as my poor hero! Let them make to me all the advances they will.
I never made any to them, and never shall." Eleanor Corde's Swift (*Dean
Swift: A Drama,* 1922), inexplicably speaking with a brogue, tells Vanessa he
sees matrimony as a plague, "Wi' its attendant children—sickness—discord
and loathing—." Fear as well as loathing is cited as a reason for Swift's re-
pugnance in Yeats's *Words Upon the Window-pane* (1934), where Swift am-
biguously alludes to his horror of bringing a child into the world—"I have
something in my blood that no child must inherit." (Vertigo? Madness?
Syphilis? The Sin of Wit?) Winston Clewes's Swift (in *The Violent Friends,*
1945) is afraid of his own sexuality. Stella reproves him, saying, "You have
made. . . . your flesh a devil to crush under your feet. But mind was meant
to live in flesh, Jonathan. You cannot separate them."[42]

The twentieth century applied Freud's insights with assiduity to explain
Swift's replacement of sex with excrement as a ruling passion. Aldous Huxley, in his influential essay on Swift in *Do What You Will* (1929), focuses on
a phrase in one of Swift's letters—"I have a hatred of the word *bowels,*"which
he uses as the key to Swift's disgust with humanity.[43] John Middleton Murry

expands Huxley's interpretation in a chapter of his biography entitled "The Excremental Vision" and observes, for instance, that Swift's misogyny, expressed in terms of excrement, resulted from Swift's violent reaction to the deaths of Vanessa and Stella. This premise leads Murry to argue that in Swift's mind, "the young female Yahoo who lecherously embraces [Gulliver] while he bathes, is horribly like Stella at the time that Swift first became conscious of her beauty."[44] Murry does not explain the meaning of this grotesque simile, but seems to imply that Swift, like Strephon in "The Lady's Dressing Room," suddenly realized that Stella was not an ethereal "goddess," but a very mortal animal.[45]

Twentieth-century *scientia sexualis* elaborated the thesis, first arising in the nineteenth century, that Swift was frigid only with women of his own class. In 1926, Sandor Ferenczi, for example, pronounces that "[f]rom the psychoanalytical standpoint one would describe [Swift's] neurotic behavior as an inhibition of normal potency, with a lack of courage in relation to women of good character and perhaps with a lasting aggressive tendency toward women of a lower type."[46] With this diagnosis, Ferenczi "scientifically" explains Swift's supposed rejections of Jane Waring, Esther Vanhomrigh, and Esther Johnson, concluding that Swift could only be aroused by prostitutes. Some Victorian commentators conjectured that Swift's supposed madness was the result of syphilis. The idea that Swift contracted syphilis from one of his doxies is repeated in a letter from A. G. Gordon published in the *Journal of the Royal Society of Medicine* (February, 1999), which argues that "Swift was obsessed with syphilis and admitted having it." The "proofs" Gordon offers are several allusions in Swift's works to the "pox"; Swift's love of "pippens [apples]," which Gordon (in an enormous mental leap) equates to "tarts"; and Swift's poem "To Betty the Grisette," which Gordon presumes is Swift's address to a prostitute with whom he has consorted. Gordon's Swift does not marry for fear of infecting his spouse and dies in a state of syphilis-induced dementia.[47] Although these myths of Swift's promiscuity with underclass women appeared in academic discourse, the same themes are treated in popular literature. Many of the stories collected by Mackie Jarrell, for instance, involve the Dean sending Jack out to find him a woman for the night. In Paul Vincent Carroll's play, *Farewell to Greatness* (1966), Bolingbroke searches for Swift in the brothels, and Erica Jong shows Swift's attraction to prostitutes in her novel, *Fanny* (1980).[48] Tom MacIntyre's play, *The Bearded Lady* (1984), presents a Swift who "becomes beset, inescapably but not wholly against his will, by sex." In the original production of the play, characters had to make their entrances and exits between two enormous breasts.[49]

Psychoanalytic evidence has also been used to construct an alternative scenario—that Swift is not heterosexual but homosexual, an inference drawn from his reluctance to marry. According to Dr. Phyllis Greenacre, it was Swift's "hidden tendency" toward cross-dressing that made the vocation of Anglican clergyman so attractive to him. Greenacre's sees proof of her thesis concerning Swift's sexual orientation in scenes from Brobdingnag in which Gulliver is attacked by a dwarf and a frog—both males—"adventures suggestive of . . . homosexual fantasies."[50] More recently and less tendentiously, Victoria Glendinning considers at length Swift's seeming aversion to sexual relations with women and wonders "whether [he] was, in the modern sense, gay."[51]

With the collapse of traditional frameworks in the twentieth century, the Swiftian romance acquired existential dimensions. Removing the imaginative explorations of Swift's love life from the realms of science, morality, or religion, many modern narratives represent Swift's refusal to make connections with women as an expression of his individual freedom—a freedom that compromised his happiness and the happiness of the ordinary mortals around him. In *Swift: or the Egotist* (1934), Mario Hone and Joseph Rossi define Swift's desire for personal autonomy as egotism: "Love of independence, the struggle towards liberty, obstinacy in one's own opinions . . . the egotist never abandons himself. He cannot give himself up to anything or any person." Virginia Woolf's Swift also "hated interference. If anyone laid a finger upon his liberty or hinted the least threat to his independence, be they men or women, queens or kitchen maids, he turned on them with a ferocity which made a savage of him on the spot. . . . Stella knew better than to invite such treatment." Earlier in the century, Florence Bell's Swift tells Stella, "You know that I can be no obedient husband, no slave in the bonds of marriage; you know the very thought has to me ever been impossible. Will you be content with what I can give?"[52] Characterized in this way, Swift could be seen as embodying a male fantasy of being desired by many women yet remaining free of entanglements.

That the Swiftian romance is a male fantasy is too simple a theory, however, and does not explain, for instance, the numbers of women writers attracted to him as a subject. These women might be responding to Swift's indifference to gender categories and his willingness to occupy female identities: he and Mrs. Harris are one and the same. He had an intimate knowledge of female domains, as he demonstrates in "The Lady's Dressing Room" and "A Beautiful Young Nymph Going to Bed," and possessed the domestic skills associated with women, like making butter or brewing coffee. In using direct, sometimes coarse language in his addresses to women, Swift treated them like men, and, as critics have noted, he praises the women he admires for their masculine virtues. Perhaps, then, it is not surprising that so many women have chosen to write their own versions of the Swiftian romance in drama, poetry, prose fiction and nonfiction targeted to a general audience. In addition to the women authors already mentioned—Virginia Woolf, Eleanor Corde, Florence Bell, Sibyl Le Brocquy—there are others: Anna

Jameson, *Memoirs of the Loves of the Poets* (1829); Lady Duff Gordon, *Stella and Vanessa: A Romance from the French* (1850); Mrs. Wood, *Jonathan Swift: A Novel in Three Volumes* (1883); Myrtle Reed, *Love Affairs of Literary Men* (1907); Louise Bogan, "Hypocrite Swift" (1931); Edith Sitwell, *I Live Under a Black Sun* (1939); Elizabeth Myers, *The Basilisk of St. James, A Romance* (1946); Evelyn Hardy, *The Conjured Spirit: A Study in the Relationship of Swift, Stella and Vanessa* (1959); Susan Howe, "The Liberties" in *The Defenestration of Prague* (1983).

In reference to Harlequin romances, Janice Radway (*Reading the Romance: Women, Patriarchy, and Popular Literature*) acknowledges that the reading (and, by extension, writing) of romances by women could be viewed as evidence of "female masochism, in the desire to obliterate the self, or in the wish to be taken brutally by a man," but argues instead that the romance empowers women.[53] Unlike other major genres, such as tragedy, epic, or comedy, the romance plot by definition features major female characters. Typically, the leading women of romance are strong and independent. One can think of heroines from Una in the *Faerie Queene,* to Rosalind in *As You Like It,* to the characters played by Katherine Hepburn. Swift himself endowed Vanessa and Stella with spunky self-sufficiency (aside from their need for his love). Without husbands or fathers, they manage their own money and have their own houses. Far from being trapped by home, hearth, and heritage, both women pull up stakes from England and move to Ireland. Despite the calumnies that might besmirch them, both connect themselves to Swift in unsanctioned relationships. Many versions of the Swiftian romance ascribe Swift's madness to his unhappiness in love, thus attributing great power to the women in his life. That power is also manifest, Radway argues, in the heroine's ability to elicit deeply buried emotions from men who on the surface are cold or rough. Stella and Vanessa are sometimes represented as reducing the fierce Swift to a passionate sweet-talker. Thackeray recalls, "I have heard a woman say that she would have taken Swift's cruelty to have had his tenderness."[54]

Myths concerning the relationships of Swift, Stella and Vanessa have a modern appeal that goes beyond issues of gender. Indeed, the Swiftian romances contains elements that have made the James Bond movies so popular. In *Bond and Beyond: The Political Career of a Popular Hero,* Tony Bennett and Janet Woollacott write about the Bond world, in which both men and women are free agents:

> If Bond thus embodied a male sexuality that was freed from the constraints and hypocrisy of gentlemanly chivalry, a point of departure from the restraints, a-sexuality or repressed sexuality of the traditional English aristocratic hero, 'the Bond girl'—tailored to suit Bond's needs—was likewise represented

as the subject of a free and independent sexuality, liberated from the constraints of family, marriage, and domesticity.[55]

Unlike the existences that ordinary people inhabit, neither the men nor the women in the Bond movies are proscribed by rules or obligations. No controlling authority governs them except their own wills. Church, teachers, and parents are not present, and Bond repeatedly ignores instructions from General Headquarters. Two centuries earlier, in a much more tradition-bound society, Swift characterized himself in a similar way, ignoring, in particular, the genteel strictures proscribing commerce between the sexes. Some of Swift's poems about Stella and Vanessa summon up the unconstrained atmosphere of the mythical Golden Age. "Cadenus and Vanessa" is set in Venus's Court of Love, Stella and Apollo are depicted as best friends, and both Stella and Vanessa are referred to as "nymphs," alluding to the classical world of the pastoral.

In the late twentieth century, Bond's final coupling with a bosomy bimbo might be seen as a reward for his valor, while the ending of the more archaic Swiftian romance typically involves suffering, which was read, especially in the nineteenth century, as divine punishment for sins against "family values." The Swiftian romance and the Swiftian tragedy overlap, for Swift's madness is often shown to result from Swift's inability to love or from his misery at not being able to marry his heart's desire, Stella. The reader's pain in witnessing the star-crossed spectacle is counterbalanced by the intense feelings elicited by characters who dare to ignore conventional rules and follow love where it leads them. Northrop Frye argues that in presenting unsanctioned relationships fraught with high emotion and sexual electricity, the romance plot stirs readers in primal, irresistible ways, making them feel free and alive—"The improbable, desiring, erotic, and violent world of romance reminds us that we are not awake when we have abolished the dream world: we are awake only when we have absorbed it again."[56] By associating his print alter ego with illicit love and sex, Swift created a mythical dream world of infinite narrative possibility that readers continue to crave.

The romance in general and the Swiftian romance in particular also persist because the pleasures they provide are generally disapproved. From its modern beginnings in the eighteenth century to the present, the romance has been designated as time-wasting trash. By consuming these eros-tinged stories, readers feel they are exercising their freedom to resist social pressures. As Foucault observes, "What sustains our eagerness to speak of sex in terms of repression is doubtless this opportunity to speak out against the powers that be . . . to link together enlightenment, liberation, and manifold pleasures."[57] The popularity of the Swiftian romance is directly related to the way the print persona he created is inextricably tied to unspeakable desires and personal freedom. Even though topics that were not acceptable for public discussion are now commonplace—as evidenced in television advertisements for Viagra, vaginal douches, or hemorrhoid creams, adult diapers—Swift's flouting of social norms still has the power to shock and to excite.

# Chapter Five ~

# Tragic Scenarios:
# Madness, Suffering, and Death

B oth Fate and Swift shaped Swift's life into the pattern Raglan lays out for the mythologized figure, a tragic trajectory from high promise ("reputed to be the son of a god") and high achievement (victories over enemies and successful rule) to the loss of it all ("loses favor with the gods/or his subjects, and is driven from the throne and city"), ending with a "mysterious death" alone on a hill or an "upper room." While Aristotle says tragedy evolved from ancient fertility rites, death more than life is emphasized in the old order making way for the new. While the romance genre opens up explorations of gender, sexuality, and erotic relationships, tragedy encourages meditations on the reasons for suffering, the reality of death, the meaning of life, the nature of Providence, and the way an individual responds to the overwhelming questions these issues raise.[1] Unable to conceptualize our own deaths, tragedy allows us to witness in detachment the drama of someone else's death—to look at death slantways and accommodate ourselves indirectly to the uncertainties of the future and the inevitability of an end.[2] Contrary to the inclination of most people to do the same, Swift humorously imagined the realities of his own eventual death in "Verses on the Death of Dr. Swift," a poem in which he shows himself looking calmly and clear-eyed into the void of the hereafter. Swift's self-representation bears little resemblance to the myths about his death that sprang up after his death in 1745.

The death of a celebrity—a larger-than-life figure like Swift who dominated the media in his own time—evokes elegiac thoughts about the paths of glory leading but to the grave (to paraphrase Thomas Gray) as well as a desire to know exactly how the celebrity died, especially if he had disappeared from public view prior to his demise. A market exists for any information about the state of the dying celebrity's mind, as evidenced in his demeanor or last words. On a more concrete level, readers (both then and now) are also curious about the physical condition of the dying body, the dead body, and (if relevant), the exhumed body. That a public monument can suffer and die has a morbid fascination, but arouses the hope that sifting through the wreckage of his remains will reveal secrets about the private life hidden behind the public facade. No one seemed to have more secrets than Swift.

Swift was well aware that information about his dying would be in great demand. In "Verses on the Death of Dr. Swift," he whimsically envisions the breathless rumors about his daily decay:

> "His Stomach too begins to fail:
> Last Year we thought him strong and hale;
> But now, he's quite another Thing;
> I wish he may hold out till Spring.["] (109–14)

Swift imagines that when he finally dies, the media have a field day—"Some paragraph in every paper, / To *curse* the *Dean,* or *bless* the *Drapier*" (166–8), and talk swirls about his strange bequest to found a mental hospital.

In the "Verses," Swift constructs himself as an Aristotelian hero brought down by a tragic flaw or misjudgment. In this self-depiction, Swift's misjudgment does not result from negative aspects of his character but rather, from his fearless forthrightness. His misjudgment, like that of Oedipus, dooms him to die in exile.

> HAD he but spared his Tongue and Pen,
> He might have rose like other Men. . . .
>
> . . . . . . . . . . .
> With Horror, Grief, Despair the Dean
> Beheld the dire destructive Scene:
> His Friends in Exile, or the Tower,
> Himself within the Frown of Power;
> Pursued by base envenom'd Pens,
> Far to the Land of Slaves and Fens. . . .
>
> . . . . . . . . . .
> By Innocence and Resolution,
> He bore continual Persecution;
> While Numbers to Preferment rose;
> Whose Merits were, to be his Foes.
> (359–60, 395–10, 403–6)

Following Aristotle's pattern, Swift's Swift is a character "better than we are." Indeed, he is truly noble. Hamlet-like, he suffers and dies trying to set the times right. His tragic flaw is thinking that he will be rewarded, not punished, for crusading against corruption and injustice. In the myth presented in his "Verses," Swift dies with his reason intact, fully capable of what Aristotle terms *anagnorisis,* that is, the awareness that his fall resulted from his own actions. Fate intervened to prevent Swift's imagined outcome, when on May 20, 1742, he was legally declared *non compos mentis,* a vague pronouncement that immediately started rumors about his insanity. (Now the medical consensus is that his mental dysfunction was the result of a stroke.) Unable to leave the Deanery or to write, Swift's name virtually disappeared from print until October 19, 1745, when Faulkner published his obituary.

Swift's eighteenth-century biographers fit his life into a tragic pattern— but not the noble, Hamlet-like one used by Swift's "impartial" speaker in the "Verses." Rather, the biographers tend to see Swift's miserable end as the inevitable result of his character flaws. They draw evidence of his suffering from Pope's publication of letters (1741), in which Swift wrote of the pains of exile in Ireland, the decay of his body and mind, his growing despair, and his constant thoughts about death. The other major piece of evidence supporting the premise that Swift ended his life in mental torment is the phrase in his epitaph, contained in his will published in 1745, which describes him (in an English translation) as going "where savage indignation can lacerate his breast no more." The uncontrolled rage expressed in the epitaph hints at profound disturbances in Swift's psyche and a lack of any religious solace. Orrery, Pilkington, Delany, Sheridan, and Johnson represent Swift at the end of his life as an object of pity—a *momento mori* that evokes sublime thoughts about dissolution and presents a warning against a life misspent. These scenarios emphasize that Swift died a "bad death," one in which he is helplessly dependent, isolated from the world, emotionally agitated, or insane. In this version of the Swiftian tragedy, being too good for a corrupt world is not the reason Swift ends up suffering; rather, his own vices bring him down.

Lord Orrery formulated the basic outline of the Swiftian tragedy in his *Remarks on the Life of Dr. Swift* (1751). Although rumors of Swift's madness had been circulating, Orrery was the first to publish a coherent narrative that addresses the purported malady and speculates on its causes. Instead of depicting Swift as a noble figure who falls from fortune, Orrery shows him as a base figure, whose suffering results from trying to rise above his station. Instead of blaming himself for his suffering, Orrery's Swift irrationally blames mankind in general, blasphemously likening the human race to Yahoos. Swift's misguided ambition leads to disappointment and then to misanthropy, which leads to madness, denying him the good death of the virtuous, "that calm *exit* from the stage, for which his friend Horace so earnestly supplicates Apollo" (79).

According to Michel Foucault, in the eighteenth century madness moved from being a part of everyday life to a scandal hidden behind the closed doors of the home or the asylum.[3] The Swiftian tragedy, as presented by Orrery, brings readers into Swift's sickroom and satisfies the voyeuristic impulse to see what he was "really like" when he is helpless to resist the gaze. Orrery revealed for the first time in print the secrets of Swift's last days when his mind was gone and his body was in pain. Virtually alone, confined to an upper room in the Deanery, his company—according to Orrery's account—consisted primarily of his servants; his housekeeper, Mrs. Ridgeway; and his cousin, Mrs. Whiteway, who was one of Orrery's major sources of information; and Deane Swift, Mrs. Whiteway's son-in-law and Swift's cousin. From Orrery's citation of a letter to him from Mrs. Whiteway, readers learned that during his confinement, Swift sometimes went into such a frenzy Mrs. Whiteway dared not visit him; that sometimes he did not recognize her; that he walked ten hours a day; that his meat had to be cut up for him; that his left eye had swollen up like an egg and boils had covered his body; that, while in those tortures, it took five men to restrain him (89). A letter from Deane Swift adds the information that a servant shaved Swift's cheeks once a week with a razor but had to cut the long hairs under his throat with scissors (91). With the quotation of these letters, which many viewed as a violation of Swift's right to privacy, Orrery initiated the representation of Swift as a defenseless object of curiosity—the same curiosity that compelled thousands of persons in the eighteenth century to pay a penny to view the inmates in Bedlam Hospital.

Orrery is the first to present the public with some of the last words Swift might have spoken. There is a natural fascination with utterances on the bridge between life and death, particularly those of famous men. In general, though, most last words are too well wrought to be authentic.[4] In Orrery's *Remarks,* some of Swift's supposed last words are contained in a letter from Deane Swift responding to Orrery's query about the truth of a story that "Dr. Swift's having viewed himself (as he was being led across the room) in a glass, . . . [cried] out, "O *poor old man!"* Deane Swift answers Orrery, saying that Swift did say something on one occasion when looking in a mirror, but no one heard the words. (Deane Swift's statement does not prevent scores of authors from ascribing "O poor old man" to Swift.) Deane Swift repays Orrery's curiosity, however, by supplying him with a number of Swift's pathetic and enigmatic utterances or actions in the final phase of his illness. Among them are the following: Swift tries to grab at a knife and when thwarted, rocks back and forth in his chair for six minutes repeating, "I am what I am, I am what I am"; failing to find the words to say what he wants, Swift mutters instead, "I am a fool" and another time, pointing at his head, mysteriously says, "My best understanding"; he tells a servant trying to break a coal, "That's a stone, you blockhead" (91–3). These verbal fragments will be incorporated in numberless retellings.

Heightening his version of the tragedy, Orrery describes Swift as having a horrible foreknowledge that he would die a madman, claiming that Swift was drawn to examples of great men deprived of their reason "and when he cited these melancholy instances, it was always with a heavy sigh, and with gestures that shewed great uneasiness, as if he felt an impulse of what was to happen to him before he died" (170). Orrery's introduction of the idea that Swift knew he was going to die a madman adds a gothic dimension to the tale that proved very popular. One of the most often cited anecdotes in this vein is found in Edward Young's *Conjectures on Original Composition* (1759). Young writes,

> [A]s I and others were taking with him an evening's walk, about a mile out of *Dublin,* he stopt short; we passed on; but perceiving that he did not follow us, I went back; and found him fixed as a statue, and earnestly gazing upward at a noble elm, which in its uppermost branches was much withered, and decayed. Pointing at it, he said, "I shall be like that tree, I shall die at the top."[5]

The authenticity of this well-rendered tragic scene is impossible to verify, but it underscores the idea that Swift was doomed to live past his time, an idea Orrery develops in his *Remarks* by noting the tragic irony that Swift came to resemble the pathetic Struldbruggs, the immortals who continue to age, found in the third book of *Gulliver's Travels*. Orrery points the moral, saying that Swift's living death offers readers "a providential instance to mortify [their] vanity, which is too apt to arise in the human breast" (116). Orrery's sentimental rendering of Swift's death and dying engaged the readers of the mid- to late-eighteenth century, who avidly consumed poems like *Night Thoughts* or *The Grave* to wallow in melancholia (the "English malady") or to experience the sublime distresses brought about by "sensibility," or their capacity to feel intense emotion.[6]

Following Orrery's *Remarks* by three years, the third volume of the Pilkington *Memoirs* (1754) added to the lore concerning Swift's madness. Typical of other material in Pilkington's third volume, the stories are hyperbolic beyond belief. In one, Swift invites two men into his coach and then assaults them so violently they have to call for help. Another features Georg Handel visiting the inarticulate Swift, who can barely manage the words, "'O! A German, and a Genius! A Prodigy! Admit him.' The Servant did so, just to let Mr. *Handel* behold the Ruins of the greatest Wit that ever liv'd along the Tide of Time" (316; 316n). As A. C. Elias notes, neither of these stories has any corroboration to support its credibility, and, indeed, the available historical evidence suggests that they were made up out of whole cloth. The story of Swift and Handel was a popular one, with many variations.[7] An imagined meeting of two legendary characters is a common organizing structure in folklore and popular tales. Stories about Swift meeting with the legendary Irish harpist, O'Carolan is another favorite.

In the same year Pilkington's last volume appeared, Patrick Delany published his biography, which also plots Swift's life as a tragedy ending in madness. While Orrery cites vaunting ambition as Swift's tragic flaw, Delany points to Swift's obstinacy. This obstinacy manifests itself in Swift's stubborn refusal to discipline his urge to write bagatelle, to listen to his doctors, to wear glasses, or to overcome an avarice that prevented him from treating his friends well. This obstinacy eventually softened his intellectual fiber, ruined his body, and precluded companionship—"His passions impaired his memory, and his solitude unfurnished it" (149), which sank him into a "state of idiotism" interrupted only occasionally by rational intervals (149–50). Delany's presence during one of these rational intervals allowed him to garner some more final words for readers to ponder. Delany reports that Swift told him that "*he was an ideot . . . and no more a human creature.*" Another utterance was told to Delany "on good authority"—that Swift, informed that the populace was preparing to celebrate his birthday with bonfires, answered "*[I]t is all folly, they had better let it alone*" (150–1). The most lurid tidbit in Delany's account, though, is the news that Swift's head had been sawed open after his death, revealing a brain "remarkably loaded with water" (149). Here begins the fascination with Swift's skull.

In his *Essay on the Life, Writings, and Character of Dr. Jonathan Swift* (1755), Deane Swift avoids a ghoulish interest in Swift's physical decay to focus on Swift's tragic awareness of his mental decay. Deane Swift relates that after Swift had lost his memory, his parting remark to friends was "*Well,* God *bless you; good night to you; but I hope I shall never see you again,*" implying that he hoped himself soon to be dead. When a large, heavy mirror fell moments after Swift had been standing under it, Deane Swift reports that Swift said, "I wish the glass had fallen on me" (189n). Another influential anecdote illuminating Swift's supposed despair appears in a letter from him to Mrs. Whiteway, written in 1738, and published in Deane Swift's 1768 collection.[8] Swift tells her that he intends to read the third chapter of the *Book of Job* on November 30, which Deane Swift glosses with a footnote saying, "This chapter he always read upon his birth-day" (C 5: 128, 128n2). This chapter in *Job* includes a verse that says, "Let the day perish wherein I was born, and the night in which it was said, There is a man child conceived." Of the mythmaking about Swift's last days in his own time, Deane Swift reports that "A thousand stories have been invented of him . . . and imposed on the world."

One of the most shocking rumors about Swift's final days was that he was put on display for gawkers, to which Samuel Johnson alludes in "The Vanity of Human Wishes" (1749) when he describes Swift "expir[ing] a driv'ler and a show." Ehrenpreis says this story may have come from Thomas Birch, an acquaintance of Johnson living in Dublin and the source of much malicious gossip.[9] Later, in support of the story, Walter Scott claims that "the father of the late Lord Kinedder, one of the Editor's most intimate friends, was of the number" who paid to see "this extraordinary man in this state of living death" (424–5, 425n). That Swift was ever treated this way is both denied and supported by subsequent biographers, but the truth of the matter aside, the image of Swift as a pathetic spectacle was often repeated. Strangely, though, in *Lives of the Poets* (1781) Johnson does not redeploy this image as he lays out the tragic course of Swift's life. Following Orrery and Delany, Johnson blames Swift's character flaws—particularly avarice and obstinacy—for his suffering. Responding to Orrery's comment that Swift loved to stay in cheap inns because of his love of "grossness and vulgarity," Johnson suggests the behavior may have been motivated more by Swift's "love of a shilling." In his version, Johnson introduces the idea that Swift's avarice alienated the common people who had once supported him, reporting that although Swift lent them money without interest, he pursued them viciously if they failed to repay their debts.[10] Johnson's assertion that "The clamor against him was loud and the resentment of the populace outrageous" is without warrant. Johnson follows Delany in linking Swift's obstinate refusal to wear spectacles to his psychic collapse—unable to read, "his mind [was] vacant to the vexations of the hour. . . . [and] his anger was heightened into madness."[11]

Although all of Swift's eighteenth-century biographers mix possible fact with imaginative speculation to create elements of the myth of the mad Swift, Thomas Sheridan's account (1784) is the least credible. Sheridan, like Pilkington, was a major source of humorous anecdotes about Swift that were widely circulated in hundreds of jestbooks. Some of these jests—cited by Sheridan as facts attested to by Ambrose Phillips—feature Swift's bizarre behavior at Button's Coffeehouse, which, according to Sheridan, caused Swift to be nicknamed the "Mad Parson." In one of Sheridan's stories, John Arbuthnot asks Swift for some sand to blot a letter. Swift replies that he has no sand, but he does have "gravel" (crystals in the urine)—"If you will give me your letter I'll p-ss upon it" (46–7).

Sheridan's tone becomes more somber as he discusses the tragedy of Swift's last years. Picking up the thread introduced by Delany and amplified by Samuel Johnson, Sheridan emphasizes Swift's avarice as the main cause of his suffering. To illustrate, Sheridan inserts a long conversation that purportedly took place between his father (Swift's friend, also named Thomas Sheridan) and Swift, in which Swift makes the elder Sheridan promise to tell him if he ever becomes avaricious, because it is the vice he fears most. When

Sheridan's father finally confronts Swift about his increasing penury, "the disease is past remedy." If one believes Sheridan, Swift's avarice precipitated his father's death. Supposedly, because of the rising costs of caring for him, Swift ejected Sheridan's father from the Deanery where he was recuperating from an illness. An alternative version of the story, which Sheridan denounces as a lie, is that Sheridan's father had taken refuge in Swift's house to avoid his creditors and requested a bottle, which provoked the Dean to say "[T]hough he had given him a lodging, he had not promised to furnish him with wine." Swift's avarice, in Sheridan's opinion, deadened him to the "feelings of friendship," which would have made his last days more bearable (390–3, 393n). Sheridan does not dwell on Swift's dying days, but is the first to describe—or perhaps more likely—to invent the scene in which crowds of mourners "got into the chamber where he lay, to procure, by bribes to the servants, locks of his hair . . . [I]n less than [an] hour, his venerable head was entirely stripped of all its silver ornaments, so that not a hair remained" (282). A postscript: On April 30 1913, *The London Times* reported that a lock of Swift's own hair sold at Sotheby's for 35 shillings. Without the benefit of DNA analysis, it is doubtful that the authenticity of this relic could be assured.

Instead of focusing on character flaws, such as ambition, obstinacy, or avarice as the spring of Swift's tragedy, nineteenth-century biographers are obsessed by Swift's repudiation of God and the divinity of Creation. In this narrative, Swift's madness is God's judgment on a sinner. William Henry Davenport Adams, in *Wrecked Lives; Men Who Have Failed* (1880), points out that Swift's dying in torment "uncheered by a vivid ray of faith in the Divine goodness" presents "an awful moral lesson."[12] John Churton Collins (1893) argues that Swift's inability to see light in the darkness, plunges him into a nastiness whose equal is found only in the "speeches in which the depraved and diseased mind of Lear runs riot in obscenity and rage."[13]

Earlier in the century, William Makepeace Thackeray laid the groundwork for the view that Swift's tragic misjudgment was turning away from God. Thackeray's Swift suffers from a hubris that makes it impossible for him to accept any authority. In Thackeray's reimagining, life in Sir William Temple's house was a hell for Swift because he had the status of an underling. Treated as a "servant" or "slave," he seethed in anger as he "bent down a knee as proud as Lucifer's to supplicate my lady's good graces, or run on his honour's errands." In writing an ode on Sir William's death, Thackeray's Swift comes to a tragic awareness that his failure to accept subordination means that he is incapable of fulfilling his obligations as a priest. The epiphany causes Swift to give "a mad shriek . . . and [rush] away crying his own grief, cursing his own fate, foreboding madness, and forsaken by fortune, and even hope."

[H]aving put that cassock on, it poisoned him: he was strangled in his bands. He goes through life, tearing, like a man possessed with a devil. Like Abudah in the Arabian story, he is always looking out for the Fury, and knows that the night will come and the inevitable hag with it. What a night, my God, it was! what a lonely rage and long agony—what a vulture that tore the heart of that giant!

The refusal or inability of Thackeray's Swift to exorcize the devil within transforms him into "a monster gibbering shrieks, and gnashing imprecations against mankind,—tearing down all shreds of modesty, past all sense of manliness and shame; filthy in word, filthy in thought, furious, raging, obscene."[14]

For Thackeray, the peripety, or tragic downturn in Swift's life occurred when he wrote Book IV of *Gulliver's Travels*. Before that time, "all the great wits of England had been at his feet. All Ireland had shouted after him, and worshipped him as a liberator, a saviour, the greatest Irish patriot and citizen." The Yahoos signaled that Swift's thoughts were going drastically askew; they represented "the fatal rocks towards which his logic desperately drifted." (Like many nineteenth-century writers, Thackeray assumes that Swift equated humans and Yahoos.) In the story of the archbishop's telling Delany, "You have just met the most unhappy man on earth," Thackeray infers that Swift's unhappiness results from the recognition that he was possessed by the devil and blinded to the immanence of God in Creation.[15]

Other authors embellished Thackeray's idea that Swift was a creature of Satan. Nothing else in their view could explain why he thought humans were Yahoos or why he was attracted to darkness and dirtiness. Including an essay on Swift in his book entitled *Three Devils* (1874), David Masson stresses the "*demonic* element" in Swift. Unlike Milton and Shakespeare, who could hear "angelic music and the rustling of seraphic wings, it was Swift's unhappy lot to be related rather to the darker and subterranean mysteries. . . . [H]e had far less of belief in God than of belief in a Devil."[16] George Gilfillan, who chides Thackeray and Jefferies for being too kind to the Dean, rails on about Swift's heresy in believing "the devil . . . to be the only God."[17]

Supporting this view of Swift, a letter, purportedly written by Swift, mysteriously surfaced in the middle of the nineteenth century. In it, Swift (or a Swift impersonator) describes himself as being possessed: "[A] person of great honour in Ireland . . . used to tell me, that my mind was like a conjured spirit, that would do mischief if I would not give it employment."[18] The provenance of this letter is very murky and suspect. The only copy of the letter is composed on late-eighteenth-century paper in a hand that is not Swift's. This may be the transcript of a lost original but is more likely a manufactured piece of evidence to accentuate the popular image of a Swift character pulled down by dark forces within him.[19] Swift as a "conjured spirit" became an often-repeated simile.[20]

Elaborating the conceit of Swift's madness, the myth developed that he was the first patient in the mental hospital that he had founded. (It was built after his death.) The cosmic irony was too much to resist, for what could be a more fitting end for this arrogant sinner? In "Dean Swift's Madness: A Tale of a Churn" (1834), Father Prout (Father Francis Mahony), a popular essayist who frequently contributed to *Fraser's Magazine,* compares Swift entombing himself in his own hospital—"among his fellow creatures"—to the Pharoahs burying themselves in the great pyramids.[21] Earlier *The London Times* (November 11, 1786) printed a short squib, noting "The celebrated Dean *Swift* was the first patient admitted into the Lunatic Hospital in Dublin, which he himself founded. This is an incident which in time may possibly have its parallel. Lord preserve the proposers of the *Botany Bay* scheme [for the settlement of Australia by English prisoners]."

In the spirit of the Enlightenment, nineteenth-century scientists sought to remove the discussion of Swift's affliction from the context of religion and resituate it in the context of empiricism. Among the physical causes of Swift's madness put forward were syphilis and excessive masturbation. In *The Closing Years of Dean Swift's Life* (1849), a Dublin doctor, William Wilde (Oscar's father) tries to dismiss these theories as well as the idea that Swift was insane, by doing a postmortem over one hundred years after the patient had died. In his examination, Dr. Wilde gathered all the documents and artifacts he could—Swift's account of his own symptoms, eyewitness accounts of his illness, doctors' notes on his illness, documents related to the initial postmortem (just after Swift's death) and the subsequent one in 1835, descriptions of the condition of the grave when it was opened, plaster casts of Swift's brain, and death masks.

Although his aim is to sweep away the myths surrounding Swift's terminal illness, Wilde cannot escape the confusion of fact and fiction surrounding it. Wilde assumes that the documents in his possession are trustworthy, when in actuality they may contain exaggerations or inventions. While Wilde refuses to consider the large "number of anecdotes relative to Swift, both among the gentry and the working classes" of Dublin, he cannot resist the opportunity to introduce several new stories never "before published" that he deems more reliable.[22] One example is an account of the first postmortem, a thirdhand report of "old Brennan," who "according to Dr. Houston, on the authority of Mr. Maguire," relates that "he even held the basin in which the brain was placed after its removal from the skull . . . [T]here was brain mixed with water to such an amount as to fill the basin, and by their quantity to call forth expressions of astonishment from the medical gentlemen engaged in the examination."[23]

Swift's mysteries made readers want to look into the inner sanctums of his bedroom, sickroom—and finally, the grave. To satisfy this urge, Wilde presents excerpts of reports concerning the exhumation of Swift and Stella's remains in 1835, a project supposedly necessitated by repairs to the cathedral. The doctors doing the exhumation noted the state of the coffin and the exact arrangement of the bones in addition to their appearance. For further study, the doctors removed a number of Swift's body parts. Wilde says that some of these were scientifically examined, while others became fashionable conversation pieces. The remains were passed from person to person in Dublin and eventually reassembled, all except some "ossified fragments" of his larynx, which Wilde reports were "abstracted by a bystander . . . who carried them to the city of New York."[24] Wilde reports that the skulls of Swift and Stella were appropriated by the British Association of Phrenologists, which was meeting in Dublin at the time of the exhumation. The phrenologists found that "the cerebral surface of the whole of the frontal region [of the skull] is evidently of a character indicating the presence, during the lifetime, of diseased action in the subjacent membranes of the brain."[25] Printed in Wilde's book are engravings of Swift's skull and a reconstruction of his brain from an article by J. Houston in the *Phrenological Journal.*

The persistent interest in Swift's cranium is reflected by an article, entitled "Grim Relic" in a Dublin newspaper (July 4, 1934)[26] reporting the discovery of a cache of skulls, one of them labeled "Swift" and the title of Shane Leslie's biography, *The Skull of Swift: An Extempore Exhumation* (1928). In Leslie's final chapter, "The Place of the Skulls," Leslie imagines Swift's experience in his own Golgotha: "Oh Demon! Oh God! Was he mad, mad, mad at last? This time his whole shuddering brain quailed in his skull. . . ."[27] Dr. Wilde was not able to offer a definitive diagnosis that would explain Swift's symptoms, but in the early 1880s, several scholarly articles[28] identify the source of Swift's vertigo as Meniere's disease (a disease of the inner ear), a diagnosis that was first popularized in an appendix to Henry Craik's biography, published in 1882,[29] and later by an exchange of letters in the *Times Literary Supplement* (November 28, 1918). Swift's difficulty speaking was diagnosed as aphasia, brought on by a stroke. These scientific observations did little to dislodge the myth of the mad Swift.

Inspired by Jeffreys and Thackeray, the nineteenth century had little sympathy with Swift's suffering and saw his end as distributive justice in action but, in the twentieth century, new perspectives inflect the characterization of the tragic Swift. He appears as (1) a flawed yet great man who is ultimately overwhelmed by cosmic forces; (2) a man who denies God, but who saves his life from tragedy by acknowledging Him at the eleventh hour; (3) a man whose existential strength allows him to stand alone but prevents succor; and (4) a man whose virtues disbar him from success or happiness because he lives in a thoroughly corrupt world (a return to Swift's own vision of himself through the "impartial" speaker of the "Verses").

In the first twentieth-century plotline, neither God's wrath nor Swift's character bring about Swift's madness or suffering. Rather, the overwhelming forces of Nature or Time are responsible for grinding the hero down into a pathetic, helpless antihero in his last days, ending with a whimper and not a bang. Longford's *Yahoo* shows the aged Swift, attended by a servant, sitting in a chair, surrounded by a crowd yelling, "He's mad! He's mad! He's mad!"

> **Servant.** Walk up, walk up, ladies and gentlemen, pay your money
> and see the greatest show in the Kingdom, the Mad Dean.
> Walk up, walk up! (*The crowd pay their money and walk round
> gaping and laughing* [.])
> **Swift** (*rising feebly*). I am what I am! I am what I am!
> **A Distant Voice.** And Swift expires, a driveller and a show.[30]

The final scene of Eleanor Corde's *Dean Swift* presents a quasi-comatose Swift who is "the shadow of his former self. Shrunken form, lustreless eyes, his snowy hair falling to his shoulders . . . [his] head . . . [rolling] from side to side." On hearing the crowd shouting acclamations of his triumph as the Drapier, "he rises, raises his hand with the authority of other days—makes an effort to speak—suddenly collapses" and dies.[31] Edith Sitwell's novelized biography of Swift, *I Live Under a Black Sun* also features Swift's irresistible disintegration:

> [W]hen his meat was brought to him, cut into mouthfuls as though he were a wild beast, he, having left it till it stood for an hour, would eat it walking. Only twice, during all the time of his raging madness, did he speak. . . . a voice coming from the depths of unutterable misery was heard. It said "I am what I am . . . I am what I am. . . ."
>
> And silence fell.
>
> But sometimes an appalling hollow booming noise echoed down the long corridors and in the empty rooms . . . a crashing, rushing noise and the sound of an orangoutang beating its bosom.
>
> The madman was summoning his mate, Darkness.
>
> Then would come roar after roar. Black roar after roar.
>
> And darkness answering.[32]

Sitwell's translation of the story to the World War I era identifies Swift's persona with the plight of twentieth-century humans desperately trying to shore the fragments of a collapsed world up against their ruin, to paraphrase T. S. Eliot's line in *The Wasteland* (1922). Swift's popular last words, "I am what I am what I am" reflect existential and epistemological crises of this age. Living in an irrational or inscrutable universe and overwhelmed by forces beyond one's control, how does one decide to live, when even Swift, with all his power, is crushed in the end? In this myth, the tableau of the helpless Swift epitomizes the tragedy of modern man.

In the second new scenario, some twentieth-century authors rescue Swift from his tragic agnosticism or atheism by creating myths in which he affirms his faith at the last minute. (He never published anything that resembled such an affirmation.) While Longford shows Swift's existential collapse, he arranges an eleventh-hour epiphany in which Swift ecstatically apprehends God and repents of his sin of pride. Breaking into the nobility of blank verse, Swift praises his Maker:

> O Thou most beautiful, most great, most pure
> That art unblemish'd in Thy godlike nature
> In Whose calm gaze nought of our foulness shows,
> Whose soaring pinions sweep the stars of the sky,
> Whose white feet cleave the mountains with a flame
> More fierce than all the thunder fires of Heaven!
> To Thee will I lament my sins at the last,
> And doff my pride, my high tumultuous pride,
> That yet could never raise me from the mire
> Wherein I was engendered as the rest. . . .[33]

Like Longford, Bernard Acworth is appalled by the idea that Swift might have died in the agonies of unbelief. To prove that he did not, Acworth scours the third chapter of the *Book of Job*—a text Swift reputedly read on his birthday—and finds the passage "I have heard of Thee by the hearing of the ear: *but now mine eye seeth Thee.* Wherefore I abhor myself, and repent in dust and ashes." Acworth reads this as evidence that Swift had asked God's forgiveness and was confident in the knowledge it had been given— "[T]he Deanery floor was Swift's Damascus road [on which Paul experienced his epiphany]. . . . His last confession to God, like Job's was that he was vile. . . . His perfectly tranquil end, so utterly unlike that which Thackeray imputes to him, is an assurance to one that Swift, outcast in this world, is one of the great ones in the next."[34] These narratives are generated by an ardent desire to rescue Swift from the tragic mistakes of thinking he could be autonomous and of not placing his life in God's hands.[35]

In the third variant of the tragic plot in the twentieth century, Swift does not call on God, but rather nobly endures without Him or any other supports, such as family and friends. He decides to be self-sufficient despite the suffering it will cause. An influential version of this narrative is found in Rossi and Hone's *Swift, or the Egotist* (1934). Aiming to sweep away the "novelized" Swift built up from false reports and overt fictions—a character "out of all human proportions, the life of a madman, and of a strange, perhaps impotent lover of many women, and of a miser"—and to present an authoritative analysis that resolves the paradoxes of "this towering and tragic figure," Hone and Rossi create their own myth. In a chapter called "The Doom," Rossi and Hone argue that Swift chose to live a tragic, isolated life because he could endure no other. Viewing Swift as the prototype of modern man living in an existential void, Rossi and Hone admire his courage. He neither committed suicide nor became insane. Without illusion, he stood and withstood: "In his final egotism he had refused to be covered before death. . . . He would affront death, master death, alone."[36] Similarly, John Middleton Murray is struck by Swift's stoic rejection of the beliefs that make life bearable. Citing Swift's famous epitaph, Murry notes that "It is silent on any Christian hope. . . . Death is not the opening of a gate, but the closing of a wound."[37]

Evelyn Hardy, in *The Conjured Spirit* (1949), uses Rossi and Hone as a foundation, with some added support from Sigmund Freud, to explore the roots of Swift's tragic isolation. She finds them in the early childhood traumas of his father's death and his kidnapping by his nurse:

> Extremely sensitive, inclined to be anxious and melancholy by nature, Swift felt these early disruptions profoundly. They made him apprehensive, suspicious, fearful of committing himself to female care, ignorant of family life, distrustful of his powerful but wavering emotions and therefore of those of others. The fount of love had been dangerously divided and poisoned for him at its source.[38]

Victoria Glendinning also follows Rossi and Hone when she, in summary, suggests that Swift's egotism allowed him to prevail, yet damaged his ability to be fully realized as a human being:

> Swift's walled-in self-centredness hardened, unchecked. Out of this centre poured his polemics, out of this centre his imagination blackly flowered, his ambition grew and was thwarted by the world's rules. . . . Swift does not love himself. But himself—adamantine, *mere*—is all that there is.

In conclusion, Glendinning cites Deane Swift's image of Swift rocking back and forth and repeating, "I am what I am, I am what I am. I am what I am."[39]

In the twentieth century, the Hamlet-like narrative initiated by Swift in "Verses on the Death of Dr. Swift"—that he suffered slings and arrows trying to right social wrongs—is resurrected and joins the other variations of the Swiftian tragedy. In this version, Swift is not insane, weak, or blamable but consciously takes actions that he knows will result in personal tragedy. Instead of accommodating himself to the corruptions of the world, this Swift makes war on it with courage and wears his persecution as a medal of honor. Carl Van Doren portrays Swift in this way: "Swift never waited for tragedy to come to him. He had always run to meet it. He had, dramatic and perverse, insisted upon playing the most tragic parts. . . ."[40] Similarly, W. B. C. Watkins, in *Perilous Balance: The Tragic Genius of Swift, Johnson, and Sterne* (1939), makes the comparison between Swift and Hamlet, saying they both adhere to high principles that prevent them from accepting the immorality of their times:

> [Swift's] problem is identically the problem of Hamlet, though he had no ghost to give him injunctions, no uncle-father to kill.
> Swift's melancholia is the melancholia of Hamlet, and its root is very much the same—a dichotomy of personality expressing itself in an abnormal sensitivity to the disparity between the world as it should be and the world as one sees it.[41]

Frank Stier Goodwin's novelized biography, *Jonathan Swift: Giant in Chains* (1940), explores how Swift's principled belief in social equality caused him to be persecuted in "an intolerant and undemocratic England," an oppression that took its toll on his body and his mind.[42] David Nokes's biography, *Jonathan Swift, A Hypocrite Reversed* (1985) also depicts a Swift tragically unsuited for the hypocritical hierarchical world in which he moved. Nokes suggests that Swift's unwillingness to play the games required of him—or even *seem* to play the games—caused him to conceal his good qualities and "even to put on the semblance of their contraries," provoking Bolingbroke to call him "a hypocrite reversed." Refusing to justify himself or be a hypocrite, he scotched all chances for high positions in the church or state.[43]

Yeats's Swift also suffers because of his high ideals. But unlike the Swifts of Van Doren, Watkins, Goodwin, and Nokes, Yeats's Swift is not oppressed by the governing class but by the growing power of the common folk. Through his gifts of prophecy, he can foresee the revolution that will overthrow the British caste system:

> He foresaw the ruin to come, Democracy, Rousseau, the French Revolution; that is why he hated the common run of men. . . . [T]hat is why he wrote *Gulliver,* that is why he wore out his brain, that is why he felt *saeva indignatio,* that is why he sleeps under the greatest epitaph in history.[44]

The suffering in these narratives does not inspire pity or fear, but, rather, admiration for Swift's epic heroism in refusing to compromise his vision. David Nokes concludes his biography of Swift by making this point:

He left us with the carefully cultivated image of a lonely misanthrope, chiseling his savage indignation on his tombstone, and leaving, as his benefactions to mankind, a privy and a madhouse. Only by acknowledging the ineradicable self-interest that makes each human being his own tempter, tormentor, and judge, can we face up to the challenge of Swift's ironies, and recognize the essential honesty and humanity that made him prefer to seem a monster rather than a hypocrite.[45]

In this rendering of the tragedy, Swift is represented as a secular saint, a martyr to his own integrity. While this version of Swift's tragedy follows the plot he imagined in his "Verses on the Death of Dr. Swift," it is just one of the many plots that focus on the fall of this verbal master into muteness, this powerful man into helplessness. Because knowing how Swift died is crucial to understanding his mysterious life, the tragic tableau of his last days has become a necessary element in any biographical treatment. That search for truth, however, may mask the desire to speak of another unspeakable subject, not sex (as in the romance narratives), but death.

# Chapter Six ∼

# Jestbook Swift:
# The Return of the Repressed

B y the early twentieth century, the narratives of Swift's tangled amours and his tormented death dominated his biography. What got left behind was the image of the comic Swift that had circulated widely in print for one and a half centuries. Some writers argued that Swift had been stripped of the humorous qualities that had made him so famous in his own time, but these protests were ignored or repudiated. In 1927, in a work called *Literary Blasphemies*, Ernest Boyd laments that one could no longer openly relish Swift's love of laughter, manifest in the coarse and silly things he published, and complains that an overemphasis on Swift's epitaph and his final illness had distorted Swift's essential nature.[1] Also taking issue with the prominence of the doomed and dour Swift character, W. D. Taylor, writing in 1933, says,

> [O]ne is inclined to protest that he is after all a humorist, that he provokes us to laughter, not to tears. . . . All that stupendous force of indignant passion which threatens to carry everything headlong before it, comes surging about us as laughter, at times bitter harsh laughter, at times the laughter of him who knows that the game is up.[2]

This chapter recuperates the comic Swift of the jestbooks, widely distributed compendia of laughter-producing material read by all classes of people. In the jestbooks, Swift appears as the author of light verse (most of which he did not write) and as a comic character in humorous or witty anecdotes. Unlike the tragic Swift character, the comic one lacks an inner dimension, is immune to change, and enjoys life. The myths of the comic Swift, like those of the romance and tragic Swifts, grow directly out of Swift's contradictory construction of himself in print.

The reading public of the eighteenth and nineteenth centuries probably knew Swift primarily as a comic character and a comic writer. Swift's first successful publications, *A Tale of a Tub* and his Bickerstaff hoax, both appearing as *jeux d'esprit* without clear corrective aims, created the expectation that he always had a joke up his sleeve. The Whigs libeled Swift as a buffoon and jester, a reputation Swift encouraged with his humorous publications and his facetious self-representations. He caricatured himself in poems like "The Grand Question Debated" (1732), "A Panegyric on the Dean" (1735), and "Verses on the Death of Dr. Swift" (1739) to name a few, and did not protest when works that did him no credit were fathered on him, two of the most popular being *Ars Punica . . . or the Art of Punning* (1719) and *The Wonderful Wonder of Wonders, being an accurate description of . . . mine A-se* (1721). Stories involving Swift's eccentric behavior and his humorous trifles became popular fare in the universally read jestbooks. At least one jestbook uses Swift's name as a come on—*Swift's Jests, or a Compendium of Wit and Humour* (1759).[3] Throughout the British empire, jestbooks were mined by publishers of periodicals for fillers, spreading the material even further. In the eighteenth century, the number of jests about Swift in American newspapers, for example, exceeded those about all other characters.[4]

Jestbooks, published from the time of Caxton to the end of the nineteenth century, are cheaply printed compilations of jokes, anecdotes, riddles, light verse, songs, and other laugh-provoking material. Their titles suggest their tone, content, and audience: *Dr. Merryman; or Nothing but Mirth. Being a poesy of pleasant poems and witty jests* (n.d.); *The Merry Fellow; or Companion: Being the wit's pocketbook and entertaining magazine* (1757); *The Jester's Gimcrack; or Two Pennyworth of Fun. . . . The whole adapted to the capacities of youth, as well as infants six feet high* (1772); *Fun Upon Fun, or the Jolly Fellow's Budget Broke Open* (1797); *Laugh and Grow Fat; or A Cure for Melancholy* (1797); *New Joe Miller; or The Tickler, containing upwards of five hundred good things* (1801); *The New Care-Killer, or Laughing Philosopher's Legacy to Dull Mortals, containing many diverting tales. . . .' Including Dean Swift and the Post Boy* (n.d.);[5] *Fun for the Million or, The Laughing Philosopher consisting of several thousand of the best witticisms, puns, epigrams, humorous stories and witty compositions* (1835).[6] With laughter as their aim, jestbooks were considered underclass reading. The upper-class attitude toward laughter is summed up by Lord Chesterfield, who is repulsed by the "disagreeable noise" and "shocking distortions of the face" it produces. It is, for him, the way "the mob expresses their silly joy, at silly things."[7] In satire, wit and humor could be used to reinforce moral norms, but much of what Swift wrote lacked clear didactic purpose and seemed designed only to amuse, often in a very coarse way. Although Alexander Pope tries to put his friend in the best light by situating him in the tradition of Rabelais, Swift's reputation as an author and subject of jestbook material was a scandal many could not overlook.[8]

Swift, though, recognized the relationship of jestbooks to mythmaking. He has his *Tale of a Tub*-teller choose to immortalize himself and his work by allying it with "those Productions designed for the Pleasure and Delight of Mortal Man; such as *Six-Peny-worth of Wit,* Westminster *Drolleries, Delightful Tales, Compleat Jesters,* and the like; by which the Writers of and for *GRUB-STREET,* have in these latter Ages so nobly triumph'd over Time (PW 1: 39). The *Tale*-teller's mock heroic language celebrates the immortality of the constantly recirculated materials of the jestbook, which remain relatively constant despite the public's addiction to the "newest and the latest" encouraged by the print marketplace. Swift's understanding that jestbooks reflect and shape basic cultural assumptions is also evident in a letter to Lord Bathhurst, in which Swift complains that jestbooks have unfairly created the myth that all Irishmen are Pat and Mike characters—irredeemably stupid, capable only of "bulls" or ignorant blunders. To create a counter myth, Swift tells Bathhurst that "a certain Wag, one of my followers, is collecting materials for a tolerable Volume of English Bulls, in revenge of the reproaches you throw upon us [Irish]. . . . The Author is a great reader of jest books. . . . All of these [materials] are to be gathered, others invented, and many transplanted from here to England. All the Bulls fathered upon names at Length, with their places of abode" (C 3: 411). By describing how he would create an alternative folklore stereotyping the English as dumb, Swift lays bare the process by which myths are made: creating narratives that compel retelling and become familiarized as common knowledge.

Although Swift did not explicitly write jests about himself, he created a public image that encouraged their production, making himself into a comic character that became a jestbook staple. Several jests were published in the *St. James's Evening Post* in 1735.[9] One is entitled "A trick played by Dean Swift on some of his friends which ended unfavorably for himself," which probably is the oft-repeated story of Swift and a group of his friends walking to a nobleman's house, where they were all going to spend the night. Swift decides to walk ahead to secure the best bed, but his friends, realizing his intention, send word ahead to have a servant at the estate tell Swift on his arrival that the nobleman's family is afflicted with smallpox.

> [T]he Dean, who had never had the distemper, alarmed at the news, took up his residence at the end of a garden, where he supped alone, and passed several melancholy hours, while his friends at the mansion were laughing very heartily at his situation. At length taking pity of [*sic*] him, they revealed the jest, and promised that on no future occasion the best bed should deprive them of his company.[10]

Even the biographers of Swift who saw themselves as serious litterateurs were unable to forbear introducing jests into their accounts, perhaps because the public expected them or because the comic dimension of Swift could not be repressed. Interspersed jests oddly interrupt the solemn narrations in the some of the accounts, for the comic Swift does not resemble in the least the tortured lover of Stella or the man who reads the *Book of Job* on his birthday. The eighteenth-century biographies of Swift became a major source of supply for the jestbook compilers.

Swift, protean figure that he is, plays not one comic role, but many. He appears as the joker and the butt of jokes; as a prankster and a witty moralist; a jocular companion of servants and an insensitive master. While Swift's eighteenth-century biographers often claim their humorous anecdotes are eyewitness accounts or reports from reliable sources, it seems strange that (1) few of the anecdotes have any corroboration other than the biographer's say-so; (2) most of them emerge long after Swift dies; and (3) they are patterned on folklore motifs found in classical facetiae and medieval fabliaux.[11] As time goes along, new jests are added to Swiftian trove, some the effect of "Joe Miller's Law," a term coined by James Osborne to describe the phenomenon in which the name of a current celebrity replaces that of a no-longer popular one in an existing jest.[12] Although some critics have argued that the stories mingle fact and fiction, their highly formulaic nature and their merely coincidental parallels to the documented elements of Swift's life suggest that they are almost wholly imaginative, products of a mythopoeic dynamic set in motion by Swift himself. Through repetition, many of the stories about Swift attained the hardness of biographical fact.

Laetitia Pilkington can be credited for making jests a conventional feature of accounts of Swift's life and for creating some of the most popular stories about Swift. These were routinely plagiarized by other biographers and included in many jestbooks. The central narrative of Pilkington's *Memoirs* (1748–52) concerns her alternately humorous and melodramatic sexual adventures, but her tangential stories about Swift proved quite a draw. Swift's appearance in Pilkington's *Memoirs* added to the sense he was beyond the pale, for it connected him in print to a woman who joked about her adultery and was characterized as a harlot in the popular press.[13] Similar to the Swift she depicts, though, Pilkington seems oblivious to the embarrassment she ought to feel and holds the comic mask before her face to keep people guessing, a strategy she predicts will make her immortal: "*That I, like the Classics, shall be read / When Time, and all the World are dead.*" (87). Her prophecy was correct, for her *Memoirs* have never been out of print. In her own century, Pilkington's notoriety was used to market a jestbook entitled *Mrs. Pilkington's Jests: Or the Cabinet of Wit and Humour* (1759).[14] A frontispiece engraving to the second edition shows a satyr leering from behind a

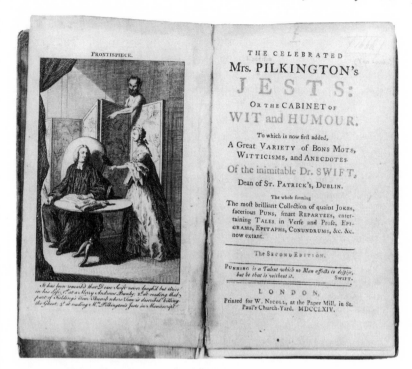

6.1. Frontispiece and title page, *Mrs. Pilkington's Jests* (2nd edition, 1764). Mrs. Pilkington introduced into circulation some of the most popular jests about Swift. They were plagiarized by other biographers and by compilers of jestbooks such as this one. Material from the hundreds of jestbooks was recirculated as fillers in periodicals. Courtesy of the Library of Congress.

screen at Pilkington (who is standing) and Swift (who is seated at a table reading a copy of *Pilkington's Jests*—an impossibility since he had died 14 years before). The caption to the frontispiece reads, "It has been remarked that Dean Swift never laughed but thrice in his life. 1st at a Merry Andrews Pranks [*sic*]; 2nd at reading that part of Fielding's Tom Thumb where Tom is described killing the Ghost; 3rd at reading Mrs. Pilkington's Jests in Manuscript." The frontispiece identifies Swift with popular culture, not only by reinforcing his relationship with Pilkington and her sleazy *Memoirs*, but also by suggesting that he occupied himself by reading chapbooks.

Pilkington's jests about Swift are allied to the medieval fabliaux by their crudity, misogyny, and sensationalism.[15] She constructs a comic Swift in the trickster mode, for she depicts him as a character who "take[s] great delight in deceiving and depriving other people" and in flouting the rules to pursue his selfish pleasures.[16] Pilkington's Swift specializes in aggressively disrupting social gatherings, especially meals. His manners are not elevated by the presence of women. In fact, he seems to go out of his way to humiliate and to offend them. Below are several anecdotes from Pilkington on this theme. When plagiarized in jestbooks, her first person-narration is changed to third person and details are added, omitted, or altered.

> I heard the Dean tell of a Lady, who had given him an Invitation to Dinner: As she heard he was not easily pleased, she had taken a Month to provide for it. When the Time came, every Delicacy which could be purchased, the Lady had prepared, even to Profusion (which you know *Swift* hated). However, the Dean was scarce seated, when she began to make a ceremonious Harangue; in which she told him, that she was sincerely sorry she had not a more tolerable Dinner, since she was apprehensive there was not any thing there fit for him to eat; in short, that it was a bad Dinner: *Pox take you for a B*[itch], said the Dean, *why did you not get a better? Sure you had Time enough! but since you say it is so bad, I'll e'en go Home and eat a Herring.* (284)

> I remember Doctor *Swift* told me, he once dined at a Person's House, where the Part of the Table-Cloth, which was next to him, happened to have a small Hole in it, which says he, I tore as wide as I could; then asked for some Soop, and fed myself through the Hole. . . . The Dean . . . did this to mortify the Lady of the House. (264)

> The last time he was in *London,* he went to dine with the Earl of *Burlington,* who was then but newly married. My Lord being willing, I suppose, to have some Diversion, did not introduce him to his Lady, nor mention his Name: 'Tis to be observed, his Gown was generally very rusty, and his Person no Way extraordinary.—After Dinner, said the Dean, 'Lady *Burlington,* I hear you can sing; sing me a Song.' The Lady looked on this unceremonious manner of asking a Favour with Distaste, and positively refus'd him; he said, she should sing, or he would make her. . . . As the Earl did nothing but laugh at this Freedom; the Lady was so vext that she burst into Tears, and retired.
>     His first Compliment to her when he saw her again, was, 'Pray Madam, are you as proud and as ill-natur'd now, as when I saw you last?' to which she answered with great good Humour,—'No, Mr. Dean, I'll sing for you, if you please.' (38)

> [I] digress to relate a Compliment of his to some Ladies, who supped with him, of which I had the Honour to be One: The Dean was giving us an Account of some Woman, who, he told us, was the nastiest, filthiest, most stinking old Bitch that ever was yet seen, except the Company, Ladies! except the Company! for that you know is but civil. We all bowed, could we do less? (178)

These anecdotes accentuate the image of the pointedly unchivalric Swift that caused an uproar when it appeared in such poems as "The Journal of Part of a Summer" or "The Lady's Dressing Room." Fantasylike, this character can act on his atavistic impulses without pangs of conscience or fear of reprimand.

Recalling the cuckolding scenarios of the fabliaux, Pilkington creates a sexually charged triangle consisting of herself, her husband, and Swift, in which Swift's humiliation of Matthew Pilkington is a source of laughter. For example, Pilkington's Swift brags that he made Matthew drink the dregs, saying, "I always keep some poor Parson to drink the foul Wine for me" (31). In other stories, though, Swift and Matthew gang up on Laetitia. One involves a Christmas gathering at which Swift blackens Laetitia's face with burnt cork, makes her take off her stockings to see whether she has "foul toes," and takes a vote as to what sex she is. Matthew Pilkington declares she is a man, and the rest agree, so they force a tobacco pipe in her mouth "in Spite of [her] Petticoats" (309–10). These cruel jests elicit the laughter Hobbes characterizes as "sudden glorying," when the reader identifies with Swift's domination of others.

In Volume III of the *Memoir*, Laetitia Pilkington is depicted as the particular object of Swift's rough jesting. At one point, however, she (or it might be her son Jack, who published this volume) relates how Swift had agreed to be godfather to her unborn child, but only if it were a boy, saying "[I]f it be a little Bitch I'll never answer for her" (310). According to Pilkington's account, by the time Swift read her note telling him that she gave birth to a son, the little boy had died. Arriving at the Pilkingtons' house unaware of the child's death, he asks, "Where was his God-son elect?"

> I told him in Heaven. The Lord be praised, said he, I thought there was some good News in the way, your Husband look'd so brisk: Pox take me, but I was in Hopes you were dead yourself; but 'tis pretty well as it is, I have sav'd by it, and I should have nothing by you. (315)

Making light of the death of a child and the possible death of its mother (to her face) recalls the grim humor of *A Modest Proposal.* The jest might be read as playful sarcasm, yet the horrific inferences about the nature of the jester cannot be dismissed.

Like the classic trickster, Pilkington's Swift is a shape-shifter, who keeps the reader off-balance by assuming various identities. A sadistic misogynistic man in one story, for example, he appears as a misanthropic woman in another. The incident may actually have occurred, but more likely, Pilkington is building on the reputation Swift acquired from productions like "Mrs. Harris's Petition" or "Mary the Cookmaid's Letter," in which he speaks with a female voice.

> [T]aking up Part of his Gown to fan himself with; and acting in Character of a prudish Lady, he said, "Well, I don't know what to think; Women may be

honest that do such things, but, for my Part, I never could bear to touch any Man's Flesh—except my Husband's, whom perhaps,' says he, 'she wished at the Devil.['] (28)[17]

Role reversal and transvestitism are favorite motifs in the folk and fabliaux tradition, and are still crowd-pleasers.[18] Such narratives confuse gender boundaries and offer a vision of identity free of categorical restraints. Pilkington's Swift seems to have no aversion to assuming the forms of creatures at the lower end of the Great Chain of Being, such as servants, women, or animals. Indeed, Pilkington narrates an account of one party in which Swift and his companions imitate the animal that most "suited their Inclination" (312). An annoying omission in the story is that Pilkington does not tell the reader what animal Swift chose to be. (A horse?)

Many of Pilkington's anecdotes exploit the provocative ambiguities of Swift's attitudes toward the underclass that aroused so much commentary during his lifetime. In some stories, Pilkington's Swift is presented as a moral superior, for instance, when he reproves a beggar with dirty hands, saying, "Water was not so scarce but she might have washed" (28). In another, he sarcastically admonishes the cook (in later versions of the story often named "Sweetheart") who had burned his roast—telling her to take it back and "do it less." After the cook says it is impossible, he chastises her for "committing a Fault which cannot be amended" (28). In these cases, Pilkington's Swift underlines class distinctions, but at other times he effaces them, for example, by playfully addressing "old Beggar-women and Cinder-pickers" as the "Fair Sex" (178).

In Pilkington's story of Swift's Saturnalia, the world is turned upside down in an elaborate episode of clowning that draws its effect from the social taboo of crossing class lines. In this anecdote, Swift proposes that he and his friends switch places with the servants for an evening meal. All goes well until the servant playing the part of Swift imitates Swift's obstreperous behavior as master too exactly and throws his food into Swift's face. In Pilkington's story, Swift immediately steps out of his part and beats the man heartily (280). Although Swift reasserts his class-based authority in this skit, his behavior allies him more with the stereotypical violence of the underclass. The numbers of subsequent jests involving Swift and underlings— with the underlings often triumphing—suggest that the comic Swift may be a way to explore repressed fears about class warfare, anxieties about the validity of social categories, or fantasies about freedom from hierarchical order. Such narratives link Swift to Mikhail Bakhtin's concept of carnival, where, in the spirit of fun, social distinctions are vertiginously blurred, suspended, or inverted, creating a temporary alternative to the rigidity, seriousness, prohibitions, and repressive structures of "official" culture.[19]

While Pilkington offers no judgments about Swift's carnivalesque qualities, Orrery openly deplores them. His *Remarks on the Life of Dr. Swift* (1751) is really an argument about why Orrery himself, by virtue of his dignity, nobility, and erudition, should be more famous than Swift, who made himself the butt of laughter by playing the fool. In an annotation to a copy of his *Remarks,* Orrery makes his position clear:

> The Light in which Dr. Swift's character generally stands, makes him rather appear in the manner of a drol [*sic*] buffoon wit, than of a distinguished eminent writer. His trifling manner in writing and conversing have put him in this disadvantagious situation. Name him, and some ridiculous jest is expected to follow. His Puns and Rebusses are still hoarded up in Cabinets: I mean the few which have escaped Print.
>
> All dignity of character seems lost, partly owing to the low stuff which he has printed, and partly to the want of distinction in the generality of readers. . . . Dignity is far from being his characteristic.[20]

To Orrery, Swift "composing riddles, is like TITIAN painting draught-boards, which must be inexcusable, while there remained a sign-post painter in the world" (83). *Directions to Servants* totally flabbergasts Orrery: "What an intenseness of thought must have been bestowed on the lowest, and most slavish scenes of life? . . . A man of SWIFT'S exalted genius, ought constantly to have soared into higher regions" (180). He concludes that Swift's refusal to write in a way befitting his station might be an early symptom of his final madness. A little too late, Orrery issues the exhortation, "Let him jest with dignity, and let him be ironical on useful subjects" (180–81), indicating that Swift should have asserted his superiority by publishing satires his peers would admire, rather than Grubstreet foolery to amuse the "generality of readers." Educated elites, like Chesterfield and Orrery, are uncomfortable with comic laughter, as opposed to the corrective laughter of satire, because it dissolves rather than reinforces hierarchical distinctions. As George Meredith observes in his *Essay on Comedy,* "[Of] Comedy they have a shivering dread, for Comedy enfolds them with the wretched host of the world, huddles them with us all in an ignoble assimilation, and cannot be used by any exalted variety as a scourge and a broom."[21] Satire presumes the authority of the writer to rid society of folly and vice, while Comedy puts on no such airs.

While Orrery harps on the horror of Swift's disappointed ambitions, his thwarted love life, and his miserable decline, he cannot resist introducing several anecdotes that portray Swift as a joker—a characterization completely at odds with the rest of the account. Orrery's purported rationale for inserting these jests is to emphasize that Swift's lowliness made him incapable of maintaining the decorum that his position as dean required. No doubt the popularity of the anecdotes about Swift in Pilkington's *Memoirs,* published three years before, also inspired Orrery's decision. The following story—which Orrery represents as fact—was widely repeated and sparked a spate of subsequent mythmaking about Swift and Roger, or about Roger by himself.[22]

> When Swift went to his first parish, which was very scantily populated with Church of Ireland communicants, he gave public notice to his parishioners, that he would read prayers on every Wednesday and Friday. Upon the subsequent Wednesday the bell was rung, and the Rector attended in his desk, when after having sat some time, and finding the congregation to consist only of himself, and his clerk Roger, he began with great composure and gravity, but with a turn peculiar to himself, '*Dearly beloved Roger, the scripture moveth you and me in sundry places.*' And then proceeded regularly through the whole service. (20)

Here Orrery's Swift impishly replaces the word "brethren" with "Roger" in the liturgy from the *Book of Common Prayer,* an irreverence to be expected from one associated with *A Tale of a Tub* or *Dean Jonathan's Parody of the Fourth Book of Genesis.*[23] Dodging any suggestion that he might enjoy the story of Swift and Roger, Orrery assures his son (the addressee of the *Remarks*) that he includes it only for didactic purposes: "I mention this trifling [story] only to shew you, that he could not resist a vein of humour whenever he had an opportunity of exerting it" (20).

That a love of clowning makes Orrery's Swift indifferent to the boundary between the sacred and profane is exemplified in another jest Orrery inserts to show Swift's "abhorrence to all kind of reserve: even to discretion. Solemnities and outward forms were despised by him."

> Soon after [Swift] had been made Dean of St. Patrick's, he was loitering one Sunday in the afternoon at the house of Dr. Raymond (with whom he had dined) at *Trim,* a little town near *Dublin,* of which the Doctor was vicar. The bell had rung: the parishioners were assembled, for evening prayers: and Dr. Raymond was preparing to go to the church, which was scarce two hundred yards from his house. "Raymond, said the Dean, I'll lay you a crown I will begin prayers before you this afternoon." "I accept the wager," replied Dr. Raymond: and immediately they both ran as fast as they could towards the church. . . . Swift never slackened his pace, but, running up the isle [*sic*], left Dr. Raymond behind him in the middle of it, and stepping to the reading desk, without putting on a surplice, or opening the prayer-book, began the liturgy in an audible voice . . . long enough to win his wager. (122–3)

In these two anecdotes, Orrery shows Swift acting like a child, who plays when he has serious responsibilities to fulfill.

Orrery's Swift can also act properly superior, like a hero in a comedy of manners, who uses wit to put presumptuous clods in their place. In one story, Swift, while attending a municipal feast in Dublin, becomes annoyed at a drunken squire's attempts at raillery and calls out to the Lord Mayor, *"My Lord, here is one of your bears at my shoulder, he has been worrying me this half hour, I desire you will order him to be taken off"* (146). Orrery's juxtaposition of a farcical Swift with a high-comedy Swift is typical of the early biographies and of the jestbooks that plagiarize from them. Such contradictions and inconsistencies underline the idea that with Swift, the master of surprises, anything is possible and nothing can be ruled out.

No doubt spawned by Orrery's inclusion of Swiftian jests, a pirated and altered edition of the *Remarks*—retitled *Memoirs of the Life and Writing of Swift* (1751)—appeared with a number of new stories.[24] One story builds on the reputation, reinforced by Pilkington, that Swift loved to insult hostesses. In this case, however, the hostess shows him that turnabout is fair play.

> The Dean frequently visited the late PETER LUDLOW, of Arsala, in the County of Meath. Mrs. LUDLOW, was so remarkable for her Prudence and good Understanding, that the Dean, often entertained her with his Poems. Dining together one Day, she helped him with some Beef, and assured him, better could not be got in the Country, 'what Woman,' says the Dean, 'it is full of Maggots;' The Lady instantly replyed, 'I affirm to you, Sir, not so full as your Head.'

Despite the misleading particularity, this jest (and others like it) is almost certainly fictional. Sheridan later reshapes the anecdote by replacing Mrs. Ludlow with a serving "wench," thus fitting the story into the Swift-and-servants jest formula.

Several stories in the pirated *Memoirs* return to the popular theme of Swift's attraction to people and genres of a lower class. In one, Swift asks a gentleman who just sold a large part of his estate how he will be content to live in diminished circumstances. The gentleman resents the implication and pointedly calls attention to Swift's activities as a balladmaker to embarrass him. Another story is introduced by the idea that the "Dean was very fond of talking to mechanics" and involves his learning that *A Tale of a Tub* is the Bible of the Free Masons. Another has Paddy Drogheda, a street hawker, reply to Swift's attempt to silence him, with "Get away raw head and bloody bones. / Here is a boy does not fear you." According to the pirated *Memoirs,* "This was such a turn of humour, (the Dean being the reputed author of that song,) that it did not pass unrewarded." The attribution to Swift of the phrase, "raw head and bloody bones"—in circulation from at least the sixteenth century—adds to the myths citing Swift as the innovator of uncouth diction. (One accusation is that he brought the taboo British epithet *bloody* into the language.) In contrast to these depictions of a Swift who fraternizes with the vulgar sort and speaks their language, other stories in the pirated *Memoirs* create a very different Swift who, as a magisterial figure, polices the boundaries of class. In one tale, Swift punishes a shoemaker locked in his garden by "forgetting" he was there, just as the shoemaker forgot to finish his shoes on time. In another, Swift pretends not to recognize his publisher, George Faulkner, who appears at the door dressed far above his rank.

Patrick Delany makes it his particular goal to discredit Orrery's characterization of Swift as more fit for the jestbooks than the Temple of Worthies. Delany vehemently rejects Orrery's statement that after Swift arrived in Ireland, "his choice of companions . . . shewed him of a very depraved taste." Delany snaps back, reacting to Orrery's slur on his own reputation, "They were men of fortune, scholars, men of parts, men of humour, men of wit, and men of virtue" (96). Unlike Pilkington's Swift, who speaks crudely even in mixed company, Delany's Swift is "remarkably delicate and pure" in his ideas and style, chastising others for not being the same (75). Delany's Swift does not converse with the lower orders, but engages in witty repartee with his peers, which Delany illustrates with a series of erudite jests. One story concerns Swift seeing "a lady wisking about her long train (long trains were then in fashion) [which] swept down a fine fiddle, and broke it. . . . [prompting him to cry,] *Mantua ve miserae nimium vicina cremonae,"* a line from Virgil's ninth eclogue that puns on the place names Mantua and Cremona as also signifying a lady's garment and cremona (a type of violin) respectively. But the cleverness may not be Swift's. Delany has taken a pun ascribed to an anonymous "Dr.————" in Thomas Sheridan's *Ars Punica* (1719) and put it in Swift's mouth.[25]

To defend Swift against Orrery's charge that he wrote only trifles, Delany discusses the excellencies of Swift's Latin poems and the classical antecedents of his puns and riddles. Acknowledging Swift's use of offensive images, Delany justifies it as one of the necessary tools of satirists from ancient times, who as "physicians" to the culture, must use "strong emeticks [and] . . . all the most nauseous, and offensive drugs, and potions, that could be administered" (198). Delany's Swift is an Augustan who uses his verbal talent to correct human folly and vice. One jest features a pert young man who declares to Swift, "You must know, Mr. Dean, that I set up for a wit. Do you so, says the Dean, then take my advice, and sit down again" (219). In another story, Swift reproves the Duke of Wharton (the son of the Earl whom Swift "hated like a Toad") for his wildness, recommending that he "take a frolic to be virtuous; take my word for it, that one will do you more honour than all the other frolicks of your whole life" (216). Although Delany agrees with Orrery that *Gulliver's Travels* was a complete waste of Swift's time and that Swift sometimes published things of questionable taste or value, Delany argues that these lapses prove the rule of Swift's superiority—a superiority that qualifies him as laureate, "the fittest man of his age to be raised to that high station." (A4v).

Delany situates Swift among the most genteel writers of the age, not among mechanics, servants, or artisans. Delany relates, for example, that Swift refused to introduce the poet Thomas Parnell to Lord Oxford, saying that Oxford should introduce himself to Parnell, since "a man of genius was a character superior to that of a Lord in a high station" (29). Another story involves a conversation between Addison and Swift, "each of them . . . remarkably distinguished, for two excellencies: a great fund of true humour, and a fine *English* style." In the anecdote, the two authors argue about who is the most admirable character in the Old Testament. Swift supports Joseph, while Addison supports Jonathan. Suddenly they realize each has chosen characters with the first name of the other (32–3). The linkage of Swift with Addison is a strategic one—Addison was known for his classicism, decorum, and Christian faith. In various other jests, Delany's Swift is a satiric scourge of those who violate Addisonian standards of politeness by acting in ways that are ignorant, unrefined, or immoral.

Although Delany makes a concerted attempt to restore Swift's dignity, he introduces some stories into his biography that have the opposite effect. Supposedly trying to clear Swift of the charge of avarice, for instance, Delany relates incidents that reinforce the image of the comically penurious Swift that began to be popular in the 1720s. One of Delany's most widely circulated anecdotes describes Swift's giving his dinner guests a shilling each to supply their own meal (181). Another joke answers Orrery's charges that Swift had a "seraglio" of gentlewomen who doted upon him. Delany asserts that Swift's real "mistresses" were some beggar women he had befriended: "Some of these we are told . . . he named thus for distinction's sake, and partly for humour; CANCERINA, STUMPA-NYMPHA, PULLAGOWNA, FRITTER-ILLA, FLORA, STUMPANTHA" (133n). Although Delany offers this story as a sign of Swift's compassion, it reinforces Orrery's view that Swift is far too familiar with the underclass.

The next contributor to the Swiftian comic tradition was Swift's Irish publisher, George Faulkner. In his 1762 edition of Swift's *Works,* he elaborates Pilkington's image of Swift dressed up as a servant at the Saturnalia with stories about Swift assuming all sorts of underclass identities. According to Faulkner, as a child Swift roamed with the gypsies.

At other Times he was a Waggoner's Boy, a Boot Catcher, an Ostler, Waiter at a Tavern; would sometimes dress himself like a Weaver, a Shoe-maker and other Journeymen in *London*. . . . But his greatest Desire was to be Footman

to a Lady, for which purpose he would hire Livery Cloaths. . . . He took a
Frolick [once] . . . to borrow Beggar's Cloaths, in which Disguise he went to
a neighboring Farmer's . . . pretending to be very lame and helpless. . . .[26]

The gentleman or prince putting on the garb of persons below his station is
a common motif in folklore. In *Robin Hood's Garland, Being a Compleat History of all the notable and merry exploits perform'd by him and his men* (1719),
for example, one finds ballads entitled "Robin Hood and the Bishop; shewing how Robin went to an old Woman's House and chang'd Cloaths with her
to 'scape from the Bishop" and "Robin Hood and the Beggar: Shewing how
he and the Beggar fought, and changed Cloaths; and How he went a begging in Nottingham."

In his biography published in 1784, Thomas Sheridan, like Delany before
him, professes his desire to show Swift as a high-minded Augustan—"a pattern
of such perfect virtue, as was rarely to be found in the annals of the ancient Republic of Rome" (A1r). This ambition notwithstanding, Sheridan does more to
add to the treasury of farcical Swiftian jests than any author since Laetitia Pilkington.[27] Sheridan integrates (not very smoothly) a few comic stories concerning Swift's behavior as the "Mad Parson" of Button's coffeehouse into his
biography proper, but is at a loss about what to do with the scores of other humorous stories (many drawn from the accounts of Pilkington, Orrery, and Delany) that also he wants to include. His solution is to contain them in a separate
appendix entitled "Various Anecdotes of Swift."[28] This 125-page appendix of
anecdotes testifies to the consumer demand for humorous Swiftiana.[29]

Taken as a whole, Sheridan's *Life* is an odd volume: it is a hagiography
with a jestbook tacked on. Anticipating criticism that his collection of anecdotes is a sideshow, Sheridan argues that Plutarch had demonstrated that
seemingly trivial incidents often reveal the true nature of a person. This begs
the question, What did Sheridan think he was doing in the 282-page biography that precedes the appendix? Similar to justifications of the tabloid
press for publishing photos or information sure to embarrass the celebrities
involved, Sheridan notes,

> There is a wonderful curiosity in mankind to pry into the secret actions of
> men, who have made a distinguished figure in public, as it is from private
> Anecdotes alone that a true estimate can be formed of their real characters,
> since the other may be assumed only to answer the purposes of ambition.
> Even circumstances in themselves trifling, often lead to this, and on that account are registered with care, and read with avidity. (395)

Sheridan realizes that a compendium of Swiftian jests would generate larger
sales for his book, but he cannot say that directly. Rather, he pretends that

their inclusion is necessary to his search for the truth about Swift. Although most are patently fictional, Sheridan vouches for all of the stories: "I shall . . . set down none which I have not good reason to believe authentic; as I received most of them from my father; others from the Dean's intimate friends; and some came within my own knowledge" (396). With some nerve and much hypocrisy, Sheridan sharply differentiates himself from tellers of tall tales: "We see it every day practised, that witty Sayings, Blunders, and things of Humour, are constantly fathered upon the most remarkable Wit, Blunderer, or Humourist of the times, whether they belong to them or not" (455).

In the anecdotes he contributes to Swiftian lore, Sheridan, like Pilkington, favors the trickster pattern. Sheridan's Swift engages in intricately planned humiliations of his victims, which sometimes involve the donning of underclass disguises, a motif introduced by Pilkington and Faulkner. Sheridan's anecdote appendix, for example, begins with a long narrative describing Swift's joke on a college friend named Gibbons, in which Swift dresses up like an impoverished clergyman named Jodrel, and pretends to seek work as an usher. At a meal with Gibbons, Swift/Jodrel displays atrocious manners, holding his plate with both hands and stretching across the table until Gibbons is forced to call him a "dunce" and "even to give him a slap on the wrist with the flat of his knife." Later, Swift metamorphoses back into the Dean "dressed . . . in as high a style as the clerical function will allow; in a paduasoy gown, square velvet cap, &c.," which causes Gibbons much chagrin when he recognizes him (395–99). Following that story is the oft-repeated account of Swift and Dr. Sheridan (the biographer's father) donning rags to attend a beggars' wedding in the neighborhood: Sheridan impersonates a blind fiddler and Swift, his lead man. The next day, they return to the beggars. Sheridan gives back the money they had paid him for fiddling, and Swift lectures them on the need to find employment. In contrast to those showing Swift in disguise, other stories depict Swift taking a moralistic view toward those who do not dress appropriately, for instance, in the anecdote in which he pretends not to recognize the wife of a gentleman farmer who has elaborately adorned herself to receive his visit (405–6). The latter story, of course, is just another version of an earlier anecdote in which Swift reproves George Faulkner for "disguising" himself in high fashion clothes.[30]

Like Pilkington's Swift, Sheridan's is sadistic. Three of Sheridan's most replicated jests show Swift in this mode. One tells of Swift announcing to a mob gathered in front of the Deanery to see a scheduled eclipse that he was going to postpone it until the next day: "The mob upon this notice immediately dispersed; only some, more cunning than the rest, swore they would not lose another afternoon, for that the Dean, who was a very comical fellow, might take it into his head to put off the eclipse again, and so make fools of them a second time" (429). This jest mocks the mob for failing to realize that eclipses are beyond Swift's power to control. The second one shows Swift commanding a maid halfway to her sister's wedding ten miles distant to come back and shut the door properly, just one example of the "whimsical contrivance[s] to punish his servants for any neglect of his orders." To soften Swift's cruelty, Sheridan seems compelled to add "But not to carry the punishment too far, he then permitted her to pursue her journey." Finally, Sheridan tells how Swift agreed to read a man's playscript and eliminate the errors in it. When Swift returns the manuscript, the man is chagrined to see that Swift had blotted out every other line. Sheridan adds, "Nor was it in the power of the unfortunate author to conceal his disgrace, as his friend, from whom I had the story, thought it too good a joke to be lost" (441–3).

Sheridan also provides the pleasure of seeing the trickster tricked or the bully bullied, often by those much lower in social status than he. In one anecdote, Swift asks the way to Market Hill and becomes furious when a local Irishman cannot tell him. Ascertaining that Swift had previously visited Market Hill, the Irishman snorts, "Then what a damned English blockhead are you . . . to find fault with me for not directing you the way to a place where I never had been, when you don't know it yourself, who have been there. . . . [The Irishman's rejoinder provided] no small entertainment of the company; who, however, were not sorry that the Dean had met with his match" (408). In another widely reprinted story, the Dean ridicules an alderman throughout a dinner: "Toward the latter end of the meal, Swift happened to be helped to some roasted duck, and desired to have some apple sauce on the same plate; upon which the Alderman bawled out, 'Mr. Dean, you eat your duck like a goose.' [Applesauce was considered a condiment specifically for goose.] This unexpected sally threw the company into a long continued fit of laughter, and Swift was silent the rest of the day" (430). In a similar vein, Swift reproaches a farmer who gives him directions that fail to prevent him from taking the wrong turn. "'Why,' said Swift, 'did you not tell me I could not miss it?' 'No more you could,' said the farmer, 'if you had not been a fool'" (432).

Delany's Swift offers learned witticisms, but Sheridan's Swift spouts off homey axioms. To a man who has fallen in a slough, Sheridan's Swift says, "The more dirt, the less hurt." Tempted by a peach tree, he says, "Always pull a peach, when it lies in your reach" (432). Swift's reputation for creating "instant" folklore may derive from the sayings cobbled together in the dialogues of *Polite Conversation* or from the playful rhymes interspersed in the *Journal to Stella*.[31] As Sheridan notes, Swift "often used to coin proverbs of that sort, and pass them [off] for old" (432), many of which remain in circulation, as a peek in Bartlett's *Familiar Quotations* reveals. Swift's reputation as a folk philosopher, enhanced by Sheridan, has inspired authors to credit him with witticisms he never uttered or with devising old saws in existence for centuries, like "Necessity is the mother of invention."

Early in the nineteenth century, Swift's lack of seriousness was amplified by Thomas Wilson's two-volume *Swiftiana* (1804), full of little extracts (mostly humorous) drawn from eighteenth-century biographies of Swift, Swift's writing, and unknown sources. The image of Swift as a scapegrace was also emphasized at this time by Dr. John Barrett's publication in 1808 of records concerning Swift's misbehavior while a student at Trinity College, Dublin, where his fines for misconduct far exceeded those of his peers.[32] Around the same time, Sir Walter Scott introduced more comic stories, primarily in the notes to his *Life* (1814). As is his style, Scott offers each with authenticating sources. One features a man recounting how Swift ordered him to eat the stalks of the asparagus ("[I]f you had dined with Dean Swift, . . . you would have obliged to eat your stalks too!") (25–6n). Another "well-attested anecdote, communicated by the late Mr. William Waller of Allanstown, near Kells, to Mr. Theophilus Swift" tells of Waller's meeting with Swift and his servant one day near his father's house. Swift is on horseback reading a book. When asked where they were going, the servant replies, "To Heaven, I believe . . . for my master's praying and I am fasting." Earlier the servant had refused to clean Swift's boots, telling him they would only get dirty again. Swift turned that logic against him by refusing to give him breakfast, since he would only get hungry again (402–3n).

Trifles by Swift, such as "Elegy on Demar," were popular items in the jestbooks, encouraging others to ascribe light verse to him. Typically, the verse is framed in a prefatory story that explains how Swift was prompted into rhyme. Most of the verses attributed to Swift in the jestbooks almost certainly were not written by him and appeared well after his death. Faulkner was accused of including bogus items to swell his volumes, a sin of which many of Swift's editors are guilty. Sir Harold Williams includes 100 pages of these "poems attributed to Swift" in his standard edition of Swift's *Poems,* but this is a mere fraction of the number laid at his feet. Of the most widely circulated poems is one Swift supposedly uttered when he married a couple under a tree during a thunderstorm. Some framing stories locate this event in Lichfield, others at Quilca. In some versions the woman is visibly pregnant. The title varies, but most often it is called "Certificate of Marriage."[33] In it, Swift declaims

> Under an oak, in stormy weather,
> I join'd this rogue and whore together;
> And none but he who rules the thunder
> Can put this whore and rogue asunder.
> (P 3: 1146)

Another favorite is "Grace after Dinner," allegedly uttered by Swift after finally being served dinner by a rich miser with whom he was staying:

> Thanks for this miracle!—this is no less,
> Than to eat manna in the wilderness.
> Where raging hunger reign'd we've found relief,
> And seen that wondrous thing, a piece of beef.
> Here chimneys smoke, that never smoked before,
> And we've all ate, why ere we shall eat no more!
> (P 3: 1146)

George Faulkner is the source of several poems attributed to Swift, one of which Swift purportedly composed after seeing the arms and motto of the city of Waterford covered with filth:

> A Thistle is the *Scottish* Arms,
> Which to the Toucher threatens Harms:
> What are the Arms of *Waterford?*
> That no Man touches—but a T[ur]d.[34]

One of the favorite epigrams attributed to Swift appeared long after his death in *Lloyd's Evening Post* and was reprinted in the *Annual Register* for 1759. The framing story explains that one day after he had lost his senses, Swift was taken out for air and encountered a building he had never seen before. When told it was a magazine for holding gunpowder and rifles to protect the city, Swift composed these verses, "the last he ever wrote."

> Behold! a proof of *Irish* sense!
> Here *Irish* wit is seen!
> When nothing's left, that's worth defence,
> We build a magazine.
> (P 3: 843)

This last bit of apocrypha is so nicely turned that people want to believe that it is Swift's. Some biographers offer it as evidence of Swift's state of mind in his terminal years.

The jestbook Swift also specializes in composing verses for shop and inn signs: For the King's Head and Bell in Dublin—"May the King live long. / Dong, ding, ding dong"; for a barber who also ran a pub, "The Dean took out his pencil and wrote the following couplet. 'Rove not from pole to pole, but step in here / Where nought excels the shaving, but the beer.'" A related specialty is epitaphs. One of the most popular was "Epitaph on Judge Boat." Full of the punning associated with Swift, the final couplet is "Tis needless to describe him fuller, / In short he was an able *sculler*."[35] Because of Swift's reputation for graveyard humor, antiquaries have been fond of crediting epitaphs to him. In a Gloucester historical society newsletter of 1791–2, Ralph Bigland, for example, attributes a verse on Dicky Pearce's headstone to Swift.[36] Subsequently, this item was reprinted by the *Gentleman's Magazine* and incorporated in John Nichols's edition of Swift's works (1801), where it remained in the canon until the twentieth century.[37] One can safely say that Swift wrote none of the items above.

Other humorous ephemera ascribed to Swift include riddles, words on windowpanes, and mock-Latin spoofs. Swift's identity as a riddler probably began when a riddle posed by Delany and answered by Swift was published as a broadside in Dublin in 1726. Faulkner included a number of riddles in his 1746 edition and added more in his 1762 edition. Both erudite and coarse, they were very popular and stimulated others to add to the store. Harold Williams warns that "It is impossible to say which, if any, of these riddles are by Swift" (P 3: 927). One short example is as follows:

> Ever eating, never cloying,
> All devouring, all destroying,
> Never finding full Repast,
> Till I eat the World at last. (Answer: Time)
>
> (P 3: 930).

In his 1735 edition, Faulkner also included four sets of epigrams Swift had supposedly etched on windowpanes with a diamond. The numbers of these doubtful verses multiplied through time. A story in *Swiftiana* (1804) tells of Swift stopping at an inn called the "Three Crosses," which had a very disagreeable landlady whom he felt slighted him. To get revenge, "he took from his pocket a diamond, and wrote on every pane of glass in her bettermost room" a poem inscribed to the landlord: "There hang three crosses at thy door: / Hang up thy wife, and she'll make four."[38] The site of this desecration varies from publication to publication—some say it happened between Dunchurch and Daventry, some say Watling-street in Warwickshire.

Sheridan and Swift enjoyed exchanging tomfoolery in verse and prose. Many of these items were published after their deaths in editions of their works and in biographies. Some of the most reprinted items are their writings in mock Latin, reminiscent of a schoolboy game. One short example is an epigram, first printed by Faulkner in 1746: "Dic heris agro at, an da quarto fine ale, / For a ringat ure nos, and da stringat ure tale" (P 3:1039). [Dick, here is a groat, and a quart of fine ale. / For a ring at your nose, and a string at your tail.] Swift's spoofing inspired others to imitate his silliness. One example comes from *the London Times* (November 19, 1785). Thinking Swift stupid, an officious chaplain asks him to translate a passage in Latin—*Romanos rerum dominos, gentemque togatam.*

> [Swift] began the translation thus: Dominos romanos—*damn all Roman noses;* gentemque togatam—*and all State Chaplains.* Highly gratified with these answers, and expecting further entertainment, the Chaplain asked what he intended to do with the word—rerum. Oh! Says the Dean, that is latin for *rare rum.* This brought peals of laughter. . . .

Throughout the nineteenth and early twentieth centuries, Swiftian anecdotes with headers like "An Anecdote of Dean Swift," Dean Swift's Advice," "Swift's Proverbs," or "A Joke on the Dean" appeared in periodicals published in London and Dublin, including the *London Times, Illustrated London News, John O'London's Weekly, T. P.'s Weekly,* and many more. By the late nineteenth century, jestbooks were supplanted by collections of anecdotes about "English Eccentrics," "British Worthies," "Books and Authors," and "World Celebrities," as well as treasuries of light verse and witticisms.[39] The disappearance of the jestbook was also hastened by the emergence of comic books, a genre that became popular in the first decades of the twentieth century.

In Ireland, Swift stories circulated in the oral tradition (both in English and Gaelic), a phenomenon brought to the attention of modern scholars by Mackie Jarrell, who studied the archive collected by the Irish Folklore Commission in the 1940s. Many of the stories collected by the commission are similar to printed jestbook stories, but whether the oral versions were a source of the printed versions, or vice versa, is impossible to tell. In many cases, Swift is made the subject of traditional Irish jests that previously featured other characters. The comic tales circulating in Ireland often involve "Jack and the Dane [Dean]." They focus on Swift's relationship with his uppity servant, Jack, who usually gets the best of him. Mackie notes that the familiar stories about Swift and servants found in the early biographies and reprinted in English jestbooks—for example, his telling the cook to "do [the roast] less" or calling the maid back to close the door—do not appear in the Folklore Commission archive, suggesting that there was independent myth-making in Ireland.

Some of the oral Irish stories are much more ribald than anything found in the English jestbooks. One Irish jest hinges on a misunderstanding that results when Swift brings a traveler home to dinner. Before they arrive, Jack eats the two ducks prepared for the meal. To save himself a beating, Jack tells the traveler, while Swift has gone to the kitchen to carve the birds, that his master has a room full of testicles and intends to castrate the visitor to add to his collection. The visitor starts running away. When Swift comes back, Jack tells him the visitor has stolen the ducks. Swift runs after the visitor with his carving knife in his hand. "'Give me one of them,' roared the Dean. . . . 'Oh no, oh no,' cried the poor fellow, 'I want the two of them myself'" Another tells of Swift's sending Jack out to find him a woman for the night when they are away from home. Jack brings back a woman who is old, ugly, or deformed. When Swift wakes up and sees his bedmate, he fires Jack. "When Jack is asked why he has been fired, his answer is that the Dean sent him out to get a chicken and he brought him an old hen." Some versions of the story give Swift a wife, who pleads with him to hire Jack back because he couldn't be expected to know anything about fowl. Swift, pleased that Jack has successfully deceived his wife, hires him back and rewards him.[40]

Without the jestbooks and the newspaper fillers derived from the jestbooks, readers in the twentieth century lost contact with the oft-told tales about Swift's humorous adventures, witty rejoinders, and eccentric behavior. As mythmaking about Swift's last days and tortured amours took center stage, the number of imaginative fictions in the comic vein dwindled. An exception proves the rule. In Erica Jong's novel *Fanny* (1986), Swift is shown taking the novel's namesake—a prostitute—to a horse pasture, where he gallops around the field with her riding on him piggyback and naked. His object is to see whether the stallions will mount her. The anecdote is capped by the Dean's words: "A Man in Heat will mate with any Hole that presents itself to his View! . . . But a Horse, a Noble Horse . . . is far more rational than Man!"[41]

Although Swift as a comic character is no longer prominent in popular literature, he still has some reputation as a comic writer, thanks to the continued popularity of *Gulliver's Travels* and to collections of quotations, like Bartlett's. Of the 36 items listed under "Swift" in the 1980 edition, 18 are humorous sayings from *Polite Conversation*. Here are a few:

> -'Tis very warm weather, when one's in bed.
> -An old saying and a true [one], "much drinking, little thinking"
> -'Tis as cheap sitting as standing.
> -I won't quarrel with my bread and butter.
> -May you live all the days of your life.[42]

Large numbers of print-producers refer to books of quotations on a regular basis. Through this mechanism, Swift's witty wisdom is plugged into advertisements, websites, speeches, and other places a chuckle is needed.

At the end of the eighteenth century, English critics and historians attempted to separate Swift from his jestbook reputation and make him a worthy member of the English literary tradition. The effort was not easy, given the plethora of works by and about Swift that violate the moral and aesthetic proprieties expected of great writers. One hundred years later, at the beginning of the twentieth century, George Saintsbury was still having trouble making Swift into an Augustan, an idea that seemed at first to him like "an idle paradox or a wanton absurdity." Saintsbury achieves his goal only by censoring the "anecdotes and gossip" about Swift as well as works like "Mrs. Harris' Petition" and *Directions to Servants* ("mere filth, unrelieved by any naughty *haut goût*.").[43] In the next chapter, I show how the campaign to sanitize and enoble Swift created a character very different from the scandalous Swifts found in the myths governed by the conventions of romance, tragedy, and comedy.

# Chapter Seven ∾

# Taboo to Totem: Swift as Epic Hero

In *The Image: A Guide to Pseudo-Events in America,* Daniel J. Boorstin contrasts the genesis of a "celebrity" with that of a "hero": "The hero is made by folklore, sacred texts, and history books, but the celebrity is the creature of gossip, of public opinion, of magazines, newspapers, and the ephemeral images of movie and television screen. The passage of time, which creates and establishes the hero, destroys the celebrity."[1] In violation of this principle, Swift's fame proves the reverse. The gossip about his life and character continued long after his death, but in tandem, he begins to be hailed as a paragon of virtue, excellence, and heroism. In this mode, while Swift does not exactly resemble Aeneas or Ulysses, he assumes epic functions: as an epitome of national values, as a leader on whom the destiny of nations depends, as an heroic warrior who challenges enemies far larger than he, as an idealist willing to sacrifice and suffer for a higher cause, as a demi-god gifted with prophecy and supernatural powers, as an object of reverence. Some versions of Swift's life accentuate the epic features Raglan associates with the mythic hero: He is "reputed to be the son of a god," vanquishes a "king and/or giant, dragon, or wild beast," becomes a king himself, "prescribes laws," and "has one or more holy sepulchres [*sic*]." The epic Swift often exists not as a bodied character, but as an abstract icon.

Making Swift into an epic hero or icon, though, was troubled, to say the least, by the scandals concerning his love life, madness, coarseness, and apostasy. The solution was to separate Swift from his history, to suppress works that did no credit to his name, or to create new myths. As Bronislaw Malinowski explains, such mythologizing is "an indispensable ingredient of all culture. It is . . . constantly regenerated; every historical change creates its mythology, which, however, is but indirectly related to historical fact. Myth is a constant by-product of living faith, which is in need of miracles; of sociological status, which demands precedent; of moral rule, which requires sanction."[2]

The epic hero plays a role in the determining the destiny of his nation and, as its representative, embodies national virtues. Swift, however, mystified his national origins, which made it difficult for either England or Ireland to claim him without significant provisos. The indeterminacy of Swift's nationhood, though, may add to his mythic aura. Raglan notes that the mythologized figure has an ambiguous birth and crosses borders during his life, when he is "spirited away" as a youth and "reared . . . in a far country," when he returns to reign, and when he "is driven from the throne and city" into exile. After death, he still remains unrooted because "his body is not buried." Like the questions about Swift's faith, his relationships with women, and his sanity, the question of Swift's allegiances generated speculation and mythmaking. While he was born in Ireland and became a popular hero in Ireland for his role as the Drapier, he described Ireland as the "land of slaves," was an Anglican dean hoping for preferment in England, and said at one point he wanted to be buried across the sea from Dublin. Because of the traditional enmity between England and Ireland, Swift's Irish associations tainted him for the English, and his English associations tainted him for the Irish, yet authors from both nations have claimed him as one of their own.

After Swift's death in 1745, his biographers try to sort out his national loyalties. Swift's decision to use chapbook-style pamphlets to organize the populace against Wood's half pence and his self-glorification as a popular hero troubled Lord Orrery, who felt such activities were beneath Swift's dignity and had a destabilizing political effect. In his typically ungenerous interpretation of Swift's motives, Orrery explains that Swift took a leadership role in Ireland because of his failure to be appointed an English bishop and because of his need for adulation. Although Orrery reports that Swift never denied the country of his birth and that "his patriotism was as manifest as his wit" (45), he quotes Swift as saying, "I am not of this vile country, I am an Englishman" (4). Prefaced with doubts about the wisdom of "the lower class of people" and the violent "flux and reflux of popular love and hatred" (45), Orrery says Swift "became the idol of the people. . . . In this state of power, of popular love and admiration, he remained till he lost his senses" (47–8). Quite uncomfortable with what he sees as Swift's demagogic tactics, Orrery ends up praising Swift's "patriotism" in the abstract.

Because London was the center of England's far flung imperial culture, most Anglo-Irish writers wanted fame as English writers. In that light, Orrery commends Swift as one of the "brightest sons of fame among our English authors" (153), but this remark seems out of place given the pages and pages of Orrery's account that condemn Swift's writing. It also begs the question of whether a man who baldly criticized the Crown, the ministry, and the aristocracy of England can really be said to possess English values, an issue that arises later in the century when England begins to write literary histories that chart its epic rise to empire. Always cautious on political issues, Delany in his account (1754) says little about Swift's role in Irish politics, but praises Swift's stewardship of St. Patrick's as well as his superiority as a writer. In doing so, Delany counters Orrery's allegations that Swift's devotion to the church was lukewarm and that his writings were mostly "weeds and sour small-beer" (246). By highlighting Swift's identities as an Anglican Dean and a laureate, Delany implicitly underscores Swift's English virtues.

Deane Swift (1755) was the first biographer to represent Swift in a heroic vein. At the same time he heralds Swift's battle for Irish rights, however, Deane Swift emphasizes that Swift did so as an Englishman with a sense of *noblesse oblige*. Because Swift's father was driven out of his homeland by Cromwell's fanatics, according to Deane Swift, Swift's sole aim and desire was to resettle himself in what he considered his native country: "Sometimes he would declare, that he was not born in *Ireland* at all; and seem to lament his condition, that he should be looked upon as a native of that country, and would insist, that he was stolen from *England* when a child, and brought over to *Ireland* in a band-box" (26). Even though his heart yearned for England, Swift could not let the "errors and the blunders of his deluded countrymen [the English]" go unchallenged (183)—"*Swift*, armed with genius and fired with a zeal for *Liberty and Public Interest,* flew directly to the charge" (185) to protect Ireland. Deane Swift exhorts his fellow citizens not forget the sacrifices Swift made for their country and to heed his lessons, for "the time may come for want of a patriot inspired like *Dr. Swift* to apprize them of their danger, they may be doomed to chains and slavery. . . . Read therefore and imbibe the political principles of *Dr. Swift;* engrave them on the tablet of your hearts; teach them to your children's children . . ." (198). In these passages, Deane Swift echoes the rhetoric in *The Intelligencer* regarding the importance of Swift-as-Drapier in Irish history as a freedom fighter. Of course, in Swiftian mythologies, every thesis has one or more antithesis. While Deane Swift extols Swift's devotion to Ireland, an anonymous pamphlet published in London—*Some Account of the Irish. By the late J. S.* (1753)—characterizes Swift as the quintessential Englishman who sees the Irish as the "Rubbish . . . cast out at this Back-door of Europe."[3]

In *Lives of the Poets* (1781), Samuel Johnson states that when Swift left England in 1714, "much against his will, he commenced Irishman for life." Johnson chronicles Swift's role in rescuing Ireland from very oppressive and predatory measures, but at the same time, alludes to the love of adulation provided by Orrery as Swift's motive for action and his pride in his power over the populace. Johnson introduces the story of Swift being reprimanded for his demagoguery by Archbishop Boulter and replying, "If I had lifted up my finger, they would have torn you to pieces." On the whole, Johnson admires Swift's zeal but is annoyed by Swift's mystification of his national identity: "He was contented to be called an Irishman by the Irish, but would occasionally call himself an Englishman. The question may, without regret, be left in the obscurity in which he delighted to involve it." As for Swift's contribution to English letters, Johnson damns it with faint praise, saying "[T]he peruser of Swift wants little previous knowledge; it will be sufficient that he is acquainted with common words and common things." Of *Gulliver's Travels*, Johnson observes that the book's stunning popularity obscured the fact that it was "written in open defiance of truth and regularity." Like Orrery, Johnson has difficulty viewing Swift as a great literary figure.[4]

Sheridan (1784), like Deane Swift, echoes *The Intelligencer* (written by his father and Swift) and portrays Swift as an Irish hero. Although resolved to stay out of politics once in Ireland, Sheridan's Swift cannot stand idly by and watch the "cruel acts of oppression and injustice under which his country labored." Sheridan reports a conversation in which Swift asks Delany, "'Whether the corruptions and villanies of men in power, did not eat his flesh, and exhaust his spirits? Answered, 'that in truth they did not,' he then asked in a fury why—why—'how can you help it?' how can you avoid it?'" (228) Sheridan emphasizes that Swift loved Ireland, and that Ireland loved him. When Swift dies, Sheridan reports, "[C]itizens gathered from all quarters, and forced their way in crowds into the house, to pay the last tribute of grief to their departed benefactor." Many of them, according to Sheridan, bribed the servants into giving them locks of Swift's hair, "to be handed down as sacred relicks to their posterity" (282).

Despite (or maybe because of) the disparagement of Orrery, Johnson, and other critics, editions of Swift's collected works were in great demand in the last half of the eighteenth century. One title page quotes Lord Chesterfield as saying: "Any one in the three kingdoms who has one book, has Swift."[5] Faulkner in his editions, of course, claims Swift's glory for Ireland by showcasing *The Drapier's Letters* and inserting a frontispiece of Swift, crowned with laurel, accepting the homage of the Irish people from his throne. Henry Jones ("The Bricklayer Poet") and William Dunkin hail Swift as Ireland's Apollo,[6] but both Swift's ambivalences and the English domination of Ireland's culture militated against Swift being exalted in Ireland as an Irish writer. In *Jonathan Swift: The Irish Identity*, Robert Mahony characterizes the Irish attitude toward Swift in the last half of the eighteenth century as "diffident."[7] One sign of that diffidence was that despite many proposals (one spearheaded by George Faulkner), efforts to erect a public monument to Swift all collapsed in failure. In the meantime, on the other side of the Irish Sea, some Englishmen were eager to claim Swift's achievements for their nation.

In the mid-to-late eighteenth century, England became self-conscious about its role as an imperial power responsible for spreading its civilization

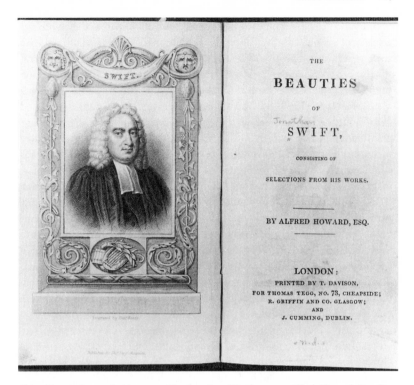

7.1. Frontispiece and title page, *The Beauties of Swift,* comp. Alfred Howard (London: Thomas Tegg, n.d. [ca. 1805]. Collections of beauties, gleanings, specimens, or extracts popularized selected quotations from Swift as part of a canon-building effort to transform him from a scandalous figure into a moral and stylistic exemplar. Bartlett's *Familiar Quotations* and the *Oxford Book of Quotations* (and many other collections) are modern versions of this genre and supply most of the statements attributed to Swift on the Internet. Courtesy of the Library of Congress.

throughout its domain. In order to do so, England had to determine what texts or authors quintessentially represented that civilization. During the same period, underclass and middle-class readers clamored for publications that would provide the knowledge they needed for upward mobility, which included an appreciation of the English literary tradition. With heavy censorship and ingenious rationalization, the name Swift becomes a sign of English Augustanism, an aesthetic characterized by wit, propriety, erudition, and an obligation to uplift manners, morality, and taste. Canonized as an English author, Swift is not an epic hero in the strict sense of the term, but functions as one in that he epitomizes his nation's values and is heralded for his contribution toward making England the pinnacle of civilization.

England's elevation of Swift began with the publication in the eighteenth century of canon-defining collections or dictionaries of national biography, such as Thomas Flloyds's *Biobliotheca Biographica* (1760), Thomas Mortimer's *British Plutarch* (1762), *Biographia Britannica* (1763), John Noorthouck's *Historical and Classical Dictionary* (1776), Samuel Johnson's *Lives of the English Poets* (1779–81) and Robert Anderson's *Works of the British Poets* (1795), among others. Although eighteenth-century literary historians and grammarians tout Swift as an author who occupies one of the "highest niches in the temple of our literature," they are often at a loss to find a specific work that meets their approval. Some of them get around this problem by praising his style in isolation. In a *Short Introduction to English Grammar* (1762), Robert Lowth pronounces Swift to be "one of the most correct, and perhaps our very best prose writer." In *Lectures on Rhetoric and Belles Lettres* (1783), a widely reprinted manual of style—Hugh Blair holds Swift up as the "standard of the strictest Purity and Propriety" in English prose and uses carefully selected excerpts from Swift's writings as examples of perfection.

Popularization of Swift as a great writer was accelerated by the enormous numbers of works designed for classroom instruction and self-improvement that appeared under the titles of *gleanings, beauties, extracts,* or *specimens*.[8] Usually printed without biographies, these books sometimes offer context-less sentences from the English classic authors under useful headings such as "Discretion," "The Benefits of Reading," or "Good Manners," which are among the categories found in Thomas Tegg's edition of *The Beauties of Swift*.[9] Another approach is evident in *A Poetical Dictionary; or the Beauties of the English Poets, Alphabetically Displayed* (1761), which takes short poems from a range of authors and arranges them alphabetically. The Rs contain, *rage, raillery, rain, rainbow,* and so on. Swift's "Description of city shower" is cited under *rain*.[10] In his preface, the editor of *A Poetical Dictionary* explicitly expresses his aim to celebrate the national heritage and to help educate those most in need of learning about it for their own improvement:

> [N]o modern language more happily adapted to express the various and delightful stiles of poetry than the English . . . [N]o nation can boast of greater poetical ornaments. . . . [T]o . . . make the rising generation pay a due tribute to the merits of their countrymen, is one of the ends of this collection . . . by exhibiting, as it were, the essence of her most refined geniuses . . . [T]he editor has kept clear of every quotation that favors in the least of obscenity, immorality, or vice: every quotation tends to enforce a contempt of vice; to paint virtue in her most pleasing colours; to promote the love of liberty, patriotism, and religion. . . .[11]

Shorn of his life, his words carefully excerpted and put in a moral frame, Swift appears without the taint of taboo that made him so popular during his lifetime. Instead, he assumes a new identity as an exemplar of the most refined English values. The gleanings and beauties genre democratized literary knowledge and brought Swift into popular culture in a new guise.

Purified of the scandalous myths about his personal life and his heterodox beliefs, the epic Swift could serve as a moral leader. While still mythologized as the cruel lover of multiple women and a husband who refused openly to claim his wife, Swift is cited in this new context, for example, as an authority on courtship and marriage based on his authorship of *Letter to a Very Young Lady on her Marriage* (1727), a piece in the courtesy tradition of giving advice to mothers, fathers, daughters, sons, wives, and husbands. Before Swift's works started to be mined for their moral instruction, the *Letter* had no market value, but suddenly in the late eighteenth century it began appearing in collections of essays designed for young ladies. One of these collections, *The Lady's Pocket Library* (Philadelphia, 1792), lists Swift's letter in the following company: "Miss [Hannah] More's Essays, Dr. Gregory's Legacy to his Daughters, Lady Pennington's Unfortunate Mother's Advice, Marchioness of Lambert's Advice of a mother to her daughter, Mrs. Chapone's Letter on the Government of the Temper."[12] At the same time the doings of a fleshly Swift are being embellished in biographies, a sanctified Swift becomes a foot soldier in the war against impropriety.

The nineteenth century brought changes to the way Swift was represented in the epic mode in both Ireland and England. In Ireland, Swift's stock as an Irish patriot rose considerably as Irish writers who envisioned their nation encompassing both Protestant and Catholic identities used him as a symbol of unity that transcends sectarianism. Swift's apparent secularism (a liability in other contexts) proved a virtue in the Irish situation where religious division was rife. In 1830, for example, an Irish Catholic, Francis Sylvester Mahony, writing as "Father Prout," salutes Swift as a hero, whose noble deeds on behalf of Ireland will eventually be recognized:

> The long arrears of gratitude to the only true disinterested champion of her people will then be paid—the long-deferred apotheosis of the patriot-divine will then take place—the shamefully-forgotten debt of glory which the lustre of his genius shed around his semi-barbarous countrymen will be deeply and feelingly remembered . . . and due honour will be rendered by a more enlightened age to the keen and scrutinizing philosopher, the scanner of whate'er lies hidden in the folds of the human heart, the prophetic seer of coming things. . . .[13]

During the same period, the staunchly Protestant *Dublin University Magazine* offers a similar view of a Moses-like Swift, leading Ireland to the promised land of peace and prosperity.

[A]ll . . . parties have drank at the same fountain—all are unconsciously ador-
ers at the same altar—all are worshippers of the same divinity—followers of
the beckoning shadows of Swift. . . . [W]hen shall the great spirit of nationality, which the patriot called from the grave, assert its dignity . . . [and bring]
the country safe to grandeur and to happiness. This spirit was evoked by
Swift; he stood like the patriarch in a desert, and with the power that God had
given him, he smote the dry rock. . . .[14]

Both nineteenth-century Catholics and Protestants cite Swift's successful resistance against England as a model for their own battles—Catholics, for full civil
rights and the creation of a more Catholic Ireland; Protestants, for economic
and political equity with England as part of the United Kingdom of Great
Britain or for complete independence as a separate nation. All along, though,
there were those who did not believe that Swift could represent Ireland. Especially for some Catholics, the idea of a Protestant Irishman was an oxymoron,
and besides, many believed Swift was not Irish in lineage, but English.

Ireland could not write its own history while it was controlled by England, for the domination of Ireland is an essential element of the English
epic. Notwithstanding *The Cabinet of Irish Literature* published in Dublin in
1880, there were no focused efforts to recover a "native" literary tradition in
the nineteenth century because as a dependency of England, Ireland was expected to look to London, the center of imperial power, as a beacon of culture. For this reason, Swift's literary lack of "Irishness" was considered a
virtue even in Ireland. W. E. H. Lecky, an Anglo-Irish historian who ab-
horred the idea of home rule for the Irish, commends Swift for "his complete freedom from the characteristic defects of the Irish temperament. His
writings exhibit no rhetoric or bombast, no fallacious images or far-fetched
analogies, no tumid phrases in which the expression hangs loosely and inac-
curately around the meaning."[15]

In England during the meantime, canon-builders were consolidating the
English literary legacy. In the nineteenth century, English literature became a
standard feature of curricula in English-speaking countries, English colonies,
and former English colonies, such as the United States. Grade school and un-
dergraduate students as well as those taking advanced programs in prepara-
tion for careers in teaching or the foreign service were required to pass
examinations about England's literary heritage. The result was an increased
production of biographical dictionaries, literary histories, anthologies, encyclopedias, collections of quotations, manuals of style, and other works for
readers eager to learn what they needed to ensure their success.[16]

Four issues caused problems for Victorians who wanted to make Swift
part of the epic sweep of England's literary history: his birth in Dublin; his
criticism of England and English institutions; his eschewal of Augustan and

"polite" literary standards; and his disreputable life. Thackeray easily deals with the problem of Swift's nativity, arguing that a true Englishman can be born anywhere:

> [Swift] was no more an Irishman than a man born of English parents at Cal-cutta is a Hindoo. Goldsmith was an Irishman and always an Irishman: Steele was an Irishman, and always an Irishman: Swift's heart was English. . . . He never indulges in needless extravagance of rhetoric, lavish epithets, profuse imagery. . . . Dreading ridicule too, as a man of his humour—above all an Englishman in his Humour—certainly would, he is afraid to use the poetical power which he really possesses. . . .[7]

Edmund Gosse supports Thackeray's point, saying Swift had "nothing Irish about him except the accident of being born in Dublin. His father was a Herefordshire man, and his mother was a Leicestershire woman."[18] Case closed. Just as the travels of Aeneas and Ulysses do nothing to alter their tribal identities, so the essentially English Swift is unaffected by his tragic birth and wanderings in the barbarous landscape of Ireland.

Swift's virulent hatred of England and his sympathy with Ireland during the 1720s and 1730s is another inconvenient feature of English narratives that attempt to reclaim him as a paragon of England's values and genius. In what became the standard line in English historiography of the nineteenth century, Swift's expressions of opposition were depicted as neither anti-English nor pro-Irish. The English Swift loathed the Irish as much as any other of his countrymen. The narration in the *Encyclopedia Britannica* (9th edition, 1887) assures the reader that Swift never became an "Irish patriot in the strict sense of the term . . . [H]e was proud of being an Englishman, who had been accidentally 'dropped in Ireland'; he looked upon the indigenous population as conquered savages; but his pride and sense of equity alike re-volted against the stay-at-home Englishmen's contemptuous treatment of their own garrison, and he delighted in finding a point in which the tri-umphant faction [the Whig party] was still vulnerable." In this depiction, Swift's anger is not directly at England but at certain politicians who thwarted his efforts to civilize the "savages" in his outpost of empire.

Only through judicious excerpting and omission could Swift be made to exemplify the refinement of the Queen Anne Period. Victorian textbooks usually include inoffensive sections of his most famous prose works, *Gul-liver's Travels* and *A Tale of a Tub;* his most classically influenced poetry ("Description of Morning," "Baucis and Philomen," "Cadenus and Vanessa," "The Fable of Midas"); and perhaps some acceptable jestbook fa-vorites ("An Elegy on Demar," "Inventory of Goods," "Verses Written in a Lady's Ivory Tablebook"). As John Aikin notes in his *Letters to a Young Lady on a Course of English Poetry* (1804), the Swiftian canon can only be read in a highly selective way, since a "large portion must be left unvisited" because it is "grossly tainted with indelicacies."[19]

During this period, *Gulliver's Travels* continued to instill awe in readers world-wide, who placed it beside the masterpieces of Dante, Cervantes, and Voltaire. A nineteenth-century engraving by J. J. Grandeville (the pseudonym of Jean Ignace Isidore Gérard), frequently used as a frontispiece to editions of *Gulliver's Travels,* emblematizes the universal acclaim for this work. Gulliver (one presumes) holds half the globe over his head and straddles a shrine with Swift's name at the top and Gulliver's at the bottom. Inside the shrine, what looks like a map of the world provides a backdrop to a Houyhnhnm subduing a Yahoo. Kneeling before the enormous shrine is a tiny worshipper (the reader?), offering incense. Even Francis Jeffreys, who had little good to say about Swift, admires the "success, spirit, and originality . . . [of this] celebrated performance."[20] Others commend the book for its moral influence. William Monck Mason, for example, exalts Swift's genius at satisfying the "fastidious taste of the literary adept, and of gratifying, at the same time, the most vulgar or infantine capacity" in order "to instruct the whole race of mankind, [which] was the benevolent purpose of its philanthropic author."[21] Of course, for every Victorian writer who praises *Gulliver's Travels* there are an equal number, in the vein of Thackeray, who condemn it for its nastiness and nihilism. To make this classic acceptable to children and other innocents, it was often printed in heavily bowdlerized form, with the scenes of Gulliver putting out fire in Lilliput and perching on the nipples of the maids-of-honor omitted or altered.[22]

Many nineteenth-century textbooks anthologies and literary histories carry brief biographies that ignore the unsavory lore about Swift's life. Thomas Campbell, editor of *Specimens of the British Poets,* however, omits Swift's life altogether, a move the editor of the second edition applauds heartily, for the following reasons:

> The life of this hateful fellow was one continuous growl of discontent. His loves, if loves they were, a series of shuffles, to be accounted for alone by a charitable supposition [that he was already insane]. . . . He is obscene and outspoken as Lord Rochester, and writes rather in the style of the stews than the pulpit. . . . No one's writings need castration more. This done, and the clergyman and his beastliness forgotten, how indignant and admirable his satire, how pleasant and pointed his humour.[23]

Other textbooks authors rehearse the scandals of Swift's life to warn naive students about what kind of man Swift was. William Francis Collier, in *A History of English Literature* (1880)—designed for classroom use—describes

7.2.   J. J. Grandeville (the pseudonym of Jean Ignace Isidore Gérard), frontispiece to *Gulliver's Travels* (1832). The immediate and persistent worldwide popularity of *Gulliver's Travels* as well as its original and prophetic visions inspired reverence for Swift's power as a writer, which is illustrated by Grandeville's frequently reprinted engraving. Courtesy of the Library of Congress.

Swift as a man "possessed of an evil spirit, which does not quite abandon its wretched prey even when a pall of darkness settles on his ruined mind." Of *Gulliver's Travels,* Collier remarks, "Greatness and wisdom mark every page of the wonderful fiction; but such greatness and wisdom are often the attributes of a fiend." Like other nineteenth century commentators, Collier takes Swift to task for making the women who loved him "victims" of his cruelty, for which God curses him with madness. The entry on Swift in the *Critical Dictionary of English Literature* (1870) references this point, noting that because of Swift's behavior toward Varina, Stella, and Vanessa, many point "the finger of admonition at the cage of the wretched maniac, [and] exclaim, 'Behold an awful monument of the retributive justice of Almighty God!'" *English Literature: an Illustrated Record* (1903), opens its discussion of Swift by describing him as one whose "enthusiasms were negative, and his burning imagination, even when he applied it to religion, revealed not heaven but hell to him." These demonic energies produced that "sinister and uncomparable masterpiece, *Gulliver's Travels.*" In these myths, Swift—like a Byronic hero—is portrayed as great, but not good.[24]

When Swift became an important part of English literary history, the Established Church was proud to own him again, arguing that he was not only great, but good. His pamphlet attacks on Catholics and Presbyterians showed he was a soldier of the (Anglican) cross. His sermons were reprinted, in, for example, *The Churchman Armed Against the Errors of the Times . . . by the Society for the Distribution of Tracts in Defence of the United Church of England and Ireland* (1814). In this vein, an anecdote in material published by the Religious Tract Society characterizes Swift as a righteous warrior: "When Dr. Swift was arguing one day with great coolness, with a gentleman who had become exceedingly warm in the dispute, one of the company asked him how he could keep his temper so well. "'The reason is,' replied the dean, 'I have truth on my side.'"[25] Elbert Hubbard, in *Journeys to the Homes of Good Men and Great* (1895) also commends Swift for his strong defenses of the church. Like other mythologizers, Hubbard puts words in Swift's mouth, quoting him as saying, "I believe in religion—it keeps the masses in check" and "if [religion] is abolished the stability of the Church might be endangered" [!][26] Then, too, Swift is not necessarily always represented as a defender of the Anglican faith. Mackie Jarrell notes a tradition of stories "in and out of Ireland" that Swift was a secret Catholic and secluded himself at the end of his life so that he could practice his religion unmolested.[27]

In the twentieth century, the English view of Swift as a exemplary churchman, great writer, and defender of English values settled into orthodoxy. But in Ireland, the appropriateness of considering Swift an Irish hero or writer became a central issue in the political debates that accompanied the tumultuous transitions from the Irish Union, to the Irish Free State, to the Republic of Ireland, or Eire. Faced with the prospect of exclusion by a Catholic majority who had won their political rights, Protestants mythologized Swift as an icon of Irish liberty that promised to encompass and equally empower both colonial Protestants and native Catholics. W. B. Yeats, in particular, sought to bridge the ancient schisms by conceiving of Irish culture as an amalgam of Celtic and Protestant traditions, whose heroes include Swift, whom Yeats credits with "creat[ing] the political nationality of Ireland." Rejecting the idea that longtime Anglo-Irish citizens could in any way be called English, Yeats asserts that the colonists "soon intermarried with an older stock, and that older stock had intermarried again and again with Gaelic Ireland. . . . Ireland . . . is as much one race as any modern country.[28] In general, Protestant writers acknowledge Swift's negative remarks about Catholics but stress his hatred of English absentee landlords and his desire to benefit all Irish, including the Catholic majority, who, they say, looked on him as a savior. P. S. O'Hegarty, for instance, argues that although Swift was a Church of Ireland man, his desire for Irish independence inspired both Catholic and Protestant leaders alike, "not only Flood and Grattan but every Irish leader after them down to Arthur Griffith. That public opinion that he so magnificently called into being . . . was the same public opinion which O'Connell recreated. . . ."[29]

Militant Catholic nationalists would have none of this myth. Writing mid-century, Daniel Corkery, in "Ourselves and Dean Swift," declares that Swift's having sympathy for the Catholics of Ireland "is just about as wrong as an idea can be," since Swift hated and despised them. Of Swift's presence in the native folklore, Corkery sarcastically notes that "It is true we come on stories about the Dean in the Gaeltacht, comic and scurrilous stories only. . . . [T]hey still bear the marks of having been translated from the English." Corkery cites the tale of the native Irish "wish[ing Swift] a God of their Gaelic Olympus and even imagin[ing] that he was secretly of their faith," snorting, "So are 'correct' ideas of Irish history spread abroad in the world."[30] Referring to Swift as "the enemy" throughout his essay in the *Catholic Bulletin,* Dermot Curtin, writing on the same theme, emphasizes that the glorification of Swift as the Father of Irish Nationalism is another Ascendancy [Protestant Anglo-Irish] tactic to enslave the natives. Real Irishmen should reject Swift and his Anglo-Irish boosters for "these men detest the whole heart of our national and spiritual being: they seek to impose themselves on it as its overlords and judges."[31]

After Irish constitutional issues were settled in 1949, the heated rhetoric died down. Various factions had mythologized Swift as a national figure, but in the last part of the twentieth century it became more of a fact. In this emanation, Swift usually stands for no particular political agenda, but is invoked as an totem of generalized Irish greatness. An exception proves the rule: a paraphrase of Swift's (literally) incendiary statement (in the *Universal Use of Irish Manufacture*), "Burn everything English but their coal," continues to be used as the IRA motto.[32] Notwithstanding, in 1978 a new Irish ten-pound note was issued, featuring a portrait of Swift, behind which is the section of Swift's will that bequeathed money to build a mental hospital in Dublin. Few now would argue that this gift was not a noble gesture. Few now would argue, either, that Swift's international celebrity has not had concrete benefits to the Emerald Isle because of the tourists it draws.

Supposed linkages to Swift have put on the Irish tourist trail a number of places that perhaps function as modern-day equivalents of the shrines typically inspired by mythologized figures, a phenomenon Raglan notes. At any rate, the significance of the sites derives from the myths associated with them, and modern travel guides keep the myths alive in the present. *The Oxford Illustrated Literary Guide to Great Britain and Ireland* (1992) identifies Swift as "Dublin's greatest citizen" and points the traveler to plaques commemorating his birthplace, St. Patrick's Cathedral, and the Deanery, where he suffered from "periods of insanity" at the end of his life. During the time of Vanessa's final illness, Swift took a long trip to the south of Ireland, about which virtually nothing is known. The gap in information has been fertile ground for mythmaking. The *Oxford Guide* quotes Charles Smith's *Present State of the County and City of Cork* (1750) as saying Swift enjoyed sailing up and down the coast of Cork, an activity that inspired his Latin poem "Carberiae Rupes," which "according to the Somerville family records Swift wrote in a ruined tower, known as 'Swift's Tower,' at Castletownshend, a town in which he named one of the houses 'Laputa.'" Although the *Oxford Guide* accurately states that on this southern trip, it "is not certain with whom [Swift] stayed," it asserts, nonetheless, that he spent some time in the rectory of Unionhall ("the original house still stands").[33] By contrast, *Let's Go Ireland* describes Unionhall as "a hangout for Jonathan Swift and family"![34] While the *Oxford Guide* advises tourists to visit Lake Lamor as the site that supposedly inspired Swift to write *Gulliver's Travels*,[35] *Let's Go Ireland* locates the moment of conception at Lough Ennell, now graced by a "Jonathan Swift Park."[36] At Gosford Castle in Markethill (Armagh)—the home of his friends, Sir Arthur and Lady Acheson—tourists can see "Swift's Well," "Swift's Chair," and "Swift's Walk."[37]

The Swiftian romance has endowed a number of places with special meaning. The *Oxford Guide* points out Celbridge Abbey as the place where Vanessa "built a rustic bower" to meet Swift, where Swift came to bid her an angry final farewell, and where she is buried[38]—the first two "facts" almost certainly untrue, and the last, verifiably false. The grounds of the Abbey have been turned into a mini-theme park, complete with cardboard cut-outs of Cadenus and Vanessa and marked trails leading to the spots where they supposedly trysted.[39] Stella-related sites have also generated interest. In her biography of Swift, Sophie Shilleto Smith inserts a picture identified as "Stella's Cottage in Laracor,"[40] a structure that local officials considered restoring in 1963 (according to an article in the *Irish Independent*) and the subject of a brochure published by Thomas Murray in 1991, complete with poems invoking visions of "The winding road that Swift with Stella strolled." A native of Laracor, Murray notes that in those parts, "rumour turned to half truth and half truth became tradition. Everyone it seemed had a story to tell and in the center of it all stood Stella's cottage." There is, however, significant doubt that Stella ever lived in the house.[41]

Despite the efforts of Lady Gregory, W. B. Yeats, and other proponents of the so-called Irish Renaissance to make Swift a key figure in the history of Irish literature, he more often than not has been classified in Ireland as a "classical English writer" or an Ascendancy writer.[42] In recent times, though, there has been a tendency to see some essential "Irishness" uniting all writers who have called Ireland home. In the Spring 1989 *Visitor,* a complimentary magazine published by the Irish Hotel federation and distributed to hotel guests, sums up the Irish literary situation for a general audience:

> In spite of the obvious differences between these groups [the ancient Gaelic writers, the Ascendency writers, and the modern Irish writers of both Gaelic and English], they all show definite marks of Irishness. . . . There is a freshness of invention that comes from the fact that English is always, in a remote but perceptible way, a foreign language. This means that they can look at it from the outside, and their use of it is all the more amusing and incisive for that fact.[43]

The recuperation of Swift as an Irish writer is also evidenced by the publication of *Jonathan Swift: The Man Who Wrote Gulliver* (1990) in the O'Brien Junior Biography Library, a series on Irish history for children.[44] In the book, Swift's battles against England and his confrontation with Bettesworth are described in heroic terms. Across the Atlantic, in 1981 the editors of the MLA *International Bibliography* transplanted Swift from the English to the Irish section, where he now rubs shoulders with Seamus Heaney and Flann O'Brien. Despite these gestures, no consensus exists in Ireland about Swift's identity as a native son. There is still no public monument erected to him, although the new high-speed ferry between Holyhead and Dublin was christened the *Jonathan Swift.*[45]

Unlike the Irish, the English during the twentieth century were not debating Swift's loyalties or the nature of his genius. It was obvious. They were both English. At the beginning of the period, the *Encyclopedia Britannica* (11th edition, 1910–11) observes that as "the author of *Gulliver* he is still read the world over, while in England discipleship to Swift is recognized as one of the surest passports to a prose style. Among those upon whom Swift's influence has been most discernible may be mentioned Chesterfield, Smollet, Cobbett, Hazlitt, Scott, Borrow, Newman, Belloc." At the end of the century, writers looked to Swift for a different reason. In an article entitled "Britain's Writers Embrace the Offbeat," ["Arts Section," *New York Times,* July 5, 1990, C11], Michiko Kakutani explains how "a new generation of British writers has begun to produce ambitious novels that employ a hodgepodge of styles and post-modernist pyrotechnics to tackle the daunting themes of history, time, politics, social change, and art. . . . Sterne and Swift have succeeded Austen and Waugh as models. . . . [T]he results are larger, less organic novels that abandon old-fashioned storytelling for more complicated, self-referential forms. . . ."

Textbook anthologies, literary histories, biographical dictionaries, and encyclopedias published in England in the modern period continued to categorize Swift an Augustan and to emphasize his Englishness. The content of textbook anthologies has remained basically unchanged since the Victorian period, but recently, "The Lady's Dressing Room" has been included in a few collections, with a note to students that Swift's offensive imagery is essential to his satire. Lest the reader worry that Swift's birth and long-term residence Ireland had corrupted his taste, for example, the entry on Swift in *Chambers's Cyclopedia of English Literature* (1903) assures the reader that "his characteristics were not in the slightest degree Irish—in fact, few of the distinguished men of the three kingdoms had been more thoroughly English."[46] The English Swift views the Irish as "the other," possessing qualities antithetical to those of his own tribe. In his *History of English Literature* (1973), Peter Quennell summarizes the point of *A Modest Proposal* as follows: "[Swift's] chief target is the Irish people themselves, whose neglect of reason, decency and Christian precepts had reduced them to their current plight."[47] *The Oxford Anthology of English Literature* (1973) refers to Swift's "long exile" in Ireland, during which he sought "to stir the Irish to self-respect and to resistance against English exploitation," a view that implicitly blames the Irish for their victimhood.[48] The *Concise Dictionary of National Biography: From Earliest Time to 1985* (1992) tells readers that Swift, "though always contemptuous of the Irish, was led, by his personal antipathies to the Whigs to acquire a sense of their unfair dealings with Ireland." *The Illustrated History of English Literature* (1987) states that two of the most important influences on Swift were "his stress on his Englishness despite the way others saw him as Irish [and] his nevertheless increasing outrage at the oppression of Ireland," which, it is implied, is caused not by English malice but by the "workings of the cash nexus."[49]

Michael Foot, former head of the Labour Party, however, dramatizes Swift more concretely as an epic hero doing battle for his nation. Although

Swift's defeat of Wood's half-pence would seem best to exemplify Swift's heroism as a journalist, in *The Pen and the Sword* (1959) Foot chooses to focus on Swift's defeat of the Duke of Marlborough:

> Jonathan Swift has been called 'the prince of journalists.' The Duke of Marlborough is regarded as the greatest of English soldiers. . . . [B]etween September 1710 and Christmas 1711—the paths of these men crossed. The pen and the sword fought a duel. The two foremost figures of Queen Anne's England—at least the two whose genius is most firmly acknowledged centuries later—found themselves matched against one another.[50]

In Foot's narrative, Swift is an English knight fighting on English soil for an English cause, in this case, the defense of the commonweal against the unrestrained power and insatiable greed of Marlborough and the Whigs who propped him up.

In the twentieth century, more Church of England and Ireland clerics stepped forward to embrace Swift as a good Christian soldier of their faith, for example, Sidney Dark in *Five Deans* (1928); Robert Wyse Jackson in *Jonathan Swift, Dean and Pastor* (1939) and *Dean Swift and his Circle* (1945); and A. R. Winnett in *Jonathan Swift, Churchman* (1968). In a review of Winnett's book, Richard Rodino notes the mental gyrations required of the author to excuse "the bad taste of Swift's writings in the name of his 'true Christian piety.'"[51] Storytelling about Swift in his priestly role continued to produce attributions to Swift of Christian sentiments he probably never uttered. In 1922, *The London Times* published a filler about an extremely short sermon Swift purportedly delivered, in which all he said was "He that giveth to the poor lendeth to the Lord." The result, according to the account, was an enormous collection. Strangely, but in keeping with the nature of mythmaking, *The Times* published the same story two days apart, August 24 and August 26. One is identified as a story told to a Mr. James Mulligan by a "farm labourer in Ireland to whom it had been handed down by his ancestors," and the other, as a story told the Rev. J. F. Heyes by his mother, Mary Heyes, "whose father brought it from Dublin."

While much of Swift's epic status is related to the histories that both England and Ireland want to tell about themselves, Swift also became a totem of values that have nothing in particular to do with national identity. In the last ten years, Swift's cultural authority has been magnified because thousands of websites on the Internet use his words—drawn from Bartlett's or other collections of quotations—to bless, to elevate, or to give historical precedence to a wide variety of causes or points of view. In addition, Swift's uncanny prescience about issues and discoveries of the twentieth and twenty-first centuries evokes awe, conferring on him the prophet's mantle. In the aftermath of World War II, R. C. Churchill, for example, expresses his amazement at Swift's uncanny understanding of modern warfare—"[F]rom our aeroplanes [we can see] that the enemy are the most diminutive of Lilliputians, not creatures of flesh and blood and bowels like ourselves; it was 'most amusing', Bruno Mussolini said, to the bombed Abyssinians 'bursting open like a rose.'"[52] A number of articles published in popular magazines over the years marvel at Swift's anticipation of modern scientific developments. A few examples will suffice: In 1919, a letter to *The London Times* applauding Swift's anticipation of the antivivisection movement ("Dean Swift and Dogs"); an article on "Swift's Forecast of Mars' Satellites" in *Sky and Telescope* (1956)); "The Astonishing Prediction in Gulliver's Travels" in *The Mathematics Teacher* (1961).[53] With the baby boomers reaching middle and old age, Swift's depiction of the Struldbruggs seems prophetic and is alluded to, for instance, in "Can—or Should—We Conquer Aging?" (Health Section; *Washington Post,* November 24, 1987). *Gulliver's Travels* also seems to anticipate post-colonial criticism, the animal rights movement, the abortion debate, and many other contemporary phenomena.

Swift's prophetic powers are celebrated in book form by A. L. Rowse, whose *Jonathan Swift, Major Prophet* (1975) hails Swift's condemnation of the Concorde supersonic transport, the Labor party's "Ground-nut Scheme," the Value-Added Tax (VAT), drug use, and computers. Rowse also commends Swift's early realization that "Leftist liberal cant—about the educability of everybody, and everybody being not only but the same, and what not" is misguided.[54] Others credit Swift's foresight in promoting ideas that only in the twentieth century have been accepted as standard practice. A pamphlet prepared for the 250th anniversary of St. Patrick's Hospital eulogizes Swift, its founder, for "anticipating by nearly two centuries the belief that psychological and physical disorders are closely linked." Because Swift seemed to have a visionary grasp of modern economic principles, a headline in *The Irish Press* (June 8, 1932), for example, calls for a return to "Dean Swift's Fourteen Points" as a way out of the Depression, and in the Fall 1992 issue of *History of Political Economy,* Bruce Bartlett heralds Swift as the "Father of Supply-Side Economics" and the inventor of "the Laffer curve" (the centerpiece of Reaganomics), which indicates that higher tariffs do not necessarily produce higher government revenues.[55]

Not only is Swift honored as prophet in the twentieth century, he is cited as an inspiration to those fighting unpopular yet (in their eyes) worthy battles against oppressors of different kinds. Sophie Shilleto Smith characterizes him in these terms:

> A sense of vocation inspired him throughout his life. A feeling that he had duties to perform, greater than the majority, taught him that their small inter-

ests were not for him, that he must enter greater lists. Knowing his danger, fully aware of the risk of failure, he entered the greatest lists that any man can enter. . . .[56]

In the narrative implied by Smith's depiction, Swift is an epic warrior, fighting not for a particular nation, but for truth, justice, or morality against the forces of orthodoxy, convention, and hypocrisy that threaten them. Of course, this is how Swift portrayed himself through the words of the "impartial speaker" in "Verses on the Death of Dr. Swift." Viewed in this perspective, Swift embodies the heroism necessary to upend the corrupt status quo and change the course of history.

For his devastating analyses of economic, political, and social oppression, Swift becomes a favorite text of revolutionaries or would-be revolutionaries. Some Marxists embraced him, for example, because they believed that he shared their hatred of bourgeois ideology. In the preface of an edition of *Gulliver's Travels* published in Moscow during the Stalinist regime, Dimitry Mirsky spells out the relationship between Swift and dialectical materialism, observing that Swift's criticisms of the class system and private property "sapped the foundation of the feudal world and prepared the way for the [French] Revolution." Mirsky notes that while others place Swift in the forefront of progressive thought for inspiring useful critiques of capitalism and religion, his bedrock pessimism is at odds with the utopian world that Marxism promises.[57] On the World Wide Web, an anarchist-socialist website entitled "The Daily Bleed" features Swift's oft-quoted maxim—"Whoever could make two ears of corn, or two blades of grass, to grow upon a spot of ground where only one grew before, would deserve better of mankind, and do more essential service to his country, than the whole race of politicians put together"[58]—presumably as a reproof to capitalists seeking their own profit.

Long after Jonathan Swift died in 1745, "Jonathan Swift," "Dean Swift, Jr." and "Swift Redivivus" continued to publish revolutionary tracts on the "present times" or to inspire others to do so.[59] In an opener to an article on the surreal Florida vote-counting crisis culminating the race between Bush and Gore for the presidency of the United States in 2001, Swift's understanding of the "present times" is invoked—"'Where is Jonathan Swift when we need him?' Mr. [Charles Taylor] fairly bellowed in the Fall Plaza shopping mall parking lot, singling out English literature's classical satirist of human folly as the only commentator qualified for what has been happening to the 2000 election." (Francis X. Clines, "Counting the Vote: The Voices," *New York Times,* November 23, 2000, A41). On the Internet, one website proclaims, "Jonathan Swift resurrected to fix the world and all its problems!" as a come-on for a book called *Swift Solutions* by Carkan Moil.[60]

The lack of explicit evidence about Swift's faith has caused some twentieth-century religious skeptics or nonbelievers to honor him as a hero for his defiant nonconformity. An edition of *Argument Against Abolishing Christianity* is advertised on the Manic Press website with a blurb describing it as a work "showing the absurdity of organized religion." The cover of the book features the words "Abolishing Christianity" and shows an angel spearing a cross. In similar homage, Swift appears on another website containing "The Celebrity Atheist List" because of his sentiment that "We have just enough religion to make us hate but not enough religion to make us love one another."[61] Not surprisingly, Swift can also be found on the opposite side of the religion issue, as a supporter of Christian orthodoxy. The Family Friendly Libraries website suggests *Gulliver's Travels* be read as an antidote to the "religion of witchcraft" promoted by J. K. Rowlings's Harry Potter books, implying that bell, book, candle, and Swift will protect us from the newest forms of Satanism.[62]

The aphorism about "just enough religion to make us hate one another" is popular with groups oppressed by institutional religion, in particular, gays. In her *Just a Mom* (about giving emotional support to a gay child), Betty DeGeneres, mother of actress Ellen DeGeneres (a lesbian who played a lesbian on the American sitcom *Ellen)* uses the quotation in her last chapter, where she touches on religious bigotry.[63] Another Swiftian allusion found on Internet sites advocating acceptance of homosexual unions is a biblical passage attributed to Swift because he quoted it: "What they do in heaven we are ignorant of; what they do not we are told expressly, that they neither marry, nor are given in marriage." Two websites invoking this passage—presumably because it suggests that heterosexual unions are not divinely authorized—are *Love Makes a Family* and *The Uniting Church in Australia, an Inclusive Church.*[64]

In general, Swift's assault on received opinion, especially evident in *Gulliver's Travels,* implies a dissatisfaction with the traditional binaries, especially those concerning gender. Praising "The Perv," a book of short stories dealing with homosexuality by Rabih Alameddine, Greg Burkman (in the online *Seattle Times)* states his admiration for the way, "like Swift and [Lenny] Bruce, the cumulative effect of these stories transcends gay/straight, foreign/domestic and all of these structural limitations of the ways we think."[65] For the same reason, perhaps, *The Quill: Queer Individual Liberty* lists *Gulliver's Travels* in a list of ten "must-reads."[66] Despite his association with misogyny, Swift was cited as one of the "Fathers of Feminism" on a website celebrating Women's History Month in 1996.[67]

Today in popular culture, Swift appears as the epitome of the artist-as-hero, brave enough to do epic battle against the philistines and the self-styled arbiters of morality by expressing the truth as he sees it, regardless of dangers to himself. The work most frequently used as an example of Swift's bravery is *A Modest Proposal.* In an action that received worldwide news coverage in 1984, Peter O'Toole read from *A Modest Proposal* at the reopening of Dublin's Gaiety Theater and prompted a mass walk-out of dignitaries. "O'Toole defends 'disgusting' reading" is the headline from the *Toronto Globe and Mail* (October 28, 1984), which quotes the actor as saying he wanted to capture Swift's "savage indignation" by reading a piece that had "a little something to offend everybody." In 1986, a satiric television show in England called *The Spitting Image* used the strategies of *A Modest Proposal* to lampoon Thatcherite economic policies in a puppet show. In the skit, a Margaret Thatcher puppet declares that the solution to the unemployment problem is for the poor to eat their own children. An article entitled "The Queen May Not be Amused, but Millions Are" reports that this "Swiftian satire was carried to a graphic extreme when the hand of the nationally known television interviewer who was supposed to have been questioning Mrs. Thatcher was placed in a food processor. What happened then—the foam rubber caricature of one of Mrs. Thatcher's closest Cabinet colleagues dutifully poured out a pinkish fluid from the food processor and gulped it down—might have been assumed some kind of acme in tasteless lampooning" (*New York Times,* April 10, 1986, A2).

Controversial pop stars frequently invoke the revered precedents of Jonathan Swift and Lenny Bruce to defend their artistic freedom and to argue that, like good Augustans, the offensive element in their works is necessary to promote moral or social reform. For example, in an interview, comedian/satirist Buddy Cole (featured in *The Kids in the Hall,* a widely rebroadcast Canadian television series) discusses his highest hopes for his latest book: "All I'm looking for in a review is that one word: Swiftian. Then I will be *so* happy. . . . I mean, when Jonathan Swift wrote "A Modest Proposal" about eating the Irish, people wanted to kill him, because people didn't understand. In my career, people have wanted to hurt me. . . . because they mistake content for intent."[68] Praising a rapper—Kool Keith [Thornton]—Alec Hanley Bemis (in the *Miami New Times Online)* cites the precedents of Swift and Bruce, and then asks, "When . . . Swift proposed eating the children of Ireland to alleviate hunger, it was a shocking idea. So why, at the end of the Twentieth Century, when Keith's Dr. Doom persona resorts to cannibalism to rid the world of bad rappers, are people still a little taken aback?"[69] Using a similar strategy, Nick Gillespie (in *ReasonOnline),* disputes Linda Chavez's declaration in *USA Today* that Howard Stern, the notorious New York talk show host, "is no satirist, [no] latter-day Jonathan Swift making 'a modest proposal.'" Gillespie retorts that "Stern *is* indeed a latter-day Jonathan Swift—and not just because he is nasty, crude and scatological. . . . Stern's search-and-destroy highjinks puncture the pretensions of all manner of fakes and phonies. . . . [He is] a national treasure."[70]

Hardly a week goes by without seeing in print or on the Internet "A Modest Proposal for _____," or some other reference to the work. The prominence of *A Modest Proposal* in popular culture may be a result of its predictable inclusion in readers for high school and university students. In Fall 2001, the AltaVista search engine pulled up 15,000 hits for *A Modest Proposal,* 2,000 of which make specific reference to Swift. Many of these references, no doubt, occur on syllabi. One, however, was an advertisement for a comic book version of *Modest Proposal* from the Tome Press, illustrated by Phillip ("Swamp Thing") Hester.[71] Whether the popularity of *A Modest Proposal* derives from its ironic advocacy of humane treatment for the Irish or for its hair-raising representation of cannibalism is difficult to gauge. Hester's cover design for the Tome Press edition shows Swift lifting the lid off of a stew pot with skulls and bones in the background.

In an influential essay called "The Excremental Vision," Norman O. Brown commends Swift for ignoring the *cordon sanitaire* surrounding the issue of excrement. In doing so, Swift, in Brown's eyes, works like the psychotherapist, who makes his patients healthy by forcing them to face their repressed thoughts. In Swift's case, the patient is modern civilization.[72] Others credit Swift for speaking openly not only about excrement, but also about sex. On a website entitled *So you want to be a writer?,* an article by Ray Girvan surveys the market for erotica, noting that the boundary between pornography and literary fiction has become very porous, a line Swift breached well before it became acceptable to do so.[73] Swift's frank treatments of taboo subjects are not as shocking as they used to be, with the slippage in aesthetic decorum at the end of the twentieth century that allows the f-word, excretion, sex (both hetero- and homosexual)—and recently, scenes of people on the toilet—to appear in Hollywood movies and television shows. The lapse in genteel standards of taste permitted viewers of a 1995 NBC miniseries production of *Gulliver's Travels* (starring Ted Danson) to see Gulliver's urination on the Lilliputian castle as well as his "rape" by a naked female Yahoo. The time has not yet come, however, when Swift's works do not have the power to shock and to amaze.

With the rapid deconstruction of the nineteenth-century literary canon, in the twenty-first century fewer and fewer people may be exposed to print-published works of Jonathan Swift in school. No doubt, though, *Gulliver's Travels,* now available in multiple video versions as well as many inexpensive paper editions, will remain familiar to future generations, as will the blood-curdling premise of *A Modest Proposal,* which promises to remain a fixture in textbook anthologies. An abstractly epic Swift has now supplanted the romance, tragic, and comic Swifts in popular culture, largely through the expansion of the Internet, where his gnomic pronouncements in Bartlett's and other collections, are used to give authority to a bewildering variety of causes. Neil Postman—author of many books critical of the fragmenting effects of modern electronic media—calls for a return to the ordered, rational world of the eighteenth-century epitomized by—among others—Jonathan Swift.[74] In that context, the authoritative axioms of Jonathan Swift provide an anchor of common sense, until one realizes they are invoked by warring tribes to equal effect.

Swift's current body-lessness has much to do with the rise of his identity as an abstract icon or a name to conjure with and the decline of narratives featuring him as a rounded character. That decline started with television's rise to dominance circa 1960, when the faces, figures, and voices of celebrities (singers, film stars, athletes, television personalities) provided the main impetus to modern mythmaking. If, however, the tales of the love triangle, the fall into madness, the humorous tricks, or the epic battles were appropriated by Hollywood or the television studios, Swift might come alive again as a folkloric figure. With that in mind, I am thinking that my next project might be a screenplay.

# Notes

## Introduction, pp. 1–11

1. Maurice Johnson describes this process in his analysis of the oft-repeated story of Dryden dashing Swift's literary hopes by telling him, "Cousin Swift, you will never become a poet." "A Literary Chestnut: Dryden's 'Cousin Swift,'" *PMLA* 62 (1952), 814–27.

2. Ronald Paulson defines phenomena in popular culture as those that become "part of the consciousness of the learned or educated as well as of the uneducated; read or seen or talked about by so many people that we can say they were taken for granted as part of the environment." *Popular and Polite Art in the Age of Hogarth and Fielding* (Notre Dame, IN; London: University of Notre Dame Press, 1979), x. Paulson avoids the errors of assuming that popular literature is the product of the semiliterate or the illiterate, that it is necessarily subversive, or that it has "primitive" features.

3. Instead of typographically differentiating Swift (the man, the facts of whose life have been established by scholarly research) from "Swift" (the media-projected alter ego or namesake), I use Swift for both. Identifying the media construct with quotation marks would create a very cluttered text and, besides, the distinction between the two Swifts is clear from the syntax.

4. I benefited from the discussion of notoriety, history, and fame by Linda Charnes, *Notorious Identity: Materializing the Subject in Shakespeare* (Cambridge, MA, and London: Harvard University Press, 1993).

5. Daniel Boorstin makes a distinction between celebrity, which he identifies with ephemeral prominence given to essentially unworthy persons, and fame, which memorializes the worthy. I, however, use *fame, renown,* and *celebrity* synonymously, a more standard practice. Daniel Boorstin, *The Image: A Guide to Pseudo-Events in America* (New York: Vintage Books, 1961; rpt. 1992), 57. With an emphasis different from mine, Alan Chalmers discusses Swift's consuming interest in fame and posterity in *Jonathan Swift and the Burden of the Future* (Newark, DE: University of Delaware, 1995).

6. Lawrence Klein, *Shaftesbury and the Culture of Politeness: Moral Discourse and Cultural Politics in Early Eighteenth-Century England* (Cambridge: Cambridge University Press, 1994), 4–8.

7. E. S. Turner's *Unholy Pursuits: The Wayward Parsons of Grub Street* (Lewes, Sussex, England: Book Guild, 1998) recounts the careers of eighteenth– and nineteenth-century Anglican clergymen, whose inappropriate publications led some of them to the gibbet.

8. Laetitia Pilkington claims that Swift gave himself this title. *The Memoirs of Mrs. Laetitia Pilkington,* ed. A. C. Elias, 2 vols. (Athens: University of Georgia Press, 1997), 1: 35. Further citations to this work will be included parenthetically in my text.

9. John Boyle, Earl of Orrery, *Remarks on the Life and Writings of Dr. Jonathan Swift* (London, 1751), 21. My citations come from the 2nd London edition (corrected), published in 1752. Further citations to this work will be included parenthetically in my text.

10. Thomas Sheridan, *The Life of the Rev. Dr. Jonathan Swift, Dean of St. Patrick's, Dublin* (London, 1784), A2r. Further citations to this work will be included parenthetically in my text.

11. Virgil, *Aeneid,* John Dryden, trans., Howard Clarke, ed. (University Park: Pennsylvania University Press, 1989), 93, Book 4, line 271.

12. Bartholomew Gill, *The Death of an Ardent Bibliophile* (New York: William Morrow, 1995), 187–8.

13. Irvin Ehrenpreis, *Swift: The Man, His Work, and the Age,* 3 vols. (London: Methuen, 1962–83), 1: ix. My debt to Ehrenpreis is profound and pervasive. I have depended on him for the facts of Swift's life.

14. I am indebted for much of my understanding of print culture to Elizabeth Eisenstein's work, especially *The Printing Press as an Agent of Change: Communications and Cultural Transformations in Early Modern Europe,* 2 vols. (Cambridge, UK: Cambridge University Press, 1979).

15. Lord Raglan, FitzRoy Richard Somerset, Baron, *The Hero: A Study in Tradition, Myth, and Drama* (London: Methuen, 1936), 179–84.

16. Ibid., 189.

17. The *Dictionary of National Biography* (*DNB*) denies that Robin Hood was a living person and notes that multiple candidates have been put forth as the prototype for his character. Other sources offer evidence that Robin Hood was an actual person. In *Robin Hood: An Anthology of Scholarship and Criticism,* ed. Stephen Knight (Cambridge, UK: D. S. Brewer, 1999), see W. F. Prideaux, "Who was Robin Hood?," 51–58; R. H. Hilton, "The Origins of Robin Hood," 197–210; and "The Birth and Setting of the Ballads of Robin Hood," 233–56. In *Robin Hood in Popular Culture: Violence, Transgression, and Justice,* ed. Thomas Hahn (Cambridge: D. S. Brewer, 2000), see essays by R. B. Dobson, "Robin Hood: The Genesis of a Popular Hero," 61–78 and Stephen Knight, "Which Way to the Forest? Directions in Robin Hood Studies," 111–28.

18. Victoria Glendinning, *Jonathan Swift: A Portrait* (New York: Henry Holt, 1998), 3–4.

19. Because these mythologized names have become part of popular culture, I will use them to designate the two women in my discussion. Swift is re-

sponsible for coining the name Vanessa, a portmanteau word combining syllables from each of Esther Vanhomrigh's two names.

20. I take this phrase from the title of Susan Stewart's *Crimes of Writing: Problems in the Containment of Representation* (Durham, NC: Duke University Press, 1994).

21. John B. Vickery, *Myths and Texts: Strategies of Incorporation and Displacement* (Baton Rouge, LA: Louisiana State University Press, 1983), pp. 173–4.

22. Roland Barthes, *The Pleasure of the Text,* trans. Richard Miller with a note on the text by Richard Howard (New York: Hill and Wang, 1975), 20–1; and Roland Barthes, *Mythologies,* trans. Annette Lavers (New York: Hill and Wang, 1995), 117–19.

23. John Dunton, *The Life and Errors of John Dunton* (London, 1704), 388.

24. Andy Warhol, *The Philosophy of Andy Warhol* (San Diego, CA: Harcourt Brace, Jovanich, 1975) quoted by Charnes, *Notorious Identity,* 48.

25. S. Elizabeth Bird, *For Enquiring Minds: A Cultural Study of Supermarket Tabloids* (Knoxville: University of Tennessee Press, 1992), 39.

26. Thomas Brown, "Letters to Ladies and Gentlemen," in *The Works of Mr. Thomas Brown, in Prose and Verse,* 4 vols. (London: Printed for S. Briscoe, 1707), 3: 99–100.

27. The following works offer useful discussions of the process by which narratives such as rumor and myth are generated and shaped. Elizabeth Bird, *For Enquiring Minds,* op. cit.; Frederick Koenig, *Rumor in the Marketplace: The Social Psychology of Commercial Hearsay* (Dover, MA: Auburn House, 1985), 19–20; Linda Dégh, Chapter 1 "The Variant and the Folklorization Process in the Basic Forms of Narration," *American Folklore in the Mass Media* (Bloomington: University of Indiana Press, 1994, 12–33; Hayden White, *The Content of the Form: Narrative Discourse and Historical Representation* (Baltimore, MD: Johns Hopkins University Press, 1987); Gordon Allport and Leo Postman, Chapter 8, "The Basic Patterns of Distortion," *The Psychology of Rumor* (New York: Holt, 1947), 134–99.

28. Leo Braudy, *The Frenzy of Renown: The History of Fame* (New York: Oxford University Press, 1986), 15.

## Chapter One, pp. 13–40

1. Many scholars have identified the 1690s as a turning point in English literary culture. For Harold Love, it was a transition from an aristocratic scribal culture to a democratic print culture (*Scribal Publication in England* [Oxford: Clarendon Press, 1993]); for Jürgen Habermas, it marked the emergence of a "public sphere" created by print and coffeehouses (*The Structural Transformation of the Public Sphere: An Inquiry into a Category of Bourgeois Society,* trans. Thomas Burger with Frederick Lawrence [Cambridge, MA: MIT University Press,1989]); for Frank Ellis, it was the beginning of public opinion as a political force ("Introduction," *A Discourse of the Contests and Dissensions,* ed. Frank Ellis [Oxford: Clarendon University Press, 1967]); for Brean Hammond, it was marked by the growth of

professional writing driven by market forces (*Professional Imaginative Writing in England, 1670–1740: Hackney for Break* [Oxford: Clarendon Press, 1997]); for Terry Belanger, it was the point at which print became a significant part of most people's lives and England could be called a "well developed print culture" ("Publishers and Writers in Eighteenth-Century England," in *Books and their Readers in Eighteenth-Century England,* ed. Isabel Rivers [New York: Leicester University Press/St. Martin's Press, 1982, 6]); for Peter Stallybrass and Allon White, it was when "high culture" began to define itself in opposition to the gross energies of the popular fair, and by implication, popular literature (*The Politics and Poetics of Transgression* [Ithaca, NY: Cornell University Press, 1986]); for Lawrence Klein it was when the ideology of "politeness" emerged in response to the collapse of traditional hierarchies and institutions (*Shaftesbury and the Culture of Politeness: Moral Discourse and Cultural Politics in Early Eighteenth Century England*); and for J. Paul Hunter, it was a time when the tastes of the young, urban, ambitious, mobile, and outward looking middle class altered the modes of literary production by demanding publications full of news and novelty in accessible styles (*Before Novels: The Cultural Contexts of Eighteenth-Century Fiction* [New York: Norton, 1990]).

2. Hammond, *Hackney,* 8. See also Stephen Zwicker, "Representing the Revolution: Politics and High Culture in 1689," in *The Revolution of 1688–89: Changing Perspectives,* ed. Lois Schwoerer (Cambridge, UK Cambridge University Press, 1992), 165–83.

3. Richard Helgerson, *Self-crowned Laureates: Spenser, Jonson, Milton, and the Literary System* (Berkeley: University of California Press, 1983), 282.

4. Elizabeth Eisenstein discusses "The Republic of Letters" as a product of print culture. *Printing Press,* 1: 36–40.

5. [John Dunton], *The Visions of the Soul, before it comes into the Body. In several Dialogues, Written by a Member of the Athenian Society* (London: for John Dunton, 1692), A2v.

6. Eisenstein discusses "amplification and reinforcement" as a feature print culture. It is another way to term mythopoesis in print culture. *Printing Press* 1: 26–36.

7. John Dunton brags in his autobiography that Sir William was "pleased to honour me with frequent Letters and Questions, very curious and uncommon." *Life and Errors,* 193.

8. Tom Brown, *The London Mercury* (London, 1692), quoted by Gilbert McEwen, *The Oracle of the Coffee House: John Dunton's Athenian Mercury,* (San Marino, CA: The Huntington Library, 1972), 37.

9. [Elkannah Settle], *New Athenian Comedy* (London, 1693).

10. Swift writes his cousin Thomas about how when he reads over the ode, "I am Cowley to my self" (C 1: 9). Perhaps Swift hoped that his "Ode to the Athenian Society" would become as famous as Cowley's "Ode to the Royal Society."

11. Until recently, there was no evidence that Swift's "Ode to the King" actually had been printed in 1691, and doubt whether the one published by Samuel Fair-

brother in 1735 was actually Swift's lost ode. At the Fourth Münster Symposium on Jonathan Swift in June 2000, James Woolley, in a paper entitled "Swift's First Published Poem: 'Ode to the King,'" convincingly argued that the "Ode to the King on his Irish Expedition" (Dublin, 1691) (ESTC # 181173) held by the Derry and Raphoe Diocesan Library, was written by Swift.

12. Swift was busy writing other odes during this time, but these were not published until after his death. Some of them—the ones about Sir William Temple—may have circulated in manuscript in the Moor Park household. A. C. Elias, *Swift at Moor Park* (Philadelphia: University of Pennsylvania Press, 1982), 77–94.

13. I presume that Swift was going to attach his name to this poem, as he had done in the "Ode to the Athenian Society", and as he intended to do in his unfinished "Ode to Sancroft," so that one would equate the "I" in the poem with Swift.

14. [Sir William Temple], *Letters Written by Sir W. Temple, Bart.*, 2 vols. "Published by Jonathan Swift Domestick Chaplain to his Excellency the Earl of Berkeley (London, 1700 [1699]); *Miscellanea. The Third Part*, "Published by Jonathan Swift, A.M. Prebendary of St. Patrick's, Dublin" (London, 1701).

15. I discuss these early abortive measures in "The Birth of 'Swift,'" *Reading Swift: Papers from the Second Münster Symposium on Jonathan Swift* (Munich: Wilhelm Fink, 1993), 11–24.

16. *The Source of our Present Fears Discover'd* (London, 1703), in Ellis, *Contests*, Appendix B, 229.

17. Herbert Davis, "Introduction," PW 1: xx.

18. For an excellent overview of the issues involved in the debate and a summary of the scholarship relating to Swift, see Joseph Levine, *The Battle of the Books: History and Literature in the Augustan Age* (Ithaca, NY and London: Cornell University Press, 1991).

19. I discuss these ideas in more detail in "Swift's *Battle of the Books:* Fame in the Modern Age," in the *Proceedings of the Third Münster Symposium on Jonathan Swift*, eds. Hermann Real and Helgard Stöver-Leidig (Munich: Wilhelm Fink, 1998), 91–100.

20. Although Antoine Furetière (*Nouvelle Allegorique, ou Histoire des Derniers Troubles arrivez au Royaume d'Éloquence* [Paris, 1658] and Francois Callières, *Histoire Poëtique de la guerre nouvellement declarée entre les Anciens et les Modernes* [Paris, 1688] had previously dramatized the "battle of the books," neither placed the field of combat in a library.

21. Alvin Kernan, *Printing Technology, Letters, and Samuel Johnson* (Princeton, NJ: Princeton University Press, 1987), 249–58, discusses the ideological stakes in library reorganization, a phenomenon directly related to the determination of "the canon." Indeed, our current canon wars have been called "The Battle of the Books."

22. Gabriel Naudeus [Naudé], *Instructions Concerning Erecting of a Library* (1627), trans. John Evelyn (1661) facsimile rpt. (Cambridge, MA: Houghton, Mifflin, and Co, 1903). Bentley was a member of the Royal

Society, which published Naudé's book, and a friend of John Evelyn, the book's translator. See also my "Swift's Battle of the Books," op. cit.

23. Ibid., 94.

24. See Sharon Achinstein, "The Politics of Babel in the English Revolution," in *Pamphlet Wars: Prose in the English Revolution,* ed. James Holstun (London: Frank Cass, 1992), 14–44.

25. John Hawkesworth, in a note to his edition of the *Tale* (London, 1755), glosses this passage as follows: "By calling this disorderly rout *calones* the author points both his satyr and contempt against all sorts of mercenary scriblers, who write as they are commanded by the leaders and patrons of sedition, faction, corruption, and every evil work: they are stiled *calones* because they are the meanest and most despicable of all writers, as the *calones,* whether belonging to the army or private families, were the meanest of all slaves or servants whatsoever." Quoted in Jonathan Swift, *A Tale of a Tub: to which is added The Battle of the Books and the Mechanical Operation of the Spirit,* eds. A. C. Guthkelch and D. Nichol Smith, 2nd edition (Oxford: Clarendon Press, 1958), 238n.

26. Northrop Frye, *The Secular Scripture: A Study of the Structure of Romance* (Cambridge, MA: Harvard University Press, 1976), 25.

27. For further discussion of this idea, see Remy Saisselin, "Imaginary Libraries in the Eighteenth Century" in *Studies on Voltaire and the Eighteenth Century,* 311 (1993), 115–41.

28. Harold Bloom analyzes the way new writers clear a space for themselves by "killing" their literary fathers. *The Anxiety of Influence: A Theory of Poetry* (New York: Oxford University Press, 1973).

29. I am grateful to Jayne Elizabeth Lewis's "Swift's Aesop / Bentley's Aesop: The Modern Body and the Figures of Antiquity," *The Eighteenth Century* 32:2 (1991), 99–118 for focusing my attention on the options in print culture Aesop offered Swift.

30. Ibid., 106.

31. For further discussion of Aesop's legacy, see Ben Edwin Perry, *Studies in the Text History of the Life and Fables of Aesop* (Haverford, PA: American Philological Association, 1936). The online English Short Title Catalog (ESTC) lists 17 eighteenth-century editions with a life of Aesop appended.

32. Roger L'Estrange, *Fables of Aesop and Other Eminent Mythologists* (London, 1692), A1r, quoted in Annabel Patterson, *Fables of Power: Aesopian Writing and Political History,* Durham, NC: Duke University Press, 1991), 17

33. One of the books directly behind the figure of Swift in Jervas's portrait is that of Aesop. Swift alludes to Aesop on multiple occasions and shares with him an appreciation of the similarities between man and animal, for example, in the poem, "The Beast's Confession."

34. [John Dunton], *Miscellaneous Letters, Giving an Account of the Works of the Learned* (London, 1699), 157–67 quoted in Levine, *Battle of the Books,* 83.

35. Phillip Harth, *Swift and Anglican Rationalism* (Chicago: University of Chicago Press, 1961), 154.

36. Ehrenpreis, *Swift*, 1: 242.

37. Lawrence Lipking, *The Life of the Poet: Beginning and Ending Poetic Careers* (Chicago: University of Illinois Press, 1981), 19.

38. David Hall, in "The World of Print and Collective Mentality in Seventeenth-Century New England" (*Cultures of Print: Essays in the History of the Book* [Amherst: University of Massachusetts Press, 1996]), characterizes this kind of reading as "intensive" reading, in contrast to "extensive" reading that satisfies a demand for novelty.

39. The myth that cheaply printed books, such as chapbooks, were underclass reading has been thoroughly debunked by scholarship, such as Margaret Spufford's *Small Books and Pleasant Histories: Popular Fiction and it Readership in Seventeenth-Century England* (Athens: University of Georgia Press, 1982). When the self-styled Republic of Letters ceased to have much influence on taste in the eighteenth century, works that were once considered "low" became mainstream. In an essay for *The Tatler*, Swift describes the phenomenon: In the past, he says, a "Grub-street Book was always bound in Sheep-skin, with suitable Print and Paper; the Price never above a Shilling; and taken off wholly by common Tradesmen, or Country Pedlars. But now they appear in all Sizes and Shapes, and in all Places: They are handed about from Lapfulls in every Coffee-house to Persons of Quality; are shewn in Westminster-Hall and the Court of Requests" (PW 2: 174; italics omitted).

40. [William Wotton], *A Defense of the Reflections Upon Ancient and Modern Learning in Answer to the Objections of Sir W. Temple, and Others with Observations upon* The Tale of a Tub (London, 1705), Appendix B in *A Tale of a Tub*, eds. Guthkelch and Smith, 324, 326.

41. [William King], *Some Remarks on a Tale of a Tub* (London, 1704), 9–10, 7–8.

42. [Arthur Mainwaring], *The Medley*, June 18, 1711, in Frank Ellis, *Swift vs. Mainwaring: The Examiner and The Medley* (Oxford: Clarendon Press, 1985), 487.

43. [King], *Some Remarks*, 14–16.

44. [Wotton], *Observations*, 327.

45. *A Tale of a Tub Revers'd . . . with a Character of the Author* (London, 1705), A2r. A2v-A3r.

46. [King], *Some Remarks*, 13.

47. ESTC.

48. Much debate exists about Swift's motives for orchestrating this elaborate scheme. Some argue that the Bickerstaff episode is a serious attempt to neutralize enemies of the church and intellectual mountebanks, while others view it as a trifling joke. See N. F. Lowe, "Why Swift Killed Partridge," *Swift Studies* 6 (1991), 71–82; Herbert Davis, "Introduction," *Bickerstaff Papers* (PW 2: x-xi), and Richmond Bond "Isaac Bickerstaff, Esq," *Restoration and Eighteenth Century: Essays in Honor of Alan Dugald McKillop*, ed. Carroll Camden (Chicago: Published for William Marsh Rice University by the University of Chicago Press, 1963), 103–24.

49. For information on how almanacs shaped and reflected English popular culture, as well as specific details on John Partridge and the Bickerstaff hoax, see Bernard Capp, *Astrology and the Popular Press: English Almanacs, 1500–1800* (London and Boston: Faber, 1979).

50. Richard Steele, *The Tatler,* ed. Donald Bond, 3 vols. (Oxford: Clarendon Press and New York: Oxford University Press, 1987), 1: 22–23. Bond notes that Swift was the probable author of this essay (22n27).

51. *Squire Bickerstaff Detected; Or, the Astrologer Imposter Convicted, by John Partridge* (London, 1708), quoted in Ehrenpreis, *Swift,* 2: 207.

52. Quoted in Richmond P. Bond, "Isaac Bickerstaff, Esq," 110.

53. See George Mayhew, "Swift's Bickerstaff as an April Fool's Joke," *Modern Philology,* 61 (1964), 270–80.

54. ESTC.

55. At the time they were published, no one remarked Swift's self-depiction in "Mrs. Harris' Petition" (1709), or his allusion to his role as Bickerstaff in *A Letter Concerning the Sacramental Test* (1709). Swift suppressed *An Answer to Bickerstaff,* which links Bickerstaff and the *Tale-*teller. See Ehrenpreis 2:200–4.

56. [Daniel Defoe], *The Ballad Maker's Plea* (London, 1722), Appendix B86 in Natascha Wurzbach, *The Rise of the English Street Ballad 1550–1650,* trans. Gayna Walls (Cambridge, UK, and New York: Cambridge University Press, 1990), 284. Ballads became one of Swift's favorite genres: eighteen of his poems have the word *ballad* in their titles or the note *"sung to the tune of—"*

57. Steele, *Tatler,* 1: 462n, 1: 462.

58. Ibid., 1: 469.

59. I am speculating here based on a note in Curll's copy of the miscellany he published in 1710 that says he got the manuscript from "John Cliffe, Esq.; who had them of the Bp. Of Killala, in Ireland, whose Daughter he married & was my Lodger." Ralph Straus, *The Unspeakable Curll* (London: Chapman and Hall, 1927), 33–34. I am supposing an Irish ecclesiastical connection.

60. A discussion of the audience of Tonson's *Miscellanies* can be found in Barbara Benedict, *Making the Modern Reader: Cultural Mediation in Early Modern Literary Anthologies* (Princeton, NJ: Princeton University Press, 1996), 98–104.

61. John Tanner's almanac for 1707, for instance, alludes to "honest Dan" in a verse, with the presumption that the vast audience can easily decode the reference (*Angelus Britannicus. An Ephemeris* [London, 1707], B4r). On the relationship of Defoe and Swift, see Maximillian E. Novak, "Swift and Defoe: Or, How Contempt Breeds Familiarity and a Degree of Influence," in *Proceedings of the First Münster Symposium on Jonathan Swift,* eds. Hermann Real and Heinz Vienken (Munich: Wilhelm Fink, 1985), 157–74.

62. Steele, *Tatler,* 1: 47–8.

63. Swift's defenses of the church were often very indirect and full of discordant elements. In *Project for the Advancement of Religion,* for example, it is difficult to tell whether Swift is being serious. In contrast to the lack of response it received when it was published, there was a lively debate touched off by

Leland Peterson, who argued that Swift was being ironic. Leland Peterson, "Swift's *Project:* A Religious and Political Satire," *PMLA* 82 (1967), 54–63.

64. "Projected List of Subjects for a Volume, 1708," in Ehrenpreis, *Swift,* (Appendix B, 2: 768). Swift's imaginary table of contents resembles the real table of contents of Thomas Brown's collected works, which had been published posthumously in 1707. Brown was a professional writer, vilified as a hack and a no-account by the self-styled Augustans. Benjamin Boyce, in *Tom Brown of Facetious Memory* (Cambridge, MA: Harvard University Press, 1939), notes the extensive similarities between Brown and Swift, 178–88.

65. Steele, *Tatler,* 1: 3.

66. A few months later, the fifth edition of the *Tale* was published with an "Apology" from the *Tale*-teller, who attacks those who would see the work as anything but a defense of the church, but argues against Curll's assertion that several people wrote *A Tale of a Tub.*

67. See Alan Downie, *Robert Harley and the Press: Propaganda and Public Opinion in the Age of Swift and Defoe* (Cambridge, UK: Cambridge University Press), 1979, 117–130.

68. Ellis, "Introduction," *Swift vs. Mainwaring,* xxxi.

69. Ibid., xxxii.

70. Jonathan Swift, *Examiner* #46 (not in *The Prose Works*), in Ellis, *Swift vs. Mainwaring,* 481.

71. Ehrenpreis, *Swift,* 2 :485.

72. Sir George Macauley Trevelyan, *England Under Queen Anne,* 3 vols. (New York and London: Longman, Green and Co., 1931–4), 3: 254, quoted in Ehrenpreis, *Swift,* 2:500.

## Chapter Two, pp. 41–75

1. [Mainwaring], *The Medley* in *Swift vs. Mainwaring,* 106–7.

2. [Jonathan Swift], "Preface," *Miscellanies in Prose and Verse* (London, 1711), A4r. Italics omitted.

3. Curll's *Miscellanies* is not a pirated edition of Swift's 1711 volume but a collection of works by Swift that he had published, such as "Mrs. Harris" Petition," "Baucis and Philemon," and others. It also included *Meditation upon a Broomstick,* appearing in print for the first time.

4. Edmund Broadus, *The Laureateship: A Study in the Office of the Poet Laureate of England, with Some Account of the Poets* (Oxford: Clarendon Press, 1921), 62.

5. [Thomas Burnet], "Preface," *Essays Divine, Moral and Political . . . by the Author of the Tale of a Tub, sometime Writer of the Examiner, and the Original Inventor of the* Band-Box-Plot (London, 1714), iv.

6. *Dr. S———'s Real Diary; Being a True and Faithful Account of Himself. Containing, His entire Journal from the Time he left London to his Settling in Dublin* (London, 1715), A3r.

7. [John Oldmixon], *Reflections on Dr. Swift's Letter to the Earl of Oxford about the English Tongue* (London, 1712), Ar, 2, 15–16, 4; facsimile reprint, in *Poetry and Language,* The Augustan Reprint Society, Series 6; number 1, introduction by Louis Landa (Ann Arbor, MI: The Augustan Reprint Society, 1948).

8. [Arthur Mainwaring], *The British Academy: Being a New-Erected Society For the Advancement of Wit and Learning: With Some Few Observations Upon It,* facsimile reprint (London, 1712), 11 (included with Oldmixon, op. cit). A recent book, Ian Higgins's *Swift's Politics: A Study in Disaffection* (Cambridge, UK: Cambridge University Press, 1994), takes these Whig countercharges seriously and argues that Swift actually was a Jacobite.

9. "Plot upon Plot: A Ballad," in W. W. Wilkins, *Political Ballads of the Seventeenth and Eighteenth Centuries,* 2 vols. (London: Longman, 1860), 2: 120–3.

10. "The Plotter Found Out: or, Mine Arse in a Band-Box. To the tune of Which No Body Can Deny," in *Poems on Affairs of State,* ed. George F. deLord, 7 vols. (New Haven and London: Yale University Press, 1963–75), 7: 578.

11. Although Swift by implication is Mrs. Harris's lover in "Mrs. Harris's Petition, no notice of that reference was made during Swift's lifetime. See Richard Reynolds, "Swift's 'Humble Petition' from a Pregnant Frances Harris?" *Scriblerian,* 5 (1972), 38–9, and the endorsing note, *Scriblerian,* 13 (1980), 51.

12. "A Great Plot! The Second Part of the St. Paul's Screw Plot! Or Mine A— in a Ban-box" in *The Letters of Thomas Burnet to George Duckett 1712–22,* ed. D. Nichol Smith (Oxford: The Roxburghe Club, 1914), 225–6. The satire was published in *The Flying Post,* November 20–22, 1713.

13. The "Band-box Plot" became a persistent metaphor for Swift's dangerous abilities to create fictions that might foment mob violence. In 1712, *A Letter to the People to be left for them at the Booksellers; with a Word or Two of the Bandbox Plot* laughs at the prospect of being "Blown up with a Band-box" (15) and implies Swift was as sincere about the Band-box Plot as he was about his *Project for the Advancement of Religion* (A3v); *Essays Divine, Moral, and Political* are supposedly written by "the Author of the Tale of a Tub, sometime Writer of the Examiner, and the Original Inventor of the Band-Box Plot" (t.p.); in 1722, the *Defence of English Commodities* [supposedly] *written by Jonathan Swift* criticizes Swift for "sowing the Seeds of Discord and Contention, under the Cover of a Band-box" (115); Dean Percival in "A Description in Answer to the Journal" (Dublin, 1722) describes how Swift with "dire effect o'er the Band Box Hover'd / Venice Preserv'd and the Plots discover'd."

14. [Burnet], *Essays,* 50, i-ii.

15. "A Genuine Epistle from M[atthe]w P[rio]r, Esq.; at Paris, to the Revd. Dr. J[ontha]n S[wif]t at Windsor," in *A Farther Hue and Cry After Dr. Sw—t* (London, 1714) in *Two Rare Pamphlets Attributed to Swift,* Occasional Pa-

pers; Reprint Series No. 4 (San Francisco: California State Library), 22. [Typescript.]

16. "A Town Eclogue: or a Poetical Contest between Toby and a Minor-Poet of B-tt-n's Coffee-House . . . Inscribed to the Author of the *Tale of a Tub* [who] . . . hated *Wharton like a Toad*" (London, 1714) 17. See footnote 22 for a gloss on "Toby."

17. [Daniel Defoe], *The History of the Jacobite Clubs* (London, 1712), 12.

18. *The Tryal and Condemnation of Don Prefatio d'Asaven* (London, 1712), quoted in David Woolley, "'The Author of the *Examiner*' and the Whiggish Answer-Jobbers" in *Swift Studies,* 5 (1990), 108.

19. [Abel Boyer], *The Political State of Great Britain* (London, 1713), quoted in Ehrenpreis, *Swift,* 2: 677.

20. "A Copy of Verses fastn'd to the Gate of St. P——'s C————h D———— —r, on the Day of the I————t of a certain D—n," in An *Hue and Cry after Doctor S——t; Occasion'd by a True and Exact Copy of Part of his own Diary, found in his Pocket-Book, &c To which is added a Poem*" &c, 2nd edition (London, 1714), 14–5. I quote from the edition published in 1727.

21. *Dr. S——'s Real Diary,* 7, 26.

22. Swift attacked both men in *The Examiner* and in addition, focused particularly on Steele in *The Publick Spirit of the Whigs* (1713) and *The Importance of the Guardian Consider'd* (1713). A vicious attack on Steele, fathered on Swift, was *The Character of Richard S—le, Esq . . . By Toby, Abel's Kinsman* (London, 1713). "Toby" a dull-witted street hawker was related to Abel Roper, the Tory printer. After this appeared, Swift was often referred to as "Toby." See footnote 16. He attacked Wharton in *The Examiner* (November 30, 1710) and in *A Short Character of His Excellency, Thomas Earl of Wharton* (1711).

23. [Burnet], *Essays,* vii, 54.

24. "The First Ode of the Second Book of Horace Paraphrased and Addressed to Richard Steele, Esq.," published by Mrs. Dodd (an ally of Curll) on January 7, 1714. There has been debate about Swift's authorship of this poem. Although most editors include it in the canon, I think because of its "pox on both houses" theme, it cannot be Swift's.

25. [Burnet], *Essays,* viii-ix.

26. *Dr. S——'s Real Diary,* 2–4.

27. [Defoe], *Jacobite Clubs,* 13–14.

28. [Boyer], *Political State* in Ehrenpreis, *Swift,* 2: 677.

29. William Diaper, "An Imitation of the Seventeenth Epistle of the First Book of Horace, Address'd to Dr. Swift" (London, 1714) in *The Complete Works of William Diaper,* ed. Dorothy Broughton (London: Routledge and Kegan Paul, 1953), 92, ll. 163–66.

30. *An Hue and Cry after Doctor S—t,* 3–4.

31. *Dr. S——'s Real Diary,* 4, 6.

32. See Linda Colley, *Britons: Forging the Nation 1707–1837* (New Haven, C.T., and London: Yale University Press, 1992).

33. *Saint Patrick's Purgatory: Or, Dr. S——t's Expostulation With his Distressed Friends in the Tower and Elsewhere* (London, 1716), aa2r.

34. In addition to the two pieces discussed, from 1716 to 1718 there were only two short works by "The Author of a Tale of a Tub," in *The Agreeable Variety* (1717); a reprint of *An Argument Against the Abolishing of Christianity* (1717); and a reprint of "Baucis and Philomen," in *The Virgin Muse* (1717). *A Bibliography of the Writings of Jonathan Swift*, 2nd edition, Revised and Corrected by Hermann Teerink, edited by Arthur H. Scouten (Philadelphia: University of Pennsylvania Press, 1963.

35. [Thomas Gordon], *Dedication to a Great Man, Concerning Dedications. Discovering, amongst other wonderful secrets, what will be the present posture of affairs a thousand years hence* (London, 1718). The pamphlet was first published in 1718, but the attributions to Swift did not appear until the next year.

36. *A Letter to the Reverend Mr. Dean Swift, occasion'd by a Satire said to be written by him, entitled A Dedication to a Great Man* (London, 1719), 6.

37. "Mr. Lewis of Covent Garden, his letter to Dr. Swift," in *The Tickler,* No. III, *The Contents wherof the Author thinks fit not to mention in the Title-Page* (London, 1719), 14.

38. Reprinted as "A Letter to the Author; Occasion'd by the foregoing ODE [An Ode to the Earl of Cadogan, by D—n Sm——y]" in *Miscellaneous Poems . . . Published by Mr. Concanen* (London: 1724), 170–81.

39. Ehrenpreis, *Swift*, 3: 128–9.

40. It was appended to the *Defence of English Commodities* "written by Dean Swift."

41. "Elegy on Demar," for example, appeared in *Pinkethman's Jests: Or, Wit Refined.* London: 1721, 2nd part, 121.

42. First appearing in London, the poem was reprinted in Dublin and Edinburgh and appeared in a widely circulated engraving called *The Bubbler's Medley.* Swift's name was attached to it in John Concanen's *Miscellaneous Poems* (London, 1724).

43. After its initial appearance in 1720–21 (one Dublin edition; two London editions), the *Letter* appeared in the 1727 *Miscellanies* and Faulkner's edition of the *Works* (1735). Teerink records no subsequent publication. Another church-related tract published by Swift at this time was the anonymous *Some Arguments Against Enlarging the Power of the Bishops* (Dublin, 1723), which uses economic analysis to rebut the idea that the church should be constrained in negotiating leases for its lands. This tract was attributed to Swift by its appearance in Faulkner's 1735 edition of Swift's *Works.*

44. "A Second Poem to D—S——" (Dublin, 1725). [Broadside]

45. "A Poem on the Dean of St. Patrick's Birthday, November 30th being St. Andrews Day," Dublin, 1726. [Broadside]

46. Although the "A Modest Proposal" is one of the most anthologized essays at present, it received virtually no published response when it first appeared.

47. A. R. Hosier [pseud.], "A Poem to the Whole People of Ireland, Relating to N. B. Drapier" (Dublin, 1726). [Broadside]

48. "W——tt's Ghost Appears to the R——d D—n S——t" (Dublin, 1727). [Broadside]

49. Pat Rogers, "Notes," Jonathan Swift, *The Complete Poems,* ed. Pat Rogers (New Haven: Yale University Press, 1983), 710. Patrick Delany's "News from Parnassus" (1721), for example, dramatizes the gods' selection of Swift as Apollo's vice-regent on earth.

50. The poem is attributed both to Mary Barber and to Swift. It appeared in an undated quarto in Dublin and later in Mary Barber's *Poems on Several Occasions* (Dublin, 1734). The issue of authorship is discussed by Oliver Ferguson, "The Authorship of 'Appolo's Edict,'" *PMLA* 70 (1955), 433–40.

51. [Jonathan Smedley], "A Satyr" (Dublin, 1725). [Broadside]

52. Swift was attracted to the figure of Apollo at various times in his writing career. In addition to "Stella's Birthday," "Apollo to the Dean," and (possibly) "Apollo's Edict," he also published "Apollo Outwitted" (1711) and "Apollo: or a Problem Solved" (1735).

53. See *An Annotated List of Gulliveriana 1721–1800,* ed. and comp., Jeanne Welcher (Delmar, NY: Scholars' Facsimiles and Reprints, 1988).

54. [John Arbuthnot], *It Cannot Rains but it Pours: Or, London Strow'd with Rarities* (London, 1726), t.p.

55. [Jonathan Smedley], *Gulliveriana: or, A Fourth Volume of Miscellanies, being a Sequel of the Three Volumes published by Pope and Swift* (London, 1728), 217.

56. *Gulliver Decypher'd; Or Remarks on a late Book, intitled Travels Into Several Remote Nations of the World* (London, 1727?), 3, 9, 30.

57. *A Letter from a Clergyman to his Friend, With an Account of the Travels of Capt. Lemuel Gulliver; and a Character of the Author. To which is added, The True Reasons why a Certain Doctor was made a Dean* (London,1726), 11–12, 21; facsimile reprint, Augustan Reprint Society, Number 143, introduction by Martin Kallich (Los Angeles: University of California, 1970).

58. [Smedley], *Gulliveriana,* 332.

59. "To the Author of the Flying Post," in [Smedley], *Gulliveriana,* 280–81.

60. [Smedley], *Gulliveriana,* 4.

61. [Jonathan Swift and Alexander Pope], "Preface," and "Ode, for Musick, on the Longitude," *Miscellanies in Prose and Verse,* 3 vols. (London, 1727–8). It is unclear whether Pope, as the volumes' editor, wrote the preface by himself or whether he collaborated with Swift on it.

62. [Smedley], "The Preface," *Gulliveriana,* viii-xx. The interpretation of the frontispiece is found in Hugh Ormsby-Lennon, "*Classis?* Under the Stage Itinerant," *Swift: The Enigmatic Dean,* eds. Rudolf Freiburg, Arno Löffler, and Wolfgang Zach (Tübingen, Germany: Stauffenburg Verlag, 1998), 173–200.

63. "An Indian Tale," in [Smedley], *Gulliveriana,* 341.

64. [James Ralph], "Sawney: An Heroic Poem" (London, 1728), 21, 45.

65. *Baker's News; or the Whitehall Journal* (Jan 1722–3) and *The Weekly Journal: or British Gazeteer* (Jan 1722–3).

66. These are contained in an exchange of letters in *Baker's News; or the White-Hall Journal* in [Smedley], *Gulliveriana*, 11–2, 20.

67 [William Percival], "A Description in Answer to the Journal" (Dublin, 1722). [Broadside]

68. "An Answer to Hamilton's Bawn: or, A Short Character of Dr. S—t" [Dublin, 1732]. [Broadside]

69. "Written on the Deanery Window of St. Patrick's, Dublin. By Dr. Delany" and "Another. By the Same" first appeared in Concanen, *Miscellaneous Poems*, 137–8.

70. "A True and Faithful Inventory of the Goods Belonging to Dr. Swift, Vicar of Lara Cor; upon Lending his House to the Bishop of Meath, until his own was built" (n.p., n.d.) [Broadside]; printed in *The London Journal* on 25 June 1726 (P 3: 1044n).

71. "A Rebus on Dean Swift. By Vanessa" and "The Dean's Answer" in *Miscellanea* [ed. Edmund Curll], 2 vols. (London, 1727), 76, 77–8. Through an analysis of printers' ornaments, John I. Fischer has determined that the Dublin edition of "Cadenus and Vanessa" was published by either Aaron Rhames or John Hyde, Swift's favored printer in 1726. Fischer, however, does not believe Swift was responsible for the poem's appearance. "Love and Books: Some Early Texts of Swift's 'Cadenus and Vanessa,' and a Few Words about Love," in *Reading Swift: Papers from the Fourth Münster Symposium on Jonathan Swift*, eds. Hermann J. Real and Helgard Stöver-Leidig (München: Wilhelm Fink, forthcoming, 2002).

72. [Smedley], *Gulliveriana*, xxx.

73. Ralph, "Sawney," 21.

74. "One Epistle to Mr. A. Pope, Occasion'd by Two Epistles Lately Published" (London, 1730). [Broadside]

75. *Some Memoirs of the Amours and Intrigues of a Certain Irish Dean . . . with the Gallantries of Two Berkshire Ladies* (London, 1728), A1r–A2r.

### Chapter Three, pp. 77–104

1. *A Concordance to the Poems of Jonathan Swift* cites approximately 120 uses of the word "Dean" during the period 1729–40; 20 for variations of the word "Drapier"; and 20 for variations of the word "Swift." In each case, there is a marked increase in the appearance of those terms in poetry written or published before 1730. *A Concordance to the Poems of Jonathan Swift*, ed. Michael Shinagel (Ithaca, NY and London: Cornell University Press, 1972). The concordance includes all the poems in Harold Williams' edition, which means some were not published during the periods in which they were written or never published at all. In the poems Swift did publish, though, the focus on himself as a character is evident.

2. Swift and Carteret became good friends. To make his respect for Carteret clear, Swift published under his name *A Vindication of his Excellency the Lord*

C———t, *from the Charge of favouring none but Tories, High-Churchmen
and Jacobites* (London and Dublin, 1730).

3. Letter from Marmaduke Coghill to Edward Southwell (21 February
1729–30), quoted in Ehrenpreis, *Swift,* 3:651.

4. [James Arbuckle], "A Panegyric on the Reverend D—n S———t, in Answer
to the Libel on Dr. D———y, and a Certain Great L—d" (Dublin and London, 1729). Although formerly attributed to Swift, James Woolley convincingly argues that this poem was written by James Arbuckle. See "Arbuckle's
'Panegyric' and Swift's Scrub Libel: The Documentary Evidence," in *Contemporary Studies of Swift's Poetry,* eds. John Irwin Fischer and Donald C.
Mell (Newark, DE: University of Delaware Press, 1981), 191–210.

5. "Advice to a Certain Dean" (n.p., 1730). [Broadside.]

6. Letter from Coghill to Southwell, quoted in Ehrenpreis 3:652.

7. An example of the reaction in England is "A Letter from Dublin concerning
the presentation of the Freedom of the City to Swift," in number 5717 of
*The Flying Post; Or, Post-Master,* Thursday, March 19, 1730. (Broadside).
Notice of the awarding of the Gold Box was carried in *Universal Spectator*
and *The Weekly Journal* on June 13, 1730.

8. Mrs. Barber, who transported "Epistle to a Lady" to London, and all the
publishers involved, were arrested. The *Political State* (March 1734) reports
that "several printers and publishers, at Dublin, were taken into custody" for
being involved in the publication of "On Poetry" (P 2:640n).

9. James Woolley, "Commentary in *Mist's* and *Fog's*," Appendix D, (pp.
236–244) in [Jonathan Swift and Thomas Sheridan], *The Intelligencer,* ed.
James Woolley (Oxford: Clarendon Press, 1992), 236–7.

10. [Anthony Collins], *Discourse Concerning Ridicule and Irony in Writing, In a
Letter to the Reverend Dr. Nathanael Marshall* (London, 1729); facsimile
reprint, Augustan Reprint Society, Number 142, introduction by Edward
and Lillian Bloom (Los Angeles, CA: William Andrews Clark Library,
1970), 38.

11. "Answer to Hamilton's Bawn." [Broadside]

12. [Sheridan and Swift], *Intelligencer,* (Number 2), 52.

13. This folktale was recorded by the Irish Folklore Commission, and may have
originated with Thomas Sheridan, who inserts it in his life of Swift. For a
discussion of Swift as a character in Irish folklore, see Mackie L. Jarrell,
"'Jack and the Dane': Swift Traditions in Ireland," *Fair Liberty was All his
Cry: A Tercentenary Tribute to Jonathan Swift 1667–1745,* ed. A. Norman Jeffares (London: MacMillan; New York: St. Martin's Press, 1967), 311–341.

14. [Sheridan and Swift], *Intelligencer,* (Number 18) 197.

15. Woolley, Headnote, Ibid., 197.

16. Ibid., (Number 15), 174.

17. The relationship between Swift and Faulkner became a popular topic and
generated a number of poems and anecdotes after Swift's death. The persistence of mythmaking about Swift and Faulkner can be seen in this apocryphal story about the meeting of Swift and Faulkner, published by *The Irish*

*Independent,* November 15, 1932. Swift's printer had died, and so he sent for the publisher of the *Dublin Journal.* A man named Hoey appeared, and to the Dean's question about whether he was a printer, he answered, "I am an apology for one." The Dean then demanded that Faulkner be sent to him, and in response to his question, responds, "I *am* a printer," to which the Dean says, "You are the man I want."

18. Barry Slepian, "George Faulkner's *Dublin Journal* and Jonathan Swift," *Pennsylvania Library Chronicle,* 31 (1965), 98.

19. *Dublin Journal,* 12 Jan 1734, quoted in Ehrenpreis 3:771.

20. Sheridan's biography portrays the confrontation of Swift and Bettesworth, complete with dialogue, an account about whose accuracy Ehrenpreis and others have expressed doubts." Luis R. Gamez, in "Richard Bettesworth's Insult and 'The Yahoo Overthrow'" (*Swift Studies* 12 [1997: 80–4]), defends the truth of Sheridan's report. Walter Scott, on the authority of Theophilus Swift, tells a story in which Swift was struggling to find a rhyme for Bettesworth when he was interrupted by a porter demanding payment: "The fellow's demand being considered as exorbitant [by Swift], he wiped his forehead, saying, with the humour of a low Irishman, 'Oh! your reverence, my sweat's worth half a crown.' The Dean instantly caught at the words, 'Ay, that it is,—there's half a crown for you.'" Walter Scott, *Life,* 1:385–90. A biography published in Ireland targeted to young adults, discusses the incident and provides an illustration of a bloody-thirsty Bettesworth reading Swift's poem with a knife in his hand. Mary Moriarty and Catherine Sweeney, *Jonathan Swift: The Man Who Wrote* Gulliver, O'Brien Junior Biography Library, Number 5 (Dublin: The O'Brien Press, 1990), 64.

21. Quoted in Slepian, "Faulkner's *Dublin Journal,*" 105.

22. Ibid.

23. *Dublin Journal,* 3 December 1737, quoted in Ehrenpreis 3:865.

24. *Dublin Journal,* 12 May 1733, quoted in Ehrenpreis 3:761.

25. "Ub—Bub—A—Boo: Or, The Irish Howl. In Heroic Verse. By Dean Swift" (London, 1735—2 editions).

26. *The Advantages Proposed by Repealing the Sacramental Test, Impartially Consider'd. By the Rev. Dr. Swift, Dean of St. Patrick's* (1733); *Queries Related to the Sacramental Test* (in *The Dublin Journal,* 1732); *The Presbyterians Plea of Merit; In Order to take off the Test, Impartially Examined* (1733); *The Nature and Consequences of the Sacramental Test consider'd, With Reasons humbly offer'd for Repeal of it"* (1732); "On the Words 'Brother Protestants and Fellow Christians' So Familiarly used by the Advocates for Repeal of the Test Act in Ireland" (broadside ballad) (1733).

27. Ehrenpreis, *Swift,* 3:716.

28. One opposing response to Swift's claim to having the interests of the lower clergy most at heart is Edward Lonergan's "The Dean and the Country Parson" (Dublin, 1739), which depicts Swift as unsympathetic to the lower clergy because of his wealth and personal political ambitions. This poem was not reprinted and seems to be quite rare.

29. Swift attacks Hort in "Judas," "Advice to a Parson" and "Epigram On Seeing a Worthy Prelate Go out of Church in the time of Divine Service, to Wait on his Grace the Duke of Dorset," among others.

30. Ehrenpreis, *Swift*, 3: 859–60. In his headnote to "A Ballad," Harold Williams mentions that a broadside called *Ireland's Mourning Flagg* opened with 18 lines describing Swift's action (P 3: 840).

31. *Pue's Occurrences* (September 13, 1737), quoted in Ehrenpreis, *Swift*, 3: 859–60.

32. Quoted in Victor Jackson, *The Monuments of St. Patrick's Cathedral Dublin*, Dublin: St. Patrick's, 1987, 38.

33. "The Devil's Gratitude. A Poem in Answer to a late Poem, Intitled the Place of the Damn'd" (n.p., n.d.). [Broadside]

34. "A Curry Comb of Truth for a Certain Dean; or The Grub-street Tribunal" (Dublin, 1736), 5, 8. Reprinted in London in *S—t Contra Omnes* (1736).

35. Smedley, *Gulliveriana,*10. On the epitaph, Swift had wanted to put that McGee was his "servant and friend," but Pope convinced him to omit the word friend. Ehrenpreis, *Swift*, 3:323.

36. The only one of these likely to have been written by Swift is the "Petition of the Footmen," which appeared in Faulkner's 1735 edition of Swift's collected *Works*.

37. *Dublin Journal*, 26 November 1737, quoted in Slepian, "Faulkner's *Dublin Journal*," 105.

38. "David Mullan's Letter to Dean Swift" (Dublin, 1735), 3. Someone fathered a response onto Swift, "The Dean's Answer to David Mullan's Letter" (Dublin, 1735).

39. The online catalog of the Library of Congress lists three reprints of *Directions to Servants* from 1964 to the present.

40. "The Excremental Vision," now a widely used term, is the title of a chapter in John Middleton Murry's *Jonathan Swift, A Critical Biography* (London: Jonathan Cape, 1954).

41. Yeats, another Anglo-Irish poet, links love and excrement in the twentieth century—cf. "Crazy Jane and the Bishop": "Love has pitched his mansion / In the seat of excrement." In the late eighteenth, Smollett introduces Swiftian grossness into the novel, but this is not a practice that had many followers until the late twentieth century.

42. "Chloe Surpriz'd: or the Second Part of the Lady's Dressing Room" (Dublin and London, 1732).

43. [Lady Mary Wortley Montague], "The Dean's Provocation For Writing the Lady's Dressing Room," (London, 1734), reprinted in Robert Halsband, "'The Lady's Dressing Room' Explicated by a Contemporary," in *The Augustan Milieu: Essay Presented to Louis A. Landa*, eds. Henry Knight Miller *et al.* (Oxford: The Clarendon Press. 1970), 225–231, 228–9. Other imaginative re-visionings of Swift's poem are "The Gentleman's Study In Answer to the Lady's Dressing-Room" (London and Dublin, 1732) and "Caelia's Revenge. . . . Being an Answer to the Lady's Dressing-Room (London,1741).

44. See W. A. Speck, "Politicians, Peers, and Publication by Subscription 1700–1750 in *Books and their Readers in Eighteenth-Century England,* ed. Isabel Rivers, New York: St. Martin's Press, 1982, 47–68.

45. Ehrenpreis, *Swift,* 3:786.

46. Ibid., 3:790.

47. James Arbuckle, "Momus Mistaken: A Fable, Occasioned by the Publication of the Works of the Revd. Dr. Swift" (Dublin: 1735). [Broadside]

48. "The Draper's Apparition to G—ge F————r, A New Poem" (Dublin, 1745), 3, 6.

49. Elizabeth Malcolm, Chapter 1, "Dean Swift and Madness," 1–31, *Swift's Hospital: A History of St. Patrick's Hospital, Dublin, 1746–1989* (Dublin: Gill and Macmillan, 1989), 7–8.

50. I am using the edition published by George Faulkner. *Letters to and from Dr. J. Swift from the Year 1714, to 1738. To which are added, several Notes and Translations not in the London Edition* (Dublin, 1741).

51. John Barrett, *An Essay on the Earlier Part of the Life of Swift* (London, 1808).

### Chapter Four, pp. 105–126

1. Three reprint editions of Hay's book appeared in the 1970s.

2. Michel Foucault, *The History of Sexuality: An Introduction.* 3 vols. Trans. Robert Hurley (New York: Vintage Books [Random House], 1978; rpt. 1990), 34.

3. Ibid., 72.

4. Ibid., 35.

5. See John Sutherland's discussion of sexual secrets in *Can Jane Eyre Be Happy? More Puzzles in Classic Fiction,* which includes essays such as "Where does Fanny Hill keep her contraceptives?" and "Who is Tom Jones' Father?" (Oxford; New York: Oxford University Press, 1997) as well as William A. Cohen's *Sex Scandal: The Private Parts of Victorian Fiction* (Durham: Duke University Press, 1996).

6. Foucault, *History of Sexuality,* 57–63.

7. In "A Candid Appeal from the Late Dean Swift to the Right Hon. the Earl of O——y" (London, 1752)," Swift's ghost castigates Orrery for besmirching him. The ghost of Swift appears in another broadside to castigate George Faulkner for publishing Orrery's *Remarks*—"Ungracious Varlet. . . . shall my Printer to whom I gave my Works as a Fortune, turn Tail upon me after I am dead, join Issue with the Enemies of *Ireland,* publish their wicked Trash[?]" (A Letter from Dean Swift to George F—k—r" (Dublin, 1752). Another writer imagines the ghost of Swift confronting Orrery with the words *Et tu, Brutus* ("A Letter from a Gentleman," [Dublin, 1751]).

8. The evidence is summarized in Maxwell Gold's *Swift's Marriage to Stella* (Cambridge: Harvard University Press, 1937); Ehrenpreis rejects the evidence for any marriage, *Swift,* 3: 405.

9. "The Account of Dean Swift . . . [in] an Epitome of the Earl of Orrery's Letters to his Son," *Gentleman's Magazine* 22 (August 1752), 361. A few broadsides and pamphlets defended Orrery for his unflinching portrayal of the nasty truth, for example, "Emendations on an Appeal from the late Dean Swift. Or Right Hon. Earl of Orrery Vindicated" (London, 1752).

10. C.M.P.G.N.S.T.N.S. [Pseud.], "Anecdotes of Dean Swift and Miss Johnson," *Gentleman's Magazine* (November 1757), 490-l.

11. See Peter L. Thorslev, Jr., "Incest as Romantic Symbol," *Comparative Literature Studies* (1965), 41–58.

12. Daniel W. Wilson, "Science, Natural Law, and Unwitting Sibling Incest in Eighteenth-Century Literature," *Studies in Eighteenth Century Culture,* 13 (1984), 249–70.

13. See Julia Shaffer, "Familial Love, Incest, and Female Desire in Late Eighteenth-Century and Early Nineteenth-Century Novels, *Criticism* 41:1 (Winter 1999), 67–99.

14. Eight months before she died Pilkington advertised Volume III in the press, but she had a habit of announcing the publication of works well before she had completed them (Elias 1: xxiv).

15. A. C. Elias, "Commentary," in Pilkington, *Memoirs,* note 281.40, 2: 670.

16. In the headnote to "Jealousy" (P 2: 736n), Harold Williams also notes that it was reprinted in *The Flowers of Parnassus: Or, the Lady's Miscellany* (1736), where it was also signed merely as "By a Lady." Nichols later ascribed the other anonymous poem in Concanen's collection to Stella.

17. See Harold Williams's headnote to "Cadenus and Vanessa," (P 2: 736).

18. Significant collections of Swift's correspondence before that of Harold Williams were published in 1740, by Pope; 1741, 1746, 1765, by Faulkner; 1765, 1768 by Deane Swift; 1766, by John Hawkesworth; 1779, by John Nichols; 1814, by Walter Scott; 1899, by George Birbeck Hill; 1910, by Elrington Ball; 1910–14, by J.H. Bernard; 1921, by A. Martin Freeman; and 1935, by David Nichol Smith.

19. Sybil Le Brocquy capitalized on the inherent drama of these letters in her *A View on Vanessa; a Correspondence with Interludes for the Stage* (Dublin: Dolmen Press, 1967).

20. These poems had been previously printed in the *Gentleman's Magazine,* (April 1767) and in the *Annual Register* (1767) with authorship given to Vanessa. Another poem of dubious attribution is "To Love," which Sheridan prints in his *Works* with this note: "Found in Miss Vanhomrigh's desk, after her death, in the handwriting of Dr. Swift." Williams, headnote, 2: 717.

21. The word "victim" characterizes Vanessa and Stella, for instance, in a monitory article published in *The Penny Magazine of the Society for the Diffusion of Useful Knowledge.* "The Week" [an article prompted by Swift's birthday, November 30], 4 (November 24, 1832), 335–6.

22. For example, Samuel Phillips, "Dean Swift—Stella and Vanessa," *Essays from the London Times: A Collection of Personal and Historical Sketches* (New York: Appleton, 1852), 223.

23. [Francis Jeffreys], Review of Scott's *Works of Jonathan Swift, The Edinburgh Review,* 53 (September 1816), 40, 42. As a Whig, Jeffreys particularly disliked Swift for his political apostasy.

24. William Makepeace Thackeray, "Swift," in *The English Humourists of the Eighteenth Century* (London: Smith, Elder, and Co., 1853), 43, 53.

25. William Wilde, *The Closing Years of Dean Swift's Life . . . and Some Remarks on Stella* (Dublin: Hodges and Smith, 1849), 74.

26. Mahony, *Irish Identity,* 67.

27. *Donald M. Berwick, The Reputation of Jonathan Swift (1781–1882)* (Philadelphia, 1941), 26, 26n3.

28. Jarrell, "Jack and the Dane," 335.

29. Frances Cobb, "A Relic of Swift and Stella," *Temple Bar Magazine* 66 (1832), 570.

30. Wilde, *Closing Years,* 120n.

31. Agnes M. Winifred ("Quilca and Its Associations: Interesting Gossip about Dean Swift and the Sheridans," (n.p., n.d). This item is contained in a scrapbook of Swiftiana assembled by Dr. Francis Bourke, which contains 570 pages of clippings dating from the beginning of the nineteenth century. Unfortunately, some of the headers are cut off, so the imprint information is lost. Such is the case with this item, p. 163. The scrapbook is now in the archives of St. Patrick's Hospital, Dublin.

32. Johnston's "Weep for Polyphemus" was broadcast on BBC Radio June 18, 1938 and rewritten for the stage with the title *The Dreaming Dust,* first performed March 25, 1940. Mahony, *Irish Identity,* 157.

33. Glendinning, *Swift,* 239.

34. Ibid., 243.

35. Elizabeth Bird notes that folklorists no longer talk about the need for belief, but "suggest that what is involved in legend telling and hearing is more accurately a suspension of disbelief, during which a participant plays with notions of reality, involving other people in the game" (*Enquiring Minds,* 189).

36. Florence Eveleen Bell (Mrs. Hugh Bell), *The Dean of Saint Patrick's: A Play in Four Acts* (London: Edward Arnold, 1903).

37. Charles Edward Lawrence, *Swift and Stella: A Play in One Act* (Boston: Gowans and Gray, 1927).

38. The coffee-drinking thesis was originally propounded in the late eighteenth-century by Horace Walpole (in a letter). It did not start to circulate in popular literature until the twentieth century.

39. Bruce Arnold, *Swift: An Illustrated Life* (Dublin: Lilliput Press, 2000), 63–64.

40. Sybil Le Brocquy, *Cadenus: A Reassessment in Light of New Evidence of the Relationships between Swift, Stella, and Vanessa* (Dublin: Dolmen Press, 1962). In addition, Le Brocquy dramatized her theory in her play, *A View on Vanessa,* produced at the Lantern Theatre in Dublin, April 1967. Mahony, *Irish Identity,* 163. Le Brocquy also published a book on Stella, entitled *Swift's Most Valuable Friend* (Dublin: Dolmen Press, 1968).

41. Jarrell, "Jack and the Dane," 323. Jarrell cites a printed version of the story in O'Donoghue's *The Poets of Ireland* (Dublin, 1912).

42. Earl of Longford, Edwards Arthur Pakenham, *Yahoo: A Tragedy in Three Acts* (Dublin: Hodges and Figges, 1934).10; Eleanor Corde, *Dean Swift: A Drama* (Los Angeles, CA.: McBride, 1922), 75; William Butler Yeats, *Words on the Window-pane* (Dublin: Cuala Press, 1934), 49; Winston Clewes, *The Violent Friends* (New York and London: D. Appleton-Century, 1945), 112–13.

43. Aldous Huxley, "Swift," in *Do What You Will* (Garden City, NY: Doubleday and Doran,1929), 105.

44. Murry, *Swift*, 441.

45. Swift's coprophilia has stimulated much discussion in academic journals and monographs. Dr. Phyllis Greenacre, author of *Swift and Carroll: A Psychoanalytic Study of Two Lives* (New York: International Universities Press, 1955), blames Swift's nurse for his unhealthy obsession: "However devoted to her little charge, [she] was in some way overly conscientious and harsh in her early toilet training, and left this stamp of the nursery morals of the chamber pot forever on his character" (108). Here Greenacre is clearly mythologizing, for no documentary evidence exists about Swift's toilet training. The Swift-nurse dynamic in the toilet training narrative also excites the imagination of Donald R. Roberts, who elaborates the scenario by asserting (without any warrant whatsoever) that the nurse plied Swift "with caresses of a faintly lascivious character." By implication, this childhood molestation rendered Swift frigid. "A Freudian View of Jonathan Swift," *Literature and Psychology*, 4 (1956), 10.

46. Sandor Ferenczi, "Gulliver Phantasies," *International Journal of Psychoanalysis*, 9 (1928), 299.

47. A. G. Gordon, "Letter to the Editor," *Journal of the Royal Society of Medicine* 92 (February 1999), 102. Earlier in the twentieth century, T. G. Wilson had considered and rejected the syphilis diagnosis in his article, "Swift's Deafness and his Last Illness" *Irish Journal of Medical Science* 162 (1939), 241–56.

48. Erica Jong, *Fanny, being the true History of the Adventures of Fanny Hack-about-Jones* (New York: Signet, 1980).

49. Mahony, *Irish Identity,*167.

50. Greenacre, *Swift and Carroll*, 109, 114.

51. Glendinning, *Swift*, 258. Robert Mahony notes that *Dr. S—t's Real Diary* satirically alludes to a homosexual relationship between Swift and Lord Oxford: Swift remembers "when I was to your Lordship *a mensa & secretis* [privy to your table and secrets] (the world was never so wicked as to say *a thoro* [to your bed]. *Irish Identity*, 31.

52. Mario Hone and Joseph Rossi, *Swift; or the Egotist* (London: Gollancz, 1934), 16; Virginia Woolf, "Swift's 'Journal to Stella,'" in *The Second Common Reader* (New York: Harcourt, Brace and World, 1932; rpt. 1966), 63; Bell, *The Dean of Saint Patrick's*, 75–6.

53. Janice Radway, *Reading the Romance: Women, Patriarchy, and Popular Literature* (Chapel Hill: University of North Carolina Press, 1984), 155.

54. William Makepeace Thackeray, *English Humorists,* 45.

55. Tony Bennett and Janet Woollacott, *Bond and Beyond: The Political Career of a Popular Hero* (New York: Methuen, 1987), 35

56. Frye, *Secular Scripture,* 61.

57. Foucault, *History of Sexuality,* 7.

### Chapter Five, pp. 127–142

1. See Timothy J. Reiss, *Tragedy and Truth: Studies in the Development of a Renaissance and Neoclassical Discourse* (New Haven, CT: Yale University Press, 1980). Reiss argues that "Tragedy in itself does not reveal any cosmic law. It does not show the impossibility of overcoming fate; it does not settle or unsettle the place of man in a divine order. Tragedy is a . . . textual . . . machine that enable use subsequently to make such readings" (15).

2. See A. D. Nuttall, *Why Does Tragedy Give Pleasure?* (Oxford: Clarendon Press, 1985) and Susan Letzer Cole, *The Absent One: Mourning Ritual, Tragedy, and the Performance of Ambivalence* (University Park: Pennsylvania University Press, 1985).

3. Michel Foucault, Chapter 2, "The Great Confinement," 38–64, *Madness and Civilization: A History of Insanity in the Age of Reason,* trans. Richard Howard (New York: Random House, 1965; reprinted 1973).

4. Eighty items are listed under the subject heading "last words" in the Library of Congress online catalog. One current example is *Famous Last Words: apt observations, pleas, curses, benedictions, sour notes, bon mots, and insights from people on the brink of departure,* comp. by Alan Brisport (San Francisco: Pomegranate, 2001).

5. Edward Young, *Conjectures on Original Composition. In a Letter to the Author of Sir Charles Grandison* (London, 1759), 64–5.

6. Max Byrd, Chapter Five, "Madness at Mid-Century: Melancholy and the Sublime," 113–44, *Visits to Bedlam: Madness and Literature in the Eighteenth Century* (Columbia: University of South Carolina Press, 1974).

7. The visit is dramatized in John O'Donovan's "The Fiddler and the Dean" in *Jonathan, Jack, and GBS: Four Plays about Irish History and Literature,* ed. Robert Hogan; with a reminiscence by James Plunkett (Newark: University of Delaware Press, 1993), 85–101.

8. *Letters written by the Late Jonathan Swift, D.D . . . and Several of his Friends from the Year 1710 to 1742. Published from the Originals,* ed. Deane Swift (London, 1768).

9. Birch, for example, said that "Dr. Swift has lately awakened from a mere animal life into a thorough misanthropy and brutality of lust; for he can hardly be restrained from knocking every man on the head . . .or from attempting every woman that he sees." Ehrenpreis, *Swift,* 3: 919–20.

10. Samuel Johnson, "Swift," *Lives of the Poets* in *Selected Poetry and Prose,* Frank Brady and W. K. Wimsatt, eds. (Berkeley and Los Angeles, CA; London: University of California Press, 1977), 447.

11. Ibid., 464–5.

12. William Henry Davenport Adams, *Wrecked Lives: Men Who Have Failed,* First series (London: Society for Promoting Christian Knowledge; New York: Pott, Young and Co, 1880), 225.

13. John Churton Collins, *Jonathan Swift: A Biographical and Critical Study,* London: Chatto and Windus, 1893, facsimile reprint, Norwood, PA: Norwood Editions, 1978, 230.

14. Thackeray, *English Humourists,* 16–17, 23, 31–32, 40, 41–42.

15. Ibid., 41–42.

16. David Masson, "Dean Swift," in *The Three Devils: Luther's, Milton's, and Goethe's, with other essays* (London: MacMillan, 1874), 289. First published inthe *British Quarterly Review* (1854).

17. George Gilfillan, "Satire and Satirists," *Scottish Review* (January 1856); reprinted in *A Gallery of Literary Portraits* (London, 1909), 236–7. Quoted in Berwick, *Reputation,* 93.

18. "Literary Curiosity. An Original Letter by Dean Swift," *The Midland Counties Historical Collector,* 1:4 (1854), 62–3.

19. See Williams' rehearsal of the evidence (C 1:3).

20. Evelyn Hardy chooses the phrase for the title of her biography *The Conjured Spirit; Swift, a Study in the Relationship of Swift, Stella and Vanessa* (London: Hogarth Press, 1949); David Nokes, for the first chapter of his biography; and Carl Van Doren, for his final chapter of *Swift* (1931), where he characterizes Swift as a man at war with his spirit, which has "enough angelic light, enough diabolic pride, to make it restless in its human flesh." (London: Martin Secker, 1931), 241, Van Doren also uses the phrase as the title of an essay in *Saturday Review of Literature* 7 (September 1930, 117–18). In addition, "Conjured Spirit" was used as the title for a review of Stephen Gwynn's *Life and Friendships of Dean Swift* in *The Saturday Review of Literature* 10 (December 1933), 321.

21. [Rev. Francis Mahony], "Dean Swift's Madness: A Tale of a Churn," *The Works of Father Prout,* ed. Charles Kent (London: Routledge, 1881), 76–7. First published in *Fraser's Magazine,* July 1834.

22. Wilde, *Closing Years,* 122. One story involves Swift suggesting to the vicar of Carlow that one way to repair his church was to give to the papists, let them fix it up, and then take it back (98).

23. Ibid., 56–9, 58n.

24. Ibid., 61. For this information, Wilde cites "*The Phrenological Journal,* vol. ix. p. 606."

25. Ibid., p. 57. Wilde is quoting a report by Dr. Houston in *The Phrenological Journal* cited above.

26. This item was included in Dr. Bourke's scrapbook. See footnote 31, Chapter 4.

27. Leslie Shane, *The Skull of Swift: An Extempore Exhumation* (Indianapolis: Bobbs-Merrill, 1928), 335.

28. J. Wickam Legg and J. C. Bucknill, "Letter," *Academy* 19 (June 25, 1881), 241–56. J. C. Bucknill, "Dean Swift's Disease," *Brain: A Journal of Neurology,* 4 (January 1882), 291–305.

29. Henry Craik, *The Life of Jonathan Swift* (London: J. Murray, 1882).

30. Longford, *Yahoo,* 63–4.

31. Corde, *Dean Swift,* 166, 168.

32. Edith Sitwell, *I Sit Under a Black Sun* (Garden City, NY: Doubleday, Doran, 1938), 322–3.

33. Longford, *Yahoo,* 64–65.

34. Bernard Acworth, *Swift* (London: Eyre and Spottiswoode, 1947), 219–20. Acworth's argument also depends on his reading of an apocryphal piece of Swiftiana, first printed by Scott in 1814, entitled "An Evening Prayer." The prayer, unlike anything Swift ever wrote, explicitly invokes Christ's mercy and the hope of resurrection. Acworth reprints the "Evening Prayer," 241–3.

35. One early example of this kind of narrative in the eighteenth century is part of a anonymous broadside eulogizing Swift on his death, in which a Swift persona acknowledges God at the end and apologizes for his offensive writings, saying "GOD alone knows my heart . . . to HIM I appeal for all my thoughts." *A Funeral Elegy on the Father of his Country, the Rev. Dr. Jonathan Swift . . . by J———n N———n* (Dublin, 1745). [Broadside]

36. Rossi and Hone, 41, 39, 172.

37. Murry, *Swift,* 484.

38. Hardy, *The Conjured Spirit,* 14.

39. Glendinning, *Swift,* 287.

40. Van Doren, *Swift,* 244.

41. W. B. C. Watkins, *Perilous Balance: The Tragic Genius of Swift, Johnson, and Sterne* (Princeton: Princeton University Press, 1939), 1–2.

42. Frank Stier Goodwin, *Jonathan Swift: Giant in Chains,* (New York: Liveright, 1940), v.

43. David Nokes, *Jonathan Swift: A Hypocrite Reversed* (Oxford; New York: Oxford University Press, 1985), t.p. Nokes takes the title of his book and his epigraph from Sheridan, who is paraphrasing Bolingbroke.

44. Yeats, *The Words Upon the Window-pane, op. cit.* 39–40.

45. Nokes, *Hypocrite Reversed,* 413.

## Chapter Six, pp. 143–164

1. Ernest Boyd, "Swift," in *Literary Blasphemies* (New York and London: Harper and Brothers, 1927), 74–105.

2. W. D. Taylor, *Swift: A Critical Essay* (London: Peter Davies, 1933), 305.

3. *Swift's Jests, or a Compendium of Wit and Humour. Being the Facecious jokes . . . of the most eminent Wits, viz. Swift* [et al.] (London, 1759). Figures known for their wit, humor, and eccentricity become jestbook staples and

are often cited in jestbook titles. These include comic actors (Richard Tarl-
ton, Samuel Foote, and most famously, Joe Miller), comic writers (John
Skelton, Ben Jonson, William Shakespeare, the Earl of Rochester), comic
characters from novels (Peregrine Pickle, Laurence Sterne's Yorick), or folkloric characters (Simple Simon, Long Meg, John Barleycorn).

4. Robert Winans (Gettysburg College), in a paper delivered at the East-Central
American Society for Eighteenth-Century Studies at Dickinson College, October 25–27, 1990, reported that fillers about Jonathan Swift in American
newspapers during the eighteenth century outnumber those about all other
personalities.

5. "Dean Swift and the Post Boy" was a popular story whose origins are mysterious. The story goes as follows. Swift had lampooned other clergy but still
was on good terms with the Bishop of Dublin, who wanted to send him a
large salmon. (In some retellings, it is a haddock.) Because it was rainy and
cold, the bishop's butler did not want to make the delivery, especially since
Swift, known for his cheapness, would not give him food or money. A post
boy pipes up to say he will do the job and bets the butler that Swift will reward him. Arriving at the Deanery, the boy greets Swift with great rudeness.
Shocked, the Dean rebukes the boy and insists that they trade roles, so he
can show him how he ought to act. As the boy in the instructional skit, the
Dean is properly deferential. In response, the boy, acting the Dean, says,
"Take this lad down; give him something to eat and drink; and give him a
half guinea for his trouble." Outwitted by the boy, the Dean does as he asks,
and the boy wins the wager with the butler. Hermann Real reported to me
that he possesses an engraving of the story; published by Bowles and Carter,
Feb. 3 1806. The fish in Real's engraving is a turbot.

6. Some of these items are included in the *Catalogue of English and American
ChapBooks and Broadside Ballads in Harvard College Library,* ed. William
Coolidge Lane (Cambridge, MA: Harvard College Library, 1905). In addition to the works cited in this chapter, useful scholarship on the jestbooks
includes Ronald Paulson's, "The Joke and Joe Miller's Jests," Chapter 6, *Popular and Polite Art in the Age of Hogarth and Fielding* and Derek Brewer's
"Prose Jest-Books Mainly in the Sixteenth to Eighteenth Centuries in England," in *A Cultural History of Humour From Antiquity to the Present Day,*
eds. Jan Bremmer and Herman Roodenberg (Cambridge, UK: Polity Press,
1997) 90–111.

7. Letter # 144, March 9, 1748. The constraints against laughter also gain support from religion; laughter is associated with sin because Christ never was
reported to have laughed. Johan Verbeckmoes, *Laughter, Jestbooks, and Society in the Spanish Netherlands* (New York: St. Martin's Press, 1999), 76.

8. The ESTC records no editions of Rabelais after 1750, but the bawdy humor
of Rabelais lived on in the coarse witticisms ascribed to Swift.

9. The three stories are listed as item 1629 in the Scouten-Teerink bibliography. Unfortunately, the issues of the *St. James's Post* in which they appear are
missing. The stories are described as follows in the bibliography: "Number

3030, March 22–5, 1735, contains the story of a trick played by Dean Swift on some of his friends which ended unfavorably for himself . . . Numb. 3098, Aug. 28–30, 1735, contains Dean Swift's Country Post. Numb. 4002, Sept. 6–9, 1735, contains the story of Dean Swift riding on the strand, and being in danger of being thrown from his horse by a clergyman shooting his gun too near him, in spite of Swift's warning." This last story seems to be a variation of Swift's ostensibly unpublished account of a similar encounter in 1715 with Lord Blayney (PW 5: 199–200). "Swift's Country Post" may be the original of the story of Swift preaching in a remote church to a congregation consisting only of his clerk, Roger. The jest, which is capped by Swift's altering the liturgy to "Dearly Beloved, Roger" was reprinted by Orrery and then became one of the most widely circulated.

10. Reprinted in many jestbooks, this version appears in *Scrapeana. Fugitive Miscellany* (n. p., 1792), 242.

11. For many of the jests she cites, Mackie Jarrell provides the index numbers from Stith Thompson's *Motif-Index of Folk-Literature* (Bloomington: University of Indiana, [1955–58]).

12. James M. Osborne, "Introduction," Joseph Spence, *Anecdotes,* 2 vols., ed. James M. Osborne (Oxford: The Clarendon Press, 1966), 1: xxii.

13. See Elias, "Introduction," Pilkington, *Memoirs,* 1: xlvii-liv.

14. *Mrs. Pilkington's Jests; or the Cabinet of Wit and Humor. Being a choice collection of the most brillant [sic] jokes, facetious puns, smart repartees, and entertaining tales, in prose and verse* (London, 1759); a second edition was printed in 1764, to which a frontispiece was added. Pilkington's prophecy of continued fame has proved true. Using the AltaVista Search engine (October 2001), her name brings up 50 "hits," many resulting from the recent anthologizing of her poetry and the reprintings of Virginia Woolf's *The Common Reader,* which contains an essay on her. Sections of her *Memoirs* were read over BBC Radio 3 on Saturday, August 11, 1990. The script was adapted from the *Memoirs* by Donald Bancroft, the reading was done by Samantha Bond, and the broadcast directed by Penny Gold. My thanks to Hermann Real for alerting me to this item and sending it to me.

15. Misogyny in the fabliaux is discussed by Norris J. Lacy, Chapter 5, "Women in the Fabliaux" in *Reading Fabliaux* (Birmingham, AL: Summa Publications, 1999), 60–78.

16. Mahadev L. Apte, *Humor and Laughter: An Anthropological Approach* (London and Ithaca, NY: Cornell University Press, 1985), 226–30. A variety of theories exist to explain why audiences react to the trickster character with laughter: his extreme nonconformity creates an inherently comic incongruity (P. E. McGhee); his humiliation of his adversaries vicariously produces the feeling of superiority, or "sudden glorying" over others (Hobbes); his unembarrassed pursuit of repressed pleasures (sex, excrement, aggression, profanity) enacts the secret urges of the audience (Sigmund Freud); his organic fluidity is a life-affirming reproof to deathlike social rigidity (Henri Bergson); his character embodies the spirit of carnivalesque popular culture

(comic, irreverent, unstable, egalitarian) in opposition to the "monolithically serious" "official" hierarchies (Mikhail Bakhtin).

17. Victoria Glendinning cites this anecdote in her discussion of whether Swift might have been gay: the episode "could be interpreted as Swift being 'camp' (though he was, perhaps, just re-enacting the intimate raillery of coffee-making with Vanessa)." *Swift,* 260.

18. For example, cross-dressing is a prominent feature in television shows like *Monty Python* and *Benny Hill* as well as Hollywood box office successes like *Tootsie* and *Mrs. Doubtfire.*

19. Mikhail Bakhtin, Chapter 3, "Popular-Festive Forms in Rabelais," *Rabelais and His World* (1965), trans. Helene Iswolsky (Cambridge, MA: M. I. T. University Press, 1968), 196–277. Bakhtin assumes that popular culture is necessarily revolutionary and that popular culture is the culture of the underclass, both positions I reject. Building on Bakhtin's idea of carnival, Peter Stallybrass and Allon White cite the "popular fair" as a subversive force that the civilizing ideology of the early eighteenth century, embodied in *The Spectator,* needed to suppress. Chapter 2, "The Grotesque Body and the Smithfield Muse: Authorship in the Eighteenth Century," in *The Politics and Poetics of Transgression* (Ithaca, NY: Cornell University Press, 1986) 80–124. Stallybrass and White argue that Swift, like Dryden and Pope, spent much energy "exorcising [the low and grotesque], charging it to others, using and adopting its very terms whilst attempting to purify the language of the tribe" (105), a view implying Swift was essentially an Augustan, also a position I reject.

20. John Boyle, Fifth Earl of Cork and Orrery, "Manuscript Notes (Houghton MS Eng. 218.14)" in *Remarks on the Life and Writing of Dr. Jonathan Swift,* ed. João Froés, 329–64, (Newark: University of Delaware Press, 2000), 330.

21. George Meredith, *An Essay on Comedy and the Uses of the Comic Spirit* (Westminster: Archibald Constable, 1903), 27.

22. Examples of stories about Roger: (1) One Sunday, as Roger Cox, Dean Swift's clerk, was going to church, his scarlet caught Swift's eye; Roger bowed, and observed that he wore scarlet because he belonged to the *church militant;* (2) When Swift was in Laracor, there happened to be a sale of farm and stock, the farmer being dead. Swift chanced to go past during the auction, just as a pen of poultry had been offered at auction. Roger bid for them: he was overbid by a farmer by the name of *Hatch.* "What, Roger, won't you buy the poultry?" exclaimed Swift. "No, sir," said Roger, "I see they are just *a' going to Hatch."* R. Wyse Jackson, in *Swift and his Circle* (Dublin: Talbot Press, 1945), has a whole chapter on "Roger Cox," in which he publishes poems purported authored by Roger. One has the couplet, "I love to see the Doctor [Swift] smile, / For it's the sunshine of our isle," from which Jackson infers that his stint at Laracor was "probably the happiest time in Swift's troubled life" (27). This may have been one of the anecdotes that appeared in *St. James's Evening Post,* Number 3098, August 28–30, 1735 and labeled "Dean Swift's Country Post," listed in Scouten-Teerink as #1629. Scott quotes Theophilus Swift, who says that Orrery's story about

Swift and Roger is pure fiction, designed to discredit Swift. Theophilus Swift claims that the story is a version of one he found in a jestbook "printed between 1655 and 1660" (61n).

23. A parody of the Nicene Creed attributed to Swift appears in the last part of the eighteenth century. Below is "Swift's Courtier's Creed" from a jestbook entitled *Scrapeana, op. cit.,* 172: I believe in [King George] the Second, . . . and in Sir [Robert Walpole], his only Minister, our Lord, who was begotten of Barrett the attorney, born of Mr. W. of Houghton, accused of corruption, convicted, expelled, and imprisoned. He went down into Norfolk; the third year he came up again . . . [etc.].

24. A. C. Elias, Jr., "Lord Orrery's Copy of *Memoirs of the Life of Swift* (1751)," *Eighteenth-Century Ireland,* 1 (1986), 111–25. Appendix II, (pp. 124–25) "Fresh Anecdotes of Swift," contains the texts of the stories added to Orrery's *Remarks,* from which I have quoted.

25. James Woolley pointed out to me the previous appearance of Swift's joke. *Ars Punica* was frequently attributed to Swift.

26. George Faulkner, "Some Further Account of Doctor Swift, in a Letter to the Earl of C[hesterfield]," Jonathan Swift, *Works,* 19 vols. (Dublin, 1762), 11: 249–68. The quotation comes from the 1763 edition, 309–10. For this information, my thanks to Lynne Farrington, Curator of Printed Books at the Annenberg Rare Book and Manuscript Library, University of Pennsylvania. In one later story of underclass impersonation (besides those included in Sheridan), Swift pretends to be a hangman to scare a farmer with whom he is forced to share a bed at a rustic inn. In *National Anecdotes: Interspersed with Historical Facts; English Proverbial Sayings, and Maxims, with a Collection of Toasts and Sentiments* (London: Craddock and Joy, 1812), 83. Scott says that there was a rumor that Swift visited the jailed printer of the *Drapier's Letters* disguised as "an Irish country clown, or *spalpeen"* (278).

27. Both Deane Swift and Samuel Johnson tend to repress the comic Swift in favor of the tragic one. Deane Swift repeats Orrery's "Dear Roger" story and adds a few more that illustrate Swift's rudeness, but these were not often reprinted. Samuel Johnson tells only one comic tale within his narrative, supposedly a story Pope told to Spence about how Swift insisted on reimbursing Pope and Gay because they had eaten supper before they came to visit him. Johnson notes that this "contempt of the general practice, is a kind of defiance which justly provokes the hostility of ridicule" (469).

28. During the late eighteenth century, anecdotes were very popular as a genre. All but 121 of the 1,130 items containing the keyword *anecdotes* in the ESTC were published from 1750–1800.

29. Although not all of the anecdotes in Sheridan's 125-page appendix are comic, a large proportion are.

30. Sheridan also repeats and embellishes the story of George Faulkner comingly to Swift in the latest fashion. In Sheridan's version, when Faulkner, properly chastened, returns in his usual attire, Swift tells him, "George, I am heartily glad to see you safe returned. Here was an impudent fellow in a lace waistcoat, who would feign have passed for you; but I soon sent him packing . . ." (337).

31. Swift's *Journal to Stella* is full of these proverbial sayings, some from the oral tra-
    dition and some made up on the spot as "instant" traditional lore—for exam-
    ple, "And now I'm in bed To break your head" (JS 1: 172); "Few fillings, many
    shillings. If the day be dark, my purse will be light (JS 2: 410); "If paper be thin,
    / Ink will slip in; / But if it be thick, / You may write with a stick" (JS 1: 93).
    In the note to this last squib, Herbert Davis notes "that the rhymes Swift passes
    off as old proverbs [here] were of his own invention" (JS 1: 93n12).
32. John Barrett, *Earlier Part of the Life of Swift,* 14–5.
33. Jarrell reports that this poem was first attributed to Swift in *The Agreeable
    Companion; Or, An Universal Medley* (London, 1745), 227. "Jack and the
    Dane," 333n2.
34. Faulkner, *Further Account,* 326–7. Faulkner also publishes a number of other
    new verses in a scatological vein.
35. These appeared in hundreds of places. All of them are included, for exam-
    ple, in *Fun for the Million, or The Laughing Philosopher* (London: Sherwood,
    Gilbert, and Piper, 1835).
36. Williams, "Notes," P 3: 1131–2.
37. Perhaps inspired by Swift's mock epitaphs, in 1929 a correspondent to *Notes
    and Queries* sent in two epitaphs attributed to Swift, which he claims to have
    heard recited 60 years previously by an uncle, who was a clergyman. Another
    correspondent pointed out that one of the epitaphs had already appeared in
    a differing version in *Gleanings in Graveyards,* published in 1861. See Harold
    Williams, "Notes," P 3:1147.
38. *Swiftiana,* ed. [C. H. Wilson], 2 vols. (London: Phillips, 1804), 2: 3
39. One popular item is an epigram by Swift given the title "At Home and
    Abroad," which first appeared in the Swift-Pope *Miscellanies.* It begins "As
    Thomas was cudgell'd one day by his Wife" (P 1: 327). It was published in a
    number of collections, for example, *An Anthology of Humor Verse,* eds. Helen
    and Louis Melville (London: George Harrap, Co., 1910), and reprinted as a
    filler, for example, in *Good Housekeeping Magazine* 141 (November 1955), 14.
40. Jarrell, "Jack and the Dane," 317, 320. Jarrell notes that "a crude versions of
    this [latter] anecdote appeared in *Teague-land Jests, or, Bog-Witticisms* (Lon-
    don, 1690)" (320n1), which derived from a standard formula in the fabliaux,
    into which Swift's name was inserted during the eighteenth century. This
    story is retold by Lady Gregory. "Jonathan Swift, Dean of St. Patrick's Cathe-
    dral," in *The Kiltartan History Book* (Dublin: Colin Smythe: 1909); reprinted
    as *Irish Folktales,* ed. Henry Glassie (New York: Pantheon Books, 1985), 92.
41. Erica Jong, *Fanny,* 234. The chapter heading reads "Containing a short
    Sketch of the celebrated Dean Swift of Dublin, Author, Misanthrope, and
    Horse-Fancier extraordinaire . . ." (227).
42. John Bartlett, *Familiar Quotations,* 15th edition, ed. Emily Morrison Beck
    (Boston: Little, Brown and Co, 1980), 321–3. Bartlett's *Familiar Quotations*
    has been in constant demand since it first appeared in 1855.
43. George Saintsbury, *The Peace of the Augustans: A Survey of Eighteenth Cen-
    tury Literature as a Place of Rest and Refreshment* (London: G. Bell and Sons,
    1916), 27.

## Chapter Seven, pp. 165–187

1. Boorstin, *The Image,* 63.
2. Bronislaw Malinowski, *Myth in Primitive Psychology,* Psyche Miniatures, General Series, Number 6. (London: Kegan Paul, 1926), 124.
3. *Some Account of the Irish* (London, 1753), l.
4. Johnson, "Swift," 457–67.
5. [John Nichols], *A Supplement to Dr. Swift's Works, Being the Fourteenth in* [Hawkesworth's] *Collection* (London, 1779), t. p. From Faulkner's first collection of the works to Sir Walter Scott's in the early nineteenth century, the Teerink-Scouten *Bibliography of the Writings of Jonathan Swift* lists 33 editions of Swift's complete collected works published in England, Ireland, and Scotland, most with multiple issues.
6. Henry Jones, "On his Excellency the Earl of Chesterfield's Arrival in Ireland," in *Poems on Several Occasions* (London, 1759) and William Dunkin, "Epistola ad Franciscum Bindonem," [occasioned by Bindon's portrait of Swift] (Dublin, 1740), or "An Inscription Intended for a Monument to Dr. Swift," in vol. 40 of Samuel Johnson's *English Poets* (1779). In addition, Walter Harris, in his update and translation of Sir James Wave's *De Scriptoribus Hiberniae* (1664) as *The Writers of Ireland continued down to the present century* (Dublin, 1746) includes Swift. My thanks to Hermann Real for this source.
7. Mahony, *Irish Identity,* Chapter 3, "British Canonization and Irish Diffidence, 1755–1800," 46–65.
8. The impact on English culture of these democratizing collections and anthologies is discussed by Richard Altick, *The English Common Reader: A Social History of the Mass Reading Public, 1800–1900* (Chicago, IL and London: University of Chicago Press, 1957; Leah Price, *The Anthology and the Novel: From Richardson to George Eliot* (Cambridge, UK and New York: Cambridge University Press, 2000); and Barbara Benedict, *Making the Modern Reader: Cultural Mediation in Early Modern Literary Anthologies* (Princeton, NJ: Princeton University Press, 1996).
9. The *Dictionary of National Biography* notes that Tegg is mentioned as a popularizer of literature in Thomas Carlyle's famous petition on the copyright bill in April 1839. Other Swiftian *Beauties* were published by G. Kearsley (London, 1782) and J. and R. Byrn (Dublin, 1783).
10. *A Poetical Dictionary; or the Beauties of the English Poets, Alphabetically Displayed.* 4 vols. (London: 1761), 4: 6–7.
11. Ibid., "Preface," 1: vii–xi.
12. This is item #1619 in the Scouten-Teerink. The bibliography lists eight reprints of Swift's "Letter to a Young Lady," all of them in the late eighteenth century, 380–382.
13. Mahony [Fr. Prout], "Dean Swift's Madness," 66.
14. "Swift," in *Gallery of Illustrious Irishmen,* No. ix, "Swift," *Dublin University Magazine,* 15 (May 1840), 540.
15. W. E. H. Lecky, "Biographical Introduction," *The Prose Works of Jonathan Swift,* ed. Temple Scott, 11 vols. (London: George Bell, 1897), 1: lxxv.

16. I have drawn from a number of books on canon formation: John Guillory, *Cultural Capital: The Problem of Literary Canon Formation* (Chicago: University of Chicago Press, 1993); Brian Doyle, *English and Englishness* (London and New York: Routledge, 1989); Chris Baldick, *The Social Mission of English Criticism 1848–1932* (Oxford: Clarendon Press, 1983; rev., 1987).

17. Thackeray, *English Humourists,* 14–5.

18. Edmund Gosse, *History of English Literature 1660–1780* (London and New York: MacMillan, 1889), 141.

19. John Aikin, *Letters to a Young Lady on a Course of English Poetry* (1804), 2nd edition (London: J. Johnson, 1807), 64–5.

20. Jeffreys, "Scott's Edition of Swift," 46.

21. William Monck Mason, *The History and Antiquities of the Collegiate and Cathedral Church of St. Patrick, near Dublin, from Its Foundation in 1190, to the Year 1819,* quoted in *Swift: The Critical Heritage,* ed. Kathleen Williams (London: Routledge, 1970), 335–6.

22. M. Sarah Smedman, "Like Me, Like Me Not: *Gulliver's Travels* as Children's Book" (pp. 75–100) in *The Genres of Gulliver's Travels,* ed. Frederik N. Smith (Newark: University of Delaware Press; London and Toronto: Associated University Presses, 1990), 83–5. Of course, this trend continues into the twenty-first century, where children's books and videos routinely omit Swift's scatological and sexual references.

23. Peter Cunningham, "Note," *Specimens of the British Poets,* ed. Thomas Campbell; 2nd edition, ed. Peter Cunningham (London: John Murry, 1844), 383n.

24. William Francis Collier, *A History of English Literature* (London: T. Nelson and Sons, 1880), 282, 284; S. Austin Albione [pseud.?], "Swift," in *A Critical Dictionary of English Literature,* 3 vols. (Philadelphia: Lippincott, 1870, 2313); Edmund Gosse, *English Literature: An Illustrated Record,* 4 vols. (London: Heineman, 1903), 236, 237.

25. *Moral and Christian Duties* (London: Religious Tract Society, 1840), n. p.

26. Elbert Hubbard, "Swift," in *Little Journeys: to the Homes of Good Men and Great* (New York; London: G. P. Putnam, 1895), 155–5.

27. Jarrell, "Jack and the Dane," 331.

28. Yeats, "Introduction," *Words upon the Window-Pane,* 7, 6n1.

29. P. S. O'Hegarty, "Jonathan Swift: Irishman," *The Bell,* 10 (September 1945), 487.

30. Daniel Corkery, "Ourselves and Dean Swift: [review of] Lives by Stephen Gwynn," *Studies* 18 (July 1934), 215n.

31. Dermot Curtin, "Our Gaelic Democracy: Teaching the Lessons of History (with special reference to Swift)," 23 (July 1933), 592.

32. Irish revolutionary Gerry Conlon, whose false imprisonment by the English is depicted in *In the Name of the Father,* recalls that his anger against his oppressors kept him alive during his detention. He repeated the IRA slogan, "Burn everything English except their coal" as a mantra while in jail. ("The Lying Game," *The Washington Post,* 1/19/94, C1–2).

33. Dorothy Eagle and Hilary Carnell, compilers, *The Oxford Literary Guide to Great Britain and Ireland,* 2nd edition (Oxford; New York: Oxford University Press, 1992), 68c, 268c.

34. Jenny Weiss, ed., *Let's Go Ireland 1999* (New York: St. Martin's Press, 1999), 212.

35. *Oxford Literary Guide,* 269c.

36. Weiss, *Let's Go Ireland,* 148.

37. *Oxford Literary Guide,* 195a.

38. Ibid., 47a.

39. I would like to thank Dr. Christopher Fox for this information as well as the photographs of him posing with the star-crossed couple.

40. Sophie Shilleto Smith, *Dean Swift* (London: Methuen, 1910), plate facing 244. Smith also has pictures of, among other things, Vanessa's Bower, the Dean's Well (Laracor), and willows in Laracor "planted by himself." (Willows are notoriously short-lived.)

41. Thomas Murray, *Stella's Cottage: Jonathan Swift, Esther Johnson, and Her Cottage* (Trim, Co. Meath, IR: Trymme Press, 1991), 1, 4. These doubts were expressed by, among others, Dr. Eileen Carvill in a speech, which Murray describes as a "bombshell," at the Swift Tercentenary Celebrations in Trim, as well as earlier by William R. Wilde who, in *Beauties of the Boyne and Blackwater* (1849), opined that the story that Stella lived in the cottage was "apocryphal." Quoted in Murry, 33–34.

42. Swift is lumped with other "classical English writers," such as Shakepeare and Milton on the reading requirements found on the first English literature syllabus of Trinity College, Dublin (1856). Aileen Douglas and Ian Campbell Ross, "Singularity and the Syllabus" in *Locating Swift: Essay from Dublin on the 250th Anniversary of the Death of Jonathan Swift 1667–1745,* eds. Aileen Douglas, Patrick Kelly, and Ian Campbell Ross (Dublin: Four Courts Press, 1998, 168.

43. Bruce Stewart, "A Refuge in Language," *Visitor* (Spring 1989), 17 [Official publication of the Irish Hotels Federation.] In a more scholarly venue, Vivian Mercier's article, "Swift and the Gaelic Tradition," argues that both share a belief in the power of satire and that they have had a mutual influence on one another. (In *Fair Liberty Was All His Cry: A Tercentenary Tribute to Jonathan Swift 1667–1745,* ed. Norman Jeffares (New York: St. Martin's Press, 1967), 279–89.

44. Mary Moriarty and Catherine Sweeney, *Jonathan Swift: The Man Who Wrote Gulliver,* O'Brien Junior Biography Library, no. 5 (Dublin: O'Brien Press, 1990).

45. More information on the wonders of this ship, (launched in 1999) can be found on the Internet: "Current Projects: Jonathan Swift," *The Website for the Shipbuilding Industry.* Appropriately enough, the children's play area is called Lilliput. http://www.ship-technology.com/projects/swift/ (January 21, 2002).

46. George Saintsbury, "Swift" in *Chambers's Cyclopedia of English Literature,* ed. David Patrick. 3 vols. (London and Edinburgh: Chambers, 1903), 2: 122.

47. Peter Quennell, *History of English Literature* , (London: Widenfeld and Nicolson, 1973), 215.

48. *Oxford Anthology of English Literature* eds., Frank Kermode and John Hollander, 2 vols. (New York: Oxford University Press, 1973), 1: 1734.

49. *The Oxford Illustrated History of English Literature,* ed. Pat Rogers (Oxford: Oxford University Press, 1987), 231.

50. Michael Foot, *The Pen and the Sword: A Year in the Life of Jonathan Swift* (London: Macgibbon and Kee, 1959; reprinted 1966), 9.

51. Richard Rodino, *Swift Studies: An Annotated Bibliography* (New York; London: Garland Publishing, 1984), 41.

52. Reginald Charles Churchill, *He Served Human Liberty: An Essay on the Genius of Jonathan Swift* (London: Allen and Unwin, 1946), 56.

53. *The London Times* in Bourke scrapbook, without imprint (see Chapter 4, n31); Henry C. Brinton, "Swift's Forecast of Mars' Satellites," *Sky and Telescope* 15 (September 1956), 494; Howard Eves, ""The Astonishing Prediction in *Gulliver's Travels,*" *The Mathematics Teacher,* 54 (December 1961), 625–6.

54. A. L. Rowse, *Jonathan Swift, Major Prophet* (London: Thames and Hudson, 1975), 34, 170–85ff.

55. Bartlett notes that Swift's maxim—that in "the Business of laying *heavy Impositions,* Two and Two never made more than One" because of smuggling and other evasions of customs—found its way into the writings of David Hume, Lord Kames, Adam Smith, Alexander Hamilton, and numerous other modern economists.

56. Smith, *Swift,* 324.

57. Jonathan Swift, *Gulliver's Travels,* ed. Dimitry Mirksy (Moscow: Co-operative publishing Society of Foreign Workers in the USSR, 1935), xvii-xviii. Carole Fabricant, in "Swift's Political Legacy: Remembering the Past in Order to Imagine the Future," addresses Swift's inspiration to revolutionary thinkers. (In *Locating Swift: Essays from Dublin on the 250ᵗʰ Anniversary of the Death of Jonathan Swift 1667–1745,* eds. Aileen Douglas, Patrick Kelly, and Ian Campbell Ross (Dublin: Four Courts Press, 1998), 180–200.

58. David Brown, "Recollection Used Books," *Our Daily Bleed/Calendar: October 28.* www.eskimo.com/~recall/bleed/1028.htm (January 31, 2002).

59. For instance, *The Progress of Law and Justice. A Tale.* By the Late Dean Swift (Dublin; Printed for the Editor, 1776); *Radical Rhymes for "True Blue" Times,* by Jonathan Swift Redivivus (London: Simpkin, Marshall, and Co, 1880); or *Gulliver Joe* [a political satire], by Jonathan Quick Dean of St. Rattrick's (London: Isbister, 1903).

60. Carkan Moil, "Swift Solutions" on *Writerspace,* December 10, 2000, www.writerspace.com/authorboard/messages/885.html (January 21, 2002).

61. Blink Design Homepage, Book Covers. "Manic Press edition of Abolishing Christianity," 1999, www.blinkdesign.com/abolish.html (January 21, 2002); "Josh," Atheist Conversation: Man-made.net, www.man-made.net/contrib/quotes.html (January 21, 2002).

62. Karen Jo Gounaud, *Family Friendly Libraries.* www.fflibraries.org (February 4, 2000).

63. Ann Shields, "Heartfelt Advice; Ellen DeGeneres' mother will discuss her book on love and support of a gay child" [Ventura County Edition], *Los Angeles Times* (December 9, 2000), B8.

64. "Uniting Sexuality and Faith: The Love of God Knows No Barriers," *Love Makes a Family,* www.members.tripod.com/~uniting/contents/family.html (January 21, 2002) and "Good News," *Uniting Church in Australia, an Inclusive Church,* www.geocities.com/WestHollywood/Heights/2554/frame/frnews.html (March 2, 2000).

65. Greg Burkman, "'The Perv' offers challenging reading, difficult lesson," *Online Seattle Times,* October 24, 1999, www.seattletimes.newsource.com/news/entertainment/html98/perv_1991024.html (January 21, 2002).

66. "Must-Read Books: Results of a Reader Poll," *The Quill: Queer Individual Liberty Letter,* Vol. 1, no. 2. (February 1994), www.glil.org/quill/quill/942.html February 19, 2000.

67. Lee Jaffee, "Fathers of Feminism," in "Brief Entries," *Gulliver's Travels by Jonathan Swift,* www.jaffebros.com/lee/gulliver/sources/biography.html (January 21, 2002). Ellen Pollak, in *The Poetics of Sexual Myth* (1985), says that while she believes that Swift "never fully departs from the terms of gender . . . [in] Western thought, [he] delivers us before the opening out of unspoken possibilities. Ellen Pollak, *The Poetics of Gender: Gender and Ideology in the Verse of Swift and Pope* (Philadelphia: University of Pennsylvania Press, 1985), 178.

68. Fiona Morgan, "An Audience with the Queen," Salon Entertainment www.salon.com/ent/1998/07/23int.html (August 8, 2000).

69. Alec Hanley Bemis, "Hip-Hop's Clown Heavy: Kool Keith, Crazy Like a Fox," *Miami New Times Online* (Music), September 2, 1999, www.miaminewtimes.com/issues/1999–09–02/music2.html (January 21, 2002)

70. Nick Gillespie, "American Scream" [review of Howard Stern's *Miss America*], *ReasonOnline,* www.reason.com/9603/dept.bk.STERN.text.html (January 21, 2002).

71. Caliber Comics, "Jonathan Swift's *A Modest Proposal*" (advertisement), May 16, 2000, www.calibercomics.com/Checkout4Pro/TITLES/modest_proposal.htm. (January 21, 2002).

72. Norman O. Brown, Chapter 8, "The Excremental Vision," in *Life Against Death: The Psychoanalytic Meaning of History* (Middletown, CT: Wesleyan University Press, 179–201).

73. Ray Girvan, "Erotic Fiction: A Writer's Perspective: An Essay on the Erotic Novel and its Trends," *So You Want to Be a Writer?,* 1999, www.gloriabrame.com/glory/erotalk.html (January 21, 2002). Not only pornographers but science fiction writers look to Swift for inspiration. He is cited on a number of websites listing science fiction writers; Isaac Asimov, master of science fiction, annotated and edited *Gulliver's Travels. The Annotated Gulliver's Travels,* ed. Isaac Asimov (New York: Clarkson N. Potter, 1980).

74. Neil Postman, *Building a Bridge to the 18th Century: How the Past Can Improve our Future* (New York: Knopf, 1999).

# Selected Bibliography
# of Works Cited and Consulted

## Standard Editions of Swift's Works

Davis, Herbert, et al., eds. *The Prose Works of Jonathan Swift* (14 vols.). Oxford: Blackwell, 1939–68.

Ellis, Frank. *A Discourse of the Contents and Dissensions.* Edited by Frank Ellis. Oxford: Clarendon University Press, 1967.

Guthkelch, A. C. and D. Nichol Smith, eds. *A Tale of a Tub to Which Added the Battle of the Books and the Mechanical Operation of the Spirit.* 2nd ed. Oxford: Clarendon Press, 1958.

Williams, Harold, ed. *The Correspondence of Jonathan Swift.* 5 vols. Oxford: Clarendon Press, 1963–5.

———. *Journal to Stella.* 2 vols. Oxford: Blackwell, 1974.

———. *The Poems of Jonathan Swift.* 3 vols. Oxford: Clarendon Press, 1937, rev. 1958.

Woolley, James, ed. *The Intelligencer* [by Swift and Sheridan]. Oxford: Clarendon Press, 1992.

## Scholarship on Jonathan Swift, Biographies Excluded

Berwick, Donald M. *The Reputation of Jonathan Swift (1781–1882).* Philadelphia, 1941.

Bond, Richard. "Isaac Bickerstaff, Esq." *Restoration and Eighteenth-Century: Essays in Honor of Alan Dugald Mckillop,* Edited by Carroll Camden. Chicago: University of Chicago Press, 1963.

Brown, Norman O. Chapter 8, "The Excremental Vision." 179–201. In *Life Against Death: The Psychoanalytic Meaning of History.* Middletown, CN: Wesleyan University Press, 1959.

Chalmers, Alan. *Jonathan Swift and the Burden of the Future.* Newark: University of Delaware Press, 1995.

Elias, A. C. *Swift at Moor Park.* Philadelphia: University of Pennsylvania Press: 1982.

———. "Lord Orrery's Copy of *Memoirs of the Life of Swift* (1751)." *Eighteenth-Century Ireland* 1 (1986), 111–25.

Fabricant, Carole. *Swift's Landscape.* Baltimore and London: Johns Hopkins University Press, 1982.

———. "Swift's Political Legacy: Remembering the Past in Order to Imagine the Future," 180–200. In *Locating Swift: Essays from Dublin on the 250ᵗʰ Anniversary of the Death of Jonathan Swift, 1667–1745.* Edited by Aileen Douglas, Patrick Kelly, and Ian Campbell Ross. Dublin: Four Courts Press, 1998.

Ferguson, Oliver. "The Authorship of 'Apollo's Edict,'" *PMLA* 70 (1955): 433–40.

Fischer, John, I. "Love and Books: Some Early Texts of Swift's 'Cadenus and Vanessa' and a Few Words about Love." In *Reading Swift: Papers from the Fourth Münster Symposium on Jonathan Swift.* Edited by Hermann J. Real and Helgard Stöver-Leidig. Munich: Wilhelm Fink, forthcoming, 2002.

Gámez, Luis, R. "Richard Bettesworth's Insult and 'The Yahoos Overthrow,'" *Swift Studies* 12 (1997): 80–4.

Gold, Maxwell. *Swift's Marriage to Stella.* Cambridge: Harvard University Press: 1937.

Harth, Phillip. *Swift and Anglican Rationalism.* Chicago: University of Chicago Press, 1961.

Jarrell, Mackie L. "Jack and the Dane: Swift Traditions in Ireland." In *Fair Liberty Was All His Cry: A Tercentenary Tribute to Jonathan Swift, 1667–1745.* Edited by A. Norman Jeffares. 311–341. New York: St. Martins Press, 1967.

———. "'Ode to the King': Some Contests, Dissensions, and Exchanges Among Jonathan Swift, John Dunton, and Henry Jones. *Texas Studies in Language and Literature* 7 (1965): 145–59.

Johnson, Maurice. "A Literary Chestnut: Dryden's 'Cousin Swift.'" *PMLA* 62 (1952): 814–827.

Kelly, Ann Cline. "The Birth of Swift." *Reading Swift: Papers From the Second Münster, Symposium on Jonathan Swift.* Edited by Richard H. Rodino and Hermann Real. 11–24. Munich: Wilhelm Fink, 1993.

———. "Swift's Battle of the Books: Fame in the Modern Age." *Reading Swift: The Third Münster Symposium on Jonathan Swift.* Edited by Hermann Real and Helgard Stöver-Leidig. 9–100. Munich: Wilhelm Fink, 1998.

———. "Swift's Enigma and the Mythopoeic Process in Print Culture" *The Enigmatic Dean.* Edited by Rudolf Friebury, Arno Löffler, and Wolfgang Zach. Tübingen, Germany: Stauffenburg, 1998.

Korshin, Paul. "The Earl of Orrery and Swift's Reputation." *Harvard Library Bulletin.* 16 (1968): 167–77.

Lewis, Jayne Elizabeth. "Swift's Aesop / Bentley's Aesop: The Modern Body and the Figures of Antiquity." *The Eighteenth Century.* 32:2 (1991): 99–118.

Lowe, N.F. "Why Swift Killed Partridge?" *Swift Studies.* 6 (1991): 70–82.

Mahony, Robert. *Jonathan Swift: The Irish Identity.* New Haven: Yale University Press, 1995.

Malcolm, Elizabeth. Chapter 1, "Dean Swift and Madness." In *Swift's Hospital: A History of St. Patrick's Hospital, Dublin, 1746–1989.* 1–31. Dublin: Gill and Macmillan, 1989.

Mayhew, George. "Swift's Bickerstaff as an April Fool's Joke," *Modern Philology,* 61 (1964), 270–280.

Mercier, Vivian. "Swift and the Gaelic Tradition." In *Fair Liberty Was All His Cry: A Tercentenary Tribute to Jonathan Swift 1667–1745.* Edited by A. Norman Jeffares. 279–289. New York: St. Martins Press, 1967.

Novak, Maximillian E. "Swift and Defoe: Or, How Contempt Breeds Familiarity and a Degree of Influence." *Proceedings of the First Münster Symposium on Jonathan Swift.* Edited by Hermann Real and Heinz Vienken. 157–174. Munich: Wilhelm Fink, 1985.

Ormsby-Lennon, Hugh. "*Classis?* Under the State Itinerant." In *Swift: The Enigmatic Dean.* Edited by Rudolf Freiburg, Arno Löffler, and Wolfgang Zach (Tübingen, Germany: Stauffenburg Verlag, 1998), 173–200.

Peterson, Leland D. "Swift's *Project:* A Religious and Political Satire." *PMLA* 82 (1967): 54–63.

Quinlan, Maurice J. "Swift's Project for the Advancement of Religion and the Reformation of Manners." *PMLA.* 71 (1956): 201–212.

Reynolds, Richard. "Swift's Humble Petition from a Pregnant Frances Harris?" *Scriblerian* 5 (1972): 38–9.

Rodino, Richard. *Swift Studies: an Annotated Bibliography.* New York; London: Garland Publishing, 1984.

Rogers, Pat. Notes. *The Complete Poems.* Edited by Pat Rogers. New Haven: Yale University Press, 1983.

Scouten, Arthur H. "Jonathan Swift's Progress from Prose to Poetry." in *The Poetry of Jonathan Swift: Papers Read at a Clark Library Seminar,* January 20, 1979. Edited by Maximillian Novak, 29–31. Los Angeles: William Andrews Clark Memorial Library, 1981.

Shinagel, Michael, ed. *A Concordance to the Poems of Jonathan Swift.* Ithaca, NY; London: Cornell University Press, 1972.

Slepian, Barry. "George Faulkner's *Dublin Journal* and Jonathan Swift." *Pennsylvania Library Chronicle* 31 (1965): 97–116.

Smedman, M. Sara. "Like Me, like Me Not: Gulliver's Travels as Children's Book." In *The Genres of Gulliver's Travels.* Edited by by Frederik N. Smith. 75–100. Newark: University of Delaware Press, 1990.

Teerink, Herman. *A Bibliography of the Writings of Jonathan Swift.* 2nd edition, revised and corrected. Edited by Arthur H. Scouten. Philadelphia: University of Pennsylvania Press, 1963.

Voigt, Milton. *Swift and the Twentieth Century.* Detroit, MI: Wayne State University Press, 1964.

Welcher, Jeanne, editor and compiler. *An Annotated List of Gulliveriana 1721–1800.* Delmar, NY: Scholars' Facsimiles and Reprints, 1988.

Woolley, David. "The Author of the Examiner and the Whiggish Answer-jobbers." *Swift Studies,* 5 (1990), 91–111.

Woolley, James, "Arbuckle's Panegyric and Swift's Scrub Libel: The Documentary Evidence." In *Contemporary Studies of Swift's Poetry.* Edited by John Fischer. Irwin and Donald C. Mell, 191–210. Newark, DE: University of Delaware Press, 1981.

## Modern Scholarship on Restoration
## and Eighteenth-Century Culture

Achinstein, Sharon. "The Politics of Babel in the English Revolution." In *Pamphlet Wars: Prose in the English Revolution.* Edited by James Holstun. 14–24. London; Portland, OR: Frank Cass, 1992.

Belanger, Terry. "Publishers and Writers in Eighteenth-century England." In *Books and their Readers in Eighteenth-Century England.* Edited by Isabel Rivers. 5–26. New York: Leicester University Press; St. Martin Press, 1982.

Benedict, Barbara. *Making the Modern Reader: Cultural Mediation in Early Modern Literary Anthologies.* Princeton, NJ: Princeton University Press, 1996.

Brewer, Derek. "Prose Jest-books Mainly in the Sixteenth to Eighteenth Centuries in England." In *A Cultural History of Humor from Antiquity to the Present Day.* Edited by Jan Bremmer and Herman Roodenberg, 90–111. Cambridge, UK: Polity Press, 1997.

Broadus, Edmund. *The Laureateship: A Study in the Office of the Poet Laureate of England, with Some Account of the Poets.* Oxford: Clarendon Press, 1921.

Byrd, Max. *Visits to Bedlam: Madness and Literature in the Eighteenth Century.* Columbia: University of South Carolina Press, 1974.

Capp, Bernard. *Astrology and the Popular Press. English Almanacs, 1500–1800.* London; Boston: Faber, 1979.

Cole, Susan Letzer. *The Absent One: Mourning Ritual, Tragedy, and the Performance of Ambivalence.* University Park: Pennsylvania University Press, 1985.

Colley, Linda. *Britons: Forging the nation 1707–1837.* New Haven and London: Yale University Press, 1992.

Downie, Alan. *Robert Harley and the Press: Propaganda and Public Opinion in the Age of Swift and Defoe.* Cambridge, UK: Cambridge University Press, 1979.

Foucault, Michel. *The History of Sexuality: An Introduction.* 3 vols. Translated by Robert Hurley. New York: Vintage Books, 1978; rpt. 1990.

———. *Madness and Civilization: A History of Insanity in the Age of Reason.* Translated by Richard Howard. New York: Random House, 1965; rpt. 1973.

Habermas, Jürgen. *The Structural Transformation of the Public Sphere: an Inquiry into a Category of Bourgeois Society.* Translated by Thomas Burger with Frederick Lawrence. Cambridge, MA: MIT University Press, 1989.

Hammond, Brean. *Professional Imaginative Writing in England, 1670–1740.* Oxford: Clarendon Press, 1997.

Helgerson, Richard. *Self-Crowned Laureates: Spenser, Jonson, Milton, and the Literary System.* Berkeley: University of California Press, 1983.

Hunter, J. Paul. *Before Novels: the Cultural Contexts of Eighteenth Century Fiction.* New York: Norton, 1990.

Jackson, Victor. *The Monuments of St. Patrick's Cathedral Dublin.* Dublin: St. Patrick's Cathedral, 1987.

Kernan, Alvin. *Printing Technology, Letters, and Samuel Johnson.* Princeton, NJ: Princeton University Press, 1987.

Klein, Lawrence. *Shaftesbury and the Culture of Politeness: Moral Discourse and Culture of Politeness in Early Eighteenth Century England.* Cambridge: Cambridge University Press, 1994.

Levine, Joseph. *The Battle of the Books: History and Literature in the Augustan Age.* Ithaca, NY: Cornell University Press, 1991.

Love, Harold. *Scribal Publication in England.* Oxford: Clarendon Press, 1993.

McEwen, Gilbert. *The Oracle of the Coffee House: John Dunton's Athenian Mercury.* San Marino, CA: The Huntington Library, 1972.

Nuttall, A. D. *Why Does Tragedy Give Pleasure?* Oxford: Clarendon Press, 1985.

Patterson, Annabel. *Fables of Power: Aesopian Writing and Political History.* Durham, NC: Duke University Press, 1991.

Paulson, Ronald. *Popular and Polite Art in the Age of Hogarth and Fielding.* Notre Dame: IN and London, England: University of Notre Dame Press, 1979.

Reiss, Timothy J. *Tragedy and Truth: Studies in the Development of a Renaissance and Neoclassical Discourse.* New Haven, CT: Yale University Press, 1980.

Saisselin, Remy. "Imaginary Libraries in the Eighteenth Century." *Studies on Voltaire and the Eighteenth Century* (1993): 115–41.

Shaffer, Julia. "Familial Love, Incest and Female Desire in Late Eighteenth-century and Early Nineteenth Century Novels." *Criticism.* (Winter 1999), 41:1: 67–99.

Speck, W. A. "Politicians, Peers, and Publication by Subscription 1700–1750." In *Books and their Readers in Eighteenth-Century England.* Edited by Isabel Rivers. 47–68. New York: St. Martin's Press, 1982.

Stallybrass, Peter and Allon White. "The Grotesque Body and the Smithfield Muse: Authorship in the Eighteenth Century." In *The Politics and Poetics of Transgression.* Chapter 2. Ithaca, NY: Cornell University Press, 1986.

Straus, Ralph. *The Unspeakable Curll.* London: Chapman and Hall, 1927.

Torrance, Robert M. *The Comic Hero.* Cambridge, MA: Harvard University Press, 1978.

Turner, E. S. *Unholy Pursuits: the Wayward Parsons of Grub Street.* Lewes, Sussex, England: Book Guild, 1998.

Wilson, Daniel. "Science, Natural Law, and Unwitting Sibling Incest in Eighteenth-century Literature." *Studies in Eighteenth Century Culture* 13 (1984), 249–70.

Wurzbach, Natascha. Appendix B86 in *The Rise of the English Street Ballad 1550–1650.* Cambridge, UK; New York: Cambridge University Press, 1990.

Zwicker, Stephen. "Representing the Revolution: Politics and High Culture in 1689." In *The Revolution of 1688–89: Changing Perspectives.* Edited by Lois Schwoerer, 165–183. Cambridge: Cambridge University Press.

### Scholarship and Theory on Myth, Fame, Culture Formation, Popular Culture, Authorship, Publication, Reading, and Genre

Allport, Gordon and Leo Postman. *The Psychology of Rumor.* New York: Holt, 1947.

Altick, Richard. *The English Common Reader: A Social History of the Mass Reading Public, 1800–1900.* Chicago; London: University of Chicago Press, 1957.

Apte, Mahadev L. *Humor and Laughter: an Anthropological Approach.* London; Ithaca, NY: Cornell University Press, 1985.

Bakhtin, Mikhail. *Rabelais and His World.* Translated by Helene Iswolsky. Cambridge: MA: MIT University Press, 1968.

Baldick, Chris. *The Social Mission of English Criticism 1848–1932.* Oxford: Clarendon Press, 1983.

Barthes, Roland. *Mythologies.* Translated by Annette Lavers. New York: Hill and Wang, 1972.

———. *The Pleasure of the Text.* Translated by Richard Miller. New York: Hill and Wang, 1975.

Bird, S. Elizabeth. *For Enquiring Minds: A Cultural Study of Supermarket Tabloids.* Knoxville: University of Tennessee Press, 1992.

Bennett, Tony and Janet Woollacott. *Bond And Beyond: The Political Career of a Popular Hero.* New York: Methuen, 1987.

Bloom, Harold. *The Anxiety of Influence: A Theory of Poetry.* New York: Oxford University Press, 1973.

Boorstin, Daniel. *The Image: A Guide to Pseudo-events in America.* New York: Vintage Books, 1961; rpt. 1992.

Braudy, Leo. *The Frenzy of Renown The History of Fame.* New York: Oxford University Press, 1986.

Charnes, Linda. *Notorious Identity: Materializing the Subject in Shakespeare.* Cambridge, MA; London: Harvard University Press, 1993.

Dégh, Linda. *American Folklore in the Mass Media.* Bloomington: University of Indiana Press, 1994.

Dobson, R. B. "Robin Hood: The Genesis Of Popular Hero." In *Robin Hood in Popular Culture: Violence, Transgression, and Justice.* Edited by Thomas Hahn 61–78. Cambridge: D.S. Brewer, 2000.

———and J. Taylor *Rymes of Robyn Hood: an Introduction to the English Outlaw.* Pittsburgh: University of Pittsburgh Press, 1976.

Doyle, Brian. *English and Englishness.* London and New York: Routledge, 1989.

Douglas, Aileen and Ian Campbell Ross. "Singularity and the Syllabus." In *Locating Swift: Essay from Dublin on the 250$^{th}$ Anniversary of the Death of Jonathan Swift 1667–1745.* Edited by Aileen Douglas, Patrick Kelly, and Ian Campbell Ross. 167–179. Dublin: Four Courts Press, 1998.

Eisenstein, Elizabeth. *The Printing Press as an Agent of Change. Communications and Cultural Transformations in Early Modern Europe,* 2 vols. Cambridge, UK; New York: Cambridge University Press, 1979.

Frye, Northrop. *The Secular Scripture: a Study of the Structure of Romance.* Cambridge, MA: Harvard University Press, 1976.

Guillory, John. *Cultural Capital: the Problem of Literary Canon Formation.* Chicago: University Press, 1993.

Hall, David. *Culture of Print. Essays in the History of the Book.* Amherst: University of Massachusetts Press, 1996.

Hilton, R.H. "The Origins of Robin Hood." In *Robin Hood: an Anthology of Scholarship and Criticism.* Edited by Stephen Knight, 197–210. Cambridge, UK: D. S. Brewer, 1999.

———. "The Birth and Settling of the Ballads of Robin Hood. In *Robin Hood: an Anthology of Scholarship and Criticism.* Edited by Stephen Knight. 233–256. Cambridge, UK: D.S. Brewer, 1999

Hodges, Jack. *The Genius of Writers: The Lives of English Writers Compared.* New York: St. Martin's Press, 1994.

Knight, Stephen. "Which Way to the Forest? Directions in Robin Hood Studies." In *Robin Hood in Popular Culture: Violence, Transgression and Justice*. Edited by Thomas Hahn. 111–128. Cambridge, UK: D.S. Brewer, 2000.

Koenig, Fredrick. *Rumor in the Marketplace: The Social Psychology of Commercial Hearsay.* Dover, MA: Auburn House, 1985.

Lane, William Coolidge, Edited by *Catalogue of English and American Chap-Books and Broadside Ballads in Harvard College Library.* Cambridge, MA: Harvard College Library, 1905.

Lipking, Lawrence. *The Life of the Poet: Beginning and Ending Poetic Careers.* Chicago: University of Illinois Press, 1981.

Lynch, Aaron. *Thought Contagion: How Belief Spreads Through Society: The New Science of Memes.* New York: Basic Books, 1996.

Malinowski, Bronislaw. *Myth in Primitive Psychology.* Psyche Miniatures, General Series, Number 6. London: Kegan Paul, 1926.

Marshall, R. David, *Celebrity and Power: Fame in Contemporary Culture.* Minneapolis; London: University of Minnesota Press, 1997.

Mullan, John and Christopher Reid, "Introduction." In *Eighteenth-Century Popular Culture: A Selection.* Edited by John Mullan and Christopher Reid. 1–28. Oxford: Oxford University Press, 2000.

Perry, Edwin. *Studies in the Text History of the Life and Fables of Aesop.* Haverford, PA: American Philological Association, 1936.

Price, Leah. *The Anthology and the Rise of the Novel: From Richardson to George Eliot.* Cambridge, UK: Cambridge University Press, 2000.

Prideaux, W. F. "Who Was Robin Hood?" In *Robin Hood: an Anthology of Scholarship and Criticism.* Edited by Stephen Knight. 51–58. Cambridge: Cambridge University Press, 1999.

Radway, Janice. *Reading the Romance: Women, Patriarchy, and Popular Literature.* Chapel Hill: University of North Carolina Press, 1984.

Raglan, Lord. [Somerset, FitzRoy Richard]. *The Hero: A Study in Tradition, Myth, and Drama.* London: Methuen, 1936.

Spufford, Margaret. *Small Books and Pleasant Histories: Popular Fiction and its Readership in Seventeenth-Century England.* Athens: University of Georgia Press, 1982.

Stewart, Susan. *Crimes of Writing: Problems in the Containment of Representation.* Durham: Duke University Press, 1994.

Torrance, Robert. *The Comic Hero.* Cambridge, MA: Harvard University Press, 1978.

Verbeckmoes, Johan. *Laughter, Jestbooks, and Society in the Spanish Netherlands.* New York: St. Martin's Press, 1999.

Vickery, John B. *Myths and Texts: Strategies of Incorporation and Displacement.* Baton Rouge, La: Louisiana State University Press, 1983.

Watt, Tessa. *Cheap Print and Popular Piety, 1550–1640.* Cambridge, UK: Cambridge University Press, 1991.

White, Hayden. *The Content of the Form: Narrative Discourse and Historical Representation.* Baltimore, MD: John Hopkins University Press, 1987.

## Biographies of Swift
### as Well as Other Works in which Swift is
### Referenced, Discussed or Characterized—Organized by Century.

*1. The Eighteenth Century*

"The Account of Dean Swift . . . an Epitome of the Earl of Orrery's Letters to his Son," *Gentleman's Magazine* 22 (August 1752), 360–2.

"Advice to a Certain Dean." n.p., 1730.

"An Answer to Hamilton's Bawn, Or, a Short Character of Dr. S—t." [Dublin, 1732].

[Arbuckle, James]. "Momus Mistaken: A Fable, Occasioned by the Publication of the Works of the Revd. Dr. Swift." Dublin, 1735.

[———]. "A Panegyric on the Reverend D—n S—t, in Answer to the Libel on Dr. D——y, and a Certain Great Lord." Dublin and London, 1729.

[Arthbuthnot, John]. *It Cannot Rains but it Pours: Or, London Strow'd with Rarities.* London, 1726.

Berkeley, George-Monck. *Literary Relics . . . To which is prefix'd, An Inquiry into the Life of Dean Swift.* London, C. Elliot, *et al.,* 1789.

[Boyer, Abel]. *The Political state of Great Britain.* London, 1713.

[Burnet, Thomas, attrib.]. *Essays Divine, Moral and Political . . . by the Author of the Tale of a Tub, Sometime Writer of the Examiner, and Original Inventor of the Band-box-plot.* London, 1714.

"Caelia's Revenge . . . Being and Answer to the Lady's Dressing-room." London, 1732.

"A Candid Appeal from the Late Dean Swift to the Right. Hon. The Earl of O——y." London, 1752.

"Chloe Surpriz'd: or the Second Part of the Lady's Dressing Room. Dublin and London, 1741.

C.M.P.G.N.S.T.N.S. [pseud.] "Anecdotes of Dean Swift and Miss Johnson." *Gentleman's Magazine.* (November, 1757): 487–91.

Collins, Anthony. *Discourse Concerning Ridicule and Irony in Writing. In a Letter to the Reverend Dr. Nathanael Marshall.* (London, 1729). Facsimile reprint. Augustan Reprint Society, Number 142. Introduction by Edward and Lillian Bloom. Los Angeles, CA: William Andrews Clark Library, 1970.

"A Curry Comb of Truth for a Certain Dean; or the Grub-stress Tribunal." Dublin, 1736.

[Defoe, Daniel, attrib.]. *The History of the Jacobite Clubs.* London, 1712.

Delany, Patrick. *Observations on Lord Orrery's Remarks on the Life and Writings of Dr. Jonathan Swift.* London, 1754.

Diaper, William. "An Imitation of the Seventeenth Epistle of the First Book of Horace, Address'd to Dr. Swift." In *The Complete Works of William Diaper.* Edited by Dorothy Broughton. London: Routledge and Kegan Paul, 1953.

"The Devil's Gratitude. A Poem in Answer to a Late Poem, Intitled the Place of the Damn'd." n.p., n.d.

*Dr. S——'s Real Diary: Being a True and Faithful Account of Himself. Containing His Entire Journal from the Time He Left London to His Settling in Dublin.* London, 1715.

"The Draper's Apparition to G——ge F————r, a New Poem." Dublin, 1745.

Dunkin, William. "Epistola ad Franciscum Bindonem." Dublin, 1740.

"An Epistle to Mr. A. Pope, Occasion'd by Two Epistles Lately Published." London, 1730.

Faulkner, George, ed. *The Works of J.S., D.D., D.S., P.D.* 4 vols. Dublin, 1735.

———. "Some Further Account of Doctor Swift, in a Letter to the Earl of C[hesterfield]." *Works.* 19 vols. Dublin, 1762. 11: 249–68.

"A Great Plot! The Second Part of the St. Paul's Screw Plot Or, Mine A—in a Banbox." In *The letters of Thomas Burnet to George Duckett: 1712–22.* Edited by D. Nichol Smith, 225–6. Oxford: The Roxburghe Club, 1914.

"The Gentleman's Study in Answer to the Lady's Dressing Room." London and Dublin, 1732.

"A Genuine Epistle from M[atthe]w P[rio]r, Esq. At Paris; to the Revd. Dr. J—n S—t at Windsor." In *A Farther Hue and Cry After Dr. Sw—T (London, 1714).* In *Two Rare Pamphlets Attributed to Swift.* Occasional papers; Reprint Series No. 4. San Francisco: California State Library. (Typescript).

*Gulliver Decypher'd: or Remarks on a Late Book, Intitled Travels into Several Remote Nations of the World.* London, 1727.

Hosier, A. R.[pseud.]. "A Poem to the Whole People of Ireland, Relating to N. B. Drapier." Dublin, 1726.

*An Hue and Cry after the Examiner. Dr. Swift. Occasion'd by a True and Exact Copy of Part of His Own Diary . . .* London, 1714.

"An Indian Tale." In Smedley, *Gulliveriana: Or, A fourth volume of Miscellanies, being a sequel of the three volumes published by Pope and Swift.* London, 1728.

Johnson, Samuel. "Swift." *Lives of the Poets in Selected Poetry and Prose.* Edited by Frank Brady and W. K. Wimsatt. 445–72. Berkeley and Los Angeles, CA; London: University of California Press, 1977.

Jones, Henry. "On His Excellency the Earl of Chesterfield's Arrival in Ireland." In *Poems on Several Occasions.* London, 1759.

[King, William.] *Remarks on a Tale of a Tub.* London, 1704.

*A Letter from Dean Swift to George F—k—r.* Dublin, 1752.

*A Letter from a Clergyman to His Friend, with an Account of the Travels of Capt. Lemuel Gulliver; and a Character of the Author. To Which Is Added, the True Reasons Why a Certain Doctor Was Made a Dean.* London, 1726.

*A Letter to the Reverend Mr. Dean Swift, Occasion'd by a Satire Said to Be Written by Him, Entitled a Dedication to a Great Man.* London, 1718.

Lonergan, Edward. "The Dean and the Country Parson." Dublin, 1739.

Mainwaring, Arthur. *The British Academy: Being a New-erected Society for the Advancement of Wit and Learning: With Some Few Observations Upon It.* Facsimile reprint. In *Poetry and Language,* The Augustan Reprint Society, Series 6; number 1, introduction by Louis Landa (Ann Arbor, MI: The Augustan Reprint Society, 1948).

———. *The Medley.* In *Swift vs. Mainwaring: The Examiner and The Medley.* Edited by Frank H. Ellis. Oxford: Clarendon Press, 1985.

"Mr. Lewis of Covent Garden, His Letter to Dr. Swift." In *The Tickler,* No III. London, 1719.

*Mrs. Pilkington's Jests; or the Cabinet of Wit and Humor. Being a Choice Collection of the Most Brilliant [sic] Jokes, Facetious Puns, Smart Repartee, and Entertaining Tales, in Prose and Verse.* London, 1759.

[Mullan, David, attrib.], "David Mullan's Letter to Dean Swift." Dublin, 1735.

[J———n N————n]. "A Funeral Elegy on the Father of his Country, the Rev. Dr. Jonathan Swift." [Dublin, 1745.]

Nichols, John. *A Supplement to Dr. Swift's Works, Being the Fourteenth in* [Hawkesworth's] *Collection* [of Swift's Works]. London, 1779.

"The Ode-Maker." reprinted as "A Letter to the Author; Occasion'd by the Foregoing Ode [An Ode to the Earl of Cadogan, by D-n Sm–y]. *Miscellaneous Poems . . . Published by Mr. Concanen.* London, 1724.

[Oldmixon, John], *Reflections on Dr. Swift's Letter to the Earl of Oxford about the English Tongue.* Facsimile reprint. In *Poetry and Language,* The Augustan Reprint Society, Series 6; number 1, introduction by Louis Landa (Ann Arbor: The Augustan Reprint Society, 1948).

"One Epistle to Mr. A. Pope, Occasion'd by Two Epistles Lately Published." (London, 1730).

Orrery and Cork, Earl. (John Boyle, 5th Earl). "Manuscript Notes." In *Remarks on the Life and Writing of Dr. Jonathan Swift.* Edited by João Froés. 329–64. Newark: University of Delaware Press, 2000.

———. *Remarks on the Life and Writings of Dr. Jonathan Swift.* Dublin; London, 1751. (I quote from the second "corrected edition," London, 1752).

Percival, William. "A Description in Answer to the Journal." Dublin, 1722.

Pilkington, Laetitia. *Memoirs . . .* 1748–54. 2 vols. Edited by A. C. Elias. Athens, GA: University of Georgia Press, 1982.

Pilkington, Matthew. *Poems on Several Occasions . . . Revised by the Reverend Dr. Swift.* 2nd edition (with the frontispiece honoring Swift). London, 1731.

"The Plotter Found Out: Or, Mine Arse in a Band-box." 1712. In *Poems on Affairs of State.* Edited by George deLord et al. 7 vols. 7:578. New Haven, CT and London: Yale University Press, 1963–75.

"Plot Upon Plot: A Ballad." 1712. In *Political Ballads of the Seventeenth and Eighteenth Centuries.* Edited by W. W. Wilkins. London: Longman,1860.

"A Poem on the Dean of St. Patrick's Birthday, November 30th Being St. Andrews Day." Dublin, 1726.

*A Poetical Dictionary; or the Beauties of the English Poets, Alphabetically Display'd.* 4 vols. London, 1761.

[Ralph, James]. "Sawney: An Heroic Poem." London, 1728.

*Saint Patrick's Purgatory: Or, Dr. S———t's Expostulation with His Distressed Friends in the Tower and Elsewhere.* London, 1716.

"A Second Poem to D—S—." Dublin, 1725.

Sheridan, Thomas. *The Life of the Rev. Dr. Jonathan Swift, Dean of St. Patrick's Dublin.* London, 1784.

[Smedley, Jonathan.] *Gulliveriana: Or, a Fourth Volume of Miscellanies, Being a Sequel of the Three Volumes Published by Pope and Swift.* London, 1728.

[———.] "A Satyr." Dublin, 1725.

[————.] "Verses Fasten'd to the Gate of St. P[atrick's] C[hurc]h D[oo]r, on the Day of I[nstallmen]t of a Certain D[ea]n." In *An Hue and Cry after the Examiner. Dr. Swift. Occasion'd by a True and Exact Copy of Part of His Own Diary . . .* London, 1714. (I quote from the 1727 edition.)

*Some Memoirs of Amours and Intrigues of a Certain Irish Dean . . . and the Gallantries of Two Berkshire Ladies.* London, 1729.

Swift, Deane. *An Essay upon the Life, Writings, and Character of Dr. Jonathan Swift* London, 1755.

Swift, Jonathan, [attrib.]. "The Dean's Answer to David Mullan's Letter." Dublin, 1735.

————, [attrib.]. "Ub–Bub–A-Boo: Or, The Irish Howl. In Heroic Verse." London, 1735.

*Swift's Jests, or a Compendium of Wit and Humour. Being the Facetious Jokes . . . Of the Most Eminent Wits, Viz. Swift* [et al.] London, 1759.

*A Tale of a Tub Revers'd . . . With a Character of the Author.* London, 1705.

"A Town Eclogue: or a Poetical Contest between Toby and a Minor-Poet of B-tt-n's Coffee-house . . . Inscribed to the Author of the *Tale of a Tub.*" London, 1714.

[Vanhomrigh, Esther, attrib.]. "A Rebus on Dean Swift." In *Miscellanea.* Compiled by Edmund Curll, Edited by 2 vols. London, 1727.

"W[hitshe]d's Ghost Appears to the R————d D—n S——t." Dublin, 1727.

Wortley, Mary, Lady Montague. "The Dean's Provocation for Writing the Lady's Dressing Room." 1734. Reprinted in Robert Halsband, "'The Lady's Dressing Room' Explicated by a Contemporary." In *The Augustan Milieu Essays Presented to Louis A. Landa.* Edited by Henry Knight Miller, et al. Oxford: The Clarendon Press, 1970.

Wotton, William. *A Defense of the Reflections upon Ancient and Modern Learning in Answer to the Objections of Sir W. Temple, and Others with Observations upon the Tale of a Tub, in a Tale of a Tub.* Appendix B. In *A Tale of a Tub to Which Added the Battle of the Books and the Mechanical Operation of the Spirit.* Edited by A. C. Guthkelch and D. Nichol Smith. 2d Edited by Oxford: Clarendon Press, 1958.

Young, Edward. *Conjectures on original composition. In a letter to the author of Sir Charles Grandison.* London, 1759.

## 2. The Nineteenth Century

Adams, William Henry Davenport. *Wrecked Lives: Men Who Have Failed.* First Series. London: Society for Promoting Christian Knowledge; New York: Pott, Young and Co., 1880.

Aikin, John. *Letters to a Young Lady on a Course of English Poetry.* 2nd edition. London: J. Johnson, 1807.

Albione, S. Austin [pseud.?] *A Critical Dictionary of English Literature.* 3 vols. Philadelphia, PA: Lippincott, 1870.

Barrett, John. *An Essay on the Earlier Part of the Life of Swift.* London: J. Johnson, 1808.

Bartlett, John, compiler. *Familiar Quotations.* Boston, 1855. The book is now in its nineteenth edition.

Cobb, Frances. "A Relic of Swift and Stella." *Temple Bar Magazine,* 66:1832), 570.

Collier, William Francis. *A History of English Literature in a Series of Biographical Sketches.* London: T. Nelson and Sons, 1880.

Collins, John Churton. *Jonathan Swift: a Biographical and Critical Study.* London: Chatto and Windus, 1893. Facsimile reprint. Norwood, PA: Norwood Editions, 1978.

Corkery, Daniel. 1934. "Ourselves and Dean Swift: [review of] Lives by Stephen Gwynn." *Studies.* 18 (July 1934): 203–18.

Craik, Henry. *The Life of Jonathan Swift.* London: J. Murray, 1882.

Cunningham, Peter, ed. *Specimens of the British Poets.* London: John Murry, 1844. *Fun for the Million, or The Laughing Philosopher.* London: Sherwood, Gilbert and Piper, 1835.

"Swift." In *Gallery of Illustrious Irishmen,* Number 10, *Dublin University Magazine,* 15 (February 1840)—part 1), 131–44 ; (March 1840—part 2), 333–44; (May 1840—part 3), 538–56; (June 1840—part 4), 634–61.

Gilfillan, George. "Satire and Satirists." *Scottish Review* (January 1856). Reprinted in *A Gallery of Literary Portraits.* London, 1909.

Gosse, Edmund. *History of English Literature, 1660–1780.* London and New York: Macmillan, 1889.

Howard, Alfred. *The Beauties of Swift, Consisting of Selections from his Work.* London: Thomas Tegg [circa 1820].

Hubbard, Elbert. "Swift." In *Little Journeys: to the Homes of Good Men and Great.* New York; London: G. P. Putman, 1895.

[Jeffreys, Francis]. "Review of Scott's *Works of Jonathan Swift.*" *The Edinburgh Review.* 53 (September 1816), 1–52.

Lecky, W. E. H. "Biographical Introduction." *The Prose Works of Jonathan Swift.* Edited by Temple Scott, 11 vols. 1: xiii-xci. London: George Bell, 1897.

Legg, J. Wickam and J. C. Bucknill. "Letter." *Academy.* 19 (June 25, 1881), 241–56.

"Literary Curiosity. An Original Letter By Dean Swift." *The Midland Counties Historical Collector.* 1:4 (854), 62–3.

[Mahony, Revd. Francis]. "Dean Swift's Madness: A Tale of a Churn." In *The Works of Father Prout.* Edited by Charles Kent. 64–82. London: Routledge, 1881.

Mason, William Monck. *The History and Antiquities of the Collegiate and Cathedral Church of St. Patrick, near Dublin, from its Foundation in 1190, to the Year 1819.* Dublin: W. Folds, 1820.

Masson, David. "Dean Swift." *The Three Devils: Luther's Milton's and Goethe's, with Other Essays.* London: Macmillan, 1874.

*Moral and Christian Duties.* London: Religious Tract Society, 1840.

*National Anecdotes: Interspersed with Historical Facts. English Proverbial Sayings, and Maxims, with a Collection of Toasts and Sentiments.* London: Craddock and Joy, 1812.

Phillips, Samuel. "Dean Swift—and Vanessa." In *Essays from the London Times: A Collection of Personal and Historical Sketches.* New York: Appleton, 1852.

Scott, Sir Walter. "Memoirs of Jonathan Swift, D. D." In *The Works of Jonathan Swift 2nd edition.* 19 vols. Edited by Sir Walter Scott. Volume 1. London: Bickers and Son, 1883. Scott's edition of the works was originally published in 1814 in Edinburgh.

Thackeray, William Makepeace. "Swift." In *The English Humourists of the Eighteenth Century.* 1–54. London: Smith, Elder, and Co., 1853, 1–54.

[Wilson, C.H.]. *Swiftiana.* 2 vols. London: Phillips, 1804.

Wilde, William. *The Closing Years of Dean Swift's Life . . . and Some Remarks on Stella.* Dublin: Hodges and Smith, 1849.

Windsor, Arthur Lloyd. *Ethica: Or, Characteristics of Men, Manners and Books.* London: Smith and Elder, 1860.


### 3. The Twentieth and Twenty-first Centuries

Acworth, Bernard. *Swift.* London: Eyre and Spottiswoode, 1947.

Arnold, Bruce. 2000. *An Illustrated Life.* Dublin: Lilliput Press, 2000.

Asimov, Isaac. *The Annotated Gulliver's Travels.* New York: Clarkson N. Potter, 1980.

Bartlett, John, comp. *Familiar Quotations,* 15th edition. Edited by Emily Morrison Beck. Boston: Little, Brown and Co.,1980.

Bell, Florence Eveleen. *The Dean of Saint Patrick's: A Play in Four Acts.* London: Edward Arnold, 1903.

Bemis, Alec Hanley. "Hip-Hop's Clown Heavy: Kool Keith, Crazy Like a Fox," *Miami New Times Online* (Music). September 2, 1999, www.miaminewtimes.com/issues /1999–09–02/music2.html (January 21, 2002).

Blink Design Homepage. Book Covers. "Manic Press edition of Abolishing Christianity," 1999. www.blinkdesign.com/abolish.html (January 21, 2002).

Boyd, Ernest. "Swift." In *Literary Blasphemies.* New York and London: Harper and Brothers, 1927, 74–105.

Brown, David. "Recollection Used Books," *Our Daily Bleed/Calendar: October 28.* www.eskimo.com/~recall/bleed/1028.html (January 31, 2002).

Burkman, Greg. "'The Perv' offers challenging reading, difficult lesson," *Online Seattle Times.* October 24, 1999, www.seattletimes.newsource.com/news/entertainment/html98/perv_1991024.html (January 21, 2002).

Caliber Comics. "Jonathan Swift's *A Modest Proposal*" (advertisement). May 16, 2000, www.calibercomics.com/Checkout4Pro/TITLES/modest_proposal.htm (January 21, 2002).

Churchill, Charles, Reginald. *He Served Human Liberty: An Essay on the Genius of Jonathan Swift.* London: Allen and Unwin, 1946.

Clewes, Winston. *The Violent Friends.* New York and London: D. Appleton-Century, 1945.

Corde, Eleanor. *Dean Swift: A Drama.* Los Angeles, CA: McBride, 1922.

"Current Projects: Jonathan Swift." *The Website for the Shipbuilding Industry.* www.ship-technology.com/projects/swift/ (January 21, 2002).

Curtin, Dermot. "Our Gaelic Democracy: Teaching the Lessons of History." *Catholic Bulletin.* 23 (July 1933): 587–92.

Eagle, Dorothy and Hilary Carnell, eds. *The Oxford Literary Guide to Great Britain and Ireland,* 2nd edition. Oxford; New York: Oxford University Press, 1992.

Ehrenpreis, Irvin. *Swift: The Man, His Work, and the Age.* 3 vols. London: Methuen, 1962–83.

Eves, Howard. "The Astonishing predication in Gulliver's Travels." *The Mathematics Teacher.* 54 (December 1961), 625–6.

Ferenczi, Sandor. "Gulliver Phantasies." *International Journal of Psychoanalysis* 9 (1928), 283–300.

Foot, Michael. *The Pen and the Sword: A Year in the Life of Jonathan Swift.* London: Macgibbon and Kee, 1959; rpt. 1966.

Gill, Bartholomew. *The Death of an Ardent Bibliophile.* New York: William Morrow, 1995

Gillespie, Nick. "American Scream" [review of Howard Stern's *Miss America*], *ReasonOnline,* www.reason.com/9603/dept.bk.STERN.text.html (January 21, 2002).

Girvan, Ray. "Erotic Fiction: A Writer's Perspective: An Essay on the Erotic Novel and its Trends," *So You Want to Be a Writer?,* 1999. www.gloria-brame.com/glory/erotalk.html (January 21, 2002).

Glendinning, Victoria. *Jonathan Swift: A Portrait.* New York: Henry Holt, 1998.

"Good News." *Uniting Church in Australia, an Inclusive Church,* www.geocities.com/WestHollywood/Heights/2554/frame/frnews.html (March 2, 2000).

Goodwin, Frank Stier. *Jonathan Swift: Giant in Chains.* New York: Liveright, 1940.

Gordon, A. G. "Letter to the Editor." *Journal of the Royal Society of Medicine* (February 1999), 92:102.

Gosse, Edmund. *English Literature: An Illustrated Record.* 4 vols. London: Heineman, 1903.

Gounaud, Karen Jo. *Family Friendly Libraries* www.fflibraries.org (February 4, 2000).

Greenacre, Phyllis. *Swift and Carroll: A Psychoanalytic Study of Two Lives.* New York: International Universities Press, 1955.

Hardy, Evelyn. *The Conjured Spirit: Swift, a Study in the Relationship of Swift, Stella and Vanessa.* London: Hogarth Press, 1949.

Hone, Mario and Joseph Rossi. *Swift: or the Egotist.* London: Gollancz, 1934.

Huxley, Aldous. "Swift." In *Do What You Will.* 97–112. Garden City, NY: Doubleday, Doran, 1929.

Jackson, Robert Wyse. *Jonathan Swift, Dean and Pastor.* London: Society for Promoting Christian Knowledge; New York: MacMillan, 1939.

———. *Swift and His Circle: A Book of Essays.* With a foreword by Seamus O'Sullivan. Dublin: Talbot Press, 1945.

"Jonathan Swift, Dean of St. Patrick's Cathedral" in *The Kiltartan History Book.* Compiled by Lady G. Dublin: Colin Smythe, 1909. Rpt. as *Irish Folktales.* Edited by by Henry Glassie. New York: Pantheon Books. 1985.

Johnston, Denis. *In Search of Swift.* Dublin: Hodges and Figges, 1959.

Jong, Erica. *Fanny, Being the True History of the Adventures of Fanny Hackabout-Jones.* New York: New American Library,1980.

"Josh." Atheist Conversation: Man-made.net www.man-made.net/contrib/quotes.html (January 21, 2002).

Lawrence, Charles Edward. *Swift and Stella: A Play in One Act.* Boston: Gowans and Gray, 1927.

Le Brocquy, Sybil. *Cadenus: A Reassessment in Light of New Evidence of the Relationships Between Swift, Stella, and Vanessa.* Dublin: Dolmen Press, 1962.

———. *Swift's Most Valuable Friend.* Dublin: Dolmen Press, 1968.

———. *A View on Vanessa: a Correspondence with Interludes for the Stage.* Dublin: Dolmen Press, 1967.

Longford, Edwards Arthur Pakenham, earl of, *Yahoo: A Tragedy in Three Acts.* Dublin: Hodges and Figges, 1934.

Moil, Carkan. "Swift Solutions" on *Writerspace.* December 10, 2000, www.writerspace.com/authorboard/messages/885.html (January 21, 2002).

Morgan, Fiona. "An Audience with the Queen." *Salon Entertainment.* July 7, 1998. (August 8, 2000).

Moriarty, Mary and Catherine Sweeney. *Jonathan Swift: The Man Who Wrote Gulliver.* O'Brien Junior Biography Library, no. 5. Dublin, O'Brien Press, 1990.

Mirsky, Dimiti. "Introduction." *Gulliver's Travels.* Moscow: Co-operative Publishing Society of Foreign Workers in the USSR, 1935.

Murray, Thomas. *Stella's Cottage: Jonathan Swift, Esther Johnson and Her Cottage.* Trim Co. Meath: Trymme Press, 1991.

Murry, John Middleton. *Jonathan Swift, A Critical Biography.* London: Jonathan Cape, 1954.

"Must-Read Books: Results of a Reader Poll." *The Quill: Queer Individual Liberty Letter.* Vol. 1, no. 2. February 1994. www.glil.org/quill/quill/942.html (February 19, 2000).

Nokes, David. *Jonathan Swift, A Hypocrite Reversed: A Critical Biography.* Oxford: Oxford University Press, 1985.

O'Donovan, John. "The Fiddler and the Dean," *Jonathan, Jack, and GBS: Four Plays About Irish History and Literature.* Edited by Robert Hogan. Newark: University of Delaware; London, Cranbury, NJ: Associated University Presses, 1993.

O'Hegarty, P.S. "Jonathan Swift: Irishman." *The Bell.* 10:6 (October 1945), 501–10.

Pakenham, Edward Arthur. *Yahoo: A Tragedy in Three Acts.* Dublin: Hodges and Figges, 1934.

Postman, Neil. *Building a Bridge to the 18th Century: How the Past Can Improve Our Future.* New York: Knopf, 1999.

Quennell, Peter. *History of English Literature.* London: Widenfield and Nicolson, 1973.

Rogers, Pat. *The Oxford Illustrated History of English Literature.* Oxford: Oxford University Press, 1987.

Rowse, A.L. *Jonathan Swift, Major Prophet.* London: Thames and Hudson, 1975.

Saintsbury, George. *The Peace of the Augustans: A Survey of Eighteenth Century Literature as a Place of Rest and Refreshment.* London: G. Bell and Sons, 1916.

———. "Swift" in *Chambers's Cyclopedia of English Literature.* Edited by David Patrick. 3 vols. (London and Edinburgh: Chambers, 1903), 2: 122.

Shane, Leslie. *The Skull of Swift: An Extempore Exhumation.* Indianapolis: Bobbs-Merill, 1928.

Shields, Ann. "Heartfelt Advice; Ellen Degeneres' Mother Will Discuss Her Book on Love and Support of a Gay Child." *Los Angeles Times.* (December 9, 2000) B8.

Sitwell, Edith. *I Sit under a Black Sun.* Garden City, NY: Doubleday, Doran, 1938.

Smith, Sophie Shilleto. *Dean Swift.* London: Methuen, 1910.

Stewart, Bruce. "A Refuge in Language." *Visitor.* Spring, 1989. [Official publication of the Irish Hotels Federation.]

Taylor, W. D. *Swift: A Critical Essay.* London: Peter Davies, 1933.

"Uniting Sexuality and Faith: The Love of God Knows No Barriers." *Love Makes a Family,* www.members.tripod.com/~uniting/contents/family.html (January 21, 2002).

Van Doren, Carl. *Swift.* London: Martin Secker, 1931.

Watkins, W. B. C. *Perilous Balance: The Tragic Genius of Swift, Johnson and Sterne.* Princeton, NJ: Princeton University Press, 1939.

Weiss, Jenny. *Let's Go Ireland 1999.* New York: St. Martin's Press, 1999.

Woolf, Virginia. "Swift's 'Journal to Stella.'" In *The Second Common Reader.* New York: Harcourt, Brace and World, 1932; rpt. 1966.

Yeats, William Butler. *Words on the Window-pane* Dublin: Cuala Press, 1934; rpt. 1973.

# Index